Jack Vance was born in 1916 and educated at the University of California, first as a mining engineer, then majoring in physics and finally in journalism. He has since had a varied career: his first story was written while he was serving in the US Merchant Marine during the Second World War. During the late 1940s and early 1950s, he contributed a variety of short stories to the science fiction and fantasy magazines of the time. His first published book was *The Dying Earth* (1950). Since then he has produced several series of novels – for example, the *Planet of Adventure*, *Durdane* and *Demon Princes* series – as well as various individual novels.

Jack Vance has won the two most coveted trophies of the science fiction world, the Hugo Award and the Nebula Award. He has also won the Edgar Award of the Mystery Writers of America for his novel *The Man in the Cage* (1960). In addition, he has written scripts for television science fiction series.

Jack Vance's non-literary interests include blue-water sailing and early jazz. He lives in California in a house he designed and largely built himself.

By the same author

The Five Gold Bands	*Demon Princes* Series
Son of the Tree	*Star King*
Vandals of the Void	*The Killing Machine*
To Live Forever	*The Palace of Love*
Big Planet	*The Face*
The Languages of Pao	*The Book of Dreams*
The Man in the Cage	
The Dragon Masters	*Planet of Adventure* Series
The Houses of Iszm	*City of the Chasch*
Future Tense	*Servants of the Wankh*
The Moon Moth	*The Dirdir*
The Blue World	*The Pnume*
The Last Castle	
Emphyrio	*Durdane* Series
Fantasms and Magics	*The Anome*
Trullion: Alastor 2262	*The Brave Free Man*
Marune: Alastor 933	*The Asutra*
Wyst: Alastor 1716	
Showboat World	*The Dying Earth* Series
The Best of Jack Vance	*The Dying Earth*
Lyonesse I	*The Eyes of the Overworld*
Lyonesse II The Green Pearl	*Cugel's Saga*
Araminta Station	*Rhialto the Marvellous*

JACK VANCE

Lyonesse III

Madouc

GraftonBooks
A Division of HarperCollins*Publishers*

GraftonBooks
A Division of HarperCollins*Publishers*
77–85 Fulham Palace Road,
Hammersmith, London W6 8JB

Special overseas edition 1991
9 8 7 6 5 4 3 2 1

First published in Great Britain by
Grafton Books 1990

The Author asserts the moral right to be
identified as the author of this work.

ISBN 0-586-20450-4

Printed in Great Britain by
HarperCollinsManufacturing Glasgow

Set in Times

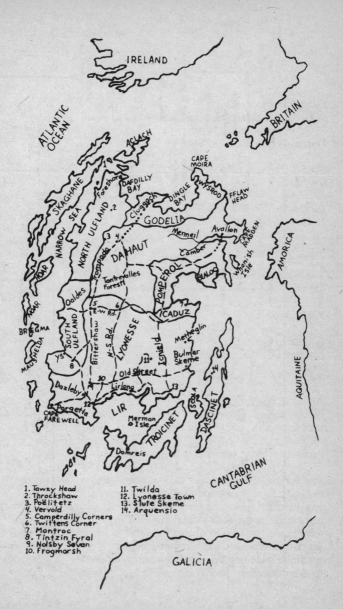

1. Tawzy Head
2. Throckshaw
3. Poëlitetz
4. Vervold
5. Camperdilly Corners
6. Twittens Corner
7. Montroc
8. Tintzin Fyral
9. Nolsby Sevan
10. Frogmarsh
11. Twilda
12. Lyonesse Town
13. Slute Skeme
14. Arquensio

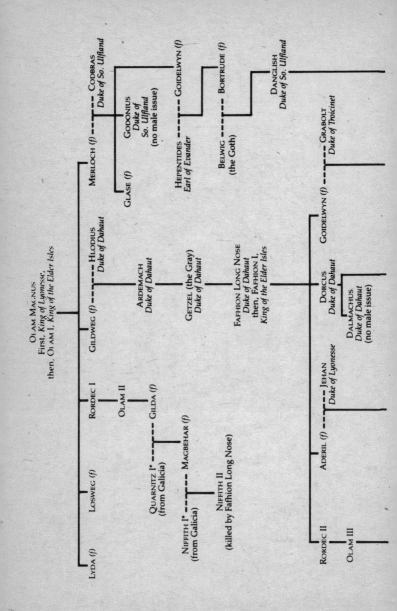

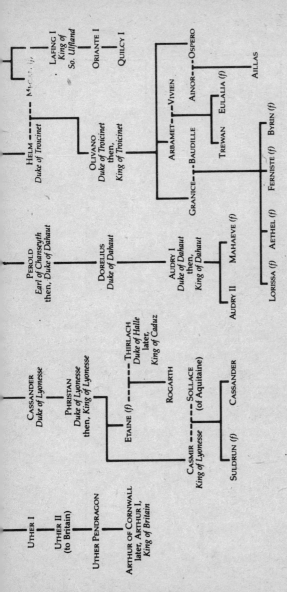

Female Issue = (f)

*The Galician Cuckoos

Siblings away from chain of descent,
collateral lines, and grass-marriages are not
indicated to avoid over-complexity.

1

I

South of Cornwall, north of Iberia, across the Cantabrian Gulf from Aquitaine were the Elder Isles, ranging in size from Gwyg's Fang, a jag of black rock most often awash under Atlantic breakers, to Hybras, the 'Hy-Brasill' of early Irish chroniclers: an island as large as Ireland itself.

On Hybras were three notable cities: Avallon, Lyonesse Town and ancients Ys[1], along with many walled towns, old gray villages, castles of many turrets and manor houses in pleasant gardens. The landscapes of Hybras were varied. The Teach tac Teach, a mountain range of high peaks and upland moors, paralleled the length of the Atlantic foreshore. Elsewhere the landscape was more gentle, with vistas over sunny downs, wooded knolls, meadows and rivers. A wild woods shrouded the entire center of Hybras. This was the Forest of Tantrevalles, itself the source of a thousand fables, where few folk ventured for fear of enchantment. The few who did so, woodcutters and the like, walked with cautious steps, stopping often to listen. The breathless silence, broken, perhaps, by a far sweet bird call, was not reassuring in itself and soon they would stop to listen again.

In the depths of the forest, colors became richer and

---

[1] In primeval times a land bridge briefly connected the Elder Isles to Old Europe. According to myth, the first nomad hunters to arrive on Hybras, when they crossed the Teach tac Teach and looked down along the Atlantic foreshore, discovered the city Ys already in existence.

9

more intense; shadows were tinged with indigo or maroon; and who knows what might be watching from across the glade, or perched at the top of yonder stump?

The Elder Isles had known the coming and going of many peoples: Pharesmians, blue-eyed Evadnioi, Pelasgians with their maenad priestesses, Danaans, Lydians, Phoenicians, Etruscans, Greeks, Celts from Gaul, Ska from Norway by way of Ireland, Romans, Celts from Ireland and a few Sea Goths. The wash of so many peoples had left behind a complex detritus: ruined strongholds; graves and tombs; steles carved with cryptic glyphs: songs, dances, turns of speech, fragments of dialect, place-names; ceremonies of purport now forgotten, but with lingering flavor. There were dozens of cults and religions, diverse except that, in every case, a caste of priests interceded between laity and divinity. At Ys, steps cut into the stone led down into the ocean to the Temple of Atlante; each month in the dark of the moon priests descended the steps by midnight, to emerge at dawn wearing garlands of sea flowers. On Dascinet, certain tribes were guided in their rites by cracks in sacred stones, which none but the priests could read. On Scola, the adjacent island, worshippers of the god Nyrene poured flasks of their own blood into each of four sacred rivers; the truly devout sometimes bled themselves pale. On Troicinet, the rituals of life and death were conducted in temples dedicated to the earth-goddess Gaea. Celts had wandered everywhere across the Elder Isles, leaving behind not only place names, but Druid sacrifices in sacred groves, and the 'March of the Trees' during Beltane. Etruscan priests consecrated their androgynous divinity Votumna with ceremonies repulsive and often horrid, while the Danaans introduced the more wholesome Aryan pantheon. With the Romans came Mithraism, Christianity, Parsh, the worship of Zoroaster,

10

and a dozen other similar sects. In due course, Irish monks founded a Christian monastery[2] on Whanish Isle, off the coast of Dahaut near Avallon, which ultimately suffered the same fate as Lindisfarne far to the north, off the coast of Britain.

For many years the Elder Isles were ruled from Castle Haidion at Lyonesse Town, until Olam III, son of Fafhion Long Nose, removed the seat of government to Falu Ffail at Avallon, taking with him the sacred throne Evandig and the great table Cairbra an Meadhan, 'the Board of Notables'[3], and the source of a whole cycle of legends.

Upon the death of Olam III, the Elder Isles entered upon a time of troubles. The Ska, having been expelled from Ireland, settled on the island Skaghane, where they rebuffed all attempts to dislodge them. Goths ravaged the coast of Dahaut; sacking the Christian monastery on Whanish Isle, sailing their longboats up the Cambermouth as far as Cogstone Head, from which they briefly menaced Avallon itself. A dozen princelings vied for power, shedding much blood, wreaking much grief and bereavement, exhausting the land, and in the end achieving nothing, so that the Elder Isles became a patchwork of eleven kingdoms, each at odds with all the rest.

Audry I, King of Dahaut, never abandoned his claim to sovereignty over all the Elder Isles, citing his custody of the throne Evandig as basis for his assertion. His claim was angrily challenged, especially by King Phristan of Lyonesse, who insisted that Evandig and Cairbra an Meadhan were his own rightful property, wrongfully

---

[2] Somewhat later, King Phristan of Lyonesse allowed a Christian bishopric at Bulmer Skeme, on the east coast of Lyonesse, insisting only that no wealth be exported to Rome. Perhaps for this reason, the church received little support from abroad, and the bishop exercised no great influence, either at Bulmer Skeme or at Rome.

[3] In years to come Cairbra an Meadhan would serve as model for the 'Round Table' which graced King Arthur's court at Camelot.

11

sequestered by Olam III. He named Audry I traitor and caitiff; in the end the two realms went to war. At the climactic battle of Orm Hill the two sides succeeded only in exhausting each other. Both Phristan and Audry I were killed, and finally the remnants of the two great armies straggled sadly away from the bloody field.

Audry II became king of Dahaut and Casmir I was the new king of Lyonesse. Neither abandoned the ancient claims, and peace between the two realms was thereafter fragile and tentative.

So went the years, with tranquility only a memory. In the Forest of Tantrevalles halflings, trolls, ogres and others less easily defined, bestirred themselves and performed evil deeds which no one dared punish; magicians no longer troubled to mask their identities, and were solicited by rulers for aid in the conduct of temporal policy.

The magicians devoted ever more time to sly struggles and baneful intrigue, to the effect that a goodly number had already been expunged. The sorcerer Sartzanek was one of the chief offenders; he had destroyed the magician Coddefut by means of a purulence, and Widdefut through the Spell of Total Enlightenment. In retaliation, a cabal of Sartzanek's enemies compressed him into an iron post which they emplaced at the summit of Mount Agon. Sartzanek's scion Tamurello took refuge at his manse Faroli, deep within the Forest of Tantrevalles and there protected himself by dint of careful magic.

That further events of this sort might be avoided, Murgen, most potent of the magicians, issued his famous edict, forbidding magicians employment in the service of temporal rulers, inasmuch as such activity must inevitably bring magicians into new conflicts with each other, to the danger of all.

Two magicians, Snodbeth the Gay, so-called for his

jingling bells, ribbons and merry quips, and Grundle of Shaddarlost, were brash enough to ignore the edict, and each suffered a severe penalty for his presumption. Snodbeth was nailed into a tub to be devoured by a million small black insects; Grundle awoke from his sleep to find himself in a dismal region at the back of the star Achernar, among geysers of molten sulphur and clouds of blue fume; he too failed to survive.

Although the magicians were persuaded to restraint, travail and dissension elsewhere were rife. Celts who had been placidly settled in the Daut province Fer Aquila became inflamed by bands of Goidels from Ireland; they slaughtered all the Dauts they could find, elevated a burly cattle-thief named Meorghan the Bald to the kingship and renamed the land Godelia, and the Dauts were unable to recapture their lost province.

Years passed. One day, almost by chance, Murgen made a startling discovery, which caused him such vast consternation that for days he sat immobile, staring into space. By degrees his resolution returned and at last he set himself to a program which, if successful, would slow and finally halt the momentum of an evil destiny.

The effort preoccupied Murgen's energies and all but eliminated the joy in his life.

The better to guard his privacy, Murgen set out barriers of dissuasion along the approaches to Swer Smod, and, further, appointed a pair of demoniac gatekeepers, the better to turn back obstinate visitors; Swer Smod thereupon became a place of silence and gloom.

Murgen at last felt the need for some sort of alleviation. For this reason he brought into existence a scion, so that he might, in effect, live two existences in tandem.

The scion, Shimrod, was created with great care, and was by no means a replica of Murgen, either in appearance or in temperament. Perhaps the differences were larger

13

than Murgen had intended, since Shimrod's disposition was at times a trifle too easy, so that it verged on the frivolous: a condition which was at discord with current conditions at Swer Smod. Murgen, nevertheless, cherished his scion and trained him in the skills of life and the arts of magic.

In the end Shimrod became restless and with Murgen's blessing he departed Swer Smod in all good cheer. For a period Shimrod wandered the Elder Isles as a vagabond, sometimes posing as a peasant, more often as a peregrine knight in search of romantic adventure.

Shimrod at last settled into the manse Trilda on Lally Meadow, a few miles into the Forest of Tantrevalles.

In due course the Ska of Skaghane perfected their military apparatus and invaded North and South Ulfland, only to be defeated by Aillas, the gallant young King of Troicinet, who thereupon became King of both North and South Ulfland, to the grievous distress of Casmir, King of Lyonesse.

Less than a dozen magicians remained extant throughout the Elder Isles. Some of these were Baibalides of Lamneth Isle; Noumique; Myolander; Triptomologius the Necromancer; Condoit of Conde; Severin Starfinder; Tif of the Troagh; and a few more, including some who were little more than apprentices, or tyros. A goodly number of others had recently passed from existence: a fact suggesting that magic might be a dangerous profession. The witch Desmei for reasons unknown had dissolved herself during the creation of Faude Carfilhiot and Melancthe. Tamurello also had acted imprudently; now, in the semblance of a weasel skeleton he hung constricted within a small glass globe in Murgen's great Hall at Swer Smod. The weasel skeleton crouched in a tight curl, skull thrust forward between the crotch formed by the upraised haunches, with two small black eyes glaring from the glass, conveying an almost palpable will to work evil upon anyone who chanced to glance at the bottle.

II

The most remote province of Dahaut was the March, governed by Claractus, Duke of the March and Fer Aquila – a title somewhat hollow, since the old Duchy of Fer Aquila had long been occupied by the Celts for their kingdom Godelia. The March was a poor land, sparsely populated, with a single market town, Blantize. A few peasants tilled barley and herded sheep; in a few tumbled old castles a rag-tag gentry lived in little better case than the peasants, consoled only by their honor and devotion to the doctrines of chivalry. They ate more gruel than meat; draughts blew through their halls, flickering the flames in the wall sconces; at night ghosts walked the corridors, mourning old tragedies.

At the far west of the March was a wasteland supporting little but thorn, thistle, brown sedge and a few spinneys of stunted black cypress. The wasteland, which was known as the Plain of Shadows, met the outlying fringes of the great forest in the south, skirted the Squigh Mires in the north and to the west abutted the Long Dann, a scarp generally three hundred feet high and fifty miles long, with the upland moors of North Ulfland beyond. The single route from the plain below to the moors above led through a cleft in the Long Dann. During ancient times a fortress had been built into the cleft, closing the gap with stone blocks, so that the fortress effectively became part of the cliff A sally port opened upon the plain, and high above a line of parapets fronted a terrace, or walkway. The

15

Danaans had named the fortress 'Poëlitetz': 'the Invulnerable'; it had never been taken by frontal assault. King Aillas of Troicinet had attacked from the rear, and so had dislodged the Ska from what had been their deepest salient into Hybras.

Aillas with his son Dhrun now stood on the parapets, looking out over the Plain of Shadows. The time was close upon noon; the sky was clear and blue; today the plain showed none of the fleeting cloud shadows which had prompted its name. Standing together, Aillas and Dhrun seemed much alike. Both were slender, square-shouldered, strong and quick by the action of sinew rather than massive muscle. Both stood at middle stature; both showed clear clean features, gray eyes and light brown hair. Dhrun was easier and more casual than Aillas, showing in his style the faintest hint of carefully restrained flamboyance, along with an indefinable light-hearted elegance: qualities which gave charm and color to his personality. Aillas, constrained by a hundred heavy responsibilities, was somewhat more still and reflective than Dhrun. His status required that he mask his natural passion and intensity behind a face of polite indifference: to such an extent that the trait had become almost habitual. Similarly, he often used a mildness close upon diffidence to disguise his true boldness, which was almost an extravagance of bravado. His swordsmanship was superb; his wit danced and flickered with the same sure delicacy, coming in sudden flashes like sunlight bursting through the clouds. Such occasions transformed his face so that for a moment he seemed as youthful and jubilant as Dhrun himself.

Many folk, observing Aillas and Dhrun together, thought them to be brothers. When assured otherwise, they tended to wonder at Aillas' precocity in the fathering of his child. Dhrun, in point of fact, had been taken as an infant to Thripsey Shee; he had lived among the fairies – how many years: eight, nine, ten? There was no way of knowing. Meanwhile time in the outer world had advanced but a single year. For compelling reasons, the circumstances of Dhrun's childhood had been kept secret, despite speculation and wonder.

The two stood leaning on the parapets, watching for those they had come to meet. Aillas was moved to reminisce of earlier times. 'I am never comfortable here; despair seems to hang in the air.'

Dhrun looked up and down the terrace, which in the bright sunlight seemed inoffensive enough. 'The place is old. It must be impregnated with misery, which weighs upon the soul.'

'Do you feel it, then?'

'Not to any great extent,' Dhrun admitted. 'Perhaps I lack sensitivity.'

Aillas, smiling, shook his head. 'The explanation is simple: you were never brought here as a slave. I have walked these very stones with a chain around my neck. I can feel the weight and hear the jangle; I could probably trace out where I placed my feet. I was in a state of utter despair.'

Dhrun gave an uneasy laugh. 'Now is now; then is then. You should feel exultation in that you have more than evened the score.'

Aillas laughed again. 'I do indeed! Exultation mixed with dread makes for an odd emotion!'

'Hmf,' said Dhrun. 'That is hard to imagine.'

Aillas turned to lean again on the parapet. 'I often wonder about "now" and "then" and "what is to be", and how one differs from the other. I have never heard a sensible explanation, and the thinking makes me more uneasy than ever.' Aillas pointed to a place down upon the plain. 'See that little hillock yonder, with the scrub

17

growing up the slopes? The Ska put me to digging in a tunnel, which was to extend out to that hillock. When the tunnel was finished, the tunnel gang would be killed, in order to secure the secret. One night we dug up to the surface and escaped, and so I am alive today.'

'And the tunnel: was it ever finished?'

'I would expect so. I have never thought to look.'

Dhrun pointed across the Plain of Shadows. 'Riders are coming: a troop of knights, to judge by the glint of metal.'

'They are not punctual,' said Aillas. 'Such indications are meaningful.'

The column approached with stately deliberation, and finally revealed itself to be a troop of two dozen horsemen. In the van, on a high-stepping white horse, rode a herald, clad in half-armor. His horse was caparisoned in cloths of rose-pink and gray; the herald carried high a gonfalon showing three white unicorns on a green field: the royal arms of Dahaut. Three more heralds followed close, holding aloft other standards. Behind, at a dignified distance, rode three knights abreast. They wore light armor and flowing cloaks of rich colors: one black, one dark green, one pale blue. The three were followed by sixteen men-at-arms, each holding high a lance from which fluttered a green pennon.

'They make a brave show, despite their journey,' observed Dhrun.

'So they have planned,' said Aillas. 'Again, such indications are significant.'

'Of what?'

'Ah! Such meanings are always more clear in retrospect! As for now, they are late, but they have troubled to make a fine arrival. These are mixed meanings, which someone more subtle than I must interpret.'

'Are the knights known to you?'

'Red and gray are the colors of Duke Claractus. I know

18

him by reputation. The company would be riding from Castle Cirroc, which is the seat of Sir Wittes. He is evidently the second knight. As for the third – ' Aillas looked along the terrace and called to his herald Duirdry, standing a few yards distant. 'Who rides in the company?'

'The first standard is that of King Audry: the company comes on royal business. Next, I note the standards of Claractus, Duke of the March and Fer Aquila. The other two are Sir Wittes of Harne and Castle Cirroc, and Sir Agwyd of Gyl. All are notables of long lineage and good connection.'

'Go out upon the plain,' said Aillas. 'Meet these folk with courtesy and inquire their business. If the response comes in respectful language, I will receive them at once in the hall. If they are brusque or minatory, bid them wait, and bring me their message.'

Duirdry departed the parapets. A few moments later he emerged from the sally port with two men-at-arms for escort. The three rode black horses furnished with simple black harness. Duirdry displayed Aillas' royal standard: five white dolphins on a dark blue field. The men-at-arms carried banners quartered in the arms of Troicinet, Dascinet, North and South Ulfland. They rode a hundred yards out upon the plain, then drew up their horses and waited in the bright sunlight, with the dun scarp and fortress looming behind them.

The Daut column halted at a distance of fifty yards. After a pause of a minute while both parties sat immobile, the Daut herald rode forward on his white horse. He reined to a halt five yards in front of Duirdry.

Watching from the parapets, Aillas and Dhrun saw the Daut herald speak the message dictated by Duke Claractus. Duirdry listened, made a terse response, turned about and rode back into the fortress. Presently he reappeared on the terrace and made his report.

'Duke Claractus extends his greetings. He speaks with the voice of King Audry, to this effect: "In view of the amicable relations holding between the Kingdoms of Troicinet and of Dahaut, King Audry desires that King Aillas terminate his encroachment upon the lands of Dahaut with all possible expedition and withdraw to the recognized borders of Ulfland. By so doing, King Aillas will eliminate what is now a source of grave concern for King Audry and will reassure him as to the continuation of the harmony now existent between the realms." Duke Claractus, speaking for himself, desires that you now open the gates to his company that they may occupy the fortress, as is their duty and their right.'

'Return,' said Aillas. 'Inform Duke Claractus that he may enter the fortress, with an escort of two persons only, and that I will grant him an audience. Then bring him to the low hall.'

Again Duirdry departed. Aillas and Dhrun descended to the low hall: a dim chamber of no great size cut into the stone of the cliff. A small embrasure overlooked the plain; a doorway gave on a balcony fifty feet above the mustering yard at the back of the sally port.

Upon instructions from Aillas, Dhrun stationed himself in an anteroom at the front of the hall; here he awaited the Daut deputation.

Duke Claractus arrived without delay, along with Sir Wittes and Sir Agwyd. Claractus marched heavily into the chamber, and halted: a man tall and massive, blackhaired, with a short black beard and stern black eyes in a harsh heavy face. Claractus wore a steel war-cap and a cloak of green velvet over a shirt of mail, with a sword swinging from his belt. Sir Wittes and Sir Agwyd were accoutered in similar style.

Dhrun spoke: 'Your Grace, I am Dhrun, prince of the realm. Your audience with King Aillas will be informal

20

and therefore is not a suitable occasion for the display of weapons. You may doff your helmets and place your swords on the table, in accordance with the usual precepts of chivalry.'

Duke Claractus gave his head a curt shake. 'We are not here seeking an audience with King Aillas; that would be appropriate only in his own realms. He now visits a duchy within the Kingdom of Dahaut, such duchy being governed by myself. I am paramount here, and the protocol is different. I deem this occasion to be a field parley. Our attire is appropriate in every respect. Lead us to the king.'

Dhrun politely shook his head. 'In that case I will deliver the message of King Aillas and you may return to your company without further ado. Listen closely, for these are the words you must convey to King Audry.

'King Aillas points out that the Ska occupied Poëlitetz over a period of ten years. The Ska also controlled the lands along the top of the Long Dann. During this time they encountered neither protest nor forceful counteraction from King Audry or yourself or from any other Daut agency. By the tenets of the common law dealing with cases of uncontested settlement, the Ska by their acts and in default of Daut counteracts gained ownership in full fee and title to Poëlitetz, and the lands along the top of the Long Dann.

'In due course the Ulfish army, commanded by King Aillas, defeated the Ska, drove them away, and took their property by force of arms. This property thereby became joined to the Kingdom of North Ulfland, with full right and legality. These facts and the precedents of history and common practice are incontestable.'

Claractus stared long and hard at Dhrun. 'You crow loudly for such a young cockerel.'

'Your Grace, I merely repeat the words taught me by

King Aillas, and I hope that I have not offended you. There is still another point to be considered.'

'And what is that?'

'The Long Dann is clearly the natural boundary between Dahaut and North Ulfland. The defensive strength of Poëlitetz means nothing to Dahaut; however, it is invaluable to the kingdoms of North and South Ulfland, in the case of attack from the east.'

Claractus gave a hoarse laugh. 'And if the attacking armies were Daut, what then? We would bitterly regret failing to claim our territory, as we do now.'

'Your claim is denied,' said Dhrun modestly. 'I might add that our concern is not for the Daut armies, valorous though they may be, but for the forces of King Casmir of Lyonesse, who hardly troubles to conceal his ambitions.'

'If Casmir dares to venture a single step into Dahaut, he will suffer a terrible woe!' declared Claractus. 'We will chase him the length of Old Street, and bring him to bay at Cape Farewell, where we will cut him and his surviving soldiers into small bits.'

'Those are brave words!' said Dhrun. 'I will repeat them to my father, for his reassurance. Our message to King Audry is this: Poëlitetz and the Long Dann are now part of North Ulfland. He need fear no aggression from the west, and therefore may apply his full energies against the Celt bandits who have caused him so much travail in Wysrod.'

'Bah,' muttered Claractus, unable for the moment to make any remark more cogent.

Dhrun bowed. 'You have heard the words of King Aillas. There is no more to be said and you have my permission to go.'

Duke Claractus glared a single moment, then swung on his heel, gestured to his companions and with no further words left the chamber.

From the embrasure Aillas and Dhrun watched the column receding across the Plain of Shadows. 'Audry is somewhat languid and even a bit airy,' said Aillas. 'He may well decide that in this case his honor is not truly compromised. So I hope, since we need no more enemies. Nor, for that matter, does King Audry.'

III

During the Danaan incursions, Avallon had been a fortified market town hard by the estuary of the Camber, notable only for the many turrets rearing high above the town walls.

The Danaan power ran its course; the tall hazel-eyed warriors who fought naked save for bronze helmets disappeared into the fog of history. The walls of Avallon decayed; the mouldering turrets protected only bats and owls, but Avallon remained the 'City of Tall Towers'.

Before the Time of Troubles, Olam III made Avallon his capital and by dint of vast expenditure made Falu Ffail the most magnificent palace of the Elder Isles. His successors were not to be outmatched in this regard, and each vied with his predecessors in the richness and splendor of his contribution to the fabric of the palace.

When Audry II came to the throne, he applied himself to the perfection of the palace gardens. He ordained six fountains of nineteen jets, each surrounded by a circular promenade with cushioned benches; he lined the central pleasance with marble nymphs and fauns to the number of thirty; at the terminus was an arcaded cupola where musicians played sweetly from dawn till dark, and sometimes later by moonlight. A garden of white roses flanked a similar expanse of red roses; lemon trees, clipped to the shape of spheres, bordered the square lawns where King Audry was wont to stroll with his favorites.

Falu Ffail was notable not only for its gardens but also for the pomp and extravagance of its many pageants. Masques, fêtes, spectacles, frivolities: they followed close one after another, each more lavish in its delights than the last. Gallant courtiers and beautiful ladies thronged the halls and galleries, clad in garments of marvellous style and complexity; each appraising the others with care, wondering as to the effect of his or her image, so carefully contrived. All the aspects of life were dramatized and exaggerated; every instant was heavy as honey with significance.

Nowhere was conduct more graceful nor manners more exquisite than at Falu Ffail. The air rustled with murmured conversations; each lady as she passed trailed a waft of scent: jasmine or floris of orange-clove, or sandalwood, or essence of rose. In dim salons lovers kept rendezvous: sometimes secret, sometimes illicit; very little, however, escaped notice, and every incident, amusing, grotesque, pathetic or all three, provided the grist of gossip.

At Falu Ffail intrigue was the stuff of both life and death. Under the glitter and glisten ran dark currents, of passion and heartbreak, envy and hate. There were duels by daybreak and murders by starlight, mysteries and disappearances, and royal banishments when indiscretions became intolerable.

Audry's rule was generally benevolent, if only because all his juridical decisions were carefully prepared for him by his chancellor Sir Namias. Nonetheless, sitting on the throne Evandig in his scarlet robes and wearing his golden crown, Audry seemed the very definition of benign majesty. His personal attributes enhanced the kingly semblance. He was tall and imposing in stature, if somewhat heavy of hip and soft in the belly. Glossy black ringlets

24

hung beside his pale cheeks; a fine black mustache graced his ripe upper lip. Under expressive black eyebrows his brown eyes were large and moist, if set perhaps too closely beside his long disdainful nose.

Queen Dafnyd, Audry's spouse, originally a princess of Wales and two years older than Audry, had borne him three sons and three daughters; now she no longer commanded Audry's ardors. Dafnyd cared not a whit and took no interest in Audry's little affairs; her own inclinations were adequately soothed by a trio of stalwart footmen. King Audry disapproved of the arrangement, and frowned haughtily upon the footmen when he passed them in the gallery.

During fine weather, Audry often took a leisurely breakfast in a private part of the garden, at the center of a large square of lawn. The breakfasts were informal, and Audry was usually attended only by a few cronies.

Toward the end of such an occasion, Audry's seneschal, Sir Tramador, approached to announce the arrival of Claractus, Duke of the March and Fer Aquila, who desired an audience at King Audry's earliest convenience.

Audry listened with a grimace of annoyance; such tidings were seldom the source of good cheer and, worse, often required that Audry spend hours in tedious consultation.

Sir Tramador waited, smiling the most gentle of smiles to see King Audry wrestling with the need to exert himself. Audry at last groaned in irritation and jerked his heavy white fingers. 'Bring Claractus here; I will see him at this moment, and be rid of the matter.'

Sir Tramador turned away, mildly surprised to find King Audry so brisk. Five minutes later he ushered Duke Claractus across the lawn. From the evidence of dusty skin and soiled clothing, Claractus had only just alighted from his horse.

Claractus bowed before King Audry. 'Sire, my excuses! I have ignored punctilio in order that I might report to you as soon as possible. Last night I slept at Verwiy Underdyke; by dint of early rising and hard riding I am here now.'

'I commend your zeal,' said Audry. 'If I were served everywhere as well I would never cease to rejoice! Your news, then, would seem to be of moment.'

'That, Sire, is for you to judge. Shall I speak?'

Audry pointed to a chair. 'Seat yourself, Claractus! You are acquainted, or so I presume, with Sir Huynemer, Sir Archem and Sir Rudo.'

Claractus, glancing toward the three, gave a curt nod. 'I took note of them on my last visit; they were enjoying a charade and all three were dressed as harlequins, or clowns, or something of the sort.'

'I fail to recall the occasion,' said Sir Huynemer stiffly.

'No matter,' said Audry. 'Speak your news, which I hope will elevate my spirits.'

Claractus gave a harsh chuckle. 'Were this the case, Sire, I would have ridden all night. My news is not gratifying. I conferred, as instructed, with King Aillas, at the fortress Poëlitetz. I expressed your views in exact words. He gave his response with courtesy, but yielded no substance. He will not vacate Poëlitetz nor the lands at the top of the Long Dann. He states that he conquered these places from the Ska, who had taken them by force of arms from the Daut realm and into their ownership. The Ska, he points out, had maintained this ownership in the absence of challenge from your royal armies. Thus, so he asserts, title to fortress and lands have devolved upon the Kingdom of North Ulfland.'

Audry uttered a sibilant ejaculation. 'Sarsicante! Does he hold my favor in such small regard, to flout me thus?

26

He would seem to scoff both at my dignity and at the might of Daut arms!'

'Not so, Sire! I would be remiss if I gave that impression. His tone was polite and respectful. He made it clear that he guards Ulfland not against Dahaut but rather against the possibility of King Casmir's aggressive intent, which, so he states, is general knowledge.'

'Bah!' snapped Audry. 'That is most farfetched! How could Casmir arrive on the Plain of Shadows without first defeating the entire armed strength of Dahaut?'

'King Aillas feels that the contingency, while remote, is real. In any event, he relies most strongly upon his first argument, to wit: that the lands are his by right of conquest.'

Sir Rudo cried out in scorn: 'An argument specious and incorrect! Does he take us for lumpkins? The boundaries of Dahaut are grounded in tradition; they have been immutable for centuries!'

'Precisely true!' declared Sir Archem. 'The Ska must be regarded as transient interlopers, no more!'

King Audry made an impatient gesture. 'Obviously it is not so easy! I must give the matter thought. Meanwhile, Claractus, will you not join us at our breakfast? Your dress is somewhat at discord, but surely no one with a conscience will cry you shame.'

'Thank you, Sire. I will gladly eat, for I am famished.'

The conversation shifted to topics more agreeable, but the mood of the breakfast had been roiled and presently Sir Huynemer again condemned the provocative conduct of King Aillas. Sir Rudo and Sir Archem endorsed his views, each advising a stern rebuff to put the 'young Troice upstart' in his place.

Audry leaned heavily back in his chair. 'All very well! But I wonder how this chastening of Aillas is to be accomplished.'

'Aha! If several strong companies were despatched into the March, with clear indications that we intended to take back our lands by force, Aillas might well chirp from a different branch!'

King Audry rubbed his chin. 'You feel that he would yield to a show of resolution.'

'Would he dare challenge the might of Dahaut?'

'Suppose that, through folly or recklessness, he refused to yield?'

'Then Duke Claractus would strike with his full might, to send young Aillas and his Ulf bantlings bounding and leaping across the moors like so many hares.'

Claractus held up his hand. 'I am chary of so much glory. You have envisioned the campaign; you shall be in command and lead the charge.'

Sir Huynemer, with raised eyebrows and a cold glance for Claractus, qualified his concepts. 'Sire, I put this scheme forward as an option to be studied, no more.'

Audry turned to Claractus. 'Is not Poëlitetz considered impregnable to assault?'

'This is the general belief.'

Sir Rudo gave a skeptical grunt. 'This belief has never been tested, though it has cowed folk for generations.'

Claractus smiled grimly. 'How does one attack a cliff?'

'The sally port might be rammed and sundered.'

'Why trouble? The defenders at your request will be pleased to leave the portcullis ajar. When a goodly number of noble knights – say, a hundred or more – has swarmed into the yard, the portcullis is dropped and the captives are destroyed at leisure.'

'Then the Long Dann itself must be scaled!'

'It is not easy to climb a cliff while enemies are dropping rocks from above.'

Sir Rudo gave Claractus a haughty inspection. 'Sir, can you offer us nothing but gloom and dismal defeat? The king has stated his requirements; still you decry every proposal intended to achieve the goal!'

'Your ideas are impractical,' said Claractus. 'I cannot take them seriously.'

Sir Archem struck the table with his fist. 'Nevertheless, chivalry demands that we respond to this insulting encroachment!'

Claractus turned to King Audry. 'You are fortunate, Sire, in the fiery zeal of your paladins! They are paragons of ferocity! You should loose them against the Celts in Wysrod, who have been so noxious a nuisance!'

Sir Huynemer made a growling sound under his breath. 'All this is beside the point.'

Audry heaved a sigh, blowing out his black mustaches. 'For a fact, our Wysrod campaigns have brought us little glory and less satisfaction.'

Sir Huynemer spoke earnestly: 'Sire, the difficulties in Wysrod are many! The gossoons are like specters; we chase them over tussock and bog; we bring them to bay; they melt into the Wysrod mists, and presently attack our backs, with yells and screams and insane Celtic curses, so that our soldiers become confused.'

Duke Claractus laughed aloud. 'You should train your soldiers not for parades but for fighting; then they might not fear mists and curses.'

Sir Huynemer uttered a curse of his own: 'Devilspit and dogballs! I resent these words! My service to the king has never been challenged!'

'Nor mine!' declared Sir Rudo.

'The Celts are a minor vexation which we will soon abate!'

King Audry pettishly clapped his hands. 'Peace, all of you! I wish no further wrangling in my presence!'

Duke Claractus rose to his feet. 'Sire, I have spoken

hard truths which otherwise you might not hear. Now, by your leave, I will retire and refresh myself.'

'Do so, good Claractus! I trust that you will join us as we dine.'

'With pleasure, Sire.'

Claractus departed. Sir Archem watched him stride across the lawn, then turned back with a snort of disapproval. 'There goes a most prickly fellow!'

'No doubt loyal, and as brave as a boar in rut: of this I am sure,' declared Sir Rudo. 'But, like most provincials, he is purblind to wide perspectives.'

'Bah!' said Sir Huynemer in disgust. '"Provincial" only? I find him uncouth, with his horse blanket cloak and blurting style of speech.'

Sir Rudo spoke thoughtfully: 'It would seem part and parcel of the same attribute, as if one fault generated the other.' He put a cautious question to the king: 'What are Your Majesty's views?'

Audry made no direct response. 'I will reflect on the matter. Such decisions cannot be formed on the instant.'

Sir Tramador approached King Audry. He bent and muttered into the royal ear: 'Sire, it is time that you were changing into formal robes.'

'Whatever for?' cried Audry.

'Today, Sire, if you recall, you sit at the assizes.'

Audry turned an aggrieved glance on Sir Tramador. 'Are you certain of this?'

'Indeed, Sire! The litigants are already gathering in the Outer Chamber.'

Audry scowled and sighed. 'So now I must finick with folly and greed and all what interests me least! It is tedium piled on obfuscation! Tramador, have you no mercy? Always you trouble me during my trifling little periods of rest!'

'I regret the need to do so, Your Highness.'

'Ha! I suppose that if I must, I must; there is no escaping it.'

'Unfortunately not, Your Majesty. Will you use the Grand Saloon[4] or the Old Hall?'

Audry considered. 'What cases await judgment?'

Sir Tramador tendered a sheet of parchment. 'This is the list, with the clerk's analysis and comments. You will note a single robber to be hanged and an innkeeper who watered his wine, for a flogging. Otherwise there seems nothing of large import.'

'Just so. The Old Hall it shall be. I am never easy on Evandig; it seems to shudder and squirm beneath me, an anomalous sensation to say the least.'

'So I would think, Your Majesty!'

The assizes ran their course. King Audry returned to his private quarters, where his valets dressed him for the afternoon. However, Audry did not immediately leave the chamber. He dismissed his valets and, dropping into a chair, sat brooding upon the issues raised by Duke Claractus.

The prospect of retaking Poëlitetz by force was, of course, absurd. Hostilities with King Aillas could benefit only Casmir of Lyonesse.

Audry rose to his feet, to pace back and forth, head bowed, hands clasped behind his back. When all was taken with all, so he reflected, Aillas had spoken only stark and unvarnished truth. Danger to Dahaut came not from the Ulflands, nor from Troicinet, but from Lyonesse.

Claractus not only had brought no cheer, but also had hinted at some unpleasant realities which Audry preferred to ignore. The Daut troops in their fine uniforms made a brave show at parades, but even Audry conceded that their conduct on the battlefield might be held suspect.

---

[4] Also known as the Hall of Heroes, where Evandig the throne and Cairbra an Meadhan the round table are situated.

31

Audry sighed. To remedy the situation called for measures so drastic that his mind jerked quickly back, like the fronds of a sensitive plant.

Audry threw his hands high into the air. All would be well; unthinkable otherwise! Problems ignored were problems defeated! Here was the sensible philosophy; a man would go mad trying to repair each deficiency of the universe!

Thus fortified, Audrey called in his valets. They settled a smart hat with a cocked crown and a scarlet plume upon his head; Audrey blew out his mustaches and departed the chamber.

IV

The Kingdom of Lyonesse extended across South Hybras, from the Cantabrian Gulf to Cape Farewell on the Atlantic Ocean. From Castle Haidion at the back of Lyonesse Town King Casmir ruled with a justice more vigorous than that of King Audry. Casmir's court was characterized by exact protocol and decorum; pomp, rather than ostentation or festivity, dictated the nature of events at Haidion.

King Casmir's spouse was Queen Sollace, a large languid woman almost as tall as Casmir. She wore her fine yellow hair in bundles on top of her head, and bathed in milk, the better to nourish her soft white skin. Casmir's son and heir-apparent was the dashing Prince Cassander; also included in the royal family was Princess Madouc, purportedly the daughter of the tragic Princess Suldrun, now nine years dead.

Castle Haidion overlooked Lyonesse Town from the shoulder of a low rise, showing from below as an interlocked set of ponderous stone blocks, surmounted by seven towers of differing styles and shape: the Tower of Lapadius[5], and the Tall Tower[6], the King's Tower, the West Tower, the Tower of Owls, Palaemon's Tower, and the East Tower. The ponderous structure and the towers provided Haidion a silhouette which, if graceless, archaic and eccentric, was in total contrast to the fine façade of Falu Ffail at Avallon.

In much the same manner, the person of King Casmir contrasted with that of King Audry. Casmir was florid and seemed to throb with strong and ruddy blood. Casmir's hair and beard were mats of crisp blond ringlets. Audry's complexion was as sallow as ivory, and his hair was richly black. Casmir was burly, thick of torso and neck, with round china-blue eyes staring from a slab-sided face. Audry, while tall and ample of girth, was measured of posture and carefully graceful.

The court of neither king lacked for regal comfort; both enjoyed their perquisites, but while Audry cultivated the company of his favorites, of both sexes, Casmir knew no intimates and kept no mistresses. Once each week he paid a stately visit to the bedchamber of Queen Sollace, and there addressed himself to her massive and lethargic white body. On other less formal occasions, he made shift to ease himself upon the quivering body of one of his pretty page boys.

The company Casmir liked best was that of his spies and informers. From such sources he learned of Aillas' intransigence at Poëlitetz almost as soon as had King Audry himself. The news, though it came as no surprise, aroused Casmir's vigorous displeasure. Sooner or later he intended to invade Dahaut, destroy the Daut armies and consolidate a quick victory before Aillas could effectively bring

---

[5] Also known as the Old Tower.
[6] Known as the Eyrie.

to bear his own power. With Aillas ensconced at Poëlitetz, the situation became more difficult, since Aillas could instantly counterattack with Ulfish troops across the March and there would be no swift decision to the war. Definitely, the danger posed by the fortress Poëlitetz must be eliminated.

This was no sudden new concept. Casmir had long worked to foment dissension among the Ulfish barons, that they might enter upon a fullscale rebellion against the rule of their foreign king. To this end he had recruited Torqual, a renegade Ska turned outlaw.

The enterprise had yielded no truly gratifying results. For all Torqual's ruthlessness and cunning, he lacked tractability, which limited his usefulness. As the months passed, Casmir became impatient and dissatisfied; where were Torqual's achievements? In response to Casmir's orders, transmitted by courier, Torqual only demanded more gold and silver. Casmir had already disbursed large sums; further he suspected that Torqual could easily meet his needs by means of plunder and depredation, thus saving Casmir unnecessary expense.

For conferences with his private agents, Casmir favored the Room of Sighs, a chamber above the armory. In olden times, before construction of the Peinhador, the armory had served as the castle's torture chamber; prisoners awaiting attention sat above in the Room of Sighs, where the sensitive ear – so it was said – might still detect plaintive sounds.

The Room of Sighs was bleak and stark, furnished with a pair of wooden benches, a table of oak planks, two chairs, a tray with an old beechwood flask and four beechwood mugs, to which Casmir had taken a fancy.

A week after receiving news of the impasse at Poëlitetz, Casmir was notified by his under-chamberlain Eschar that the courier Robalf awaited his convenience in the Room of Sighs.

Casmir at once took himself to the cheerless chamber over the armory. On one of the benches sat Robalf: a person gaunt and thin-faced with darting brown eyes, sparse brown hair and a long crooked nose. He wore travel-stained garments of brown fust and a high-peaked black felt cap; upon the entrance of Casmir he jumped to his feet, doffed the cap and bowed. 'Sire, I am at your service!'

Casmir looked him up and down, gave a curt nod and went to sit behind the table. 'Well then, what is your news?'

Robalf responded in a reedy voice: 'Sire, I have done your bidding, tarrying not a step along the way, pausing not even to empty my bladder!'

Casmir pulled at his chin. 'Surely you did not perform this function on the run?'

'Sire, haste and duty make heroes of us all!'

'Interesting.' Casmir poured wine from the beechwood flask into one of the mugs. He gestured toward the second chair. 'Be seated, good Robalf, and divulge your tidings in comfort.'

Robalf gingerly perched his thin haunches upon the edge of the chair. 'Sire, I met with Torqual at the appointed place. I delivered your summons, that he must come to Lyonesse Town, using your words and speaking with your kingly authority. I bade him make ready at once, that we might ride the Trompada south together.'

'And his response?'

'It was enigmatic. At first he spoke not at all, and I wondered if he had even heard my voice. Then he uttered these words: "I will not go to Lyonesse Town."'

'I remonstrated with all urgency, citing again Your

Majesty's command. Torqual at last spoke a message for your ears.'

'Ho ha!' muttered Casmir. 'Did he now? What was the message?'

'I must warn, Sire, that he used little tact and scamped the appropriate honorifics.'

'Never mind. Speak the message.' Casmir drank from his beechwood mug.

'First of all, he sent his best and most fervent regards, and his hopes for Your Majesty's continued good health: that is to say, he addressed certain odd sounds to the wind and this is how I interpreted their sense. He then stated that only fear for his life precluded full and instant obedience to Your Majesty's instructions. He then made a request for funds either of silver or of gold, in quantity adequate to his needs, which he described as large.'

Casmir compressed his lips. 'Is that the whole of his message?'

'No, Sire. He stated that he would be overjoyed for the privilege of meeting with Your Majesty, should you deign to visit a place called Mook's Tor. He supplied directions for arriving at this place, which I will communicate as Your Majesty requires.'

'Not at the moment.' Casmir leaned back in the chair. 'To my ears, this message carries a flavor of casual insolence. What is your opinion?'

Robalf frowned and licked his lips. 'Your Majesty, I shall render my frank assessment, if that is what you wish.'

'Speak, Robalf! Above all, I value frankness.'

'Very well, Your Majesty. I apprehend in Torqual's conduct not so much insolence as indifference mixed with a dark twist of humor. He would seem to live in a world where he is alone with Fate; where all other persons, your august self and I as well, are no more than colored shadows, to use a flamboyant figure. In short, rather than indulging in purposeful insolence, Torqual cares nothing one way or another for your royal sensibilities. If you are to deal with him, it must be on this basis. Such, at least, is my belief.' Robalf looked sidewise toward Casmir, whose face gave no clue as to his emotions.

Casmir spoke at last, in a voice reassuringly mild. 'Does he intend to do my bidding or not? That is the most important matter of all.'

'Torqual is unpredictable,' said Robalf. 'I suspect that you will find him no more malleable in the future than in the past.'

Casmir gave a single curt nod. 'Robalf, you have spoken to the point, and indeed have clarified the mysteries surrounding this perverse cutthroat, at least to some small extent.'

'I am happy to be of service, Sire.'

For a moment Casmir ruminated, then asked: 'Did he render any account of his achievements?'

'So he did, but somewhat as afterthought. He told of taking Castle Glen Gath, killing Baron Nols and his six sons; he mentioned the burning of Maltaing Keep, seat of Baron Ban Oc, during which occasion all within were consumed by the flames. Both of these lords were staunch in the service of King Aillas.'

Casmir grunted. 'Aillas has sent out four companies to hunt down Torqual. That is my latest information. I wonder how long Torqual will survive.'

'Much depends upon Torqual,' said Robalf. 'He can hide among the crags or down in the fastnesses, and never be found. But if he comes out to make his forays, then someday his luck must turn bitter and he will be tracked to his lair and brought to bay.'

'No doubt but what you are right,' said Casmir. He rapped on the table; Eschar entered the room. 'Sire?'

'Pay over to Robalf a purse of ten silver florins, together

with one heavy coin of gold. Then house him comfortably near at hand.'

Robalf bowed. 'Thank you, Sire.' The two departed the Room of Sighs.

Casmir remained at the table thinking. Neither Torqual's conduct nor his exploits were gratifying. Casmir had instructed Torqual to incite the barons one against the other, using ambush, false clues, rumors and deceit. His acts of plunder, murder and rapine served only to identify Torqual as a savage outlaw, against whom all hands must be turned in concert, despite old feuds and past suspicions. Torqual's conduct therefore worked to unite the barons, rather than to set them at odds!

Casmir gave a grunt of dissatisfaction. He drank from the beechwood mug and set it down on the table with a thud. His fortunes were not on the rise. Torqual, considered as an instrument of policy, had proved capricious and probably useless. He was more than likely a madman. At Poëlitetz, Aillas had entrenched himself, impeding Casmir's grand ambition. And yet another concern, even more poignant, gnawed at Casmir's mind: the prediction uttered long years before by Persilian the Magic Mirror. The words had never stopped ringing in Casmir's mind:

> Suldrun's son shall undertake
> Before his life is gone
> To sit his right and proper place
> At Cairbra an Meadhan.
>
> If so he sits and so he thrives
> Then he shall make his own
> The Table Round, to Casmir's woe,
> And Evandig his Throne.

The terms of the omen, from the first, had mystified Casmir. Suldrun had borne a single child: the Princess

Madouc, or so it had seemed, and Persilian's cantrap would appear to be sheer nonsense. But Casmir knew that this was never the way of it, and in the end, the truth was made known and Casmir's pessimism was vindicated. Suldrun's child had indeed been a boy, whom the fairies of Thripsey Shee had taken, leaving behind an unwanted brat of their own. All unwittingly King Casmir and Queen Sollace had nurtured the changeling, presenting her to the world as 'Princess Madouc'.

Persilian's prophecy was now less of a paradox, and therefore all the more ominous. Casmir had sent his agents to search, but in vain: Suldrun's first-born was nowhere to be found.

Sitting in the Room of Sighs, clasping the beechwood mug in one heavy hand, Casmir belabored his brain with the same questions he had propounded a thousand times before: 'Who is this thrice-cursed child? What is his name? Where does he bide, so demure and quiet from my knowledge? Ah, but I would make short work of it, if once I knew!'

As always, the questions brought no answers, and his bafflement remained. As for Madouc, she had long been accepted as the daughter of the Princess Suldrun, and could not now be disavowed. To legitimize her presence, a romantic tale had been concocted, of a noble knight, secret trysts in the old garden, marriage pledges exchanged in the moonlight, and at last the baby who had become the delightful little princess, darling of the court. The tale was as good as any, and for a fact corresponded closely with the truth – save, of course, for the identity of the baby. As to the identity of Suldrun's lover, no one knew nor cared any longer, except King Casmir, who in his rage had dropped the unfortunate young man into an oubliette without so much as learning his name.

For Casmir, Princess Madouc represented only an exasperation. According to accepted lore, fairy children, when nurtured upon human food and living in human surroundings, gradually lost their halfling cast and were assimilated into the realm of mortals. But sometimes other tales were heard, of changelings who never crossed over, and remained odd wild beings: fickle, sly and cantankerous. Casmir occasionally wondered which sort might be the Princess Madouc. Indeed she differed from other maidens of the court, and at times displayed traits which caused him perplexity and uneasiness.

At this time Madouc still knew nothing of her true parentage. She believed herself the daughter of Suldrun: so she had been assured; why should it be otherwise? Even so, there were discordant elements in the accounts presented by Queen Sollace and the ladies appointed to train her in court etiquette. These ladies were Dame Boudetta, Lady Desdea and Lady Marmone. Madouc disliked and distrusted all three; each thought to change her in one way or another, despite Madouc's resolve to remain as she was.

Madouc was now about nine years old, restless and active, long of leg, with a boy's thin body and a girl's clever pretty face. Sometimes she confined her mop of copper-auburn curls with a black ribbon; as often she allowed it to tumble helter-skelter across her forehead and over her ears. Her eyes were a melting sky-blue; her mouth was wide, and jerked, twisted or drooped to the flux of her feelings. Madouc was considered unruly and willful; the words 'fantastical', 'perverse', 'incorrigible', were sometimes used to describe her temperament.

When Casmir first discovered the facts of Madouc's birth, his immediate reaction was shock, then incredulity, then fury so extreme that it might have gone badly for Madouc had her neck been within reach of Casmir's hands. When he became calm, he saw that he had no choice but to put a good face on the situation; in not too many years Madouc no doubt could be married advantageously.

Casmir departed the Room of Sighs and returned toward his private chambers. The route led him across the back elevation of the King's Tower, where the corridor became a cloistered way overlooking the service yard from a height of twelve feet or so.

Arriving at the portal which gave on the cloisters, Casmir stopped short at the sight of Madouc. She stood in one of the arched openings, poised on tip-toe so that she could peer over the balustrade down into the service yard.

Casmir paused to watch, frowning in that mixture of suspicion and displeasure which Madouc and her activities often aroused in him. He now took note that on the balustrade beside Madouc's elbow rested a bowl of rotten quinces, one of which she held delicately in her hand.

As Casmir watched she drew back her arm and threw the quince at a target in the yard below. She watched for an instant, then drew back, choking with laughter.

Casmir marched forward. He loomed above her. 'What mischief do you now contrive?'

Madouc jerked around in startlement, and stood wordlessly, head tilted back, mouth half open. Casmir peered down through the arch into the service yard. Below stood Lady Desdea, staring up in a fury, while she wiped fragments of quince from her neck and bodice, her stylish tricorn hat askew. At the sight of King Casmir looking down from above, her face sagged in astonishment. For a moment she stood frozen into immobility. Then, dropping a perfunctory curtsey, she settled her hat and hurried across the yard into the castle.

Casmir slowly drew back. He looked down at Madouc. 'Why did you throw fruit at Lady Desdea?'

Madouc said artlessly: 'It was because Lady Desdea

41

came past first, before either Dame Boudetta or Lady Marmone.'

'That is not relevant to the issue!' snapped King Casmir. 'At this moment Lady Desdea believes that I pelted her with bad fruit.'

Madouc nodded soberly. 'It may be all for the best. She will take the reprimand more seriously than if it came mysteriously, as if from nowhere.'

'Indeed? And what are her faults, that she deserves such a bitter reproach?'

Madouc looked up in wonder, her eyes wide and blue. 'In the main, Sire, she is tiresome beyond endurance and drones on forever. At the same time, she is sharp as a fox, and sees around corners. Also, if you can believe it, she insists that I learn to sew a fine seam!'

'Bah!' muttered Casmir, already bored with the subject. 'Your conduct is in clear need of correction. You must throw no more fruit!'

Madouc scowled and shrugged. 'Fruit is nicer than other stuffs. I well believe that Lady Desdea would prefer fruit.'

'Throw no other stuffs either. A royal princess expresses displeasure more graciously.'

Madouc considered a moment. 'What if these stuffs should fall of their own weight?'

'You must allow no substances, either vile, or hurtful, or noxious, or of any sort whatever, to fall, or depart from your control, toward Lady Desdea, Dame Boudetta, Lady Marmone or anyone else. In short, desist from these activities!'

Madouc pursed her mouth in dissatisfaction; it seemed as if King Casmir would yield neither to logic nor persuasion. Madouc wasted no more words. 'Just so, Your Majesty.'

King Casmir surveyed the service yard once again, then continued on his way. Madouc lingered a moment, then followed the king along the passage.

2

I

Madouc's assumptions were incorrect. The event in the service yard had strongly affected Lady Desdea, but not instantly was she prompted to alter her philosophical bent, nor, by extension, her methods for teaching Madouc. As Lady Desdea hurried along the dim corridors of Castle Haidion, she felt only a great bewilderment. She asked herself: 'How have I erred? What was my fault, that I have so incited His Majesty? Above all, why should he signal his disfavor in such an extraordinary manner? Is there some symbolism here which evades me? Surely he has recognized the diligent and selfless work I have done with the princess! It is truly most odd!'

Lady Desdea came into the Great Hall, and a new suspicion entered her mind. She stopped short. 'Does the matter conceivably go deeper? Am I perhaps the victim of intrigue? What other explanation is possible? Or – to think the unthinkable – does His Majesty find me personally repugnant? True enough, my semblance is one of stateliness and refinement, rather than a simpering teasing coquetry, as might be practiced by some paltry little frippet, all paste and perfume and amorous contortion. But surely any gentleman of discernment must notice my inner beauty, which derives from maturity and nobility of spirit!'

For a fact, Lady Desdea's semblance, as she herself suspected, was not instantly compelling. She was large of bone, long of shank, flat of chest and elsewhere somewhat gaunt, with a long equine face and pads of straw-colored ringlets hanging down the sides of her face. Despite all else, Lady Desdea was expert in every phase of propriety, and understood the most delicate nuances of court etiquette. ('When a lady receives the duty of a gentleman, she neither stands staring like a heron which has just swallowed a fish, nor yet will she wreath her face in a fatuous simper. Rather, she murmurs a pleasantry and shows a smile of perceptible but not immoderate warmth. Her posture is erect; she neither sidles nor hops; she wriggles neither shoulders nor hips. Her elbows remain in contact with her body. As she inclines her head, her hands may go behind her back, should she deem the gesture graceful. At no time should she look vacantly elsewhere, call or signal to friends, spit upon the floor, nor embarrass the gentleman with impertinent comments.')

In all Lady Desdea's experience, nothing had occurred to parallel the event in the service yard. As she marched along the corridor her perplexity remained as carking as ever. She arrived at the private chambers of Queen Sollace, and was admitted into the queen's parlor, to find Sollace reclining among green velvet cushions on a large sofa. Behind stood her maid Ermelgart, grooming Sollace's great masses of fine pale hair. Ermelgart had already combed out the heavy strands, using a nutritive dust of ground almonds, calomel and powdered calcine of peacock bone. She brushed the hair until it shone like pale yellow silk; then rolled it into a pair of bundles, which would at last be secured under nets studded with sapphire cabochons.

To the annoyance of Lady Desdea, there were three other persons in the chamber. At the window the Ladies Bortrude and Parthenope worked at embroidery; at Sollace's elbow, perched modestly on a stool, sat Father Umphred, his buttocks overflowing the seat. Today he wore a cassock of brown fustian, the hood thrown back. His tonsure revealed a pale flat scalp fringed with mouse-brown hair; below were soft white cheeks, a snub nose, protuberant dark eyes, a small pink mouth. Father Umphred's post was spiritual adviser to the queen; today in one plump hand he held a sheaf of drawings depicting aspects of the new basilica, now in construction near the north end of the harbor.

Lady Desdea came forward and started to speak, only to be cut short by a flutter of Queen Sollace's fingers. 'One moment, Ottile! As you see, I am occupied with important matters.'

Lady Desdea stood back, chewing her lip, while Father Umphred displayed the drawings, one after the other, eliciting small cries of enthusiasm from Sollace. She voiced only a single reproach: 'If only we could build an edifice of truly magnificent proportions, to put all others, the world over, to shame!'

Father Umphred smilingly shook his head. 'My dear queen, be reassured! The Basilica of Sanctissima Sollace, Beloved of the Angels, will lack for naught in the holy afflatus which it wafts on high!'

'Oh truly, will it be so?'

'Beyond all doubt! Devotion is never measured in terms of gross magnitude! Were it so, a brute beast of the wild would exert more notice in the halls of Heaven than some tiny babe being blessed with the sacrament of baptism!'

'As always, you place all our little problems in proper perspective!'

Lady Desdea could no longer contain herself. She crossed the chamber and bent to murmur into Queen Sollace's ear: 'I must have private words with Your Majesty, at once.'

Sollace, absorbed in the drawings, made an absent-minded gesture. 'Patience, if you please! These are discussions of serious moment!' She touched her finger to a place on the drawing. 'Despite all, if we could add an atrium here, with the toil rooms to either side, rather than across the transept, then the space would serve for a pair of lesser apses, each with its shrine.'

'My dear queen, we could follow this plan were we to shorten the nave by the requisite amount.'

Queen Sollace made a petulant sound. 'But I do not care to do this! In fact, I would wish to add another five yards to its length, and also augment the curve here, at the back of the apse! We would gain scope for a truly splendid reredos!'

'The concept is undeniably excellent,' declared Father Umphred. 'Still, it must be remembered that the foundations are already laid and in place. They control the present dimensions.'

'Cannot they be extended by just a bit?'

Father Umphred gave his head a sad shake. 'We are limited, sadly enough, by a paucity of funds! Were there an unstinting amplitude, anything might be possible.'

'Always, always the same dreary tale!' gloomed Queen Sollace. 'Are these masons and laborers and stonecutters so greedy for gold that they will not work for the glory of the church?'

'It has always been thus, dear lady! Nevertheless I pray each day that His Majesty, in the fullness of his generosity, will grant us our sufficiency.'

Queen Sollace made a glum sound. 'The splendor of the basilica is not His Majesty's highest priority.'

Father Umphred spoke in thoughtful tones. 'The king should remember an important fact. Once the basilica is whole, the financial tide reverses. Folk will come from near and far to worship and sing songs of praise and bestow gifts, of gold and silver! By this means they hope to gain the gratitude of a joyful Heaven.'

'Such gifts will bring joy to me as well, if we may thereby adorn our church with proper richness.'

'To this end we must provide goodly relics,' said Father Umphred wisely. 'Nothing loosens the purse strings like a fine relic! The king should know this! Pilgrims will enhance the general prosperity, and, by inevitable flux, the royal exchequer as well! All considered, relics are very good things.'

'Oh yes, we must have relics!' cried Queen Sollace. 'Where will they be obtained?'

Father Umphred shrugged. 'It is not so easy, since many of the best have been preempted. However, if one is assiduous, relics may still be had: by gift, by purchase, by capture from the infidels or sometimes by discovery in unexpected places. Certainly it is not too early to start our search.'

'We must discuss this matter in full detail,' said Queen Sollace, and then, somewhat sharply: 'Ottile, you are in a state of obvious discomfiture! What is the matter?'

'I am confused and baffled,' said Lady Desdea. 'That is quite true.'

'Tell us, then, what has occurred, and we will puzzle it out together.'

'I can only impart this matter to you in private.'

Queen Sollace made a pettish face. 'Just so, if you truly feel that such precautions are necessary.' She turned to Bortude and Parthenope. 'Ladies, it seems that for once we must indulge Lady Desdea in her whim. You may attend me later. Ermelgart, I will ring the bell when I am ready for you.'

Lady Bortrude and Lady Parthenope, each with nose haughtily high, departed the parlor, along with the maid Ermelgart. Father Umphred paused, but was not urged to remain and so also departed.

Without further delay Lady Desdea told of the events

47

which had caused her so much distress. 'It was time for the Princess Madouc's diction exercises, which are most necessary; she slurs and lilts like a hoyden of the docks. As I walked across the service yard on my way to the lesson, I was struck on the neck by a piece of rotten fruit, hurled from above with both accuracy and force. I am sorry to say that I instantly suspected the princess, who is sometimes prone to mischief. However, when I looked up, I found His Majesty watching me with a most curious expression. If I were an imaginative woman and the person were other than His Majesty, who of course has the best of reasons for all his deeds, I would describe the expression as a leer of triumph, or, perhaps more accurately, vindictive glee!'

'Amazing!' said Queen Sollace. 'How can it be? I am as astonished as you; His Majesty is not one to perform silly pranks.'

'Naturally not! Still – ' Lady Desdea looked over her shoulder in annoyance, as into the parlor came Lady Tryffyn, her face suffused with anger.

Lady Desdea spoke crisply: 'Narcissa, if you please, I am consulting with Her Majesty upon a most serious affair. If you will be kind enough to – '

Lady Tryffyn, as stern and doughty as Lady Desdea herself, made a furious gesture. 'Your business can wait! What I have to say must be said at this very instant! Not five minutes ago, as I crossed the kitchen yard, I was hit on the forehead by an over-ripe quince, thrown down from the arcade above.'

Queen Sollace gave a throaty cry. 'Yet again?'

'"Yet" or "again": whatever you like! It happened as I have described it! Outrage gave me vigor; I ran at speed up the stairs hoping to waylay the perpetrator, and who should come trotting from the corridor, smiling and gay, but the Princess Madouc!'

'Madouc?' 'Madouc?' cried out Queen Sollace and Lady Desdea together, as if in one voice.

'Who else? She confronted me without a qualm and even asked me to move aside so that she might continue on her way. Nevertheless, I detained her and asked: "Why did you hurl a quince at me?" She said, quite soberly: "With nothing more suitable at hand, I used quince; this was on the strong advice of His Majesty the King." I cried out: "Am I to understand that His Majesty advised you to such a deed? Why should he do so?" And she responded: "Perhaps he feels that you and Lady Desdea are inexcusably tiresome and tedious in your instruction."'

'Astonishing!' said Lady Desdea. 'I am dumbfounded!'

Lady Tryffyn went on: 'I told her: "Out of respect for your rank, I may not properly chastise you as you deserve, but I will immediately report this outrage to Her Majesty the Queen!" The princess responded with an airy shrug and continued on her way. Is it not remarkable?'

'Remarkable but not unique!' said Lady Desdea. 'I suffered in the same degree, but it was King Casmir himself who hurled the fruit.'

Lady Tryffyn stood silent for a moment, then said: 'In that case, I am confused indeed!'

Queen Sollace heaved herself erect. 'I must get to the bottom of this! Come! Before the hour is out we shall know what is what and which is which.'

The queen and her two ladies, with Father Umphred coming unobtrusively behind, found King Casmir in conference with the High Seneschal Sir Mungo and the royal secretary Pacuin.

Casmir looked around with a frown, then rose heavily to his feet. 'My dear Sollace, what is so urgent as to bring you here during my consultations?'

'I must have a word with you in private,' said Sollace.

'Be good enough to dismiss your counsellors, if only for a few moments.'

Casmir, noting Lady Desdea and her set countenance, divined the purpose of the visit. At his signal, Sir Mungo and Pacuin left the room. Casmir jerked his finger at Father Umphred. 'You may also go.'

Father Umphred, smiling his kindly smile, departed the chamber.

'Now then,' said King Casmir, 'what is the matter?'

In a tumble of words Queen Sollace explained the situation. King Casmir listened with stolid patience.

Sollace terminated her remarks. 'You now will understand my concern. Essentially, we are puzzled as to why you threw fruit at Lady Desdea and then encouraged Madouc to work the same mischief upon Lady Tryffyn.'

Casmir spoke to Lady Desdea. 'Bring Madouc here at once.'

Lady Desdea left the chamber and a few moments later returned with Madouc, who entered the room somewhat reluctantly.

King Casmir spoke in even tones. 'I ordered you to throw no more fruit.'

'Indeed you did, Sire, in the direction of Lady Desdea, and you also advised against the use of substances more offensive, in connection with Lady Desdea. I followed your advice exactly.'

'But you threw a quince at Lady Tryffyn. Was that my advice?'

'I took it to be so, since you failed to include her in your instructions.'

'Ah hah! Did you want me to name each individual of the castle and in each case name the stuffs with which he or she was not to be pelted?'

Madouc shrugged. 'As you see, Sire, when there is doubt, mistakes occur.'

'And you felt this doubt?'

'Exactly, Sire! It seemed only fair that each of the ladies should be treated alike, and enjoy the same advantages.'

King Casmir smiled and nodded. 'These advantages are subtle. Can you bring them into sharper focus?'

Madouc frowned down at her fingers. 'The explanation might be lengthy, even tedious, so that I would be committing the same fault I deplore in the Ladies Desdea and Tryffyn.'

'Please make the effort. If you bore us, we will excuse you this once.'

Madouc chose her words with care. 'These ladies are surely genteel but each day their conduct is much like that of the day before. They know neither zest nor surprise nor any wonderful new events. I thought it might be well if they were provided a mysterious adventure, which would excite their minds and reduce the tedium of their conversation.'

'Your motives, then, were totally kind and sympathetic?'

Madouc turned him a dubious glance. 'I suspected, of course, that at first they might not be grateful and perhaps even a bit gruff, but in the end they would be delighted for my help, since they would realize that the world is sometimes unexpected and strange, and they would start to look around them with gay anticipation.'

Lady Desdea and Lady Tryffyn made sounds of incredulity. Casmir smiled a small hard smile. 'So you feel that you have done the two ladies a favor?'

'I have done my best,' said Madouc bravely. 'They will remember this day to the end of their lives! Can they say the same of yesterday?'

Casmir turned to Sollace. 'The princess has made a persuasive case that both Lady Desdea and Lady Tryffyn will profit from her acts, even though they come in the form of sheer mischief. However, the altruism of the princess must be returned in kind, and I suggest that you make this day memorable for her as well, with the aid of a willow whisk or a light ferrule. In the end, everyone will profit. Lady Desdea and Lady Tryffyn will find that their lives have been enriched, and Madouc will learn that she must obey the spirit as well as the letter of the royal command.'

Madouc spoke in a voice which trembled slightly: 'Sire, all is quite clear! Her Majesty need not exert herself to make a point which is already well taken.'

King Casmir had already turned away, and spoke over his shoulder: 'Events of this sort often take on a momentum of their own, as in the present case. Her Majesty may well work up a perspiration but will suffer no real inconvenience. You have my leave to go.'

Queen Sollace, with the Ladies Desdea and Tryffyn, departed the room. Madouc lagged behind. Sollace turned and beckoned. 'Come along: smartly now; nothing is to be gained by sulking.'

Madouc sighed. 'Ah well, I have nothing better to do.'

The group returned to Sollace's parlor. Somewhere along the way Father Umphred emerged from the shadows and fell in behind.

Sollace settled herself comfortably on the sofa and summoned Ermelgart. 'Bring me three withes from a besom; let them be both stout and supple. Now then, Madouc! Attend me, if you will! Do you understand that your mischief has caused distress to us all?'

'The quinces were quite small,' said Madouc.

'No matter! The deed does not become a royal princess: most especially a princess of Lyonesse.'

Ermelgart returned with three willow withes, which she handed to Queen Sollace. Madouc watched with wide blue eyes and mouth drooping in woe.

Sollace tested the action of the withes upon a cushion, then turned to Madouc. 'Have you aught to say? Words of contrition or humility?'

Madouc, fascinated by the motion of the withes, failed to respond, and Queen Sollace, usually lethargic, became vexed. 'You feel no remorse? Now I know why you are said to be impudent! Well then, Miss Sly-puss, we shall see. You may approach.'

Madouc licked her lips. 'I do not think it sensible, if I am to be beaten for my pains.'

Sollace stared in wonder. 'I can hardly credit my ears. Father Umphred, kindly escort the princess to me.'

The priest in all affability put his hand on Madouc's shoulder and urged her across the room. Sollace swept Madouc across her great lap, raised high the skirt of Madouc's frock, and plied the withes upon the narrow little haunches. Madouc lay limp as a rag, making no sound.

The lack of response annoyed Sollace; she struck again and again, and finally pulled down Madouc's smallclothes in order to belabor the naked buttocks, while Father Umphred looked on, smiling approval and nodding in time to the strokes.

Madouc made no sound. Sollace at last becoming bored, threw down the withes, and pushed Madouc from her lap and to her feet. Tight-faced, her mouth set in a thin white line, Madouc pulled up her undergarments, settled her skirt and started to walk from the room.

Sollace called out sharply: 'I did not give you leave to go.'

Madouc halted and looked back over her shoulder. 'Do you intend to beat me again?'

'Not at this moment. My arm is tired and sore.'

'Then you are done with me.' Madouc left the parlor, with Sollace blinking slack-jawed after her.

II

Queen Sollace had been adversely affected by Madouc's conduct and also by her demeanor, which seemed deficient in the respect which Sollace conceived to be her due. She had long heard rumors in regard to Madouc's wilfulness, but the firsthand experience came as something of a shock. If Madouc were to become a truly gracious maiden and an ornament to the court, then, clearly, remedial measures were instantly necessary.

Queen Sollace discussed the problem with Father Umphred, who proposed that the little princess be allowed religious instruction. Lady Tryffyn scoffed at the idea. 'That is most impractical and would waste everyone's time.'

Queen Sollace, herself devout, was somewhat nettled. She demanded: 'Then what action do you yourself advocate?'

'I have, for a fact, given the matter thought. The instruction must continue as before, with perhaps more emphasis upon the niceties of deportment. Further, it might be well if she were provided a retinue of noble maidens, so that gracious conduct may be learned by force of example. She is almost to the age when you will be providing such a retinue in any case; I say, the sooner the better!'

Sollace gave a grudging nod. 'It is perhaps a year or two early for such an arrangement, but the circumstances are special. Madouc is as brash and insolent as a little creature of the wild, and surely needs a restraining influence.'

A week later Madouc was summoned to the morning parlor, on the second level of the East Tower. Here she was introduced to six noble damsels, who, so she was told, would serve as her maids-in-waiting. Madouc, aware that protest was futile, stood back appraising her new companions and not liking what she saw. The six maidens were all dressed in fine garments and carried themselves with an exaggerated delicacy of poise. The six, after small formal curtsies, subjected Madouc to an inspection of their own, and showed no more enthusiasm than Madouc. They had been instructed in their duties, which most of them expected to be irksome. In general, they were to provide the princess companionship, run small errands at her behest, regale her with tidbits of gossip, and share the tedium of her lessons. At Madouc's pleasure, the damsels would frolic together and play at quoits, jump-rope, catchball, blinko, mains, shuttlecock and battledore, and other such games; together they would sit at needlework, mix potpourris, compound sachets, weave flower garlands and learn the steps of those dances currently in vogue. All would take instruction in reading and writing; more importantly, they would be schooled in decorum, court convention, and the unalterable rules of precedence.

The six maidens were:

Devonet, of Castle Folize.
Felice, daughter of Sir Mungo, the High Seneschal.
Ydraint, of Damar Greathouse.
Artwen, of Kassie Keep.
Chlodys, of the Fanistry.
Elissia, of Yorn.

The six were a diverse group, all older than Madouc, save Felice, who was about her own age. Chlodys was large, blonde and somewhat ungainly; Elissia was small, dark and neat. Artwen was assertive; Felice was subdued, somewhat absent-minded, unobtrusively pretty, if frail. Ydraint was both radiant with health and definitely pretty;

Devonet was beautiful. Certain of the girls, like Chlodys and Ydraint, were noticeably pubescent; Devonet and Artwen were somewhat less so; Felice and Elissia, like Madouc, were still at the threshold of change.

In fond theory the six maidens would accompany their adored princess everywhere, chattering merry nonsense, each vying to fulfill her little duties, overjoyed to hear her praise, penitent at her kindly censure. In effect, the six would form a miniature court of virtuous and joyful damsels, over whom Princess Madouc would reign serene, like a precious jewel in a golden setting.

In practice, the situation was different. From the first, Madouc was suspicious of the new arrangement, deeming it a nuisance which could only limit her freedom. The six maidens, in their turn, showed little zeal in the performance of their duties. Madouc was considered queer and eccentric, with no penchant whatever for style and naïve to the point of vapidity.

The conditions of Madouc's birth, as understood by the court, brought her no great prestige, which the maidens also were quick to perceive. After a few days of cautious formality, the maids formed a clique from which Madouc was pointedly excluded. Madouc thereafter was treated to only a flippant pretense at courtesy; her inclinations were greeted with vacant stares; her remarks were lost in the chatter, or if heard were ignored.

Madouc was at first puzzled, then amused, then piqued; finally she decided that she cared not a whit, one way or the other and, as far as practical, followed her own pursuits.

Madouc's detachment brought even greater disapproval from the maidens, who found her to be more peculiar than ever. The guiding spirit of the cabal was Devonet: a maiden dainty and graceful, fresh as a flower, already skilled in the arts of charm. Glossy golden curls hung to her shoulders; her eyes were golden-hazel pools of innocence. Devonet was also competent at machinations and intrigues; at her signal – a twitch of the finger, a tilt of the head – the maidens would wander away from Madouc and gather in a huddle across the room, from which they would peer back at her over their shoulders, then whisper and giggle. On other occasions, they made a game of peeping around corners at Madouc, to jerk back when she looked up.

Madouc sighed, shrugged and ignored the mischief. One morning, while taking breakfast with her maids-in-attendance, Madouc discovered a dead mouse in her bowl of porridge. She wrinkled her nose and drew back in distaste. Glancing around the table, she noted the covert attention of the six maidens; clearly they were aware of what she would find. Chlodys clapped a hand over her mouth to restrain a giggle; Devonet's gaze was limpid and bland.

Madouc pushed the bowl aside, pursed her lips, but made no comment.

Two days later Madouc, by a series of mysterious acts and feigned stealth, so aroused the curiosity of Devonet, Chlodys and Ydraint that they followed her surreptitiously, in order to spy out the reason for her strange conduct. Clearly, it could only be scandalous, and the potentialities were delicious indeed. So tempted, they followed Madouc to the top of the Tall Tower, and watched as Madouc climbed a ladder up to a range of abandoned dovecotes. When at last she descended the ladder and hurried off down the stairs, Devonet, Chlodys and Ydraint emerged from their hiding places, climbed the ladder, pushed through a trap door and cautiously explored the dovecotes. To their disappointment, there was nothing to be found but dust, dirt, a few feathers and a bad smell, but no evidence of depravity. Glumly they returned to the trap door, only to discover that the ladder had been removed, with the stone floor a daunting twelve feet below.

At noon the absence of Devonet, Chlodys and Ydraint was noticed, to the general perplexity. Artwen, Elissia and Felice were questioned, but could supply no information. Lady Desdea put a sharp question to Madouc, who likewise professed puzzlement. 'They are very lazy; perhaps they still lie asleep in their beds.'

'Not likely!' said Lady Desdea crisply. 'I find the situation most peculiar!'

'So do I,' said Madouc. 'I suspect that they are up to no good.'

The day passed, and the night. Early the next morning, when all was still, a kitchen maid, crossing the service yard, thought to hear a thin wailing sound coming from a source she could not at once identify. She stopped to listen, and finally fixed upon the dovecotes at the top of the Tall Tower. She reported her findings to Dame Boudetta, the housekeeper, and the mystery was at last resolved. The three girls, dirty, frightened, cold and aggrieved, were rescued from their high prison. In hysterical voices they denounced Madouc and blamed her for all their discomfort. ('She wanted us to go hungry and starve!' 'It was cold, and the wind blew, and we heard the ghost!' 'We were frightened! She did it all on purpose!')

Lady Desdea and Lady Tryffyn listened with stony faces, but were at a loss to adjudicate the situation. The issues were confused; further, if the case were brought to the attention of the queen, Madouc might well bring accusations of her own, in regard to dead mice in the porridge, for instance.

In the end, Chlodys, Ydraint and Devonet were brusquely advised that climbing around abandoned dovecotes was behavior unsuitable for highborn young ladies.

Up to this time, the affair of the rotten quinces, along with King Casmir's embarrassment and Madouc's subsequent travail, had been sternly suppressed. Now, through some clandestine source, the news reached the ears of the six maids-in-waiting, to their delight. Over needlework, Devonet spoke softly: 'What a sight, what a sight, when Madouc was beaten!'

'Kicking and squalling, bare bottom high!' said Chlodys quietly, as if awed by the thought.

'Was it truly so?' marvelled Artwen.

Devonet nodded primly. 'Indeed! Did you not hear the dismal howling?'

'Everyone heard it,' said Ydraint. 'Still, no one knew where it came from.'

'Everyone knows now,' said Chlodys. 'It was Madouc, roaring like a sick cow!'

Elissia spoke with sly mirth: 'Princess Madouc, you are so quiet! Are you discontented with our conversation?'

'Not altogether. I am amused by your jokes. Sometime you shall repeat them for me.'

'How so?' asked Devonet, puzzled and alert.

'Can you not imagine? Someday I will marry a great king and sit on a golden throne. At that time I may well command the six of you to my court, that you may produce some of this "dismal howling" which seems to be so amusing.'

The maidens fell uneasily silent. Devonet was the first to recover her composure. She gave a tinkle of laughter. 'It is not certain, nor even likely, that you shall marry a king – since you have no pedigree! Chlodys, has Princess Madouc a pedigree?'

'No pedigree whatever, poor thing.'

Madouc asked innocently: 'What is a pedigree?'

Devonet laughed again. 'It is something you do not have! Perhaps we should not tell you this, but truth is truth! You have no father! Elissia, what is a girl who lacks a father?'

'She is a bastard.'

'Exactly true! Sad to say, the Princess Madouc is a bastard, and no one will ever want to marry her!'

Chlodys gave an exaggerated shudder. 'I am glad that I am not a bastard.'

'But you are wrong,' said Madouc in a voice of sweet reason. 'I do have a father. He is dead, or so it is said, along with my mother.'

Devonet spoke with disdain: 'Perhaps he is dead, perhaps not. They threw him into a hole, and there he is today. He was a vagabond, and no one even troubled to ask his name.'

'In any event,' said Chlodys, 'you lack a pedigree, and so you shall never marry. It is hard news, but it is best that you learn the facts now, so that you may become inured to them.'

'Just so,' said Ydraint. 'We tell you this because it is our duty to do so.'

Madouc controlled the quaver in her voice. 'It is your duty to tell only the truth.'

'Ah, but we have done so!' declared Devonet.

'I do not believe it!' said Madouc. 'My father was a noble knight, since I am his daughter! How could it be otherwise?'

Devonet looked Madouc up and down, then said: 'Very easily.'

III

Madouc had no sure understanding as to what might be a 'pedigree'. She had heard the word used once or twice before, but its exact significance had never been made clear. A few days past she had gone to the stables to groom her pony Tyfer; nearby a pair of gentlemen were discussing a horse and its 'fine pedigree'. The horse, a black stallion, had been notably well-hung; but this would not seem to be the determining factor, and certainly not so far as Madouc was concerned. Devonet and the other maidens could not reasonably expect her to flaunt an article of this sort.

It was all very puzzling. Perhaps the gentlemen had been alluding to the quality of the horse's tail. As before, and for much the same reason, Madouc rejected the theory. She decided to speculate no further, but to make inquiries at the first opportunity.

Madouc was on tolerably good terms with Prince Cassander, only son to King Casmir and Queen Sollace, and heir-apparent to the crown of Lyonesse. Cassander over the years had become something of a gay blade. His physique was robust. Under tight blond curls his face was round, with small stiff features and round blue eyes. From his father Cassander had inherited, or had learned, a whole set of curt gestures and habits of command; from Sollace had come his fine pale pink skin, small hands and feet, and a temperament easier and more flexible than that of King Casmir.

Madouc discovered Cassander sitting alone in the orangery, writing with concentration upon a parchment with a quill pen. Madouc stood watching a moment. Did Cassander spend his energies upon poetry? Song? An amorous ode? Cassander, looking up, caught sight of Madouc. He put his pen aside and dropped the parchment into a box.

Madouc slowly approached. Cassander seemed in a jovial mood, and gave Madouc a heavily facetious greeting: 'Hail and thrice hail, to the avenging Fury of the castle, clothed in darts and spasms of purple lightning! Who will be next to know the sting of your awful wrath? Or – I should say – the impact of your over-ripe quinces?'

Madouc smiled wanly and settled herself upon the bench beside Cassander. 'His Majesty has issued exact orders; I may no longer do what needs to be done.' Madouc sighed. 'I have decided to obey.'

'That is a wise decision.'

Madouc went on, in a wistful voice. 'One would think that, as a royal princess, I might be entitled to throw quinces in whatever direction and as often as I chose.'

'So one might think, but the act is not considered decorous, and above all, decorum is the duty of a royal princess!'

'What of my mother, the Princess Suldrun – was she decorous?'

Cassander, raising his eyebrows, slanted a quizzical glance down upon Madouc. 'What an odd question! How should I answer? In all honesty, I would be forced to say something like: "not altogether".'

'Because she lived alone in a garden? Or because I was born to her when she was not married?'

'Neither form of conduct is considered truly decorous.'

Madouc pursed her lips. 'I want to know more about her, but no one will speak. Why is there so much mystery?'

Cassander laughed ruefully. 'There is a mystery because no one knows what went on.'

'Tell me what you know of my father.'

Cassander said ponderously: 'I can tell you next to nothing because that is all I know. Apparently he was a handsome young vagabond who chanced to find Suldrun alone in the garden and imposed himself upon her lonely condition.'

'Maybe she was glad to see him.'

Cassander spoke with unconvincing primness: 'She acted without decorum, and only that may be said for Suldrun. But his was insolent conduct! He made a fleering mockery of our royal dignity, and well deserved his fate.'

Madouc reflected. 'It is very odd. Did Suldrun complain of my father's conduct?'

Cassander frowned. 'By no means! The poor little wight seems to have loved him. But tush! I know little of the affair, except that it was the priest Umphred who found the two together and brought the news to His Majesty.'

'My poor father was punished terribly,' said Madouc. 'I cannot understand the reason.'

Again Cassander spoke virtuously: 'The reason is clear! It was necessary to teach the churl a stern lesson, and to discourage all others of like mind.'

With a sudden quiver in her voice Madouc asked: 'Is he then still alive?'

'That I doubt.'

'Where is the hole into which he was cast?'

Cassander jerked his thumb over his shoulder. 'In the rocks behind the Peinhador. The oubliette is a hundred feet deep with a dark little cell at the bottom. It is where incorrigible criminals and enemies of the state are punished.'

Madouc looked up the hill to where the gray roof of the Peinhador could be glimpsed behind Zoltra Bright-Star's Wall. 'My father would be neither of those.'

Cassander shrugged. 'Such was the royal justice, and doubtless correct.'

'Still, my mother was a royal princess! She would not have loved just anyone who happened to look over the fence.'

Cassander shrugged, to indicate the puzzle took him beyond his depth. 'So it would seem: I grant you that. Still – who knows? Royal princess or not, Suldrun was a girl, and girls are female, and females are as wayward as dandelion fluff in the wind! Such is my experience.'

'Perhaps my father was highborn,' Madouc mused. 'No one troubled to ask.'

'Unlikely,' said Cassander. 'He was a foolish young rogue who received his just deserts. You are not convinced? This is the law of nature! Each person is born into his proper place, which he must keep, unless his king grants him advancement for valor in war. No other system is proper, right, or natural.'

'What then of me?' asked Madouc in a troubled voice. 'Where is my pedigree?'

Cassander gave a bark of laughter. 'Who knows? You have been granted the status of a royal princess; that should suffice.'

Madouc was still dissatisfied. 'Was my father put into the hole along with his "pedigree"?'

Cassander chuckled. 'If he had one to begin with.'

'But what is it? Something like a tail?'

Cassander could not restrain his mirth and Madouc indignantly rose to her feet and walked away.

IV

The Royal family of Lyonesse often rode out from Haidion into the countryside: to join a hunt, or to indulge the king's taste for falconry or simply to enjoy a pastoral excursion. King Casmir usually rode his black charger Sheuvan, while Sollace sat a gentle white palfrey, or, as often as not, the cushioned seat of the well-sprung royal carriage. Prince Cassander rode his fine prancing roan Gildrup; the Princess Madouc ranged happily here and there on her dappled pony Tyfer.

Madouc noted that many highborn ladies doted on their steeds and frequently visited the stables to pet and nourish their darlings with apples and sweetmeats. Madouc began to do likewise, bringing carrots and turnips for Tyfer's delectation, meanwhile evading the surveillance of both Lady Desdea and Lady Tryffyn, and also escaping her six maids-in-waiting.

The stable boy assigned to the care of Tyfer was Pymfyd: a tow-headed lad of twelve or thirteen, strong and willing, with an honest countenance and an obliging disposition. Madouc convinced him that he had also been appointed to serve as her personal attendant and escort when the need arose. Without demur Pymfyd acceded to the arrangement, which seemed to signalize an advancement in status.

Early one gray afternoon, with the overcast hanging low and the scent of rain in the air, Madouc donned a gray hooded cloak and slipped away to the stables. She summoned Pymfyd from his work with the manure fork. 'Come, Pymfyd, at once! I have an errand which will require an hour or so of my time, and I will need your attendance.'

Pymfyd asked cautiously: 'What sort of errand, Your Highness?'

'In due course you will learn all that is necessary. Come then! The day is short; the hours tumble past, while you doodle and dither.'

Pymfyd gave a sour grunt. 'Will you be wanting Tyfer?'

'Not today.' Madouc turned away. 'Come.'

With something of a flourish Pymfyd plunged his manure fork into the dungheap and followed Madouc on laggard steps.

Madouc marched up the path which led around the back of the castle, with Pymfyd trudging behind.

He called out: 'Where are we going?'

'It will soon be made clear to you.'

'As you say, Your Highness,' grumbled Pymfyd.

The path veered to the left, toward the Sfer Arct; here Madouc swung away to the right, to scramble up the hillside along a trail leading up the stony slope toward the gray bulk of the Peinhador.

Pymfyd voiced a querulous protest, which Madouc ignored. She continued up the slope, with the north wall of the Peinhador looming above. Pymfyd, panting and apprehensive, lunged forward in sudden alarm and caught up with Madouc. 'Princess, where are you taking us? Below those walls criminals crouch in their dungeons!'

'Pymfyd, are you a criminal?'

'By no manner of means!'

'Then you need fear nothing!'

'Not so! The innocent are often dealt the most vicious blows.'

'Allow me to do the worrying, Pymfyd, and in any case we shall hope for the best.'

'Your Highness, I suggest – '

Madouc brought to bear the full force of her blue gaze. 'Not another word, if you please.'

Pymfyd threw his arms in the air. 'As you will.'

Madouc turned away with dignity and continued up the slope beside the black masonry walls of the Peinhador, and Pymfyd came sullenly behind.

At the corner of the structure Madouc halted and surveyed the grounds at the back of the Peinhador. At the far end, at a distance of fifty yards, stood a massive gibbet, and several other machines of grim purpose, as well as three iron posts for the burning of miscreants; a firepit and griddle used for a similar purpose. Closer at hand, only a few yards distant, at the back of a barren area Madouc discovered what she had come to find: a circular stone wall three feet high surrounding an opening five feet in diameter.

Step by slow step, and despite Pymfyd's inarticulate mutter of protest, Madouc crossed the stony barrens to the circular wall and peered down into the black depths below. She listened, but heard nothing. She pitched her voice so that it might be heard in the black depths and called: 'Father! Can you hear me?' She listened: no sound returned. 'Father, are you there? It is Madouc, your daughter!'

Pymfyd, scandalized by Madouc's acts, came up behind her. 'What are you doing? This is not proper conduct, either for you or for me!'

Madouc paid him no heed. Leaning over the opening she called again: 'Can you hear me? It has been a very long time! Are you still alive? Please speak to me! It is your daughter Madouc!'

From the darkness below came only profound silence.

Pymfyd's imagination was not of a far-ranging nature; nevertheless he conceived that the stillness was not ordinary, but rather that where listeners quietly held their breath. He tugged at Madouc's arm and spoke in a husky whisper: 'Princess, there is a strong smell of ghosts to this place! Listen with a keen ear, you can hear them chittering down deep in the darkness.'

Madouc cocked her head and listened. 'Bah! I hear no ghosts.'

'You are not listening with proper ears! Come away now, before they rob us of our senses!'

'Do not talk nonsense, Pymfyd! King Casmir dropped my father down this hole, and I must learn if he still lives.'

Pymfyd peered down the shaft. 'Nothing down there lives. In any case, it is royal business, beyond our scope!'

'Not so! Is it not my father who was immured?'

'No matter; he is no less dead.'

Madouc nodded sadly. 'So I fear. But I suspect that he left some memorial as to his name and pedigree. If nothing else, this is what I wish to know.'

Pymfyd gave his head a decisive shake. 'It is not possible; now let us go.'

Madouc paid no heed. 'Look, Pymfyd! On yonder gibbet hangs a rope. With this rope we will lower you down the shaft to the bottom. The light will be poor, but you must look about to see what has transpired and what records remain.'

Pymfyd stared, mouth gaping in wonder. He stuttered: 'Have I heard rightly? You intend that I should descend into the hole? The idea lacks merit.'

'Come, Pymfyd, be quick! Surely you value my good opinion! Run to the gibbet and fetch the rope.'

A step grated on the stony ground; the two jerked around to find a ponderous silhouette looming against the gray overcast. Pymfyd sucked in his breath; Madouc's jaw sagged.

The dark shape stepped forward; Madouc recognized

Zerling the Chief Executioner. He halted, to stand heavy legs apart, arms behind his back.

Madouc previously had seen Zerling only from a distance, and the sight had always brought her a morbid little shiver. Now he stood looking down at her, and Madouc stared back in awe; Zerling's semblance was not the more lightsome for proximity. He was massive and muscular, so that he seemed almost squat. His face was heavy, with skin of a curious brownish-red color, and fringed all around with a tangle of black hair and black beard. He wore pantaloons of sour black leather and a black canvas doublet; a round leather cap was pulled low over his ears. He looked back and forth between Madouc and Pymfyd. 'Why do you come here, where we do our grim deeds? It is no place for your games.'

Madouc responded in a clear treble voice: 'I am not here for games.'

'Ha!' said Zerling. 'Whatever the case, Princess, I suggest that you leave at once.'

'Not yet! I came here for a purpose.'

'And what might that be?'

'I want to know what happened to my father.'

Zerling's features compressed into a frown of perplexity. 'Who was he? I have no recollection.'

'Surely you remember. He loved my mother, the Princess Suldrun. For punishment, the king ordered him dropped into this very hole. If he still lives, I want to know, so that I might beg His Majesty for mercy.'

From the depths of Zerling's chest came a mournful chuckle. 'Call down the hole as you like, by day or by night! You will hear never a whisper, or even a sigh.'

'He is dead?'

'He went below long ago,' said Zerling. 'Down in the dark folk do not hold hard to life. It is cold and damp, and there is nothing to do but regret one's crimes.'

Madouc looked at the oubliette, mouth drooping wistfully. 'What was he like? Do you remember?'

Zerling glanced over his shoulder. 'It is not my place to notice, nor to ask, nor to remember. I lop heads and heave at the windlass; still, when I go home of nights I am a different man and cannot so much as kill a chicken for the pot.'

'All very well, but what of my father?'

Zerling glanced once more over his shoulder. 'This perhaps should not be said, and your father committed an atrocious act – '

Madouc spoke plaintively: 'I cannot think it so, since I would not be here otherwise.'

Zerling blinked. 'These questions are beyond my competence; I confine my energies to drawing entrails and working the gibbet. Royal justice, by its very nature, is at all times correct. I must say that in this case I wondered at its severity, when a mere cropping of ears and nose, with perhaps a taste or two of the snake, would seem to have sufficed.'

'So it seems to me,' said Madouc. 'Did you speak with my father?'

'I remember no conversation.'

'What of his name?'

'No one troubled to ask. Put the subject out of your mind: that is my best advice.'

'But I want to learn my pedigree. Everyone has one but me.'

'You will find no pedigree in yonder hole! So now: be off with you, before I hang up young Pymfyd by his toes, just to maintain order!'

Pymfyd cried out: 'Come along, Your Highness! No more can be done!'

'But we have done nothing!'

Pymfyd, already out of earshot, failed to respond.

V

One bright morning Madouc came briskly along Haidion's main gallery and into the entry hall. Looking through the open portal and across the front terrace, she noticed Prince Cassander leaning against the balustrade, contemplating the town below and eating purple plums from a silver dish. Madouc looked quickly over her shoulder, then ran across the terrace and joined him.

Cassander glanced at her sidelong, first carelessly, then a second time, with eyebrows raised in surprise. 'By Astarte's nine nymphs!' swore Cassander. 'Here is a definite marvel!'

'What is so marvelous?' asked Madouc. 'That I deign to join you?'

'Of course not! I refer to your costume!'

Madouc looked indifferently down at herself. Today she wore a demure white frock with green and blue flowers embroidered along the hem, with a white ribbon constraining her copper-auburn curls. 'It is well enough, or so I suppose.'

Cassander spoke in fulsome tones. 'I see before me, not a wild-eyed scalawag escaping a dogfight, but a royal princess of delicacy and grace! Indeed, you are almost pretty.'

Madouc gave a wry laugh. 'It is not my fault. They dressed me willy-nilly, so that I might be fit for the cotillion.'

'And that is so inglorious?'

'Not altogether, since I will not be there.'

'Aha! You run grave risks! Lady Desdea will be rigid with vexation!'

'She must learn to be more reasonable. If she likes dancing, well and good; it is all the same to me. She may jig, jerk, kick high in the air and jump in a circle, so long as I may do otherwise. That is reasonable conduct!'

'But it is not the way things go! Everyone must learn to act properly; no one is exempt, not even I.'

'Why, then, are you not at the cotillion, sweating and hopping with the others?'

'I have had my share of it: never fear! It is now your turn.'

'I will have none of it, and this is what Lady Desdea must get through her head.'

Cassander chuckled. 'Such mutiny might easily earn you another beating.'

Madouc gave her head a scornful toss. 'No matter! I shall utter not a sound, and they will quickly tire of their sport.'

Cassander uttered a bark of laughter. 'Wrong, in every respect! I discussed this same topic only last week with Tanchet the under-torturer. He states that voluble types who instantly screech and blubber and make horrid noises – these are the ones who fare the best, since the torturer is quickly satisfied that his job has been well and truly done. Take my advice! A few shrill screams and a convulsion or two might save your skin a whole medley of tingles!'

'This bears thinking about,' said Madouc.

'Or – from a different perspective – you might try to be mild and meek, and avoid the beatings altogether.'

Madouc gave her head a dubious shake. 'My mother, the Princess Suldrun, was mild and meek, but failed to escape an awful penalty – which the poor creature never deserved. That is my opinion.'

Cassander spoke in measured tones: 'Suldrun disobeyed the king's command, and had only herself to blame.'

'Nevertheless, it seems very harsh treatment to visit upon one's own dear daughter.'

Cassander was not comfortable with the topic. 'Royal justice is not for us to question.' Madouc gave Cassander a cool appraisal. He frowned down at her. 'Why do you stare at me so?'

'Someday you will be king.'

'That well may be – later, so I hope, rather than sooner. I am in no haste to rule.'

'Would you treat your daughter in such a fashion?'

Cassander pursed his lips. 'I would do what I thought to be correct and kingly.'

'And if I were still unmarried, would you try to wed me to some fat bad-smelling prince, so as to make me miserable the rest of my life?'

Cassander gave an exclamation of annoyance. 'Why ask such pointless questions? You will be of age long before I wear the crown. Your marriage will be arranged by someone other than me.'

'Small chance of that,' said Madouc under her breath.

'I did not hear your remark.'

'No matter. Do you often visit the old garden where my mother died?'

'I have not done so for years.'

'Take me there now.'

'Now? When you should be at the cotillion?'

'No time could be more convenient.'

Cassander looked toward the palace, and seeing no one, gave a flippant wave of the hand. 'I should stand aloof from your vagaries! Still, at the moment I have nothing better to do. Come then, while Lady Desdea is yet dormant. I do not take kindly to complaints and reproaches.'

Madouc said wisely: 'I have learned the best response.

I feign a blank stupid perplexity, so that they weary themselves with explanations, and forget all else.'

'Ah Madouc, you are a crafty one! Come then, before we are apprehended.'

The two set off up the cloistered way toward Zoltra Bright-Star's wall: up past the orangery, through the wall itself by a dank passage and out upon the parade ground at the front of the Peinhador: a place known as 'The Urquial'. To the right, the wall veered sharply to the south; in the angle, a thicket of larch and juniper concealed a decaying postern of black timber.

Cassander, already beset by second thoughts, pushed through the thicket, cursing the brambles and the drift of pollen from the larches. He thrust at the postern and grunted at the recalcitrance of the sagging timbers. Putting his shoulder to the wood, he heaved hard; with a dismal groaning of corroded iron hinges the postern swung open. Cassander gave a grim nod of triumph for his victory over the obstacle. He beckoned to Madouc. 'Behold! The secret garden!'

The two stood at the head of a narrow vale, sloping down to a little crescent of beach. At one time the garden had been landscaped after the classic Arcadian style, but now grew rank and wild with trees and shrubs of many sorts: oak, olive, laurel, bay and myrtle; hydrangea, heliotrope, asphodel, vervain, purple thyme. Halfway down to the beach a clutter of marble blocks and a few standing columns indicated the site of an ancient Roman villa. The single whole structure to be seen was near at hand: a small chapel, now dank with lichen and the odor of wet stone.

Cassander pointed to the stone chapel. 'That is where Suldrun took shelter from the weather. She spent many lonely nights in that small place.' He gave his head a wry shake. 'And also a few nights not so lonely, which cost her dear in grief and sorrow.'

Madouc blinked at the tears which had come to her eyes and turned away. Cassander said gruffly: 'The events are many years gone; one should not mourn forever.'

Madouc looked down the long descent of the garden. 'It was my mother, whom I never knew, and it was my father, who was put in a hole to die! How can I forget so easily?'

Cassander shrugged. 'I don't know. I can only assure you that your emotion is wasted. Do you wish to see more of the garden?'

'Let us follow the path and find where it leads.'

'It goes here and there, and finally down to the beach. Suldrun whiled away her days paving the path with pebbles from the beach. Rains have undone the path; there is little to show for her work – or her life, for that matter.'

'Except me.'

'Except you! A notable accomplishment, to be sure!'

Madouc ignored the jocularity, which she found to be in rather poor taste.

Cassander said thoughtfully, 'For a fact, you are not at all like her. Evidently you resemble your father, whoever or whatever he might have been.'

Madouc spoke with feeling: 'Since my mother loved him, he was surely a person of high estate and noble character! Nevertheless, they call me "bastard" and insist that I have no pedigree.'

Cassander frowned. 'Who commits such discourtesy?'

'The six maidens who attend me.'

Cassander was shocked. 'Really! They all seem so sweet and pretty – Devonet in particular!'

'She is the worst; in fact, she is a little serpent.'

Cassander's displeasure had lost its edge. 'Ah well, girls

can be saucy at times. The facts, sadly enough, cannot be denied. Do you care to go further?'

Madouc halted in the path. 'Had Suldrun no friends to help her?'

'None who dared defy the king. The priest Umphred came occasionally; he said he wanted her for Christianity. I suspect he wanted her for something else, which was no doubt denied him. Perhaps for this reason he betrayed her to the king.'

'So Priest Umphred was the traitor.'

'I suppose he thought it his duty.'

Madouc nodded, assimilating the information. 'Why did she stay? I would have been over the wall and away inside the hour.'

'Knowing you, I well believe it! Suldrun, as I remember her, was of a dreamy gentle cast.'

'Still, she need not have remained here. Had she no spirit?'

Cassander considered. 'I suppose that she hoped always for the king's forgiveness. If she ran away, what then? She had no taste for filth or hunger, nor the cold wind by night, nor the certainty of rape.'

Madouc was uncertain as to the exact meaning of the word. 'What is "rape"?'

Cassander explained in lofty terms. Madouc compressed her lips. 'That is boorish conduct! If it were tried on me, I would not tolerate it for a moment, and I certainly would have something very sharp to say!'

'Suldrun also disliked the idea,' said Cassander. 'So ends the story, and nothing remains but memories and Princess Madouc. Have you seen enough of this old garden?'

Madouc looked all around. 'It is quiet here, and eery. The world is far away. By moonlight it must be sad, and so beautiful as to break one's heart. I want never to come here again.'

VI

An under-maid informed Lady Desdea of Madouc's return to the castle, in the company of Prince Cassander.

Lady Desdea was taken aback. Her intent had been to chide the little minx at some length and then ordain six punitive hours of dancing lessons. Prince Cassander's participation totally altered the case. To punish Madouc would imply criticism of Prince Cassander, and Lady Desdea was chary of such a risk. One day Cassander would become king, and kings were notoriously long of memory.

Lady Desdea turned on her heel and marched to the queen's parlor, where she found Sollace relaxing among her cushions while Father Umphred read psalms in sonorous Latin from a scroll. Sollace understood none of the sense, but she found Father Umphred's voice soothing, and meanwhile she refreshed herself with curds and honey from a bowl.

Lady Desdea stood impatiently to the side until Father Umphred completed his reading, then, in response to Sollace's inquiring nod, she told of Madouc's latest delinquency.

Sollace listened without emotion, supping all the while from her bowl.

Lady Desdea warmed to her subject. 'I am bewildered! Rather than acting in accordance with my instructions, she chose to saunter here and there with Prince Cassander, heedless of the arrangements. Were her rank less exalted, one could almost think her controlled by a cacodaemon, or an esper or some other malignant entity! Such is the perversity of the child.'

Queen Sollace failed to become exercised. 'She is a trifle wayward; no doubt as to that.'

Lady Desdea's voice rose in pitch. 'I am at my wit's end! She does not even trouble to defy me; she simply pays me no heed. I might as well be talking out the window!'

'I will reprimand the child later this afternoon,' said Queen Sollace. 'Or perhaps tomorrow, if I decide to beat her. At the moment, I have a dozen other matters on my mind.'

Father Umphred cleared his throat. 'Perhaps Your Highness will allow me a suggestion.'

'Of course! I value your counsel!'

Father Umphred placed the tips of his fingers together. 'Lady Desdea alluded to the possibility of an alien influence. All taken with all, I think this unlikely – but not beyond the realm of imagination, and the Holy Church recognizes such afflictions. As a precaution I would suggest that the Princess Madouc be baptized into the Christian faith and thereupon be instructed in the tenets of orthodoxy. The routines of devotion, meditation and prayer will gently but surely persuade her to those virtues of obedience and humility which we so long to inculcate in her.'

Queen Sollace put aside the empty bowl. 'The idea has merit, but I wonder if the Princess Madouc would find such a program appealing.'

Father Umphred smiled. 'A child is the last to appreciate what is pure and good. If Princess Madouc finds the environment of Haidion too stimulating, we can send her to the convent at Bulmer Skeme. The Mother Superior is both thorough and rigorous when the need exists.'

Queen Sollace sank back into the cushions of the couch. 'I will discuss the matter with the king.'

Sollace waited until King Casmir had taken his supper, and had become somewhat mellow with wine; then, as if casually, she brought Madouc's name into the conversation. 'Have you heard the latest? Madouc is not behaving as I might hope.'

'Ah bah,' growled King Casmir. 'It is no great matter. I am bored with this constant recital.'

'It is a subject not to be dismissed lightly. With full and insolent purpose she defied the instructions of Lady Desdea! Father Umphred is convinced that Madouc should be baptized and trained in Christian doctrine.'

'Eh? What nonsense is this?'

'It is scarcely nonsense,' said Sollace. 'Lady Desdea is beside herself with anxiety; she suspects that Madouc is moonstruck or possibly possessed by a familiar.'

'Absurd! The girl is full of nervous energy.' For a variety of reasons, Casmir had never informed Sollace of Madouc's provenance, nor the fact of her fairy blood. He said gruffly: 'She is a bit odd, perhaps, but no doubt she will grow out of it.'

'Father Umphred believes that Madouc is definitely in need of religious guidance and I agree.'

Casmir's voice took on an edge: 'You are far too amiable with that fat priest! I will send him away if he does not keep his opinions to himself!'

Sollace said stiffly: 'We are concerned only for the salvation of Madouc's eternal soul!'

'She is a clever little creature; let her worry about her own soul.'

'Hmf,' said Sollace. 'Whoever marries Madouc will be getting far more than he bargained for.'

King Casmir gave a frosty chuckle. 'You are correct on this account, for more reasons than one! In any event we will be off to Sarris in a week's time and everything will be changed.'

'Lady Desdea will have more difficulty than ever,' said Sollace with a sniff. 'Madouc will run wild as a hare.'

'Lady Desdea must then give chase, if she is truly in earnest.'

'You minimize the difficulties,' said Sollace. 'As for me, I find Sarris tiresome enough, without added exasperation.'

'The country air will do you a benefit,' said Casmir. 'We shall all enjoy Sarris.'

3

I

Each summer King Casmir moved with household and court to Sarris, a rambling old mansion about forty miles northeast of Lyonesse Town. The site, beside the River Glame, in a region of gently rolling parkland, was most pleasant. Sarris itself made no pretensions either to elegance or grandeur. Queen Sollace, for one, found the amenities at Sarris much inferior to those at Haidion, and described Sarris as 'a great overgrown barn of a farmhouse'. She also decried the rustic informality which, despite her best efforts, pervaded life at Sarris and which, in her opinion, diminished the dignity of the court and, further, infected the servants with slackness.

There was little society at Sarris, other than an occasional banquet at which King Casmir entertained certain of the local gentry, most of whom Queen Sollace found tedious. She often spoke to King Casmir of her boredom: 'In essence, I do not enjoy living like a peasant, with animals braying through the windows of my bedchamber and every cock of the fowl-run crying out alarums each morning before dawn.'

King Casmir turned a deaf ear to the complaints. Sarris was sufficiently convenient for the conduct of state business; for sport he played his falcons and hunted his parklands, or at times, when the chase was hot, he ranged far beyond, sometimes into the fringes of Forest Tantrevalles, only a few miles to the north.

The rest of the royal household also found Sarris to

their taste. Prince Cassander was attended by convivial comrades; daily they amused themselves riding abroad, or boating on the river, or practicing the sport of jousting, which recently had become fashionable. During the evening they fancied sport of another kind, in association with certain merry girls of the locality, using an abandoned gamekeeper's cottage for their venue.

Princess Madouc also took pleasure in the move, which, if nothing else, delivered her from the attendance of her six maids-in-waiting. Her pony Tyfer was ready at hand; every day she rode happily out on the meadows, with Pymfyd for her groom. Not all circumstances were halcyon; she was expected to comport herself in a style befitting her place. Madouc, however, paid little heed to the circumscriptions imposed by Lady Desdea, and followed her own inclinations.

Lady Desdea at last took Madouc aside for an earnest discussion. 'My dear, it is time and past time that reality enters your life! You must accept the fact that you are the Princess Madouc of Lyonesse, not some vulgar little ruffian girl, with neither rank nor responsibility!'

'Very well, Lady Desdea; I will remember this. Can I go now?'

'Not yet; in fact, I am barely started. I am trying to point out that each of your acts redounds to the credit, or discredit, not only of yourself and the royal family, but of the entire kingdom! It is awesome to think about! Are you quite clear on this?'

'Yes, Lady Desdea. And yet – '

' "And yet – " what?'

'No one seems to notice my conduct but you. So it makes little difference after all, and the kingdom is not in danger.'

'It makes a great deal of difference!' snapped Lady Desdea. 'Bad habits are easy to learn and hard to forget!

You must learn the gracious good habits that will make you admired and respected!'

Madouc gave a doubtful assent. 'I do not think anyone will ever admire my needlework or respect my dancing.'

'Nevertheless, these are skills and graces which you must learn, and learn well! Time is advancing; the days go by; the months become years while you are not even noticing. Before long there will be talk of betrothals, and then you and your conduct will be the subject of the most minute scrutiny and the most careful analysis.'

Madouc gave a disdainful grimace. 'If anyone scrutinizes me, they will need no analysis to discover what I think of them.'

'My dear, that is not the proper attitude.'

'No matter; I want nothing to do with such things. They must look elsewhere for their betrothals.'

Lady Desdea chuckled grimly. 'Do not be too positive too soon, since surely you will change your mind. In any case, I expect you to start practicing genteel conduct.'

'It would be a waste of time.'

'Indeed? Consider this case. A noble prince comes to Lyonesse, hoping to meet a princess modest and pure, of charm and delicacy. He asks: "And where is Princess Madouc, who, so I expect, is beautiful, kind and good?" For answer they point out the window and say: "There she goes now!" He looks out the window and sees you running past, helter-skelter, hair like red rope, with all the charm and grace of a banshee from hell! What then?'

'If the prince is wise, he will order up his horse and leave at once.' Madouc jumped to her feet. 'Are you finished? If so, I will be happy to leave.'

'Go.'

Lady Desdea sat still and stiff for ten minutes. Then, abruptly, she rose to her feet and marched to the queen's boudoir. She found Sollace sitting with her hands in a slurry of powdered chalk and milk of milkweed, by which she hoped to mitigate the effects of the country water.

Queen Sollace looked up from the basin of slurry. 'So then, Ottile! What a face you show me! Is it despair, or grief, or simple intestinal cramp?'

'You misread my mood, Your Highness! I have just spoken with Princess Madouc and now I must make a discouraging report.'

Sollace sighed. 'Again? I am becoming apathetic when her name is mentioned! She is in your hands. Teach her the proprieties and a few graces, together with dancing and needlework; that is enough. In a few years we will marry her off. Until then, we must bear with her oddities.'

'If she were only "odd", as you put it, I could deal with her. Instead she has become a full-fledged tomboy, and is intractable to boot. She swims the river where I can not venture; she climbs the trees and hides from my call in the foliage. Her favorite resort is the stables; always she stinks of horse. I know not how to control her.'

Sollace pulled her hand from the slurry and decided that the treatment had worked its best effect. Her maid started to wipe away the paste, prompting an outcry from Sollace: 'Take care, Nelda! You are flaying me alive with your strenuous work! Do you think I am made of leather?'

'I am sorry, Your Highness. I will be more careful. Your hands are now truly beautiful!'

Queen Sollace gave a grudging nod. 'That is why I endure such hardships. What were you saying, Ottile?'

'What shall be done with Princess Madouc?'

Sollace looked up blankly, eyes large and bovine. 'I am not quite clear on her fault.'

'She is undisciplined, free as a lark and not always tidy. There are smuts on her face and straws in her hair, if that flying red tousle deserves the word. She is careless, impudent, willful and wild.'

84

Queen Sollace sighed once again and selected a grape from the bowl at her elbow. 'Convey my displeasure to the princess and explain that I will be satisfied only with her proper deportment.'

'I have already done so ten times. I might as well be talking to the wind.'

'Hmf. She is no doubt as bored as I. This rusticity is maddening. Where are the little maids who attend her so nicely at Haidion? They are so dainty and sweet and nice; Madouc would surely profit from their example.'

'So one might imagine, in the ordinary case.'

Queen Sollace chose another grape. 'Send off for two or three of these maidens. Indicate that they are to guide Madouc in a gentle and discreet fashion. Time rushes on, and already we must look to the future!'

'Just so, Your Highness!'

'Who is that little blonde maiden, so winsome and full of pretty wiles? She is like myself at her age.'

'That would be Devonet, daughter to Duke Malnoyard Odo of Castle Folize.'

'Let us have her here at Sarris, and another as well. Who shall it be?'

'Either Ydraint or Chlodys; I think Chlodys, who is somewhat more durable. I will make arrangements at once. Still, you must expect no miracles.'

A week later Devonet and Chlodys arrived at Sarris and were instructed by Lady Desdea. She spoke dryly: 'The country air has affected Princess Madouc strangely, as if it were a vital tonic, perhaps to her excessive invigoration. She has become careless of decorum, and is also somewhat flighty. We hope that she will profit by the example you set for her, and possibly your carefully phrased advice.'

Devonet and Chlodys went to join Madouc. After long search they found her perched high in a cherry tree, plucking and eating plump red cherries.

Madouc saw the two without pleasure. 'I thought that you had gone to your homes for the summer. Are they tired of you so soon?'

'Not at all,' said Devonet with dignity. 'We are here by royal invitation.'

Chlodys said: 'Her Highness feels that you need proper companionship.'

'Ha,' said Madouc. 'No one asked me what I wanted.'

'We are supposed to set you a good example,' said Devonet. 'As a start, I will point out that a lady of refinement would not wish to be found so high in a tree.'

'Then I am a lady of refinement well and truly,' said Madouc, 'since I did not wish to be found.'

Chlodys looked speculatively up into the branches. 'Are the cherries ripe?'

'Quite ripe.'

'Are they good?'

'Very good indeed.'

'Since they are handy, you might pick a few for us.'

Madouc selected two cherries and dropped them into Chlodys' hands. 'Here are some the birds have pecked.'

Chlodys looked at the cherries with a wrinkled nose. 'Are there none better?'

'Certainly. If you climb the tree you can pick them.'

Devonet tossed her head. 'I don't care to soil my clothes.'

'As you like.'

Devonet and Chlodys moved to the side, where they settled themselves carefully in the grass and spoke in low voices. Occasionally they glanced up toward Madouc and giggled as if at some ludicrous consideration.

Madouc presently climbed down through the branches and jumped to the ground. 'How long will you stay at Sarris?'

'We are here at the queen's pleasure,' said Devonet.

She looked Madouc up and down, and laughed incredulously. 'You are wearing a boy's breeches!'

Madouc said coldly: 'If you found me in the tree without, you might have more cause for criticism.'

Devonet gave a scornful sniff. 'Now that you are on the ground, you should instantly go change. A pretty frock would be ever so much nicer.'

'Not if I should decide to go out with Tyfer for an hour or two.'

Devonet blinked. 'Oh? Where would you go?'

'Most anywhere. Perhaps along the riverbank.'

Chlodys asked with delicate emphasis: 'Who is "Tyfer"?'

Madouc gave her a wondering blue-eyed stare. 'What odd things must go on in your mind! Tyfer is my horse. What else could he be?'

Chlodys giggled. 'I was a bit confused.'

Without comment, Madouc turned away.

Devonet called out: 'Where are you going?'

'To the stables.'

Devonet screwed up her pretty face. 'I don't want to go to the stables. Let us do something else.'

Chlodys suggested: 'We can sit in the garden and play "Tittlewit" or "Cockalorum"!'

'That sounds like fine sport!' said Madouc. 'You two start the game. I will join you presently.'

Chlodys said doubtfully: 'It's no fun with just two!'

'Besides,' said Devonet, 'Lady Desdea wants us to attend you.'

'It's so that you may learn proper manners,' said Chlodys.

'That, in fact, is the way of it,' said Devonet. 'Without a pedigree you can't be expected to come by such things naturally, as we do.'

'I have a fine pedigree somewhere,' said Madouc

87

bravely. 'I am certain of it, and one day I will make a search – perhaps sooner than later.'

Devonet gave a choked gurgle of laughter. 'Do you go now to search the stables?'

Madouc turned her back and walked away. Devonet and Chlodys looked after her with vexation. Chlodys called: 'Wait for us! We will come with you, but you must behave properly!'

Later in the day Devonet and Chlodys reported to Lady Desdea. Both were thoroughly annoyed with Madouc, who had acceded to none of their wishes. 'She kept us there forever while she groomed her Tyfer horse and braided its mane!'

But worse was to come. Madouc finished with Tyfer and led him away, but failed to return. The two girls went to find her. As they picked their way fastidiously around the stable, an exit gate swung open without warning, thrusting them from the stone coping into the drainage sump, so that both stumbled and fell. At this point Madouc appeared in the opening and asked why they were playing in the manure. 'This is not what I consider ladylike behavior,' Madouc told them haughtily. 'Have you no regard for decency?'

Lady Desdea could only deplore the misfortune. 'You should be more careful. Still, Madouc need not lavish so much time on that horse. Tomorrow I shall see to it! We shall sit to our needlework, with honeycakes and sangaree for us all to enjoy.'

At twilight the three girls supped on cold fowl and onion pudding in a pleasant little room overlooking the park. Prince Cassander came to sit with them. At his order, the steward brought a flask of pale sweet wine. Cassander sat back in his chair, sipping from the goblet and talking largely of his theories and exploits. On the morrow he and his comrades intended to ride north to Flauhamet, a town on Old Street, where a great fair was in progress. 'There will be jousting,'[1] said Cassander. 'Perhaps I will take up a gage or two, if the competition is fair; we do not wish to compete against yokels and ploughboys; that goes without saying.'

Even at her relatively early age, Devonet was always ready to test her skills. 'You must be very brave, to take such risks!'

Cassander made an expansive gesture. 'It is a complicated skill, comprised of practice, horsemanship and natural ability. I flatter myself that I run a good course. You three should come to Flauhamet, at least to see the fair. Then, should we joust, we will wear your ribbons! What do you think of that?'

'It sounds splendid,' said Chlodys. 'But Lady Desdea has other plans for tomorrow.'

'In the morning we will sit at our needlework in the conservatory, while Master Jocelyn sings to the lute.' Devonet darted a glance toward Madouc. 'In the afternoon the queen holds court and we will all attend her, as is proper.'

'Ah well, you must do what Lady Desdea thinks best,' said Cassander. 'Perhaps there will be another occasion before summer is over.'

'I do hope so!' said Devonet. 'It would be most exciting to watch you vanquish your opponents, one after the other!'

'It is not so easy as that,' said Cassander. 'And there may be only bumpkins on plough horses to ride against. Still, we shall see.'

---

[1] Jousting in full armour with battle lances was not yet in vogue. During this era lances were heavily padded with pillowlike buffs, and jousting seldom caused injuries more serious than bruises and sprains.

II

In the morning, early, with the sun still red in the east, Madouc rose from her bed, dressed, took a hasty breakfast of porridge and figs in the kitchen, then ran around to the stables. Here she searched out Pymfyd and commanded him to saddle Tyfer, and his own horse as well.

Pymfyd blinked, yawned and scratched his head. 'It is neither entertaining nor sensible to ride out so early.'

'Do not attempt to think, Pymfyd! I have already made the decisions. Merely saddle the horses, and without delay.'

'I see no need for haste,' growled Pymfyd. 'The day is young and the day is long.'

'Is it not clear? I want to avoid Devonet and Chlodys! You have heard my orders; please be quick.'

'Very good, Your Highness.' Pymfyd languidly saddled the horses, and led them from the stable. 'Where do you intend to ride?'

'Here, there, up the lane, perhaps as far as Old Street.'

'Old Street? That is a goodly distance: four miles, or is it five?'

'No matter; the day is fine and the horses are eager for their run.'

'But we will not be back for our dinner! Must I go hungry on this account?'

'Come along, Pymfyd! Today your stomach is not important.'

'Perhaps not to you of the royalty, who nibble at will upon saffron cakes and tripes in honey! I am a vulgar lout with a gut to match, and now you must wait till I find bread and cheese for my dinner.'

'Be quick!'

Pymfyd ran off and returned a few moments later carrying a cloth sack which he tied to the back of his saddle.

Madouc asked: 'Are you ready at last? Then let us be off.'

III

The two rode up Sarris Way across the royal parkland: past meadows sparkling with daisies, lupines, wild mustard, flaming red poppies; past copses of ash and birch; through the shade of massive oaks where they overhung the lane.

They departed the royal domain through a stone portal and almost immediately encountered a crossroads, where Sarris Way became Fanship Lane.

Madouc and Pymfyd rode north up Fanship Lane, not without grumbling from Pymfyd, who could not understand Madouc's interest in Old Street. 'There is nothing to see but the road, which runs to the right and also to the left.'

'Just so,' said Madouc. 'Let us proceed.'

The countryside presently became marked by evidences of cultivation: fields planted to oats and barley, marked off by old stone fences, an occasional farmhouse. After a mile or two, the lane ascended a long easy slope by slants and traverses, finally, at the top of the rise, intersecting with Old Street.

Madouc and Pymfyd pulled up their horses. Looking back across the panorama to the south, they could trace the entire length of Fanship Lane to the crossroads, and beyond, across the king's park to the poplars beside the

River Glame, though Sarris itself was concealed behind trees.

As Pymfyd had asserted, Old Street continued in both directions, over the downs and out of sight. Fanship Lane, crossing Old Street, proceeded onward toward the somber loom of Forest Tantrevalles, at this point little more than a mile to the north.

At the moment Old Street was empty of traffic: a fact which seemed to excite Pymfyd's suspicions. Craning his neck, he stared first in one direction then the other. Madouc watched in puzzlement, and finally asked: 'Why are you searching so carefully, when there is nothing to be seen?'

'That is what I want to see.'

'I don't quite understand.'

'Naturally not,' said Pymfyd loftily. 'You are too young to know the woes of the world, which are many. There is also much wickedness, if one cares to look, or even if one takes care not to look.'

Madouc inspected the road: first to the east, then to the west. 'At the moment I see nothing either woeful or wicked.'

'That is because the road is empty. Wickedness often springs into view from nowhere, which makes it so fearful.'

'Pymfyd, I believe that you are obsessed by fear.'

'It may well be, since fear rules the world. The hare fears the fox, who fears the hound, who fears the kennel-master, who fears the lord, who fears the king whose fears I would not have the impudence to think upon.'

'Poor Pymfyd! Your world is built of fear and dread! As for me, I have no time for such emotions.'

Pymfyd spoke in an even voice. 'You are a royal princess and I may not call you a witless little fool, even should the thought cross my mind.'

Madouc turned him a sad blue-eyed glance. 'So that, after all, is your concept of me.'

'I will say only this: persons who fear nothing are soon dead.'

'I have a fear or two,' said Madouc. 'Needlework, Master Jocelyn's dancing lessons, one or two other things which need not be mentioned.'

'I have many fears,' said Pymfyd proudly. 'Mad dogs, lepers and leperbells, hellhorses, harpies, and witches; lightning-riders and the creatures who live at the bottom of wells; also: hop-legs, irchments and ghosts who wait by the lych-gate.'

'Is that all?' asked Madouc.

'By no means! I fear dropsy, milkeye and the pox. Now that I think of it, I very much fear the king's displeasure! We must turn back before someone sees us so far from Sarris and carries tales!'

'Not so fast!' said Madouc. 'When it is time to return I will give the signal.' She studied the signpost. 'Flauhamet is only four miles distant.'

Pymfyd cried out in quick alarm: 'Four miles or four hundred: for us one is like the other!'

'Prince Cassander mentioned the Flauhamet fair, and said it was very gay.'

'One fair is much like another,' declared Pymfyd. 'The favored resort of rogues, cheats and cut-purses!'

Madouc paid no heed. 'There are to be jugglers, buffoons, songsters, stilt-dancers, mimes and mountebanks.'

'These folk are by and large disreputable,' growled Pymfyd. 'That is common knowledge.'

'There is also a tournament of jousting. Prince Cassander may take a turn in the lists, if the competition suits him.'

'Hmf. That I doubt.'

'Oh? How so?'

Pymfyd looked off across the landscape. 'It is not fitting that I discuss Prince Cassander.'

'Speak! Your words will go no farther.'

'I doubt if he will risk the lists with so many folk to watch should he take a tumble.'

Madouc grinned. 'For a fact, he is vain. In any event, I don't care to watch the jousting. I would rather wander among the booths.'

Pymfyd's honest face took on a set of mulish obstinacy. 'We cannot ride into town so free and easy, to rub elbows with the bumpkins! Can you imagine Her Majesty's disapproval? You would be chided and I would be beaten. We must turn back, since the day advances.'

'It is still early! Devonet and Chlodys are only just settling to their needlework.'

Pymfyd gave a cry of consternation. He pointed westward along Old Street. 'Folk are approaching; they are gentry and you will be recognized! We must be gone before they arrive.'

Madouc heaved a sigh. Pymfyd's logic could not be refuted. Reining Tyfer about, she started back along Fanship Lane, only to stop short.

'What now?' demanded Pymfyd.

'A party is coming up Fanship Lane. That is Cassander on the bay horse, and it is no doubt King Casmir himself on the great black charger.'

Pymfyd gave a groan of despair. 'We are trapped!'

'Not so! We will cross Old Street and take cover up Fanship Lane until the way is clear.'

'A sound idea, for once!' muttered Pymfyd. 'Hurry! There is no time to waste; we can hide behind yonder trees!'

Touching up their horses, the two trotted across Old Street and north along the continuation of Fanship Lane, which quickly became little more than a track across the meadow. They approached a copse of poplar trees, where they hoped to take concealment.

Madouc called over her shoulder: 'I smell smoke!'

Pymfyd called back: 'There will be a crofter's hut nearby. You smell the smoke from his hearth.'

'I see no hut.'

'That is not our great concern. Quick now, into the shade!'

The two took themselves under the poplars, where they discovered the source of the smoke: a fire over which a pair of vagabonds roasted a rabbit. One was short and big-bellied, with a round flat face surrounded by a froust of black beard and black hair. The second was tall and thin as a stick, lank of arm and leg, with a face long and vacuous, like the face of a cod. Both wore ragged garments and tattered buskins. The tall vagabond wore a high piked cap of black felt; his fat comrade wore a low-crowned hat with a very wide brim. To the side were a pair of sacks in which they evidently carried their belongings. At the sight of Madouc and Pymfyd, the two rose to their feet, and stood appraising the situation.

Madouc gave the two a cold inspection in return, and concluded that never had she encountered a more unsavory pair of rogues.

The short fat vagabond spoke: 'And what are you two doing here, so fresh and airy?'

'That is none of your concern,' said Madouc. 'Pymfyd, let us proceed; we disturb these persons at their meal.'

'Not at all,' said the short vagabond. He spoke to his tall comrade without taking his eyes from Madouc and Pymfyd. 'Ossip, have a look down the lane; see who else is near.'

'All clear; no one in sight,' reported Ossip.

'Those are fine horses,' said the burly rogue. 'The saddles and fitments are also of fine quality.'

'Sammikin, notice! The red-haired brat wears a golden clasp.'

'Is it not a farce, Ossip? That some wear gold, while others go without?'

'It is the injustice of life! Were I to wield power, everyone should share alike!'

'That is a noble concept indeed!'

Ossip peered at Tyfer's bridle. 'See here! Even the horse wears gold!' He spoke with unctuous fervor: 'Here is richness!'

Sammikin snapped his fingers. 'I cannot help but rejoice! The sun shines bright and our luck has turned at last!'

'Still, we must exert ourselves in a certain way that we know of, in order to safeguard our reputations.'

'Wise words, Ossip!' The two moved forward. Pymfyd called sharply to Madouc: 'Ride off at speed!' He wheeled his own horse, but Ossip reached out a gangling arm and seized his bridle. Pymfyd kicked out vigorously and caught Ossip in the face, causing him to blink and clap his hand to his eye. 'Ah, you little viper; you have shown your teeth! Alas, my poor face! What pain!'

Sammikin had made a dancing little run toward Madouc, but she had kicked Tyfer into motion, to ride a few yards up the lane, where she halted in an agony of indecision.

Sammikin turned back to where Ossip still hung to the bridle of Pymfyd's horse, despite Pymfyd's kicks and curses. Sammikin, coming up behind, seized Pymfyd around the waist and flung him rudely to the ground. Pymfyd bellowed in outrage. Rolling to the side, he seized up a broken tree branch and, jumping to his feet, he stood at bay. 'Dogs!' He brandished the limb with hysterical bravado. 'Vermin! Come at me if you dare!' He looked over his shoulder to where Madouc sat rigid on Tyfer. 'Ride away, you little fool, and be quick! Fetch help!'

Sammikin and Ossip without haste took up their staffs and closed in on Pymfyd, who defended himself with might and main, until Sammikin's staff broke his branch into splinters. Sammikin feinted; Ossip raised his staff on high and struck Pymfyd across the side of the head, so that Pymfyd's eyes looked in opposite directions. He fell to the ground. Sammikin struck him again and again, while Ossip tied Pymfyd's horse to a tree. He started at a run toward Madouc. She finally roused herself from her stupefaction, wheeled Tyfer, and set off up the lane at a gallop.

Pymfyd's head lolled to the side, with blood trickling from his mouth. Sammikin stood back with a grunt of approval. 'This one will carry no tales! Now for the other.'

Madouc, crouching low in the saddle, galloped up the lane, stone fences to either side. She looked over her shoulder; Ossip and Sammikin were trotting up the lane in pursuit. Madouc gave a low wild cry and kicked Tyfer to his best speed. She would ride up the lane until she found a gap in one of the fences, then dash away across the downs and back to Old Street.

Behind came the vagabonds, Ossip pacing with long stately strides, Sammikin pumping his arms and scuttling like a fat rat. As before, they seemed in no great haste.

Madouc looked right and left. A ditch flowing with water ran beside the lane on one side with the stone fence beyond; to the other, the fence had given way to a hawthorn hedge. Ahead the lane curved to the side and passed through a gap in the fence. Without a pause Madouc galloped Tyfer through the gap. She stopped short in consternation, to find that she had entered a sheep-fold of no great extent. She looked here and there and all around, but discovered no exit.

Up the lane came Ossip and Sammikin, puffing and blowing from their exertion. Ossip called out in a fluting voice: 'Nicely, nicely now! Stand your horse; be calm and ready! Do not make us dodge about!'

' "Quiet" is the word!' called Sammikin. 'It will soon be over, and you will find it very quiet, so I am told.'

'That is my understanding!' agreed Ossip. 'Stand still and do not cry; I cannot abide a wailing child!'

Madouc looked desperately around the paddock, seeking a break or a low place over which Tyfer might jump, but in vain. She slid to the ground, and hugged Tyfer's neck. 'Goodbye, my dear good friend! I must leave you to save my life!' She ran to the fence, scrambled up and over and was gone from the fold.

Ossip and Sammikin called out in anger: 'Stop! Come back! It is all in fun! We mean no harm!'

Madouc turned a frightened glance over her shoulder and only fled the faster, with the dark shade of the Forest Tantrevalles now close at hand.

Cursing, lamenting the need for so much exercise, and calling out the most awful threats which came to their minds, Sammikin and Ossip scrambled over the fence and came in pursuit.

At the edge of the forest Madouc paused a moment to gasp and lean against the bole of a crooked old oak. Up the meadow, not fifty yards distant, came Ossip and Sammikin, both now barely able to run for fatigue. Sammikin took note of Madouc, where she stood by the tree, auburn curls in wild disarray. The two slowed almost to a halt, then advanced a sly step at a time. Sammikin called in a voice of syrup: 'Ah, dear child, how clever you are to wait for us! Beware the forest, where the bogles live!'

Ossip added: 'They will eat you alive and spit up your bones! You are safer with us!'

'Come, dear little chick!' called Sammikin. 'We will play a jolly game together!'

Madouc turned and plunged into the forest. Sammikin and Ossip raised cries of wrathful disappointment. 'Come back, you raddle-topped little itling!' 'Now we are angry; you must be punished, and severely!' 'Ah, vixen, but you will squeak and gasp and shudder! Our mercy? None! You had none for us!'

Madouc grimaced. Uneasy little spasms tugged at her stomach. What a terrible place the world could be! They had killed poor Pymfyd, so good and so brave! And Tyfer! Never would she ride Tyfer again! And if they caught her, they would wring her neck on the spot – unless they thought to use her for some unthinkable amusement.

Madouc stopped to listen. She held her breath. The thud and crush of heavy feet on the dead leaves came frighteningly close at hand. Madouc darted off at an angle, around a thicket of blackthorn and another of bay, hoping to befuddle her pursuers.

The forest became dense; foliage blocked away the sky, save only where a fallen tree, or an outcrop of rock, or some inexplicable circumstance, created a glade. A rotting log blocked Madouc's way; she clambered over, ducked around a blackberry bush, jumped a little rill where it trickled through watercress. She paused to look back and to catch her breath. Nothing fearful could be seen; undoubtedly she had evaded the two robbers. She held her breath to listen.

Thud-crunch, thud-crunch, thud-crunch: the sounds were faint and cautious but seemed to be growing louder, and, in fact, by fortuitous chance, Ossip and Sammikin had glimpsed the flicker of Madouc's white smock down one of the forest aisles, and were still on her trail.

Madouc gave a little cry of frustration. She turned and once more fled through the forest, picking out the most devious ways and the darkest shadows. She slid through a thicket of alders, waded a slow stream, crossed a glade and made a detour around a great fallen oak. Where the roots thrust into the air she found a dark little nook, concealed by a bank of foxgloves. Madouc crouched down under the roots.

Several minutes passed. Madouc waited, hardly daring to breathe. She heard footsteps; Ossip and Sammikin went blundering past. Madouc closed her eyes, fearing that they would feel the brush of her vision and stop short.

Ossip and Sammikin paused only an instant, to look angrily around the glade. Sammikin, thinking to hear a sound in the distance, pointed his finger and gave a guttural cry; the two ran off into the depths of the forest. The thud of their footsteps diminished and was lost in the hush.

Madouc remained huddled in the cranny. She discovered that she was warm and comfortable; her eyelids drooped; despite her best intentions, she drowsed.

Time passed – how long? Five minutes? Half an hour? Madouc awoke, and now she felt cramped. Cautiously she began to extricate herself from the cranny. She stopped short. What was that sound, so thin and tinkling? Music?

Madouc listened intently. The sounds seemed to come from a source not too far away, but hidden from her view by the foxglove foliage.

Madouc crouched indecisively, half in, half out of her covert. The music seemed artless and easy, even somewhat frivolous, with queer little trills and quavers. Such a music, thought Madouc, could not conceivably derive from threat or malice. She raised to her knees and peered through the foxglove. It would be an embarrassment to be discovered hiding in such an undignified condition. She plucked up her courage and rose to her feet, ordering her hair and brushing dead leaves from her garments, all the while looking around the glade.

Twenty feet distant, on a smooth stone, sat a pinch-faced little creature, not much larger than herself, with round sea-green eyes, nut-brown skin and hair. He wore a suit of fine brown stuff striped blue and red; a jaunty little blue cap with a panache of blackbird's-feathers, and long pointed shoes. In one hand he held a wooden sound-box from which protruded two dozen small metal tongues; as he stroked the tongues music tinkled from the box.

The creature, taking note of Madouc, desisted from his playing. He asked in a piping voice: 'Why do you sleep when the day is so new? Time for sleep during owl's-wake.'

Madouc replied in her best voice: 'I slept because I fell asleep.'

'I understand, at least better than I did before. Why do you stare at me? From marvelling admiration, as I would suppose?'

Madouc made a tactful response. 'Partly from admiration, and partly because I seldom talk with fairies.'

The creature spoke with petulance. 'I am a wefkin, not a fairy. The differences are obvious.'

'Not to me. At least, not altogether.'

'Wefkins are calm and stately by nature; we are solitary philosophers, as it were. Further, we are a gallant folk, proud and handsome, which conduces to fate-ridden amours both with mortals and with other halflings. We are truly magnificent beings.'

'That much is clear,' said Madouc. 'What of the fairies?'

The wefkin made a gesture of deprecation. 'An unstable folk, prone both to vagary and to thinking four thoughts at once. They are social creatures and require the company of their ilk; otherwise they languish. They chatter and titter; they preen and primp; they engage in grand passions

101

which occupy them all of twenty minutes; extravagant excess is their watchword! Wefkins are paladins of valor; the fairies do deeds of wanton perversity. Has not your mother explained these distinctions to you?'

'My mother has explained nothing. She has long been dead.'

'"Dead"? What's this again?'

'She is dead as Dinan's cat, and I can't help but think it inconsiderate of her.'

The wefkin blinked his green eyes and played a pensive trill on his melody box. 'This is grim news, and I am doubly surprised, since I spoke with her only a fortnight past, when she showed all her usual verve – of which, may I say, you have not been denied your full and fair share.'

Madouc shook her head in perplexity. 'You must mistake me for someone else.'

The wefkin peered closely at her. 'Are you not Madouc, the beautiful and talented child now accepted, if somewhat gracelessly, as "Royal Princess of Lyonesse" by King Bumble-head?'

'I am she,' said Madouc modestly. 'But my mother was the Princess Suldrun.'

'Not so! That is a canard! Your true mother is the fairy Twisk, of Thripsey Shee.'

Madouc stared at the wefkin in open-mouthed wonder. 'How do you know this?'

'It is common knowledge among the halflings. Believe or disbelieve, as you wish.'

'I do not question your word,' said Madouc hastily. 'But the news comes as an astonishment. How did it happen so?'

The wefkin sat upright on the stone. Rubbing his chin with long green fingers, he appraised Madouc sidelong. 'Yes! I will recite the facts of the case, but only if you request the favor – since I would not care to startle you without your express permission.' The wefkin fixed his great green eyes upon Madouc's face. 'Is it your wish that I do you this favor?'

'Yes, please!'

'Just so! The Princess Suldrun gave birth to a boy-child. The father was Aillas of Troicinet. The baby is now known as Prince Dhrun.'

'Prince Dhrun! Now I am truly astonished! How can it be? He is far older than I!'

'Patience! You shall learn all. Now then. For safety the baby was taken to a place in the forest. Twisk chanced to pass by and exchanged you for the little blond boy-baby, and that is the way of it. You are a changeling. Dhrun lived at Thripsey Shee a year and a day by mortal time, but by fairy time, many years elapsed: seven, eight, or it might be nine; no one knows since no one keeps a reckoning.'

Madouc stood in bemused silence. Then she asked: 'Am I then of fairy blood?'

'You have lived long years in human places, eating human bread and drinking human wine. Fairy stuff is delicate; who knows how much has been replaced with human dross? That is the way of it; still, all taken with all, it is not so bad a condition. Would you have it differently?'

Madouc reflected. 'I would not want to change from the way I am – whatever that is. But in any case, I am grateful to you for the information.'

'Save your thanks, my dear! It is just a little favor – barely enough to be reckoned.'

'In that case, tell me who might be my father.'

The wefkin chuckled. 'You phrase the question with a nicety! Your father might be this one or he might be that one, or he might be someone far away and gone. You must ask Twisk, your mother. Would you like to meet her?'

103

'Very much indeed.'

'I have a moment or two to spare. If you so request, I will teach you to call your mother.'

'Please do!'

'Then you so request?'

'Of course!'

'I accede to your request with pleasure, and there will be no great increment to our little account. Step over here, if you will.'

Madouc sidled from behind the foxgloves and approached the wefkin, who exuded a resinous odor, as if from crushed herbs and pine needles, mingled with bosk, pollen and musk.

'Observe!' said the wefkin in a grand voice. 'I pluck a blade of saw-grass; I cut a little slit here and another here; then I do thus, then so. Now I blow a gentle breath – very easy, very soft, and the virtue of the grass produces a call. Listen!' He blew, and the grass whistle emitted a soft tone. 'Now then: you must make just such a whistle with your own fingers.'

Madouc started to make the whistle, then, troubled by a thought which had been working at the back of her mind, paused. She asked: 'What do you mean when you speak of "our little account"?'

The wefkin made a flickering flourish of long-fingered hands. 'Nothing of large significance: in the main, just a way of speaking.'

Madouc dubiously continued her work. She paused again. 'It is well known that fairies never give without taking. Is the same true of wefkins?'

'Bah! In large transactions, this might be the case. Wefkins are not an avaricious folk.'

Madouc thought to detect evasiveness. 'Tell me, then, how I must pay for your advice?'

The wefkin pulled at the flaps of his cap and tittered as

if in embarrassment. 'I will accept nothing of consequence. Neither silver nor gold, nor yet precious stuffs. I am happy to oblige someone so quick and pretty. If only for the joys of gratitude you may kiss the end of my nose, and that will settle our account. Is it agreed?'

Madouc looked askance at the wefkin and his long pointed nose, while the wefkin made foolish and inconsequential little gestures. Madouc said: 'I will take the matter under advisement. I seldom kiss strangers; on their noses or elsewhere.'

The wefkin scowled and jerked his knees up under his chin. After a moment he resumed his bland demeanor. 'You are unlike your mother in this regard. Well, no matter. I only thought to – but again, no matter. Have you made your grass flute? Well done. Blow softly, with kind expression – ah! That is good. Stop now, and listen to my instruction. To summon your mother you must blow into the flute and sing in this wise:

> "Lirra lissa larra lass
> Madouc has made a flute of grass.
> Softly blowing, wild and free
> She calls to Twisk at Thripsey Shee.
> Lirra lissa larra leer
> A daughter calls her mother dear!
> Tread the wind and vault the mere;
> Span the sky and meet me here.
> So sing I, Madouc."'

Madouc, after a diffident rehearsal, took a deep breath to settle her nerves, then blew a soft note on the grass flute and spoke the cantrap.

Nothing seemed to occur. Madouc looked here and there, then spoke to the wefkin. 'Did I pronounce the charm correctly?'

A soft voice responded from behind the foxgloves: 'You

spoke the charm in good rendition.' Twisk the fairy damsel came forward: a supple creature with a casual fluff of pale blue hair, bound with a rope of sapphires.

Madouc called out in awe and rapture: 'Are you truly my mother?'

'First things first,' said Twisk. 'How did you agree to pay Zocco for his services?'

'He wanted me to kiss his nose. I told him that I would take advice on the matter.'

'Quite right!' declared Zocco the wefkin. 'In due course I will vouchsafe the correct advice, and that will be the end of it. We need discuss the subject no further.'

'Since I am her mother, I will provide the advice, and spare you the effort,' said Twisk.

'No effort for me! I am deft and alert in my thinking!'

Twisk paid no heed. 'Madouc, this is my advice: pick up yonder clod of dirt, and tender it to that pop-eyed little imp, speaking these words: "Zocco, with this token I both imburse and reimburse you, in full fee and total account, now and then, anon and forever, in this world and all others, and in every other conceivable respect, for each and every service you have performed for me or in my behalf, real or imaginary, to the limits of time, in all directions."'

'Sheer rigmarole and tommyrot!' scoffed Zocco. 'Madouc, pay no heed to this foolish blue-haired wiffet; you and I have our own arrangements, as you know.'

Twisk came slowly forward, and Madouc was able to see her clearly: a lovely creature with pale blue hair, skin the color of cream, features of surpassing delicacy. Her eyes, like those of Madouc, were wonderful dreaming sky-blue pools, in which a susceptible man might easily lose his wits. Twisk spoke to Madouc: 'I will remark, as a matter of casual interest, that Zocco is notorious for his lewd conduct. If you kissed his nose you would be compelled into his service, and soon would be kissing him elsewhere, at his orders, and who knows what else?'

'This is unthinkable!' declared Madouc aghast. 'Zocco seemed so affable and courteous!'

'That is the usual trick.'

Madouc turned to Zocco. 'I have now taken advisement.' She picked up the clod of dirt. 'Instead of kissing your nose, I tender you this token of my gratitude.' She spoke the disclaimer which Twisk had contrived for her use, despite Zocco's squeaks and groans of protest.

With a pettish motion Zocco cast the clod of dirt aside. 'Such tokens are useless! I cannot eat them; they are flavorless! I cannot wear them; they lack style, and they provide no amusement whatever!'

Twisk said: 'Silence, Zocco; your complaints are crass.'

'In addition to the token,' said Madouc with dignity, 'and despite your horrifying plans, I extend you my thanks, in that you have united me with my mother, and no doubt Twisk feels the same gratitude.'

'What!' said Twisk. 'I had long put your existence out of my mind. Why, may I ask, did you call me?'

Madouc's jaw dropped. 'I wanted to know my mother! I thought all the time she was dead.'

Twisk gave an indulgent laugh. 'The error is absurd. I am surcharged with vivacity, of all kinds!'

'So I see! I regret the mistake, but I was given false information.'

'Just so. You must learn to be more skeptical. But now you know the truth and I will be returning to Thripsey Shee!'

'Not yet!' cried Madouc. 'I am your beloved daughter, and you have only just met me! Also, I need your help!'

Twisk sighed. 'Is it not always the way? What then do you want of me?'

'I am lost in the forest! Two murderers killed Pymfyd and stole my horse Tyfer. They chased me and caused me a great fright; they wanted to kill me as well; also they called me a "scrawny red-headed whelp"!'

Twisk stared in shock and disapproval. 'You meekly stood by and allowed these insults?'

'By no means! I ran away as fast as possible and hid.'

'You should have brought them a waft of hornets! Or shortened their legs so that their feet adjoined their buttocks! Or transformed them into hedgehogs!'

Madouc gave an embarrassed laugh. 'I don't know how to do these things.'

Twisk sighed once more. 'I have neglected your education; I cannot deny it. Well, no time like the present, and we shall make a start at this instant.' She took Madouc's hands in her own. 'What do you feel?'

'A quiver came over me: a sensation most strange!'

Twisk nodded and stood back. 'Now then: hold your thumb and finger thus. Whisper "Fwip" and jerk your chin toward whatever nuisance you wish to abate. You may practice on Zocco.'

Madouc pressed thumb and finger together. 'Like this?'

'Just so.'

'And: "Fwip"?'

'Correct.'

'And jerk my chin – like this?'

Zocco uttered a screech and jumped four feet from the ground, twirling his feet rapidly in mid-air. 'Hai kiyah!' called Zocco. 'Put me down!'

'You have worked the spell correctly,' said Twisk. 'See how he twirls his feet, as if dancing? The spell is known as the "Tinkle-toe", or sometimes "Hobgoblin's Hopscotch".'

Madouc allowed thumb and finger to separate and

Zocco returned to the ground, sea-green eyes bulging from his head. 'Hold hard on that mischief, and at once!'

Madouc spoke contritely. 'Excuse me, Zocco! I think that I jerked my chin a bit too hard.'

'That was my own thought,' said Twisk. 'Try again, using less force.'

On this occasion Zocco jumped less than three feet into the air, and his outcries were considerably less shrill.

'Well done!' said Twisk. 'You have a natural bent for such work!'

'It has come too late,' gloomed Madouc. 'Poor Pymfyd lies dead in the ditch, and all through my insistence upon the Flauhamet fair!'

Twisk made an airy gesture. 'Did you strike Pymfyd dead?'

'No, mother.'

'Then you need feel no remorse.'

Madouc's distress was not fully relieved. 'All very well, but Ossip and Sammikin who struck the blows feel no remorse either! They beat poor Pymfyd till the blood gushed; then they chased me and stole Tyfer. I have met you and I am overjoyed for this reason, but at the same time I grieve for Pymfyd and Tyfer.'

Zocco chuckled. 'Just like a female, singing both bass and falsetto with the same breath!'

Twisk turned Zocco a glance of mild inquiry. 'Zocco, did you speak?'

Zocco licked his lips. 'An idle thought, no more.'

'Since you lack occupation, perhaps you will look into the vexations which Madouc has described.'

Zocco said peevishly: 'I see no reason to oblige either you or your unappealing brat of a daughter.'

'The choice is yours,' said Twisk graciously. She spoke to Madouc: 'Wefkins are unimaginative. Zocco, for instance, envisions a future of blissful ease, with never a pang of discomfort. Right or wrong?'

'He is wrong indeed.'

Zocco jumped to his feet. 'I find that I have a few moments to spare. It will do no harm to take a cursory look around the landscape, and perhaps make an adjustment or two.'

Twisk nodded. 'Please report your findings on the instant!'

Zocco was gone. Twisk examined Madouc from head to toe. 'This is an interesting occasion. As I mentioned, I had almost forgotten your existence.'

Madouc spoke stiffly: 'It was not very nice of you to give me away, your own darling little child, and take another in my place.'

'Yes and no,' said Twisk. 'You were not as darling as you might like to think; indeed, you were something of a rippet. Dhrun was golden-haired and sweet-natured; he gurgled and laughed, while you screamed and kicked. It was a relief to be rid of you.'

Madouc held her tongue; reproaches, clearly, would serve no useful purpose. She spoke with dignity: 'I hope that I have given you reason to change your opinion.'

'You might have turned out worse. I seem to have gifted you with a certain queer intelligence, and perhaps an inkling of my own extravagant beauty, though your hair is a froust.'

'That is because I have been running through the woods in terror and hiding under a rotten log. If you like, you may give me a magic comb, which will order my hair at a touch.'

'A good idea,' said Twisk. 'You will find it under your pillow when you return to Sarris.'

Madouc's mouth drooped. 'Am I to return to Sarris?'

'Where else?' asked Twisk, somewhat tartly.

'We could live together in a pretty little castle of our own, perhaps beside the sea.'

'That would not be practical. You are quite suitably housed at Sarris. But remember: no one must learn of our meeting: King Casmir, in particular!'

'Why so? Though I had no intention of telling him.'

'It is a complicated story. He knows that you are a changeling, but, try as he might, he has never been able to identify Suldrun's true child. Were he to know – and he would force the truth from you – he would send out assassins, and Dhrun would soon be dead.'

Madouc grimaced. 'Why should he do such a terrible deed?'

'Because of a prediction in regard to Suldrun's first-born son, which causes him anxiety. Only the priest Umphred knows the secret and he hugs it close, at least for the moment. Now then, Madouc, while this has been an interesting occasion – '

'Not yet! There is still much to talk about! Will we meet again soon?'

Twisk gave an indifferent shrug. 'I live in a constant flux; I am unable to make fixed plans.'

'I am not sure whether I live in a flux or not,' said Madouc. 'I know only that Devonet and Chlodys call me "bastard" and insist that I lack all pedigree.'

'In a formal sense, they are correct, if somewhat rude.'

Madouc spoke wistfully: 'I suspected as much. Still, I would like to know the name of my father and all the particulars of his personality and condition.'

Twisk laughed. 'You pose a conundrum I cannot even begin to solve.'

Madouc spoke in shock: 'You cannot remember his name?'

'No.'

'Nor his rank? Nor his race? Nor his appearance?'

'The episode occurred long ago. I cannot recall every trifling incident of my life.'

'Still, since he was my father, he was surely a gentleman of rank, with a very long and fine pedigree.'

'I remember no such individual.'

'It seems, then, that I cannot even claim to be a bastard of high degree!'

Twisk had become bored with the subject. 'Make whatever claim you like; no one can disprove you, not even I! In any case, bastard or not, you are still reckoned to be Princess Madouc of Lyonesse! This is an enviable estate!'

From the corner of her eye Madouc glimpsed a flicker of green and blue. 'Zocco has returned.'

Zocco reported his findings. 'Neither corpse nor cadaver made itself known, and I adjudged the issue to be moot. Proceeding eastward along Old Street, I discovered two rogues on horseback. Fat Sammikin sat high on a tall bay like the hump on a camel. Ossip Longshanks bestrode a dappled pony with his feet dragging the ground.'

'Alas, poor Tyfer!' mourned Madouc.

Twisk asked: 'And how did you resolve the case?'

'The horses are tethered in the paddock. The rogues are running across Lanklyn Down pursued by bears.'

'Sammikin perhaps should have been transformed into a toad and Ossip into a salamander,' said Twisk. 'I would also have verified Pymfyd's death more carefully, if only that I might observe the prodigy of a walking corpse.'

Madouc suggested: 'Perhaps he is not dead!'

'That, of course, is possible,' said Twisk.

Zocco grumbled: 'If he wanted to be thought dead, he should have remained in place.'

'Quite so,' said Twisk. 'Now you may go your way. In the future try no more sly tricks upon my innocent young daughter.'

Zocco grumbled: 'She is young, but I doubt if she is all

so innocent. Still, I will now bid you farewell.' Zocco seemed to fall backward off the stone and was gone.

'Zocco is not a bad sort, as wefkins go,' said Twisk. 'Now then, time presses. It has been a pleasure to meet you after so many years, but – '

'Wait!' cried Madouc. 'I still know nothing of my father, nor my pedigree!'

'I will give the matter thought. In the meantime – '

'Not yet, Mother dear! I need your help in a few other small ways!'

'If I must, I must,' said Twisk. 'What are your needs?'

'Pymfyd may be in bad case, sore and ill. Give me something to make him well.'

'That is simple enough.' Twisk plucked a laurel leaf, spat delicately into its center. She folded the leaf into a wad, touched it to her forehead, nose and chin, and gave it to Madouc. 'Rub this upon Pymfyd's wounds, for his quick good health. Is there anything else? If not – '

'There is something else! Should I use the Tinkle-toe upon Lady Desdea? She might jump so high as to cause an embarrassment, or even to injure herself!'

'You have a kind heart,' said Twisk. 'As for the Tinkle-toe, you must learn to gauge both the finesse of your gesture and the thrust of your chin. With practice, you will control the vigor of her jump to exactly a proper altitude. What else?'

Madouc considered. 'I would like a wand to do transformations, a cap of invisibility, swift slippers to walk the air, a purse of boundless wealth, a talisman to compel the love of all, a mirror – '

'Stop!' cried Twisk. 'Your needs are excessive!'

'It does no harm to ask,' said Madouc. 'When will I see you again?'

'If necessary, come to Thripsey Shee.'

'How will I find this place?'

'Fare along Old Street to Little Saffield. Turn north up Timble Way, pass first through Tawn Timble, then Glymwode, which is hard by the forest. Take directions to Wamble Path, which leads into Thripsey Meadow. Arrive at noon, but never at night, for a variety of reasons. Stand at the edge of the meadow and softly speak my name three times, and I will come. If nuisances are committed upon you, cry out: "Trouble me not, by fairy law!".'

Madouc made a hopeful suggestion: 'It might be more convenient if I called you with the grass flute.'

'More convenient for you perhaps; not necessarily for me.' Twisk stepped forward and kissed Madouc's forehead. She stood back smiling. 'I have been remiss, but that is my nature, and you must expect nothing better from me.'

Twisk was gone. Madouc, her forehead tingling, stood alone in the glade. She looked at the place where Twisk had stood, then turned away and also departed.

IV

Madouc returned through the forest the way she had come. In the sheepfold she found Tyfer and Pymfyd's bay tethered to a post. She mounted Tyfer and rode down the lane toward Old Street, leading the bay.

As she rode, she searched carefully to either side of the way, but Pymfyd was nowhere to be seen, neither alive nor dead. The circumstances caused Madouc both anxiety and puzzlement. If Pymfyd were alive, why had he lain so limp and still in the ditch? If Pymfyd were dead, why should he walk away?

Madouc, with wary glances to right and left, crossed Old Street into Fanship Way. She continued south, and presently arrived at Sarris. In a mournful mood she took the horses around to the stables, and at last the mystery in regard to Pymfyd's disappearance was clarified. Sitting disconsolately beside the dung-heap was Pymfyd himself.

At the sight of Madouc, Pymfyd jumped to his feet. 'At last you trouble to show yourself!' he cried out. 'Why have you dallied so long?'

Madouc responded with dignity: 'I was delayed by events beyond my control.'

'All very well!' growled Pymfyd. 'Meanwhile I have been sitting here on tenterhooks! If King Casmir had come before your return, I would now be crouching deep in a dungeon.'

'Your worries seem far less for me than for yourself,' said Madouc with a sniff.

'Not so! I made several guesses as to your probable fate, and was not cheered. Exactly what happened to you?'

Madouc saw no need to report the full scope of her adventures. 'The robbers chased me deep into the forest. After I eluded them I circled back to Old Street and rode home. That, in general, is what happened.' She dismounted from Tyfer, and examined Pymfyd from head to toe. 'You seem in adequately good health. I feared that you were dead, from the effect of so many cruel blows.'

'Hah!' said Pymfyd scornfully. 'I am not so easily daunted! My head is thick.'

'On the whole, and taking all with all, your conduct cannot be faulted,' said Madouc. 'You fought your best.'

'True! Still, I am not a fool! When I saw how events were going I feigned death.'

'Have you bruises? Do you hurt?'

'I cannot deny a few aches and as many pains. My head throbs like a great bell!'

115

'Approach me, Pymfyd! I will try to allay your suffering.'

Pymfyd asked suspiciously: 'What do you plan to do?'

'You need ask no questions.'

'I tend to be cautious in the matter of cures. I want neither cathartics nor clysters.'

Madouc paid no heed to the remark. 'Come here and show me where you hurt.'

Pymfyd approached and gingerly indicated his bruises. Madouc applied the poultice she had received from Twisk, and Pymfyd's pain instantly disappeared.

'That was well done,' said Pymfyd grudgingly. 'Where did you learn such a trick?'

'It is a natural art,' said Madouc. 'I also wish to commend your bravery. You fought hard and well, and deserve recognition.' She looked here and there, but discovered no implement suitable to her needs save the manure fork. 'Pymfyd, kneel before me!'

Once again Pymfyd stared in perplexity. 'Now what?'

'Do as I say! It is my royal command!'

Pymfyd gave a fatalistic shrug. 'I suppose I must humor you, though I see no reason for such humility.'

'Cease grumbling, as well!'

'Then be quick with whatever game you are playing! Already I feel a fool.'

Madouc took up the manure fork and raised it on high. Pymfyd dodged and threw his arm over his head. 'What are you up to?'

'Patience, Pymfyd! This tool symbolizes a sword of fine steel!' Madouc touched the fork to Pymfyd's head. 'For notable valor on the field of combat, I dub you Sir Pompom, and by this title shall you be known henceforth. Arise, Sir Pom-pom! In my eyes, at least, you have proved your mettle!'

Pymfyd rose to his feet, grinning and scowling at the

116

same time. 'The stable men will not care a fig one way or the other.'

'No matter! In my opinion you are now "Sir Pom-pom".'

The newly-knighted Sir Pom-pom shrugged. 'It is at least a start.'

4

I

Lady Desdea, upon receiving word from the stable of Madouc's return to Sarris, posted herself in the entry hall, where she could be sure to intercept the miscreant princess.

Five minutes passed. Lady Desdea waited with eyes glittering and arms crossed, fingers tap-tapping against her elbow. Madouc, listless and weary, pushed open the door and entered the hall.

She crossed to the side passage, looking neither right nor left as if absorbed in her private thoughts, ignoring Lady Desdea as if she were not there.

Smiling a small grim smile, Lady Desdea called out: 'Princess Madouc! If you please, I would like a word with you!'

Madouc stopped short, shoulders sagging. Reluctantly she turned. 'Yes, Lady Desdea? What do you wish?'

Lady Desdea spoke with restraint. 'First, I wish to comment upon your conduct, which has caused us all a distraction. Next, I wish to inform you of certain plans which have been made.'

'If you are tired,' said Madouc in a voice of forlorn hope, 'you need not trouble with the comment. As for the plans, we can discuss them another time.'

Lady Desdea's small smile seemed frozen on her face. 'As you wish, though the comment is most pertinent and the plans concern you both directly and indirectly.'

Madouc started to turn away. 'One moment,' said Lady

Desdea. 'I will mention only this: Their Majesties will celebrate Prince Cassander's birthday with a grand fête. Many important persons will be on hand. There will be a formal reception, at which you will sit with the rest of the royal family.'

'Ah well, I suppose it is no great matter,' said Madouc, and again started to turn away, and again Lady Desdea's voice gave her pause. 'In the interim you must school yourself in the customary social graces, that you may appear at your best advantage.'

Madouc spoke over her shoulder: 'There is little for me to learn, since all I need do is sit quietly and nod my head from time to time.'

'Ha, there is more to it than that,' said Lady Desdea. 'You will learn the details tomorrow.'

Madouc pretended not to hear and went off down the passage to her chambers. She went directly to her bed and looked down at the pillow. What would she find beneath? Slowly, and fearful that she would find nothing, she lifted the pillow, and saw a small silver comb.

Madouc gave a quiet little cry of joy. Twisk was not a totally adequate mother, but at least she was alive and not dead, like the Princess Suldrun; and Madouc was not alone in the world, after all.

On the wall beside her dressing table was a mirror of Byzantine glass, rejected by Queen Sollace by reason of flaws and distortions, but which had been considered good enough for the use of Princess Madouc, who, in any case, seldom used the mirror.

Madouc went to stand before the mirror. She looked at her reflection, and blue eyes looked back at her, under a careless tumble of copper-auburn curls. 'My hair is not such a frightful vision as they like to make out,' Madouc told herself bravely. 'It is perhaps not constrained in an even bundle, but I would not have it so. Let us see what happens.'

Madouc pulled the comb through her hair. It slid easily through the strands, with none of the usual jerks and snags; the comb was a pleasure to use.

Madouc stopped to appraise her reflection. The change, while not startling, was definite. The curls seemed to fall into locks, and arranged themselves of their own accord around her face. 'No doubt it is an improvement,' Madouc told herself. 'Especially if it helps me escape ridicule and criticism. Today has been most eventful!'

In the morning Madouc took her breakfast of porridge and boiled bacon in a sunny little alcove to the side of the kitchen, where she knew she would not be likely to encounter either Devonet or Chlodys.

Madouc decided to consume a peach, then loitered over a bunch of grapes. She was not surprised when Lady Desdea looked through the door. 'So this is where you are hiding.'

'I am not hiding,' said Madouc coldly. 'I am taking my breakfast.'

'I see. Are you finished?'

'Not quite. I am still eating grapes.'

'When you have finally eaten your fill, please come to the morning room. I will await you there.'

Madouc fatalistically rose to her feet. 'I will come now.'

In the morning room, Lady Desdea pointed to a chair. 'You may sit.'

Madouc, disliking Lady Desdea's tone, turned her a sulky glance, then slumped upon the chair, legs spraddled forward, chin on her chest.

Lady Desdea, after a glance of disapproval, said: 'Her Highness the queen feels that your deportment is unsatisfactory. I am in accord.'

Madouc twisted her mouth into a crooked line, but said nothing.

Lady Desdea went on. 'The situation is neither casual nor trivial. Of all your adjuncts and possessions the most precious is your reputation. Ah!' Lady Desdea thrust her face forward. 'You puff out your cheeks; you are in doubt. However, I am correct!'

'Yes, Lady Desdea.'

'As a princess of Lyonesse, you are a person of importance! Your renown, for good or bad, travels far and fast, as if on the wings of a bird! For this reason you must be at all times gentle, gracious and nice; you must nurture your reputation, as if it were a beautiful garden of fragrant flowers!'

Madouc said thoughtfully: 'You can help by giving good reports of me in all quarters.'

'First you must alter your habits, since I do not care to look ridiculous.'

'In that case I suppose you had better remain silent.'

Lady Desdea paced two steps in one direction, then two steps in the other. Halting, she faced Madouc once more. 'Do you wish to be known as a lovely young princess notable for her decorum, or an unprincipled little hussy, all dirty face and knobby knees?'

Madouc reflected. 'Are there no other choices?'

'These will suffice at the moment.'

Madouc heaved a deep sigh. 'I don't mind being thought a lovely young princess so long as I am not expected to act like one.'

Lady Desdea smiled her grim smile. 'Unfortunately that is impossible. You will never be thought something you are not. Since it is essential that, during the fête, you present yourself as a gracious and virtuous young princess, you must act like one. Since you seem to be ignorant of that skill, you must learn it. By the wishes of the queen,

121

you will not be allowed to ride your horse, or otherwise wander the countryside, or swim the river, until after the fête.'

Madouc looked up with a stricken expression. 'What will I do with myself?'

'You will learn the conventions of the court and good deportment, and your lessons begin at this instant. Extricate yourself from that ungainly slouch and sit erect in the chair, hands folded in your lap.'

II

The occasion of Prince Cassander's eighteenth birthday would be celebrated at a festival which King Casmir intended should surpass any which had yet enlivened the summer palace at Sarris.

For days wagons had been arriving from all directions, loaded with sacks, crocks and crates, tubs of pickled fish; racks dangling with sausages, hams and bacon; barrels of oil, wine, cider and ale; baskets laden with onions, turnips, cabbages, leeks; also parcels of ramp, parsley, sweet herbs and cress. Day and night the kitchens were active, with the stoves never allowed to go cold. In the service yard four ovens, constructed for the occasion, produced crusty loaves, saffron buns, fruit tarts; also sweetcakes flavored with currants, anise, honey and nuts, or even cinnamon, nutmeg and cloves. One of the ovens produced only pies and pasties, stuffed with beef and leeks, or spiced hare seethed in wine, or pork and onions, or pike with fennel, or carp in a swelter of dill, butter and mushrooms, or mutton with barley and thyme.

On the night previous to Cassander's birthday, a pair of oxen were set to roast over the fire on heavy iron spits, along with two boars and four sheep. In the morning two hundred fowl would join the display, that they might be ready for the great banquet which would begin at noon and continue until the hunger of the company had been totally satiated.

As early as two days before the celebration, notables began to arrive at Sarris, coming from all quarters of Lyonesse; from Blaloc, Pomperol and Dahaut; from as far afield as Aquitaine, Armorica, Ireland and Wales. The most exalted of the lords and ladies were quartered either in the east wing or the west wing of Sarris proper; late-comers and folk of lesser estate used equally pleasant pavilions on the lawn beside the river. Miscellaneous dignitaries – the barons, knights, marshals, along with their ladies – were required to make shift with pallets and couches in certain of the halls and galleries of Sarris. Most of the notables would depart on the day following the banquet, though a few might linger in order to confer with King Casmir upon matters of high policy. Immediately before the banquet, the royal family planned to sit at a reception, that they might formally greet their guests. The reception would begin at mid-morning and proceed until noon. Madouc had been duly notified that her presence at the function would be required, and she had further been advised that only her best and most maidenly conduct would suit the occasion.

Late in the evening of the day before the event, Lady Desdea took herself to Madouc's bedchamber, where she made explicit to Madouc the conduct which would be expected of her. In response to Madouc's disinterested comment she became testy. 'We will not on this occasion niggle over paltry details! Each is significant; and if you will trouble to recall your Euclid you will remember that the whole is the sum of its parts!'

'Whatever you say. Now I am tired and I will go to my bed.'

'Not yet! It is necessary that you understand the reasons for our concern. There have been rumors far and wide of your unruly behavior and wildness. Each of the guests will be watching you with an almost morbid fascination, waiting for some peculiar or even freakish demonstration.'

'Bah,' muttered Madouc. 'They can ogle as they like; it is all the same to me. Are you now done?'

'Not yet!' snapped Lady Desdea. 'I am still far from reassured by your attitude. Further, the guests will include a number of young princes. Many of these will be anxious to make suitable marriages.'

Madouc yawned. 'I care not a whit. Their intrigues are no concern of mine.'

'You had better be concerned, and intimately so! Any of these princes would happily connect with the royal house of Lyonesse! They will be studying you with keen interest, appraising your possibilities.'

'That is vulgar conduct,' said Madouc.

'Not altogether; in fact, it is natural and right. They wish to make a good match for themselves! At the moment, you are too young for any thought of marriage, but the years are swift, and when the time comes to discuss betrothal, we want the princes to remember you with approval. This will enable King Casmir to make the best possible arrangement.'

'Foolishness and absurdity, both up and down!' said Madouc crossly. 'If King Casmir likes marriage so much, let him marry off Devonet and Chlodys, or Prince Cassander, or you, for that matter. But he must not expect me to take any part in the ceremonies.'

Lady Desdea cried out in shock: 'Your talk is a scandal!' She groped for words. 'I will say no more; you may retire now. I only hope that you are more reasonable in the morning.'

Madouc deigned no reply, and marched silently off to her bed.

In the morning maids and under-maids arrived in force. Warm water was poured into a great wooden tub; Madouc was lathered with white Egyptian soap, rinsed clean in water scented with balm from Old Tingis. Her hair was brushed till it shone, after which she unobtrusively combed it with her own comb, so that the copper-golden curls arranged themselves to best advantage. She was dressed in a confection of blue lawn ruffled at shoulder and sleeve, pleated with white in the skirt.

Lady Desdea watched critically from the side. Life at Sarris, so she reflected, seemed to agree with Madouc; at times the scamp looked almost pretty, although her contours and long legs were deplorably boyish.

Madouc was not happy with the gown. 'There are too many pleats and twickets.'

'Nonsense!' said Lady Desdea. 'The gown makes the most of what little figure you have; you should be grateful. It is quite becoming.'

Madouc ignored the remarks, which pleased her not at all. She sat glowering as her hair was brushed once again 'for the sake of a job well done', as Lady Desdea put it, then confined by a silver fillet set with cabochons of lapis lazuli.

Lady Desdea gave Madouc her final instructions. 'You will be meeting a number of notables! Remember: you must engage them with your charm, and make sure of their extreme good opinion, in order that all the sour and stealthy rumors once and for all are given the lie and nailed to the wall!'

'I cannot achieve the impossible,' growled Madouc. 'If persons intend to think ill of me, they will do so, even though I grovel at their feet and implore their respectful admiration.'

'Such extreme conduct will surely not be necessary,' said Lady Desdea tartly. 'Amiability and courtesy are usually sufficient.'

'You are fitting horseshoes on a cow! Since I am the princess, it is they who must supplicate my good opinion; not I theirs. That is simple and reasonable.'

Lady Desdea refused to pursue the subject. 'No matter! Listen as the notables are introduced and greet them nicely, by title and by name. They will thereby think you gracious and kind, and instantly begin to doubt the rumors.'

Madouc made no response, and Lady Desdea continued with her instructions: 'Sit quietly; neither fidget nor scratch, neither wriggle nor writhe. Keep your knees together; do not sprawl, spraddle, slump nor kick out your feet. Your elbows must be held close, unlike the wings of a seagull as it veers on the wind. If you see an acquaintance across the room, do not set up a boisterous outcry; that is not proper conduct. Do not wipe your nose on the back of your hand. Do not grimace, blow out your cheeks; do not giggle, with or without reason. Can you remember all this?'

Lady Desdea awaited a response, but Madouc sat staring blankly across the room. Lady Desdea peered close, then called out sharply: 'Well then, Princess Madouc? Will you give me an answer?'

'Certainly, whenever you wish! Say what you wish to say!'

'I have already spoken at length.'

'Evidently my thoughts were elsewhere, and I did not hear you.'

Lady Desdea's hands twitched. She said in a metallic voice: 'Come. The reception will be underway in short order. For once in your life you must evince the conduct to be expected of a royal princess, so that you will make a good impression.'

Madouc said in an even voice: 'I am not anxious to make a good impression. Someone might want to marry me.'

Lady Desdea confined her response to a sarcastic sniff. 'Come; we are expected.'

Lady Desdea led the way: down the passage to the main gallery and the Great Hall, with Madouc lagging behind, using a loping bent-kneed gait which Lady Desdea ascribed to sheer perversity and ignored.

Folk had already gathered in the Great Hall, where they stood in groups, greeting acquaintances, appraising new arrivals, bowing stiffly to adversaries, ignoring their enemies. Each wore his most splendid garments, hoping to command, at minimum, attention or, better, admiration or, at best, envy. As the notables moved from place to place, silks and satins swirled and caught the glow of light; the room swam with color, so vivid and rich that each hue displayed a vitality of its own: lavender, purple, dead black; intense saturated yellow and mustard-ocher; vermilion, scarlet, the carmine red of pomegranate; all manner of blues: sky-blue, smalt, mid-ocean blue, beetle-wing black-blue; greens in every range.

Bowing, nodding and smiling, Lady Desdea took Madouc to the royal dais, where a pretty little throne of gilded wood and ivory, with a pad of red felt on the seat and at the back, awaited her occupation.

Lady Desdea spoke in a confidential mutter: 'For your information, Prince Bittern of Pomperol will be on hand today, also Prince Chalmes of Montferrone and Prince Garcelin of Aquitaine and several others of high degree.'

Madouc stared at her blankly. 'As you know, these persons are of no interest to me.'

Lady Desdea smiled her tight grim smile. 'Nevertheless, they will come before you, and look you over with care, to gauge your charm and discover your attributes. They will learn whether you are pocked or cross-eyed, wizened or wild, afflicted with sores or mentally deficient, with high ears and low forehead. Now then! Compose yourself and sit quietly.'

Madouc scowled. 'No one else is on hand. Why should I sit here, like a bird on a post? It is foolishness. The seat looks uncomfortable. Why did they not give me a nice cushion? Both King Casmir and Queen Sollace sit on pillows four inches thick. There is only a bit of red cloth on my seat.'

'No matter! You will be pressing your bottom against it, not your eyes! Be seated, if you will!'

'This is the most uncomfortable throne in the world!'

'So it may be. Still, do not squirm around so, as if already you wished to visit the privy.'

'For a fact, I do.'

'Why did you not think of the matter before? There is no time for that now. The king and queen are entering the chamber!'

'You may be sure that both have emptied themselves to their heart's content,' said Madouc. 'I want to do the same. Is that not my privileged right, as a royal princess?'

'I suppose so. Hurry, then.'

Madouc went off without haste, and was in no hurry to return. Meanwhile the king and queen moved slowly across the hall, pausing to exchange a word or two with especially favored personages.

In due course Madouc returned. With an opaque glance toward Lady Desdea she sat upon the gilt and ivory throne, and after a long-suffering look up toward the ceiling, she settled herself.

The king and queen took their places; Prince Cassander

entered from the side, wearing a fine buff jacket, breeches of black twill embroidered with gold thread, a shirt of white lawn. He marched briskly across the hall, acknowledging the salutes of friends and acquaintances with debonair gestures, and took his place to the left of King Casmir.

Sir Mungo of Hatch, the Lord High Seneschal came forward. A pair of heralds blew an abbreviated fanfare on their clarions, the 'Apparens Regis', and the hall became silent.

In sonorous tones Sir Mungo addressed the assemblage: 'I speak with the voice of the royal family! We bid you welcome to Sarris! We are joyful that you may share with us this most felicitous occasion – to wit: the eighteenth birthday of our beloved Prince Cassander!'

Madouc scowled and dropped her chin so that it rested on her clavicle. On sudden thought, she glanced sidewise and met the ophidian stare of Lady Desdea. Madouc sighed and gave a small despairing shrug. As if with great effort, she straightened in the chair and sat erect.

Sir Mungo concluded his remarks; the heralds blew another brief fanfare, and so commenced the reception. As the guests stepped forward, Sir Mungo called out their names and degrees of nobility; the persons so identified paid their respects first to Prince Cassander, then to King Casmir, then to Queen Sollace and finally, in more or less perfunctory style, to Princess Madouc, who responded, generally with leaden disinterest, in a manner only barely acceptable to Queen Sollace and Lady Desdea.

The reception continued for what seemed to Madouc an eternity. Sir Mungo's voice droned on at length; the gentlemen and their ladies passing before her began to look much alike. At last, for entertainment, Madouc began matching each newcomer with a beast or a bird, so that this gentleman was Sir Bullock and that one Sir

Weasel, while here was Lady Puffin and there was Lady Titmouse. On sudden thought Madouc looked to her right, where Lady Crow watched her with minatory eyes, then left, where sat Queen Milkcow.

The game palled. Madouc's haunches began to ache; she squirmed first to one side, then the other, then slouched back into the depths of the throne. By chance she met Lady Desdea's stare, and for a moment watched the angry signals with bland wonder. At last, with a painful sigh, Madouc squirmed herself once again erect.

With nothing better to do, Madouc looked around the hall, mildly curious as to which of the gentlemen present might be Prince Bittern of Pomperol, whose good opinion Lady Desdea considered so necessary. Perhaps he had already presented himself without her taking notice. Possible, thought Madouc. If so, she had surely failed to charm Prince Bittern, or win his admiration.

By the wall stood three youths, all evidently of high estate, in conversation with a gentleman of intriguing appearance though, if subtle indications were to be trusted, of no exalted rank. He was tall, spare, with short dust-colored locks clustered close around a long droll face. His bright gray eyes were alive with vitality; his mouth was wide and seemed to be compressed always against a quirk of inner amusement. His garments, in the context of the occasion, seemed almost plain; despite his apparent lack of formal rank, he carried himself with no trace of deference for the noble company in which he found himself. Madouc watched him with approval. He and the three youths, so it seemed, had only just arrived; they still wore the garments in which they had traveled. The three were of an age to be the princes Lady Desdea had mentioned. One was gaunt, narrow-shouldered and ungainly, with lank yellow hair, a long pale chin and a drooping woebegone nose. Could this be Prince Bittern?

At this moment he turned to dart a somewhat furtive glance toward Madouc, who scowled, annoyed to be caught looking in his direction.

The press in front of the royal dais diminished; the three youths bestirred themselves and came forward to be presented. Sir Mungo announced the first of the three and Madouc's pessimism was validated. In orotund accents Sir Mungo declared: 'We are honored by the presence of the gallant Prince Bittern of Pomperol!'

Prince Bittern, attempting an easy camaraderie, saluted Prince Cassander with a feeble smile and a jocular signal. Prince Cassander, raising his eyebrows, nodded politely, and inquired as to Prince Bittern's journey from Pomperol. 'Most pleasant!' declared Prince Bittern. 'Most pleasant indeed! Chalmes and I had some unexpected companionship along the way: excellent fellows both!'

'I noticed that you had come in company.'

'Yes, quite so! We had a merry time of it!'

'I trust that you will continue to enjoy yourself.'

'Indeed I shall! The hospitality of your house is famous!'

'It is pleasant to hear this.'

Bittern moved on to King Casmir, while Cassander turned his attention to Prince Chalmes of Montferrone.

Prince Bittern was greeted graciously by both King Casmir and Queen Sollace. He then turned to face Madouc with barely concealed curiosity. For a moment he stood stock-still, at a loss as to what tone to take with her.

Madouc watched him expressionlessly. At last Prince Bittern performed a bow, combining half-hearted gallantry with a trace of airy condescension. Since Madouc was only half his age and barely at the edge of adolescence, bluff facetiousness seemed in order.

Madouc was neither pleased nor impressed by Prince Bittern's mannerisms, and remained pointedly unresponsive to his lame jocularities. He bowed once more and moved quickly away.

His place was taken by Prince Chalmes of Montferrone: a stocky youth, short of stature, with coarse straight soot-black hair and a complexion marred by pocks and moles. By Madouc's calculation, Prince Chalmes could be reckoned only marginally more ingratiating than Prince Bittern.

Madouc looked at the third of the group, now paying his respects to Queen Sollace. In her preoccupation with Prince Bittern and Prince Chalmes, she had not attended Sir Mungo's announcement; still she thought to recognize this youth; somewhere, so she was assured, she had known him before. His stature was about average; he seemed easy and quick, sinewy rather than heavy of muscle, with square shoulders and narrow flanks. His hair was golden-brown, cut short across the forehead and ears; his eyes were gray-blue and his features were crisp and regular. Madouc decided that he was not only handsome but undoubtedly of a pleasant disposition. She found him instantly likeable. Now if this had been Prince Bittern, the prospect of betrothal would not seem so utterly tragic. Not welcome, of course, but at least thinkable.

The youth spoke reproachfully: 'You do not remember me?'

'I do,' said Madouc. 'But I can't remember when or where. Tell me.'

'We met at Domreis. I am Dhrun.'

III

Tranquility had come to the Elder Isles. From east to west, from north to south, throughout the numerous islands – after turbulent centuries of invasion, raid, siege, treachery, feud, rapine, arson and murder – town, coast and countryside alike were at peace.

Two isolated localities were special cases. The first of these was Wysrod, where King Audry's diffident troops marched up and down the dank glens and patrolled the stony fells in their efforts to defeat the coarse and insolent Celts, who jeered from the heights and moved through the winter mists like wraiths. The second node of trouble affected the highlands of North and South Ulfland, where the Ska outcast Torqual and his band of cutthroats committed atrocious crimes as the mood came upon them.

Otherwise the eight realms enjoyed what was at least a nominal amity. Few folk, however, considered the peace other than temporary and highly fragile. The general pessimism was based upon King Casmir's known intent to restore the throne Evandig and the Round Table, Cairbra an Meadhan – otherwise known as the 'Board of Notables' – to its rightful place in the Old Hall at Haidion. King Casmir's ambitions went farther: he intended to bring all the Elder Isles under his rule.

Casmir's plans were clear and almost explicit. He would strike hard into Dahaut, and hope to win a quick, easy and decisive victory over King Audry's enfeebled forces. Casmir would then merge the resources of Dahaut with his own and deal with King Aillas at his leisure.

Casmir was given pause only by the policy of King Aillas, whose competence Casmir had come to respect. Aillas had asserted that the safety of his own realm, which now embraced Troicinet, the Isle of Scola, Dascinet, North and South Ulfland, depended upon the separate existence of both Dahaut and Lyonesse. Further, he had let it be known that, in the event of war, he would instantly range himself on the side of the party under attack, so that the aggressor must infallibly be defeated and his realm destroyed.

Casmir, assuming an attitude of benign indifference, merely intensified his preparations: reinforcing his armies, strengthening his fortresses and establishing supply depots at strategic points. Even more ominous, he gradually began to concentrate his power in the northeast provinces of Lyonesse, though the process was sufficiently deliberate that it could not be considered a provocation.

Aillas noted these events with foreboding. He had no illusions in regard to King Casmir and his objectives: first, he would bring Pomperol and Blaloc into his camp either through alliance, facilitated by a royal marriage, or perhaps through intimidation alone. By such a process he had absorbed the old kingdom of Caduz: now a province of Lyonesse.

Aillas decided that Casmir's ominous pressure must be counteracted. To this end he despatched Prince Dhrun with a suitable escort of dignitaries first to Falu Ffail at Avallon, thence to confer with bibulous King Milo at Twissamy in Blaloc, then to King Kestrel's court at Gargano in Pomperol. In each instance, Dhrun delivered the same message, asserting the hope of King Aillas for continued peace, and promising full assistance in the event of attack from any quarter. In order that the declaration should not be considered provocative, Dhrun had been instructed to make the same pledge to King Casmir of Lyonesse.

Dhrun had long been invited to Prince Cassander's birthday celebration and had returned a conditional acceptance. As it happened, his mission went expeditiously and so, with time to spare, Dhrun set off at best speed toward Sarris.

The journey took him down Icnield Way to Tatwillow Town on Old Street; here he took leave of his escort, who would continue south to Slute Skeme and there take ship to Domreis across the Lir. Accompanied only by his squire

Amery, Dhrun rode westward along Old Street to the village Tawn Twillet. Leaving Amery at the inn, he turned aside and rode north up Twamble Lane, into the Forest of Tantrevalles. After two miles he came out on Lally Meadow, where Trilda, the manse of Shimrod the Magician, was situated at the back of a flower garden.

Dhrun dismounted at the gate which gave upon the garden. Trilda was silent; a wisp of smoke from the chimney, however, indicated that Shimrod was in residency. Dhrun pulled on a dangling chain, to prompt a deep reverberating chime to sound from deep inside the manse.

A minute passed. As Dhrun waited, he admired the garden, which he knew to be tended during the night by a pair of goblin gardeners.

The door opened; Shimrod appeared. He welcomed Dhrun with affection and took him into the manse. Shimrod, so Dhrun learned, had been making ready to depart Trilda on business of his own. He agreed to accompany Dhrun first to Sarris, and then on to Lyonesse Town. Here they would go their separate ways: Dhrun across the Lir to Domreis, Shimrod to Swer Smod, Murgen's castle on the stony flanks of the Teach tac Teach.

Three days passed by, and the time came to depart Trilda. Shimrod set out guardian creatures to protect the manse and its contents from marauders, then he and Dhrun rode away through the forest.

At Tawn Twillet they encountered another party on the route to Sarris, consisting of Prince Bittern of Pomperol, Prince Chalmes of Montferrone, with their respective escorts. Dhrun, his squire Amery, and Shimrod joined the company and all traveled onward together.

Immediately upon their arrival at Sarris they were conducted to the Great Hall, that they might participate in the reception. They went to stand at the side of the hall, waiting for an opportunity to approach the dais. Dhrun took occasion to study the royal family, whom he had not seen for several years. King Casmir had changed little; he was as Dhrun remembered him: burly, florid; his round blue eyes as cold and secret as if formed of glass. Queen Sollace sat like a great opulent statue, and somewhat more massive than the image in Dhrun's recollection. Her skin, as before, was as white as lard; her hair, rolled and piled on top of her head, was a billow of pale gold. Prince Cassander had become a swashbuckling young gallant: vain, self-important, perhaps a trifle arrogant. His appearance had changed little; his curls were as brassily yellow as ever; his eyes, like those of King Casmir, were round, an iota too close together, and somewhat minatory, or so it seemed.

And there, at the end of the dais, sat Princess Madouc, bored, aloof, half-sulking and clearly longing to be elsewhere. Dhrun studied her a moment or two, wondering how much she knew in regard to the facts of her birth. Probably nothing, he surmised; who would inform her? Certainly not Casmir. So there sat Madouc, oblivious to the fairy blood which ran in her veins and which so noticeably set her apart from all the others on the dais. Indeed, thought Dhrun, she was a fascinating little creature, and by no means ill-favored.

The press at the royal dais diminished; the three princes went to present themselves to their hosts. Cassander's greeting to Dhrun was crisp but not unfriendly: 'Ah, Dhrun, my good fellow! I am pleased to see you here! We must have a good chat before the day is out; certainly before you leave!'

'I will look forward to the occasion,' said Dhrun.

King Casmir's manner was more restrained, and even somewhat sardonic. 'I have received reports in regard to

136

your travels. It appears that you have become a diplomat at a very early age.'

'Hardly that, Your Majesty! I am no more than the messenger of King Aillas, whose sentiments to you are the same as he has extended to the other sovereigns of the Elder Isles. He wishes you a long reign and continued enjoyment of the peace and prosperity which now comforts us all. He further pledges that if you are wantonly attacked or invaded, and stand in danger, he will come to your aid with the full might of his united realms.'

Casmir gave back a curt nod. 'The undertaking is generous! Still, has he considered every contingency? Does he not have the slightest qualm that a pledge of such scope might in the end prove too far-reaching, or even dangerous?'

'I believe he feels that when peace-loving rulers stand firmly united against an aggressive threat, they ensure their mutual safety, and that danger lies in any other course. How could it be otherwise?'

'Is it not obvious? There is no predicting the future. King Aillas might someday find himself committed to excursions far more perilous than any he now envisions.'

'No doubt that is possible, Your Majesty! I shall report your concerns to King Aillas. At the moment we can only hope that the reverse is a more probable event, and that our undertaking will help to keep the peace everywhere across the Elder Isles.'

King Casmir said tonelessly: 'What is peace? Balance three iron skewers tip to tip, one upon the other; at the summit, emplace an egg, so that it too poises static in mid-air, and there you have the condition of peace in this world of men.'

Dhrun bowed once more and moved on to Queen Sollace. She favored him with a vague smile and a languid wave. 'In view of your important affairs, we had given up hope of seeing you.'

'I did my best to arrive on time, Your Highness. I would not like to miss so happy an occasion.'

'You should visit us more often! After all, you and Cassander have much in common.'

'That is true, Your Highness. I will try to do as you suggest.'

Dhrun bowed and moved aside, and found himself facing Madouc. Her expression, as she looked at him, was blank.

Dhrun spoke reproachfully: 'You do not remember me?'

'I do – but I can't remember when or where. Tell me.'

'We met at Domreis. I am Dhrun.'

Madouc's face came alive with excitement. 'Of course! You were younger!'

'And so were you. Noticeably younger.'

Madouc turned a quick glance toward Queen Sollace. Leaning back in her throne, she was speaking over her shoulder to Father Umphred.

Madouc said: 'We met even before, long ago, in the Forest of Tantrevalles. At that time we were the same age! What do you think of that?'

Dhrun stared dumbfounded. At last, trying to keep his voice light, he said: 'That meeting I do not recall.'

'I expect not,' said Madouc. 'It was of very short duration. Probably we no more than looked at each other.'

Dhrun grimaced. This was not a topic to be bruited about within the hearing of King Casmir. At last he found his voice. 'How did you chance upon this extraordinary notion?'

Madouc grinned, clearly amused by Dhrun's perturbation. 'My mother told me. You may rest easy; she also explained that I must keep the secret secure.'

Dhrun heaved a sigh. Madouc knew the truth – but how much of the truth? He said: 'Whatever the case, we can't discuss it here.'

'My mother said that he – ' Madouc jerked her head toward Casmir ' – would kill you if he knew. Is that your understanding?'

Dhrun turned a furtive glance toward Casmir. 'I don't know. We can't talk about it now.'

Madouc gave an absent-minded nod. 'As you like. Tell me something. Yonder stands a tall gentleman wearing a green cape. Like you he seems familiar, as if I have known him from somewhere before in my life. But I cannot remember the occasion.'

'That is Shimrod the Magician. No doubt you encountered him at Castle Miraldra at the same time you met me.'

'He has a most amusing face,' said Madouc. 'I think that I would like him.'

'I am sure of it! He is an excellent fellow.' Dhrun looked to the side. 'I must move on; others are waiting to speak to you.'

'There is still a moment or two,' said Madouc. 'Will you talk with me later?'

'Whenever you like!'

Madouc darted a glance toward Lady Desdea. 'What I would like is not what they want me to do. I am supposed to be on display, and make a good impression, especially upon Prince Bittern and Prince Chalmes and those others who are trying to estimate my value as a spouse.' Madouc spoke bitterly and the words came in a rush. 'I like none of them! Prince Bittern has the face of a dead mackerel. Prince Chalmes struts and puffs and scratches his fleas. Prince Garcelin's fat belly wags back and forth as he walks. Prince Dildreth of Man has a tiny mouth with big red lips and bad teeth. Prince Morleduc of Ting has sores on his neck, and little narrow eyes; I think he has a bad disposition, but perhaps he has sores elsewhere, which pain him when he sits. Duke Ccnac of Knook Keep is yellow as a Tartar. Duke Femus of Galway has a roaring voice and a gray beard and he says he is willing to marry me now.' Madouc looked at Dhrun sadly. 'You are laughing at me!'

'Are all the persons you meet so distasteful?'

'Not all.'

'But Prince Dhrun is the worst?'

Madouc compressed her lips against a smile. 'He is not as fat as Garcelin; he is livelier than Bittern; he wears no gray beard like Duke Femus nor does he roar; and his disposition seems better than that of Prince Morleduc.'

'That is because I have no sores on my rump.'

'Still – taken all with all – Prince Dhrun is not the worst of the lot.' From the corner of her eye, Madouc noticed that Queen Sollace had turned her head, and was listening to the conversation with both ears. Father Umphred, standing at her back, beamed and nodded his head, as if in enjoyment of some private joke.

Madouc gave her head a haughty toss and turned back to Dhrun. 'I hope that we will have occasion to speak again.'

'I will make sure that we do.'

Dhrun rejoined Shimrod.

'So then: how did it go?' asked Shimrod.

'The formalities are complete,' said Dhrun. 'I congratulated Cassander, warned King Casmir, flattered Queen Sollace and conversed with Princess Madouc, who is far and away the most amusing of the lot, and who also had the most provocative things to say.'

'I watched you with admiration,' said Shimrod. 'You were the consummate diplomat in every detail. A skilled mummer could have done no better!'

'Do not feel deprived! There is still time for you to present yourself. Madouc especially wants to meet you.'

'Really? Or are you concocting a fanciful tale?'

'Not at all! Even from across the room she finds you amusing.'

'And that is a compliment?'

'I took it for such, although I must say that Madouc's humor is somewhat wry and unexpected. She mentioned, quite casually, that she and I had met before, in the Forest of Tantrevalles. Then she sat grinning like a mischievous imp at my stupefaction.'

'Amazing! Where did she gain the information?'

'The circumstances are not quite clear to me. Apparently she has visited the forest and met her mother, who provided the relevant facts.'

'This is not good news. If she is as giddy and careless as her mother would seem to be, and lets the news slip to King Casmir, your life will at once become precarious. Madouc must be enjoined to silence.'

Dhrun looked dubiously toward Madouc, now engaged with the Duke Cypris of Skroy and his lady, the Duchess Pargot. 'She is not so frivolous as she appears, and surely she will not betray me to King Casmir.'

'Still, I will caution her.' Shimrod watched Madouc for a moment. 'She deals graciously enough with those two old personages, who would seem to be rather tiresome.'

'I suspect that the rumors about her are very wide of the mark.'

'So it would seem. I find her quite appealing, at least from this distance.'

Dhrun said pensively. 'Someday a man will look deep into her blue eyes and there he will drown, and never be saved.'

The Duke and Duchess of Skroy moved on. Madouc, noticing that she was the topic of discussion, sat as demurely erect on the gilt and ivory throne as ever Lady Desdea might have hoped. As it happened, she had made a favorable impression upon both Duke Cypris and Lady Pargot, and they spoke of Madouc with approval to their friends, Lord Uls of Glyvern Ware and his stately spouse Lady Elsiflor. 'How the rumors have flown about Madouc!' declared Lady Pargot. 'She is said to be bold as old vinegar and wild as a lion. I insist that the reports are either malicious or exaggerated.'

'True!' stated Duke Cypris. 'We found her as modestly innocent as a little flower.'

Lady Pargot went on. 'Her hair is like a tumble of bright copper; she is truly quite striking!'

'Still, the girl is thin,' Lord Uls pointed out. 'For adequacy and advantage, a female needs proper amplitude.'

Duke Cypris gave qualified agreement. 'A learned Moor has worked out the exact formula, though I forget the numbers: so many square inches of skin to so many hands in height. The effect must be sumptuous but neither expansive nor rotund.'

'Quite so. That would be carrying the doctrine too far.'

Lady Elsiflor gave a disapproving sniff. 'I would not allow any Moor to count the areas of my skin, no matter how long his beard, nor yet might he measure my stature in hands, as if I were a mare.'

The Duchess Pargot spoke querulously: 'Is there not a certain lack of dignity to the exposition?'

Lady Elsiflor agreed. 'As for the Princess, I doubt if she will ever conform to the Moorish ideal. But for her pretty face, she might pass for a boy.'

'All in good time!' declared Lord Uls. 'She is still young in years.'

Duchess Pargot turned a sidelong glance toward King

Casimir, whom she disliked. 'Still they are already shopping her about. I find it quite premature.'

'It is no more than display,' declared Lord Uls bluffly. 'They bait the hook and cast the line in order to learn which fish will strike.'

The heralds blew the six-note fanfare: 'Recedens Royal'. King Casimir and Queen Sollace stood from their thrones and retired from the hall, that they might change into garments appropriate for the banquet. Madouc tried to slip away, but Devonet called out: 'Princess Madouc, what of you? Shall we sit together at the banquet?'

Lady Desdea looked around. 'Other plans have been made. Come, Your Highness! You must freshen yourself and don your beautiful garden frock.'

'I am well enough now,' growled Madouc. 'There is no need to change.'

'Your opinions for once are irrelevant, in that they run counter to the queen's requirements.'

'Why does she insist upon foolishness and waste? I will wear out these clothes changing them back and forth.'

'The queen has the best of reasons for all her decisions. Come along with you.'

Madouc sullenly allowed herself to be divested of her blue gown and dressed in a costume which, so she grudgingly decided, she liked equally well: a white blouse tied at the elbows with brown ribbons; a bodice of black velvet with a double row of small copper medallions down the front; a full pleated skirt of a bronze-russet similar to but less intense than the color of her curls.

Lady Desdea took her to the queen's drawing room, where they waited until Queen Sollace had completed her own change of costume. Then, with Devonet and Chlodys following modestly behind, the group repaired to the south lawn. Here, in the shade of three enormous old oaks and only a few yards from the placid Glame, a lavish collation had been laid out upon a long trestle. Here and there around the lawn were arranged small tables, set with napery, baskets of fruit, ewers of wine, as well as plates, goblets, bowls and utensils. Three dozen stewards clad in livery of lavender and green stood at their posts, stiff as sentinels, awaiting the signal from the Seneschal to commence service. Meanwhile, the company of guests stood in knots and groups awaiting the arrival of the royal party.

On the green lawn and against the sunny blue of the sky the colors of their costumes made a gorgeous display. There were blues both light and dark, of lapis and of turquoise; purple, magenta and green; tawny orange, tan, buff and fusk; mustard ocher, the yellow of daffodil, rose pink, scarlet and pomegranate red. There were shirts and pleated bargoons of fine white silk, or Egyptian lawn; the hats were brave with many brims, sweeps, tiers, and plumes. Lady Desdea wore a relatively sedate gown of heather gray embroidered with red and black flowerets. As the royal party arrived on the lawn she took occasion to confer with Queen Sollace, who issued instructions to which Lady Desdea gave a bow of compliant understanding. She turned to speak with Madouc, only to discover that Madouc was nowhere to be seen.

Lady Desdea exclaimed in vexation and called to Devonet. 'Where is the Princess Madouc? A moment ago she stood by my side; she has darted away, like a weasel through the hedge!'

Devonet replied in a voice of whimsical and confidential scorn: 'No doubt she trotted off to the privy.'

'Ah! Always at the most awkward time!'

Devonet went on: 'She said she had severely wanted to go for the last two hours.'

Lady Desdea frowned. Devonet's manner was altogether too flippant, too knowing and too familiar. She said crisply: 'All else aside, Princess Madouc is a cherished member of the royal family. We must be careful to avoid disrespect in our references!'

'I was only telling you the facts,' said Devonet lamely.

'Just so. Still, I hope that you will take my remarks to heart.' Lady Desdea swept away and went to post herself where she could intercept Madouc immediately upon her return from within the palace.

Minutes passed. Lady Desdea became impatient: where was the perverse little brat? What could she be up to?

King Casmir and Queen Sollace settled themselves at the royal table; the Seneschal nodded to the High Steward who clapped his hands together. Those guests still standing about the lawn seated themselves wherever convenient, in the company of relatives or friends, or with other persons whom they found congenial. Stewards in pairs stalked here and there with platters and trenchers, one to carry, another to serve.

Contrary to the intentions of Queen Sollace, Prince Bittern escorted the young Duchess Clavessa Montfoy of Sansiverre – this a small kingdom immediately north of Aquitaine. The duchess wore a striking gown of scarlet embroidered with black, purple and green peacocks which suited her to remarkable advantage. She was tall, vivacious of movement, with luxuriant black hair, flashing black eyes, and an enthusiastic manner which stimulated Prince Bittern's most eager volubility.

Queen Sollace watched with cold disfavor. She had planned that Bittern should sit with Princess Madouc, that he might make her better acquaintance. Evidently this was not to be, and Sollace gave Lady Desdea a look of moist reproach, prompting Lady Desdea to peer even more earnestly toward the structure of Sarris. Why did the princess tarry so long?

In point of fact, Madouc had tarried not an instant. As soon as Lady Desdea had turned her back, she slipped around the outskirts of the company to where Dhrun and Shimrod stood, beside the most remote of the oak trees. Madouc's arrival took them by surprise. 'You come up on us with neither ceremony nor premonition,' said Dhrun. 'Luckily we were exchanging no secrets.'

'I took care to use my best stealth,' said Madouc. 'I am free at last, until someone searches me out.' She went to stand behind the bole of the oak. 'Even now I am not safe; Lady Desdea can see through stone walls.'

'In that case, before you are dragged away, I will introduce my friend, Master Shimrod,' said Dhrun. 'He too can see through stone walls, and whenever he likes.'

Madouc performed a prim curtsey, and Shimrod bowed. 'It is a pleasure to make your acquaintance. I do not meet princesses every day!'

Madouc gave a rueful grimace. 'I had rather be a magician, and see through walls. Is it difficult to learn?'

'Quite difficult, but much depends upon the student. I have tried to teach Dhrun a sleight or two, but with only fair success.'

'My mind is not flexible,' said Dhrun. 'I cannot think so many thoughts at once.'

'That is the way of it, more often than not, and luckily so,' said Shimrod. 'Otherwise, everyone would be a magician and the world would be an extraordinary place.'

Madouc considered. 'Sometimes I think as many as seventeen thoughts all together.'

'That is good thinking!' said Shimrod. 'Murgen occasionally manages thirteen, or even fourteen, but afterward collapses into a stupor.'

Madouc looked at him sadly. 'You are laughing at me.'

'I would never dare laugh at a royal princess! That would be impertinence!'

'No one would care. I am a royal princess only because

Casmir makes the pretense – and only so that he can marry me to Prince Bittern, or someone similar.'

Dhrun looked off across the lawn. 'Bittern is fickle; he would make a poor match. Already he has turned his attention elsewhere. For the moment you are safe.'

'I must issue a warning,' said Shimrod. 'Casmir is aware that you are a changeling, but he knows nothing of Suldrun's first-born son. Should he gain so much as an inkling, Dhrun would be in great danger.'

Madouc peered around the tree to where King Casmir sat with Sir Ccnac of Knook Keep and Sir Lodweg of Cockaigne. 'My mother cited the same warning. You need not worry; the secret is safe.'

'How did you happen to meet your mother?'

'I chanced to be in the forest, and there I met a wefkin named Zocco who taught me how to call my mother, and I did so.'

'She came?'

'Instantly. At first she seemed a bit cross, but in the end she decided to be proud of me. She is beautiful, if somewhat airy in her manners. Nor can I help but think her capricious, giving away her lovely baby as if it were a sausage – especially when that lovely baby was I. When I brought the subject up, she seemed more amused than otherwise, and claimed that I was subject to tantrums which made the change only sensible.'

'But you have outgrown these tantrums?'

'Oh yes, quite.'

Shimrod mused upon the subject. 'A fairy's thoughts can never be guessed. I have tried and failed; there is better hope of catching up quicksilver in your fingers.'

Madouc said wisely: 'Magicians must consort often with fairies, since both are adepts in magic.'

Shimrod gave his head a smiling shake. 'We use different magics. When first I wandered the world, such creatures

147

were new to me. I enjoyed their frolics and pretty fancies. Now I am more settled, and I no longer try to fathom fairy logic. Someday, if you like, I will explain the difference between fairy magic and sandestin magic, which is used by most magicians.'

'Hm,' said Madouc. 'I thought that magic was magic, and that was all there was to it!'

'Not so. Sometimes simple magic seems hard and hard magic seems simple. It is all very complicated. For instance – by your feet I see three dandelions. Pluck their pretty little blossoms.'

Madouc bent and picked the three yellow blooms.

'Hold them between your two hands,' said Shimrod. 'Now, bring your hands to your face and kiss both thumbs together.'

Madouc raised her hands to her face and kissed her thumbs. Instantly the soft blossoms became hard and heavy inside her hands. 'Oh! They have changed! May I look?'

'You may look.'

Madouc, opening her hands, discovered three heavy gold coins in place of the dandelion blossoms. 'That is a fine trick! Can I do it myself?'

Shimrod shook his head. 'Not now. It is not so easy as it seems. But you may keep the gold.'

'Thank you,' said Madouc. She inspected the coins somewhat dubiously. 'If I should try to spend the coins, would they become flowers again?'

'If the magic had been done by fairies: perhaps, perhaps not. By sandestin magic, your coins are gold and will remain gold. In fact, the sandestin may well have purloined them from King Casmir's strongbox, to save himself effort.'

Madouc smiled. 'More than ever I am anxious to learn some of these skills. It is useless asking my mother; she lacks all patience. I inquired about my father, but she claimed to remember nothing, not even his name.'

'Your mother seems a trifle airy, or even absent-minded.'

Madouc gave a regretful sigh. 'Absent-minded or worse, and I still can show no pedigree, either long or short.'

'Fairies are often careless in their connections,' murmured Shimrod. 'It is a sad case.'

'Just so. My maidens-in-attendance call me "bastard",' said Madouc ruefully. 'I can only laugh at their ignorance, since they are referring to the wrong father.'

'That is coarse conduct,' said Shimrod. 'I should think that Queen Sollace would disapprove.'

Madouc shrugged. 'In these cases I dispense my own justice. Tonight, Chlodys and Devonet will find toads and turtles in their beds.'

'The penalty is just, and would seem persuasive.'

'Their minds are weak,' said Madouc. 'They refuse to learn, and tomorrow I will hear it all over again. At first opportunity I intend to search out my pedigree, no matter where it lies hidden.'

Dhrun asked: 'Where will you search? The evidence would seem to be scant, even non-existent.'

'I have not thought the matter through,' said Madouc. 'Probably I will apply again to my mother and hope to stimulate her memory. If all else fails – ' Madouc stopped short. 'Chlodys has seen me! Look how she scampers off with the news!'

Dhrun frowned. 'Your present company is not necessarily a scandal.'

'No matter! They want me to beguile Prince Bittern, or perhaps Prince Garcelin, who sits yonder gnawing a pig's foot.'

'The remedy is simple,' said Shimrod. 'Let us sit at a

table and gnaw pigs' feet of our own. They will hesitate to alter such definite arrangements.'

'It is worth a trial,' said Madouc. 'However, I will gnaw no pig's foot. I much prefer a roast pheasant well-basted with butter.'

'So do I,' said Dhrun. 'A few leeks to the side and some bread will suit me nicely.'

'Well then: let us dine,' said Shimrod.

The three seated themselves at a table in the shade of the oak, and were served from great silver salvers by the stewards.

Lady Desdea meanwhile had gone to take instruction from Queen Sollace. The two engaged in a hurried conference, after which Lady Desdea marched purposefully across the lawn to the table where Madouc sat with Dhrun and Shimrod. She stopped beside Madouc and spoke in a voice carefully controlled: 'Your Highness, I must inform you that Prince Bittern has urgently begged that you do him the honor of dining in his company. The queen desires that you accede to his request, and at once.'

'You must be mistaken,' said Madouc. 'Prince Bittern is absolutely fascinated by that tall lady with the long nose.'

'That is the distinguished Duchess Clavessa Montfoy. However, please take note: Prince Cassander has persuaded her to take a turn on the river before proceeding with the banquet. Prince Bittern now sits alone.'

Madouc turned to look; indeed, Prince Cassander and the Duchess Clavessa were strolling off toward the dock, where three punts floated in the shade of a weeping-willow. The Duchess Clavessa, although perplexed by Prince Cassander's proposal, continued to exercise her usual effervescence, and chattered away at a great rate. Prince Cassander was less effusive; he conducted himself with urbane politeness but no great zest. As for Prince

Bittern, he sat looking after the Duchess Clavessa, slack-jawed and glum.

Lady Desdea told Madouc: 'As you see, Prince Bittern is anxiously awaiting your presence.'

'Not so! You misread his posture. He is anxious to join Cassander and Duchess Clavessa on the river.'

Lady Desdea's eyes glittered. 'You must obey the queen! She feels that your place is properly with Prince Bittern.'

Dhrun spoke in cold tones: 'You would seem to imply that the princess now sits in unsuitable or demeaning company. If this discourtesy is carried any farther, I will instantly protest to King Casmir, and ask him to deal with what would seem a gross breach of etiquette.'

Lady Desdea blinked and drew back. She performed a stiff bow. 'Naturally I intended no discourtesy. I am only an instrument of the queen's wishes.'

'The queen, then, must be at some misapprehension. The princess does not wish to deprive us of her company, and she seems quite at her ease; why create a fiasco?'

Lady Desdea could proceed no farther. She curtsied and departed.

With a drooping mouth Madouc watched her go. 'She will take vengeance – needlework and more needlework for hours on end.' Madouc turned a thoughtful glance upon Shimrod. 'Can you teach me to transform Lady Desdea into an owl, if only for a day or so?'

'Transformations are complicated,' said Shimrod. 'Each step is critical; if a single syllable went awry, Lady Desdea might become a harpy or an orc, with the whole countryside at peril. You must delay transformations until you are more experienced.'

'I am apt at magic, according to my mother. She taught me the "Tinkle-toe Imp-spring", that I might fend off bandits or louts.'

151

'I don't know that particular effect,' said Shimrod. 'At least, not by that name.'

'It is simple enough,' Madouc looked here and there, around the lawn and down the slope toward the river. Near the dock she took note of Prince Cassander, who was politely seating Duchess Clavessa in a punt, while at the same time making a gallant remark. Madouc arranged thumb and finger, muttered: 'Fwip!' and jerked her chin. Prince Cassander gave a startled outcry and jumped into the river.

'That was the "low strength" or "low virtue" method,' said Madouc. 'The other two "virtues" are more notable. I saw Zocco the wefkin jump a good six feet into the air.'

'That is a fine technique,' said Shimrod. 'It is neat, quick and of nice effect. Evidently you have not used the "Tinkle-toe" in any of its virtues upon Lady Desdea?'

'No. It seems a bit extreme, and I would not want her to jump past her ordinary ability.'

'Let me think,' said Shimrod. 'There is a lesser effect known as the "Sissle-way", which also comes in three gradations: the "Subsurrus", the "Sissle-way Ordinary", and the "Chatter-fang".'

'I would like to learn this effect.'

'The sleight is definite but subtle. You must whisper the activator – *schkt* – then point your little finger, thus and so, and then you must hiss softly – like this.'

Madouc jerked and twitched, her teeth rattling and vibrating. 'Ow-wow!' said Madouc.

'That,' said Shimrod, 'is the first virtue, or the "Subsurrus". As you have noticed, the effect is transient. For greater urgency, one uses the "Ordinary", with a double hiss: "sss-sss". The third level is, of course, the "Chatter-fang", where the activator is used twice.'

Dhrun asked: 'And what of three hisses and three activators?'

'Nothing. The effect is vitiated. Speak the activator, if you like, but do not hiss, since you might startle some unsuspecting person.'

'*Schkt*,' said Madouc. 'Is that correct?'

'It is close. Try again, like this: *Schkt*.'

'*Schkt*.'

'Precisely right, but you must practice until it becomes second nature.'

'*Schkt. Schkt. Schkt*.'

'Well done! Do not hiss, please.'

They paused to watch Prince Cassander slouching despondently across the lawn toward Sarris. Meanwhile Duchess Clavessa had rejoined Prince Bittern, and had resumed her conversation where it had been left off.

'All worked out well,' said Shimrod. 'And here is the steward with a platter of roast pheasants. This is culinary magic with which I cannot compete. Steward, be so good as to serve us all, and do not stint.'

IV

The celebration had run its course, and Sarris was once more tranquil. In the estimation of King Casmir, the event had gone moderately well. He had entertained his guests with suitable amplitude which, while falling short of the lavish extravagance favored by King Audry, still would go far to dispel his reputation for parsimony.

Jocundity and good fellowship had ruled the occasion. Save for Cassander's fall into the river, there had been neither bitter words nor quarrels between old enemies, nor incidents which might have provoked new resentments. Meanwhile, because of Casmir's insistence upon informality, the questions of precedence which often gave rise to embarrassing disputes were avoided.

A few disappointments marred the general satisfaction. Queen Sollace had urged that Father Umphred be allowed to utter a benediction before the banquet. King Casmir, who detested the priest, would hear none of it, and the queen indulged herself in a fit of pink-nosed sulks. Further, Princess Madouc had not perceptibly helped her prospects: perhaps to the contrary. It had long been planned that Madouc should show herself to be a mild and winsome young maiden who must inevitably develop into a lovely damsel renowned for her charm, decorum and sympathy. Madouc, while reasonably polite or, at worst, apathetic with the older guests, produced a different version of herself for the young grandees who came to study her attributes, and showed herself to be irresponsible, perverse, elusive, sarcastic, wrong-headed, supercilious, sulky and so tart in her comments as to verge upon the insulting. Morleduc's disposition, already questionable, had not been improved by Madouc's innocent question as to whether sores covered his entire body. When the vain and arrogant Sir Blaise[1] of Benwick in Armorica disposed himself before her, looked her up and down with cool detachment and remarked, 'I must say, Princess Madouc, you do not at all resemble the naughty little harridan that your reputation suggests' Madouc replied in her silkiest voice: 'That is good to hear. Nor do you seem a perfumed popinjay, as I have heard you described, since your scent is not one of perfume.' Sir Blaise bowed curtly and departed. And so it went with all the others, excepting

---

[1] Sir Blaise would eventually sire Sir Glahan of Benwick, who in his turn would sire one of King Arthur's best paladins, Sir Lancelot du Lac. Also present at the celebration was Sir Garstang of Twanbow Hall, whose son would sire another of King Arthur's most trusted comrades, Sir Tristram of Lyonesse.

only Prince Dhrun, which brought King Casmir no pleasure. A connection in this quarter would advance his policies not at all – unless, of course, Madouc could be persuaded to transmit to him the state secrets of Troicinet. King Casmir gave the idea only cursory consideration.

At the first opportunity Lady Desdea expressed her dissatisfaction to Madouc. 'Everyone is most upset with you.'

'What is it this time?' asked Madouc, her blue eyes innocent.

'Come now, young lady!' snapped Lady Desdea. 'You ignored our plans and flouted our desires; my careful instruction was no more than the droning of an insect. So then!' Lady Desdea drew herself up to her full height. 'I have taken counsel with the queen. She has decided that your conduct calls out for correction, and wishes me to use my best judgment in the matter.'

'You need not exert yourself,' said Madouc. 'The celebration is over; the princes have gone home and my reputation is secure.'

'But it is the wrong reputation. In consequence, you shall be set to double lessons for the rest of the summer. Further, you will not be allowed to ride your horse, nor even go near the stables. Is that clear?'

'Oh yes,' said Madouc. 'It is very clear.'

'You may resume your needlework at this moment,' said Lady Desdea. 'I believe that you will find Devonet and Chlodys in the parlor.'

Rainy weather came to Sarris and lingered for three days. Madouc wistfully occupied herself with the schedule arranged for her by Lady Desdea, which included not only interminable hours of needlework, but also dancing lessons of a particularly tiresome nature. Late in the afternoon of the third day heavy clouds drifted across the sky, bringing a night of rain. In the morning the clouds were gone and the sun rose into a fresh and smiling world, fragrant with the odors of wet foliage.

Lady Desdea went to the small refectory where Madouc was accustomed to take her breakfast, but found only Devonet and Chlodys, neither of whom had seen Madouc. Odd, thought Lady Desdea. Could Princess Madouc have kept to her bed, by reason of illness? Perhaps the princess had gone early to the conservatory for her dancing lesson?

Lady Desdea went to investigate, only to find Master Jocelyn standing idly by the window, while the four musicians, playing lute, pipes, drums and flute, rehearsed tunes from their repertory.

Master Jocelyn, in response to Lady Desdea's question, merely shrugged. 'And if she were here: what then? She cares nothing for what I teach her; she skips and jumps; she hops on one leg like a bird. I ask: "Is that how you will dance at the Grand Ball?" And she replies: "I am not a devotee of this foolish strutting and smirking. I doubt if I will be present".'

Lady Desdea muttered under her breath and turned away. She went outside to look up and down the terrace, just in time to discover Madouc perched proudly on the seat of a pony-cart with Tyfer trotting briskly off across the meadow.

Lady Desdea gave a cry of outrage, and sent a footman to ride after the pony-cart and bring the truant princess back to Sarris.

A few minutes later the pony-cart returned: Madouc now crestfallen and Tyfer moving at a slow walk.

'Be so good as to dismount,' said Lady Desdea.

Madouc, her face screwed up into a resentful scowl, jumped to the ground.

'Well then, Your Highness? You were expressly forbidden to use your horse or to go near the stables.'

'That wasn't what you said!' cried Madouc. 'You told

156

me that I was not to ride Tyfer, and I am not doing so! I summoned the stable boy Pymfyd and required that he bring up the cart, so I never so much as approached the stables.'

Lady Desdea stared with twitching lips. 'Very well! I will rephrase the order. You are forbidden to use your horse, or any other horse, or any other beast, be it cow, goat, sheep, dog, or bullock, or any other means of propulsion, on any sort of vehicle or mode of transportation, including carts, carriages, wagons, boats, sleds, palanquins, and litters. That should define the exact scope of the queen's command. Secondly, even as you tried to evade the queen's command, you also became remiss with your lessons. What is your response to this?'

Madouc made a brave gesture. 'Today the rain is gone and the world is bright, and I preferred to be out in the air, rather than toiling over Herodotus or Junifer Algo, or practicing calligraphy or pricking my fingers at needlework.'

Lady Desdea turned away. 'I will not argue with you the relative merits of learning versus torpid idleness. What must be done, we will do.'

Three days later Lady Desdea, in a troubled spirit, reported to Queen Sollace. 'I do my best with Princess Madouc, but I seem to achieve nothing.'

'You must not be discouraged!' said the queen.

A maid brought a silver dish on which were arranged twelve ripe figs. She placed the dish on a tabouret close by the queen's elbow. 'Shall I peel, Your Highness?'

'Please do.'

Lady Desdea's voice rose in pitch. 'Were it not disrespectful, I might declare Her Highness a red-headed little brat who needs nothing more than a good whisking.'

'No doubt she is a trial. But continue as before, and

brook no nonsense.' Queen Sollace tasted one of the figs, and rolled up her eyes in pleasure. 'Here is perfection!'

'Another matter,' said Lady Desdea. 'Something very strange is going on, which I must bring to your attention.'

Queen Sollace sighed and leaned back in the divan. 'Cannot I be spared these intricate complexities? Sometimes, my dear Ottile, and despite your good intentions, you become most tiresome.'

Lady Desdea could have wept for sheer frustration. 'It is all the more tiresome for me! Indeed, I am baffled! The circumstances transcend anything I have known before!'

Queen Sollace accepted another plump fig from the maid. 'How so?'

'I will recite to you the facts exactly as they occurred. Three days ago I had reason to reprimand Her Highness for scamping her work. She seemed unconcerned – pensive rather than remorseful. As I turned away, an extraordinary sensation struck through every fiber of my being! My skin tingled, as if I had been whipped by nettles! Blue lights flashed and flared before my eyes! My teeth set up an uncontrollable rattling that I thought must never cease! I assure you that it was an alarming sensation!'

Queen Sollace, munching at the fig, considered Lady Desdea's complaint. 'Odd. You have never taken such a fit before?'

'Never! But there is more! At the same time I thought to hear a faint sound issuing from Her Highness! A hiss, almost inaudible.'

'It might have been an expression of shock or surprise,' mused Queen Sollace.

'So it might seem. I will cite another incident, which occurred yesterday morning, as Princess Madouc took breakfast with Devonet and Chlodys. There was an exchange of banter and the usual giggling. Then as I watched dumbounded, Devonet lifted the milk jug, that she might pour milk into her bowl. Instead her hand jerked and she poured the milk across her neck and chest, and all the while her teeth were chattering like castanets. Finally she dropped the jug and rushed from the room. I followed, that I might learn the reason for her strange convulsion. Devonet declared that the Princess Madouc had prompted her to the act by uttering a soft hiss. There was no real provocation, according to Devonet. "I only said that while bastards might wet into silver chamber-pots, they still lacked the most precious of all: a fine pedigree!" I asked: "And then what?" "And then I reached for the milk jug; I lifted it and poured milk all over myself, while Madouc sat grinning and making a hissing sound." And that is what happened to Devonet.'

Queen Sollace sucked at her fingers, then wiped them on a damask napkin. 'It sounds to me like simple careless-ness,' said Queen Sollace. 'Devonet must learn to grasp the jug more firmly.'

Lady Desdea gave a scornful sniff. 'And what of Prin-cess Madouc's cryptic grin?'

'Perhaps she was amused. Is that not possible?'

'Yes,' said Lady Desdea grimly. 'It is possible. But, once again, listen to this! As a penalty, I assigned Her Highness double lessons: in orthography, grammar, needlework and dancing; also special texts in genealogy, astronomy, the geometries of Aristarchus, Candasces and Euclid. I also assigned readings from the works of Matreo, Orgon Photis, Junifer Algo, Panis the Ionian, Dalziel of Avallon, Ovid and one or two others.'

Queen Sollace shook her head in bemusement. 'I found Junifer always a bore, nor could I make head nor tail of Euclid.'

'I am sure Your Majesty was more than clever at your lessons; it reveals itself in your conversation.'

Sollace looked off across the room, and did not respond

until she had thoroughly masticated another fig. 'Well then: what of the reading?'

'I deputed Chlodys to attend Madouc as she read, to make sure that she was supplied the proper texts. This morning Chlodys reached to take a fine volume of Dalziel from the shelf and felt a spasm come over her which caused her to throw the book high into the air and set her teeth to chattering. She came running to me in complaint. I took Princess Madouc for her dancing lesson. The musicians set up a nice tune; Master Jocelyn declared that he would now demonstrate the step he wished the princess to learn. Instead he jumped six feet into the air, with his feet twirling and toes pointed as if he were a dervish. When at last he descended to the floor, Madouc said that it was a step she did not care to try. She asked me if I cared to demonstrate the step, but there was something in her smile which prompted me to refuse. Now, I am at my wits' end.'

Queen Sollace accepted a fig from the maid. 'That will be all; I am almost sated with these wonderful morsels; they are as sweet as honey!' She turned to Lady Desdea. 'Proceed as before; I can advise you no better.'

'But you have heard the problems!'

'It might be coincidence, or fancy, or even a bit of hysteria. We cannot let such silly panics affect our policy.'

Lady Desdea cried another protest, but Queen Sollace held up her hand. 'No, not another word! I have heard all I care to hear.'

The drowsy days of summer passed: fresh dawns, with dew on the lawns and bird calls floating through the air from far distances; then the bright mornings and golden afternoons, followed by orange, yellow and red sunsets; then the blue-gray dusk and at last the starry nights, with Vega at the zenith, Antares to the south, Altair in the east and Spica declining in the west. Lady Desdea had discovered a convenient way to deal with Madouc since her unproductive and frustrating report to Queen Sollace. She spoke in a grim monotone, assigning the lessons and stating the schedule, then with a scornful sniff and a stiff back she departed and gave no further heed either to Madouc or her achievements. Madouc accepted the system and pursued only the reading which interested her. Lady Desdea, in her turn, discovered that life had become less of a trial. Queen Sollace was content to hear no more of Madouc's transgressions, and in her conversations with Lady Desdea avoided all reference to Madouc.

After a week of relative placidity, Madouc delicately mentioned Tyfer and his need for exercise. Lady Desdea said crossly: 'The proscription derives not from me but from Her Majesty. I can grant no permission. If you ride your horse, you risk the queen's displeasure. But it is all one to me.'

'Thank you,' said Madouc. 'I feared that you might be difficult.'

'Ha hah! Why should I beat my head against a rock?' Lady Desdea started to turn away, then halted. 'Tell me: where did you learn that opprobrious little trick?'

'The "Sissle-way"? It was taught to me by Shimrod the magician, that I might defend myself against tyrants.'

'Hmf.' Lady Desdea departed. Madouc at once took herself to the stables, where she ordered Sir Pom-pom to saddle up Tyfer, and prepare for an excursion across the countryside.

5

I

Shimrod rode in company with Dhrun to Lyonesse Town, where Dhrun, with Amery, took passage to Domreis aboard a Troice cog. Shimrod watched from the quay-side until the tawny sails dwindled across the horizon, then went to a nearby inn and seated himself in the shade of a grape arbor. Over a platter of sausages and a mug of ale he considered the possibilities of the next few days and what might lie in store for him.

The time had come when he must take himself to Swer Smod, that he might confer with Murgen and learn whatever needed learning. The prospect did not lift his spirits. Murgen's dreary disposition blended well with the somber and darkling atmosphere of Swer Smod; his sour smile was equivalent to another man's wild frivolity. Shimrod knew well what to expect at Swer Smod and prepared himself accordingly; had he discovered good cheer and merry-making, he would have wondered as to Murgen's sanity.

Shimrod left the arbor and went to a baker's booth, where he bought two large honeycakes, each packed in a reed basket. One of the cakes was sprinkled with chopped raisins, the other was cast over with nuts. Shimrod took up the cakes and stepped around to the back of the booth. The baker, assured that Shimrod had gone to relieve himself, ran out to remonstrate. 'Hold hard, sir! Go elsewhere for such business! I want no great chife in the air; it is poor advertisement!' He halted, looking right and left. 'Where are you, sir?' He heard a mutter, a whimper, a rush of wind. Something whisked up at a blur and away from his vision, but of Shimrod there was naught to be seen.

Slow of foot the baker returned to the front of his booth but told no one of the event, for fear of being thought over-imaginative.

II

Shimrod was transported to a stony flat high on the slopes of the Teach tac Teach, with the panorama to the east swathed under the Forest of Tantrevalles out to the edge of vision. The walls of Swer Smod rose at his back: a set of massive rectangular shapes, meshed and merged, stacked and layered, with three towers of unequal height rising above all, like sentinels surveying the landscape.

Shimrod's approach to the castle was obstructed by a stone wall eight feet high. At the portal hung a sign he had not seen before. Black symbols conveyed a daunting admonition:

—:O:—

WARNING!
TRESPASSERS! WAYFARERS! ALL OTHERS!
ADVANCE AT RISK!

If you cannot read these words, cry out 'KLARO!'
and the sign will declare the message aloud.

—:O:—

PROCEED NO FARTHER, AT PERIL OF DEATH!

—:O:—

In case of need, consult Shimrod the Magician,
at his manse Trilda, in the Great Forest of Tantrevalles.

—:O:—

Shimrod halted at the portal and surveyed the yard beyond. Nothing had changed since his last visit. On guard were the same two gryphs: Vus, mottled moss-green, and maroon-red Vuwas, whose color was that of old blood, or raw liver. Both stood eight feet tall, with massive torsos clad in plaques of horny carapace. Vus displayed a crest of six black spikes, to which, in his vanity, he had affixed a number of medals and emblems. Vuwas wore across his scalp and down the nape of his neck a stiff brush of black-red fibers. Not to be outdone by Vus, he had attached several fine pearls to this bristle. Vus and Vuwas, at this moment, sat beside their sentinel box, hunched over a chessboard wrought from black iron and bone. The pieces stood four inches high, and cried out as they were moved, in derision, shock, outrage, or occasionally approval. The gryphs paid no heed to the comments and played their own game.

Shimrod pushed through the iron gate and entered the forecourt. The gryphs glared hot-eyed over their pronged shoulders. Each ordered the other to rise up and kill Shimrod; each demurred. 'Do you take me for a fool?' demanded Vuwas. 'In my absence, you would make three illicit moves and no doubt abuse my pieces. It is you who must do your duty, and at this very moment.'

'Not I!' said the moss-green Vus. 'Your remarks merely indicate what you yourself have in mind. While I killed this sheep-faced fool, you would push my reignet into limbo and baffle my darkdog into the corner.'

Vuwas growled to Shimrod over his shoulder: 'Go away; it is simpler for everyone. We avoid the trouble of killing you, and you need not worry about arranging your affairs.'

'Out of the question,' said Shimrod. 'I am here on important business. Do you not recognize me? I am Murgen's scion Shimrod.'

'We remember nothing,' grunted Vuwas. 'One earthling looks much like another.'

Vus pointed to the ground. 'Wait where you stand until we finish our game. This is a critical juncture!'

Shimrod sauntered over to inspect the chessboard. The gryphs paid him no heed.

'Ludicrous,' said Shimrod after a moment.

'Hist!' snarled Vuwas, the maroon-red gryph. 'We will tolerate no interference!'

Vus looked around challengingly: 'Do you intend insult? If so, we will tear you limb from limb on the spot!'

Shimrod asked: 'Can a cow be insulted by the word "bovine"? Can a bird be insulted by the word "flighty"? Can a pair of bumbling mooncalfs be insulted by the word "ludicrous"?'

Vuwas spoke sharply: 'Your hints are not clear. What are you trying to tell us?'

'Simply that either of you could win the game with a single move.'

The gryphs glumly examined the board. 'How so?' asked Vus.

'In your case, you need only conquer this bezander with your caitiff, then march the arch-priestess forward to confront the serpent, and the game is yours.'

'Never mind all that!' snapped Vuwas. 'How might I win?'

'Is it not obvious? These mordykes stand in your way. Strike them aside with your ghost, like this, whereupon your caitiffs have the freedom of the board.'

'Ingenious,' said Vus the mottled green gryph. 'Those moves, however, are considered improper on the world Pharsad. Further, you have called the pieces by their wrong names, and also you have disarranged the board!'

'No matter,' said Shimrod. 'Simply replay the game, and now I must be on my way.'

'Not so fast!' cried out Vuwas. 'There is still a small task to be accomplished!'

'We were not born yesterday,' stated Vus. 'Prepare for death.'

Shimrod put the reed baskets on the table. Vuwas the dark red gryph asked suspiciously: 'What is in the baskets?'

'They contain honey-cakes,' said Shimrod. 'One of the cakes is somewhat larger and more tasty than the other.'

'Aha!' said Vus. 'Which is which?'

'You must open the baskets,' said Shimrod. 'The larger cake is for whichever of you is the most deserving.'

'Indeed!'

Shimrod sauntered off across the forecourt. For a moment there was silence behind him, then a mutter, then a sharp remark, an equally sharp retort, followed by a sudden outburst of horrid snarls, bellows, thuds and tearing sounds.

Traversing the forecourt, Shimrod climbed three steps to a stone porch. Stone columns framed an alcove and a ponderous black iron door, twice his height and wider than his arms could span. Black iron faces looked through festoons of black iron vines; black iron eyes watched Shimrod with sardonic curiosity. Shimrod touched a stud; the door swung open to the grinding of iron on iron. He stepped through the opening, into a high-ceilinged entry hall. To right and left pedestals supported a pair of stone statues, of exaggerated attenuation, robed and cowled so that the gaunt faces remained in shadow. No servitor appeared; Shimrod expected none. Murgen's servitors were more often than not invisible.

The way was familiar to Shimrod. He passed through the entry hall into a long gallery. At regular intervals, tall portals opened into chambers serving a variety of functions. There was no one to be seen nor any sound to be heard; an almost unnatural stillness held Swer Smod.

Shimrod walked along the gallery without haste, looking into the chambers on either side to discover what changes had been made since his last visit. Often the chambers were dark, and usually empty. Some served conventional purposes; others were dedicated to a use less ordinary. In one of these chambers Shimrod discovered a tall woman standing before an easel, back turned to the doorway. She wore a long gown of gray-blue linen; cloud-white hair was gathered at the nape of her neck by a ribbon, then hung down her back. The easel supported a panel; using brushes and pigments from a dozen clay pots the woman worked to create an image on the surface of the panel.

Shimrod watched a moment, but could not clearly define the nature of the image. He entered the chamber, that he might observe at closer range and perhaps with better understanding, but had no great success. The pigments looked to be an identical heavy black, allowing the woman small scope for contrast, or so it seemed to Shimrod. He moved a step closer, then another. At last he was able to perceive that each pigment, anomalous and strange to his eyes, quivered with a particular subtle luster unique to itself. He studied the panel; the shapes formed by the black oozes swam before his vision; neither their definition nor their pattern were at all obvious.

The woman turned her head; with blank white eyes she looked at Shimrod. Her expression remained vague; Shimrod was not sure that she saw him, but it could not be that she was blind! The case would be self-contradictory!

Shimrod smiled politely. 'It is an interesting work that you do,' he said. 'The composition, however, is not quite clear to me.'

The woman made no response, and Shimrod wondered if she might also be deaf. In a somber mood he left the chamber and continued along the gallery to the Great Hall. No footman or other servitor stood on hand to

167

announce him; Shimrod passed through the portal, into a chamber so high that the ceiling was lost among the shadows. A line of narrow windows halfway down one of the walls admitted pale light from the north; flames in the fireplace provided a more cheerful illumination. The walls were paneled with oak but bare of decoration. A heavy table occupied the center of the room. Cabinets along the far wall displayed books, curios and miscellaneous oddments; to the side of the mantlepiece a glass globe, charged with glowing green plasma, hung by a silver wire from the ceiling; within huddled the curled skeleton of a weasel, skull peering through high haunches.

Murgen stood by the table, looking down into the fire: a man of early maturity, well-proportioned but of no particular distinction. Such was his ordinary semblance, in which he felt most comfortable. He acknowledged Shimrod's presence with a glance and casual wave of the hand.

'Sit,' said Murgen. 'I am glad that you are here; in fact, I was about to summon you, that you might deal with a moth.'

Shimrod seated himself by the fire. He looked around the chamber. 'I am here, but I see no moth.'

'It has disappeared,' said Murgen. 'How was your journey?'

'Well enough. I came by way of Castle Sarris and Lyonesse Town, in company with Prince Dhrun.'

Murgen settled into a chair beside Shimrod. 'Will you eat or drink?'

'A goblet of wine might calm my nerves. Your devils are more horrid than ever. You must curb their truculence.'

Murgen made an indifferent gesture. 'They serve their purpose.'

'Far too well, in my opinion,' said Shimrod. 'Should one

of your honored guests be late in arrival, do not be offended; it is likely that the devils have torn him to bits.'

'I entertain seldom,' said Murgen. 'Still, since you are so definite, I will suggest that Vus and Vuwas moderate their vigilance.'

A silver-haired sylph, bare-legged, drifted into the hall. She carried a tray on which rested a blue glass flask and a pair of goblets, twisted and worked into quaint shapes. She placed the tray on the table, turned Shimrod a quick side-glance and decanted two goblets of dark red wine. One of these she offered to Shimrod, the other to Murgen, then drifted from the hall as silently as she had come.

For a moment the two drank wine from the blue glass goblets in silence. Shimrod studied the suspended green-glowing globe. Black glittery beads in the small skull seemed to return his scrutiny. Shimrod asked: 'Is it yet alive?'

Murgen looked over his shoulder. The black beads again appeared to shift to meet Murgen's gaze. 'The dregs of Tamurello perhaps still exist: his tincture so to speak, or perhaps the verve of the green gas itself is responsible.'

'Why do you not destroy the globe, gas and all, and be done with it?'

Murgen made a sound of amusement. 'If I knew all there was to be known, I might do so. Or, on the other hand, I might not do so. Consequently, I delay. I am both wary and chary of disturbing what seems a stasis.'

'But it is not truly a stasis?'

'There is never a stasis.'

Shimrod made no comment. Murgen continued. 'I am warned by my instincts. They tell me of movement, furtive and slow. Someone wishes to catch me as I drowse, complacent and bloated with power. The possibility is real; I cannot look in all directions at once.'

169

'But who has the will to work such a strategy? Surely not Tamurello!'

'Perhaps not Tamurello.'

'Who else, then?'

'There is a recurrent question which troubles me. At least once each day I ask myself: where is Desmei?'

'She disappeared, after creating Carfilhiot and Melancthe: that is the general understanding.'

Murgen's mouth took on a wry twist. 'Was it all so simple? Did Desmei truly entrust her revenge to the likes of Carfilhiot and Melancthe – the one a monster, the other an unhappy dreamer?'

'Desmei's motives have always been a puzzle,' said Shimrod. 'Admittedly, I have never studied them in depth.'

Murgen gazed into the fire. 'From nothing came much. Her malice was kindled by what seems a trivial impulse: Tamurello's rejection of her erotic urge. Why, then, the elaborations? Why did she not simply revenge herself upon Tamurello? Was Melancthe intended to serve as her instrument of vengeance? If so, her plans went awry. Carfilhiot ingested the green fume, while Melancthe barely sensed its odor.'

'Still, the memory seems to fascinate her,' said Shimrod.

'It would seem a most seductive stuff. Tamurello consumed the green pearl; now he crouches in the globe, and the green suffusion surrounds him to a surfeit. He gives no evidence of joy.'

'This in itself might be considered the vengeance of Desmei.'

'It seems too paltry. For Desmei Tamurello represented not only himself but all his kind. There are no gauges to measure such malice; one can only feel and wonder.'

'And cringe.'

'It is instructive, perhaps, to note that Desmei in her

creation of Melancthe and Carfilhiot used a demon magic derived from Xabiste. The green gas may itself be Desmei, in a form imposed upon her by the conditions of Xabiste. If so, she is no doubt anxious to resume a more conventional shape.'

'Are you suggesting that Desmei and Tamurello are bottled together in the globe?'

'It is only an idle thought. Meanwhile I guard Joald and soothe his monstrous hulk, and ward away whatever might disturb his long wet rest. When time permits, I study the demon magic of Xabiste, which is slippery and ambiguous. Such are my preoccupations.'

'You mentioned that you were about to call me here to Swer Smod.'

'Quite so. The conduct of a moth has caused me concern.'

'An ordinary moth?'

'So it would seem.'

'And I am here to deal with this moth?'

'The moth is more significant than you imagine. Yesterday, just before dusk, I came through the door and, as always, took note of the globe. I saw that a moth had apparently been attracted by the green light and had settled upon the surface. As I watched, it crawled to where it could look into Tamurello's eyes. I immediately summoned the sandestin Rylf, who informed me that I saw not a moth but a shybalt from Xabiste.'

Shimrod's jaw dropped. 'That is bad news.'

Murgen nodded. 'It means that a strand of communication is open – between whatever resides in the globe and someone elsewhere.'

'What then?'

'When the moth-shybalt flew away, Rylf assumed the form of a dragonfly and followed. The moth crossed the

171

mountains and flew down the Vale of Evander to the city Ys.'

'And then, along the beach to Melancthe's villa?'

'Surprisingly, no. The shybalt might have become aware of Rylf. At Ys it darted down to a flambeau on the square, where it joined a thousand other moths, all careering around the flame, to Rylf's confusion. He remained on watch, hoping to identify the moth he had followed from Swer Smod. As he waited, considering the swirling myriad, one of the moths dropped to the ground and altered its form to that of a human man. Rylf had no way of knowing whether this was the moth he had been following, or a totally different insect. By the laws of probability, as Rylf reckoned them, the moth of his interest remained in the throng; therefore Rylf took no special note of the man, although he was still able to provide a detailed description.'

'That is all to the good, certainly.'

'Just so. The man was of average quality, clad in ordinary garments, wearing a proper hat and shod with the usual sort of shoes. Rylf also noticed that he took himself to the largest of the nearby inns, beneath the sign of the setting sun.'

'That would be the Sunset Inn, on the harbor.'

'Rylf continued to keep watch on the moths, among whom – according to the probabilities, as he calculated them – was the moth he had followed from Swer Smod. At midnight the flambeau burned out, and the moths flew off in all directions. Rylf decided that he had done his best and returned to Swer Smod.'

'Hmf,' said Shimrod. 'And now I am to try my luck at the Sunset Inn?'

'That is my suggestion.'

Shimrod reflected. 'It cannot be coincidence that Melancthe is also resident close by Ys.'

'That is for you to verify. I have made inquiry and I learn that we are dealing with the shybalt Zagzig, who lacks good repute even on Xabiste.'

'And when I find him?'

'Your task becomes delicate and even dangerous, since we will wish to question him with meticulous precision. He will ignore your orders, and attempt a sly trick of some kind; you must drop this circlet of suheil over his neck; otherwise he will kill you with a gust from his mouth.'

Shimrod dubiously examined the ring of fine wire which Murgen had placed upon the table. 'This ring will subdue Zagzig and make him passive?'

'Exactly so. You can then bring him back to Swer Smod, where our inquiries can be made at leisure.'

'And if he proves obstreperous?'

Murgen went to the mantlepiece and returned with a short sword in a scabbard of worn black leather. 'This is the sword Tace. Use it for your protection, though I prefer that you bring Zagzig submissively to Swer Smod. Come now into the tire room; we must arrange a guise for you. It is not fitting that you should be identified as Shimrod the Magician. If we must violate our own edict, at least let us do it by stealth.'

Shimrod rose to his feet. 'Remember to counsel Vus and Vuwas, so that they extend me a more civilized welcome upon my return.'

Murgen brushed aside the complaint. 'First things first. At the moment, Zagzig must be your only concern.'

'As you say.'

III

The River Evander, where it met the Atlantic Ocean, passed by a city of great antiquity, known to the poets of Wales, Ireland, Dahaut, Armorica and elsewhere as 'Ys the Beautiful', and 'Ys of the Hundred Palaces', and 'Ys of the Ocean': a city so romantic, grand and rich that all subsequently claimed it for their own.

Still and all, Ys was not a city of great ostentation, nor magnificent temples, nor public occasions of any kind; Ys, indeed, was steeped in mysteries, old and new. The single concession the folk of Ys made to prideful display were the statues of mythical heroes ranked around the four Consancts, at the back of central plaza. The inhabitants, in the language spoken nowhere else, called themselves 'Yssei': 'folk of Ys'. By tradition they had come to the Elder Isles in four companies; over the course of history the companies had maintained their identities, to become, in effect, four secret societies, with functions and rites more fiercely guarded than life itself. For this reason, and others, the society was controlled by intricate customs and delicate etiquette, subtle beyond the understanding of alien folk.

The wealth of Ys and its people was proverbial, and derived from its function as a depot of trade and transshipment between the known world and far places to the south and west. Along the Evander and up the slopes to either side the Yssei palaces gleamed white through the foliage of the old gardens. Twelve arched bridges spanned the river; avenues paved with granite flags followed each bank; with tow-paths skirting the shore, that barges laden with fruits, flowers, produce of all kinds, might be conveyed to the folk living at a distance from the central market. The largest structures of Ys were the four Consancts at the back of the plaza, where the factors of the four septs transacted their business.

The waterfront was considered a separate community by the folk of Ys; they call it 'Abri', or 'Place of Outlanders'. In the harbor district were the shops of small merchants, chandleries, foundries and forges, shipyards, sail-makers' lofts, ropewalks, warehouses, taverns and inns.

Of these inns, one of the largest and best was the Sunset Inn, identified by a sign showing a red sun sinking into an ultramarine ocean, with yellow clouds drifting above. In front of the Sunset Inn tables and benches served the convenience of those who might wish to take food or drink in the open air, while observing events in the square. Beside the door, sardines grilled over glowing coals, emitting a delectable odor and attracting customers who might otherwise have passed by unheeding.

Late in the afternoon Shimrod, in the guise of an itinerant man-at-arms, arrived at Ys. He had darkened his skin and his hair was now black, while a simple cantrap of eighteen syllables had altered his features, causing him to appear hard-bitten, crafty and saturnine. At his side hung the shortsword Tace and a dagger: weapons adequate to the image he wished to project. He went directly to the Sunset Inn where, as it might seem from Rylf's report, Zagzig the shybalt had gone to keep a rendezvous. As Shimrod approached, the odor of grilling sardines reminded him that he had not eaten since morning.

Shimrod passed through the doorway and into the common room, where he halted to take stock of the company. Which of these persons, if any, would be the shybalt from Xabiste? None sat brooding alone in a

175

corner; none hunched watchfully with hooded eyes over a goblet of wine.

Shimrod went to the service counter. Here stood the innkeeper: a person short and plump with cautious black eyes in a round red face. He nodded his head politely. 'Your needs, sir?'

'First, I want accommodation for a day or so,' said Shimrod. 'I prefer a quiet chamber and a bed free of vermin. Then I will take my supper.'

The innkeeper wiped his hands on his apron, meanwhile taking note of Shimrod's well-worn garments. 'Such arrangements can be made, and no doubt to your satisfaction. But first: a detail. Over the years I have been robbed right and left, up and down, by ruthless scoundrels, until at last my natural generosity became sour and now I am excessively provident. In short, I wish to see the color of your money before taking the transaction any farther.'

Shimrod tossed a silver florin upon the counter. 'My stay may be of several days. This coin, of good silver, should adequately cover my expenses.'

'It will at least open your account,' said the innkeeper. 'As it happens, a chamber of the type you require is ready for occupancy. What name shall I write into my general register?'

'You may know me as "Tace",' said Shimrod.

'Very well, Sir Tace. The boy will show you to your chamber. Fonsel! At once! Show Sir Tace to the large west chamber!'

'One moment,' said Shimrod. 'I wonder if a friend of mine arrived at about this time yesterday, or perhaps a bit later. I am not sure as to what name he might be using.'

'Several visitors came yesterday,' said the innkeeper. 'What is your friend's appearance?'

'He is of average description. He wears garments, covers his head with a hat and is shod with shoes.'

The innkeeper reflected. 'I cannot recall this gentleman. Sir Fulk of Thwist came at noon; he is grossly corpulent, and a large wen protrudes from his nose. A certain Janglart arrived during the afternoon, but he is tall and thin as a switch, very pale and a long white beard hangs from his chin. Mynax the sheep-dealer is average in quality, but I have never known him to wear a hat: always he uses a cylindrical sheepskin casque. No one else took rooms for the night.'

'No great matter,' said Shimrod. It was probable, he thought, that the shybalt had perched the long night through on a high gable rather than enduring the confinement of a room. 'My friend will arrive in due course.'

Shimrod followed Fonsel upstairs to the chamber, which he found satisfactory. Returning downstairs, he went out to the front of the inn and seated himself at a table, where he took his supper: first, a dozen sardines sizzling and crackling from the grill, next a platter of broad-beans and bacon with an onion for relish, along with a hunch of new bread and a quart of ale.

The sun sank into the sea. Patrons entered and left the inn; none aroused Shimrod's suspicions. The shybalt might well have done its work and departed, thought Shimrod. His attention must then inevitably focus upon Melancthe, who lived in a white villa less than a mile up the beach and who had previously acted at the behest of Tamurello, for reasons never made clear to Shimrod. Apparently, he had never been her lover, having preferred her sibling Faude Carfilhiot. The relationship might or might not have pleased Desmei – had she been alive and aware. It was, Shimrod reflected, truly a tangled skein of barely plausible possibilities and shocking realities. Melancthe's role, rather than having been clarified by events, was as ambiguous now as ever, and probably not even known to herself. Who had ever plumbed even the most superficial level of Melancthe's consciousness? Certainly not himself.

Twilight descended upon Ys of the Ocean. Shimrod rose from his table and set off along the harbor road which after leaving the docks struck off to the north beside the white beach.

The town fell behind. Tonight the wind was gone from the sky and the sea was calm. Listless surf rolled up the beach, creating a dull soothing sound.

Shimrod approached the white villa. A chest-high wall of white-washed stone enclosed a garden of asphodels, heliotrope, thyme, three slim cypresses and a pair of lemon trees.

The villa and its garden were well known to Shimrod. He had seen them first in a dream, which recurred night after night. In these dreams, Melancthe had first appeared to him, a dark-haired maiden of heart-wrenching beauty and contradictions beyond number.

On this particular evening Melancthe seemed not at home. Shimrod walked through the garden, crossed the little strip of tiled terrace, rapped at the door. He awoke no response, not even from the maid. From within came no glow of lamps or candle. Nothing could be heard but the slow thud of the surf.

Shimrod left the villa and returned down the beach to the town square and the Sunset Inn. In the common room, he found an inconspicuous table beside the wall and seated himself.

One by one, Shimrod scrutinized the occupants of the room. In the main, they seemed local folk: tradesmen, artisans, a few peasants from the surrounding countryside, a few seamen from ships in the harbor. None were Yssei, who kept themselves apart from the ruck of the townspeople.

A person sitting solitary a few tables away attracted

Shimrod's attention. He appeared stocky of physique, but of middle stature. His garments were ordinary: a peasant's smock of coarse gray weave, loose breeches, buskins with pointed curled-over toes and triangular ankle-tabs. Pulled down upon his shock of brown hair was a narrow-brimmed black hat with a tall back-sloping crown. His face was bland and still, enlivened only by the glitter and constant shift of his small black eyes. On the table before him rested a full mug of ale, which he had not tasted. His posture was stiff and queer: his chest moved neither in nor out. By these and other signs, Shimrod knew that here sat Zagzig the shybalt from Xabiste, uncomfortably disguised as a denizen of Earth. Shimrod noticed that Zagzig had carelessly failed to divest himself of the moth's middle two legs, which jerked and stirred from time to time under the gray blouse. The nape of Zagzig's neck also glistened with moth-scale, where he had failed to provide himself a proper integument of human skin.

Shimrod decided that, as usual, the simplest of available options was the best: he would wait and watch and discover what eventuated.

Fonsel the serving boy, passing close to Zagzig with a tray, by chance jostled Zagzig's tall-crowned black hat, knocking it to the table, to reveal not only Zagzig's mat of brown hair but also a pair of feathery antennae which Zagzig had forgotten to remove. Fonsel stared with mouth agape, while Zagzig angrily clapped the hat back upon his head. He uttered a terse command; Fonsel grimaced, bobbed his head and hurried away with only a confused glance back over his shoulder. Zagzig darted glances this way and that to see who might have noticed the incident. Shimrod quickly averted his eyes and pretended an interest in a rack of old blue plates hanging on the wall. Zagzig relaxed, and sat as before.

Ten minutes passed. The door was pushed ajar; in the

doorway stood a tall man in black garments. He was spare, broad-shouldered, taut and precise of movement, with a pallid complexion and black hair cut square across his forehead and tied in a rope at the back of his head. Shimrod studied the newcomer with interest; here, he thought, was a man of quick and ruthless intelligence. A scar across the gaunt cheek accentuated the menace of his already grim visage. From the evidence of his hair, his pallor and his manner of contemptuous self-sufficiency, Shimrod assumed the newcomer to be a Ska[1], from Skaghane, or the Ska foreshore.

The Ska looked around the room. He glanced first at Shimrod, then at Zagzig, then once again around the room, after which he chose a table and seated himself. Fonsel came at a run to inquire his needs, and brought him ale, sardines and bread, almost before the order had been placed.

The Ska ate and drank without haste; when he had finished, he sat back in his chair and once again appraised first Shimrod, then Zagzig. Now he placed on the table a ball of dark green serpentine, an inch in diameter, attached to a chain of fine iron links. Shimrod had seen such baubles before; they were caste-markers worn by Ska patricians.

At the sight of the talisman, Zagzig rose to his feet and crossed to the Ska's table.

Shimrod signaled Fonsel to his own table. Shimrod asked quietly: 'Do not turn your head to look, but tell me the name of that tall Ska sitting yonder.'

[1] Ska: the indigenous race of Scandinavia, with traditions and records older by far than those of the Near or Far East. Three thousand years previously, a wave of Aryans, or Ur-Goths, had migrated north from the Black Sea steppes into Scandinavia, ultimately expelling the Ska, who descended first upon Ireland, where they were known to myth as the 'Sons of Partholon'. Eventually, after defeat by the Danaans, they migrated south into Skaghane.

'I can make no sure assertion,' said Fonsel. 'I have never seen him before. However, across the room, I heard someone, in very confidential tones, use the name "Torqual". If this is the "Torqual" of evil reputation, he is bold indeed to show his face here where King Aillas would be grateful to find him and stretch his neck.'

Shimrod gave the boy a copper penny. 'Your remarks are interesting. Bring me now a goblet of good tawny wine.'

By a sleight of magic Shimrod augmented the acuity of his hearing, so that the whispers of two young lovers in a far corner were now clearly audible, as were the innkeeper's instructions to Fonsel in regard to the watering of Shimrod's wine. However, the conversation between Zagzig and Torqual had been muted by a magic as sharp as his own, and he could hear nothing of its content.

Fonsel served him a goblet of wine with a fine flourish. 'Here you are, sir! Our noblest vintage!'

'That is good to hear,' said Shimrod. 'I am the official inspector of hostelries, by the authority of King Aillas. Still – would you believe it? – I am often served poor stuff! Three days ago in Mynault, an innkeeper and his pot-boy conspired to water my wine, which act King Aillas has declared an offense against humanity.'

'Truly, sir?' quavered Fonsel. 'What then?'

'The constables took both innkeeper and pot-boy to the public square and tied them to a post, where they were roundly flogged. They will not soon repeat their offense.'

Fonsel snatched up the goblet. 'Suddenly I see that, by mistake, I have poured from the wrong flask! One moment, sir, while I put matters right.'

Fonsel, in haste, served a fresh goblet of wine, and a moment later the innkeeper himself came to the table, wiping his hands anxiously on his apron. 'I trust that all is in order, sir?'

'At the moment, yes.'

'Good! Fonsel is sometimes a bit careless, and brings our good name into disrepute. Tonight I will beat him for his mistake.'

Shimrod uttered a grim laugh. 'Sir, leave poor Fonsel be. He thought better of his mischief, and deserves a chance at redemption.'

The innkeeper bowed. 'Sir, I will ponder your advice with care.' He hurried back to the counter, and Shimrod resumed his observation of Zagzig the shybalt and Torqual the Ska.

The conversation came to an end. Zagzig tossed a purse upon the table. Torqual loosened the draw-string and peered at the contents. He raised his eyes and treated Zagzig to a stony stare of displeasure. Zagzig returned an indifferent glance, then rose to his feet and prepared to depart the inn.

Shimrod, anticipating Zagzig's move, had preceded him, and waited in the front yard. The full moon had risen to illuminate the square; the granite flags showed almost as white as bone. Shimrod sidled into the deep shade of the hemlock which grew beside the inn.

Zagzig's silhouette appeared in the doorway; Shimrod readied the loop of suheil wire which he had received from Murgen.

Zagzig moved past; Shimrod stepped from the shade and attempted to drop the loop over Zagzig's head. The tall black hat interfered. Zagzig jerked aside; the suheil wire scraped his face and caused him to whine in shock. He spun around to face Shimrod. 'Villain!' hissed Zagzig. 'Do you think so to halter me? Your time has come.' He opened wide his mouth, in order to expel a gust of poison. Shimrod thrust the sword Tace into the aperture; Zagzig uttered a groan and collapsed upon the moonlit pavement, to become a pile of pink sparks and flashes, which Shimrod fastidiously avoided. Presently nothing remained but a gray fluff so light that it drifted away on a cool air from the sea.

Shimrod returned into the common room. A young man dressed in the mode currently popular in Aquitaine had perched himself on a high stool with his lute. Striking chords and melodic passages, he sang ballads celebrating the deeds of lovelorn knights and yearning maidens, all in the mournful cadences imposed upon him by the tuning of his lute. Of Torqual there was no sign; he had departed the common room.

Shimrod summoned Fonsel, who sprang to his service on the instant. 'Your wishes, sir?'

'The person named "Torqual": is he lodged here at the Sunset Inn?'

'No, your Honor! He left only a moment ago by the side door. May I bring your Lordship more wine?'

Shimrod made a stately affirmative sign. 'Needless to say, I thirst for no water.'

'That, sir, goes without saying!'

Shimrod sat for an hour drinking wine and listening to the sad ballads of Aquitaine. At last he became restless and went out into the night, where the moon now floated halfway up the sky. The square was empty; the stone flags glimmered white as before. Shimrod strolled to the harbor and along the esplanade to where it joined the shore road. Here he halted and looked up the beach. After a few minutes he turned away. At this time of night Melancthe would not be likely to receive him graciously.

Shimrod returned to the inn. The Aquitanian jongleur had departed, along with most of the patrons. Torqual was nowhere to be seen. Shimrod went up to his chamber, and composed himself to rest.

IV

In the morning Shimrod took his breakfast at the front of the inn, where he could look out across the square. He consumed a pear, a bowl of porridge with cream, several rashers of fried bacon, a slice of dark bread with cheese and pickled plums. The warmth of the sunlight was pleasantly in contrast to cool airs from the sea; Shimrod breakfasted without haste, watchful yet relaxed. Today was market-day; a confusion of movement, sound and color enlivened the square. Everywhere merchants had set up tables and booths, from which they cried out the quality of their wares. Fishmongers held aloft their best fish and beat on iron triangles so that all might turn to look. Among the booths swirled the customers, for the most part housewives and servant-girls, chaffering, haggling, weighing, judging, criticizing, occasionally clinking down their coins.

Other folk, as well, moved across the square: a quartet of melancholy priests from the Temple of Atlante; mariners and traders from far lands; an occasional Yssei factor on his way to inspect a cargo; a baron and his lady down from their dour mountain keep; herdsmen and crofters from the moors and glens of the Teach tac Teach.

Shimrod finished his breakfast but remained at the table eating grapes, wondering how best to proceed with his investigation.

Even as Shimrod pondered, he noticed a dark-haired young woman marching across the square, her orange-brown skirt and a rose-pink blouse glowing in the sunlight. Shimrod recognized her for Melancthe's housemaid. She carried a pair of empty baskets and was evidently on het way to market.

Shimrod jumped to his feet and followed the young woman across the square. At a fruit-vendor's booth she began to select oranges from the display. Shimrod watched a moment, then approached and touched her elbow. She looked around with a blank expression, failing to recognize Shimrod in his present guise.

'Come aside with me a moment,' said Shimrod. 'I want a few words with you.'

The maid hesitated and drew away. Shimrod said: 'My business is in connection with your mistress. No harm will come to you.'

Puzzled and reluctant, the maid followed Shimrod a few steps out into the square. 'What do you want of me?'

Shimrod spoke in what he hoped was a reassuring voice. 'I do not remember your name – if, indeed, I ever knew it.'

'I am Lillas. Why should you know me? I have no recollection of you.'

'Some time ago I called upon your mistress. You opened the door for me. Surely you remember?'

Lillas searched Shimrod's face. 'You seem somehow familiar, though, in truth, I cannot place you exactly. The occasion must have been long ago.'

'So it was, but you are still in the service of Melancthe?'

'Yes. I have no fault to find with her – at least none that would prompt me to leave her.'

'She is an easy mistress?'

Lillas smiled sadly. 'She hardly notices whether I am here or there, whether I am in the house or gone. Still, she would not want me to stand here gossiping about her affairs.'

Shimrod produced a silver florin. 'What you tell me will travel no farther, and cannot be considered gossip.'

185

Lillas dubiously took the coin. 'For a fact, I am concerned for the lady. I understand no single phase of her conduct. Often she sits for hours looking out to sea. I go about my work and she pays me no heed, as if I were invisible.'

'Does she often receive visitors?'

'Seldom. Still, just this morning – ' Lillas hesitated, and looked over her shoulder.

Shimrod prompted her. 'Who was her visitor this morning?'

'He came early: a tall pale man with a scar on his face; I think he would be a Ska. He knocked at the door; I opened to him. He said: "Tell your mistress that Torqual is here".

'I drew back and he came into the hall. I went to Lady Melancthe and gave her the message.'

'Was she surprised?'

'I think she was perplexed and not well-pleased, but perhaps not altogether astonished. She hesitated only a moment, then went out into the hall. I followed, but remained behind the curtain, where I could watch through the crack. The two stood looking at each other a moment, then Torqual said: "I am told that I must obey your commands. What do you know of this arrangement?"

'The Lady Melancthe said: "I am not sure of anything."

'Torqual asked: "Did you not expect me?"

'"An intimation came – but nothing is clear and I must ponder," said my lady. "Go now! If I find commands for you, I will let you know."

'At this Torqual seemed amused. "And how will you do this?"

'"By means of a signal. If I am prompted in this direction, a black urn will appear on the wall by the gate. Should you see the black urn, then you may come again."

'At this, the man Torqual smiled, and bowed, so that

186

he seemed almost princely. Without another word he turned and left the villa. That is what happened this morning. I am happy to tell you, since Torqual frightens me. Clearly he can bring the Lady Melancthe only distress.'

'Your fears are well-founded,' said Shimrod. 'Still, she may choose not to deal with Torqual.'

'So it may be.'

'She is now at home?'

'Yes; as usual she sits looking out to sea.'

'I will call on her. Perhaps I can set matters straight.'

Lillas spoke anxiously: 'You will not reveal that we have discussed her affairs?'

'Certainly not.'

Lillas went back to the fruit-seller's booth; Shimrod crossed the square to the harbor road. His suspicions had been validated. Melancthe's involvement in the affair might so far only be passive and might remain so; still Melancthe's only sure trait was her unpredictability.

Shimrod looked to the north, toward the white villa. He could find no reason for delay, save his own reluctance to confront Melancthe. He set off to the north along the beach road, walking with long deliberate strides, and soon arrived at the white stone wall. No black urn, so he noted, was visible.

Shimrod crossed the garden, went to the door. He raised the knocker and let it fall.

There was no response.

Shimrod knocked a second time, with the same result as before.

The villa, so it seemed, was empty of its occupants.

Shimrod turned slowly away from the door, then went to stand by the side of the gate. He looked up the road to the north. In the near distance he discovered Melancthe, approaching without haste. He felt no surprise; so it had been in his dreams.

Shimrod waited, with the sunlight glaring down upon the sand of the road. Melancthe drew near: a slender dark-haired maiden wearing a white knee-length frock and sandals. With only a brief impassive stare for Shimrod, she turned through the gate; as she passed, Shimrod sensed the faint odor of violets which always accompanied her.

Melancthe went to the door. Shimrod followed soberly and entered the villa behind her. She went along the hall and into a long room with a wide arched window overlooking the sea. Moving to the window, Melancthe stood gazing pensively toward the horizon. Shimrod stood in the doorway, looking here and there, appraising the room. Little had changed since his last visit. The walls were washed white; on the tiled floor three rugs showed bold patterns of orange, red, black, white and green. A table, a few heavy chairs, a divan and a sideboard were the only furnishings. The walls were innocent of decoration; nowhere in the room were objects to indicate Melancthe's point of view or to suggest the bent of her personality. The rugs were vivid and vital, and would seem to be imports from the Atlas Mountains; almost certainly, so Shimrod surmised, they had been purchased and laid down by Lillas the maid, with Melancthe taking no particular notice.

Melancthe at last turned to Shimrod, and showed him a curious twisted smile. 'Speak, Shimrod! Why are you here?'

'You recognize me, despite my disguise?'

Melancthe seemed taken aback. '"Disguise"? I notice no disguise. You are Shimrod, as meek, quixotic and indecisive as ever.'

'No doubt,' said Shimrod. 'So much for my disguise; I

cannot conceal my identity. Have you decided upon an identity for Melancthe?'

Melancthe made an airy gesture. 'Such talk is beside the mark. What is your business with me? I doubt that you have come to analyze my character.'

Shimrod pointed to the divan. 'Let us sit; it is dreary work talking on both feet.'

Melancthe gave an indifferent shrug and dropped down upon the divan; Shimrod seated himself beside her. 'You are as beautiful as ever.'

'So I am told.'

'At our last meeting you had developed a taste for poisonous blossoms. Is this inclination still with you?'

Melancthe shook her head. 'There are no more such blossoms to be found. I think of them often; they were wonderfully appealing; do you not agree?'

'They were fascinating, if vile,' said Shimrod.

'I did not find them so. The colors were of great variety, and the scents were unusual.'

'Still – you must believe me! – they represented the aspects of evil: the many flavors of purulence, so to speak.'

Melancthe smiled and shook her head. 'I cannot understand these tedious abstractions, and I doubt if the effort would yield any amusement, since I am easily bored.'

'As a matter of interest, do you know the meaning of the word "evil"?'

'It seems to mean what you intend it to mean.'

'The word is general. Do you know the difference between, let us say, kindness and cruelty?'

'I have never thought to notice. Why do you ask?'

'Because, for a fact, I have come to study your character.'

'Again? For what reason?'

'I am curious to discover whether you are "good" or "bad".'

Melancthe shrugged. 'That is as if I were to ask whether you were a bird or a fish – and then expect an earnest answer.'

Shimrod sighed. 'Just so. How goes your life?'

'I prefer it to oblivion.'

'How do you occupy yourself each day?'

'I watch the sea and the sky; sometimes I wade in the surf and build roads in the sand. At night I study the stars.'

'You have no friends?'

'No.'

'And what of the future?'

'The future stops at "now".'

'As to that, I am not so sure,' said Shimrod. 'It is at best a half-truth.'

'What of that? Half a truth is better than none: do you not agree?'

'Not altogether,' said Shimrod. 'I am a practical man, I try to control the shape of the "nows" which lie in the offing, instead of submitting to them as they occur.'

Melancthe gave an uninterested shrug. 'You are free to do as you like.' Leaning back in the divan, she looked out across the sea.

Shimrod finally spoke. 'Well then: are you "good" or "bad"?'

'I don't know.'

Shimrod became vexed. 'Talking with you is like visiting an empty house.'

Melancthe considered a moment before responding. 'Perhaps,' she said, 'you are visiting the wrong house. Or perhaps you are the wrong visitor.'

'Ha hah!' said Shimrod. 'You seem to be telling me that, indeed, you are capable of thought.'

'I think constantly, day and night.'

'What thoughts do you think?'

'You would not understand them.'

'Do your thoughts bring you pleasure? Or peace?'

'As always, you ask questions I cannot answer.'

'They seem simple enough.'

'For you, no doubt. As for me, I was brought naked and empty into the world; it was only required that I imitate humanity, not that I should become human. I do not know what sort of creature I am. This is the subject of my reflections. They are complicated. Since I know no human emotions, I have contrived an entire new compendium, which only I can feel.'

'That is very interesting! When do you use these new emotions?'

'I use them continually. Some are heavy, others are light, and are named for clouds. Some are constant; others are fugitive. Sometimes they come to thrill me and I would like to keep them forever – just as I longed to keep the wonderful flowers! But the moods slip away before I can name them, and cherish them in my heart. Sometimes, often, they never come back, no matter how I yearn.'

'How do you name these emotions? Tell me!'

Melancthe shook her head. 'The names would mean nothing. I have watched insects, wondering how they name their emotions and wondering if perhaps they were like mine.'

'I should think not,' said Shimrod.

Melancthe spoke on unheeding. 'It may be that instead of emotion, I feel sensation only, which I think to be emotion. This is how an insect feels the moods of its life.'

'In your new set of emotions, do you have equivalents for "good" and "bad"?'

'These are not emotions! You are trying to trick me into talking your language! Very well; I shall answer. I do not know what to think of myself. Since I am not human, I wonder what I am and how my life will go.'

Shimrod sat back and reflected. 'At one time you served Tamurello: why did you do so?'

'That was the behest built into my brain.'

'Now he is pent in a bottle, but still you are asked to serve him.'

Melancthe frowned at Shimrod, mouth pursed in disapproval. 'Why do you say so?'

'Murgen has informed me.'

'And what does he know?'

'Enough to ask stern questions. How do these orders come to you?'

'I have had no exact orders, only impulses and intimations.'

'Who prompts them?'

'Sometimes I think that they are my own contriving. When these moods come on me, I am exalted and I am fully alive!'

'Someone is rewarding you for your cooperation. You must be careful! Tamurello sits in a glass bottle, nose between his knees. Do you want the same for yourself?'

'It will not happen so.'

'Is that how Desmei has instructed you?'

'Please do not utter that name.'

'It must be spoken, since it is another word for "doom". Your doom, if you allow her to use you as her instrument.'

Melancthe rose to her feet and went to the window.

Shimrod spoke to her back: 'Come with me once again to Trilda. I will purge you entirely of the green stench. We will thwart Desmei the witch. You will be wholly free and wholly alive.'

Melancthe turned to face Shimrod. 'I know nothing of any green stench, and nothing of Desmei. Go now.'

Shimrod rose to his feet. 'Today – think upon yourself and how you might want your life to go. I will return at sunset, and perhaps you will come away with me.'

Melancthe seemed not to hear. Shimrod left the room and departed the villa.

The day passed, hour by hour. Shimrod sat at his table before the inn watching the sun cross the sky. When it hung its own diameter above the horizon he set off up the beach. Presently he arrived at the white villa. He went to the front door and raising the knocker, let it fall.

The door opened a crack. Lillas the maid looked out at him.

'Good evening,' said Shimrod. 'I want to speak with your mistress.'

Lillas looked at him large-eyed. 'She is not here.'

'Where is she? Up the beach?'

'She is gone.'

'"Gone"?' Shimrod spoke sharply. 'Gone where?'

'As to that who can say?'

'What has happened to her?'

'An hour ago I answered to a knock at the door. It was Torqual the Ska. He walked past me, along the hall and into the parlor. The mistress was sitting on the divan; she jumped to her feet. The two looked at each other for a moment, and I watched from the doorway. He spoke a single word: "Come!" The mistress made no move, but stood as if irresolute. Torqual stepped forward, took her hand and led her away down the hall and out the front door. She made no protest; indeed, she walked like a person in a dream.'

Shimrod listened with a weight pressing at the pit of his stomach. Lillas spoke on in a rush: 'There were two horses in the road. Torqual lifted my mistress into the saddle of one and mounted the other. They rode away to the north. And now I do not know what to do!'

Shimrod found his voice. 'Do as usual; you have not been instructed otherwise.'

193

'That is good advice!' said Lillas. 'Perhaps she will be home in short order.'

'Perhaps.'

Shimrod returned south along the beach road to the Sunset Inn. In the morning he took himself once again to the white villa, but found only Lillas on the premises. 'You have had no word from your mistress?'

'No, sir. She is far away; I feel it in my bones.'

'So do I.' Shimrod reached to the ground for a pebble. He rubbed it between his fingers and handed it to Lillas. 'As soon as your mistress returns, take this pebble out of doors, throw it into the air and say: "Go to Shimrod!" Do you understand?'

'Yes, sir!'

'What will you do?'

'I will throw the pebble into the air and say: "Go to Shimrod!"'

'That is correct! And here is a silver florin to assist your memory.'

'Thank you, sir.'

V

Shimrod conveyed himself up over the mountains to the stony flat in front of Swer Smod. Entering the forecourt, he discovered the two gryphs sitting down to their morning meal, which included two great joints of beef, four roast fowl, a pair of suckling pigs, two trenchers of pickled salmon, a round of white cheese, and several loaves of new bread. At the sight of Shimrod they jumped up from the table in a rage and ran forward as if to rend him limb from limb.

Shimrod held up his hand. 'Moderation, if you please! Has not Murgen instructed you to milder manners?'

'He approved our vigilance,' said Vuwas. 'He advised a trifle more restraint toward persons of patently good character.'

'You do not fit that description,' said Vus. 'Hence we must do our duty.'

'Stop! I am Shimrod, and I am here on legitimate business!'

'That remains to be seen!' said the mottled green Vus. With one claw he scratched a line across the stone pavement. 'First we must be convinced of your bona fides, which we will look into as soon as we dine.'

'We have been hoodwinked before,' said Vuwas. 'Never again! Step one inch past that line and we will devour you for an appetizer.'

Shimrod performed a small spell. 'I would prefer to pass by your investigation at once, but no doubt you are anxious to join your guests.'

'"Guests"?' demanded Vuwas. 'What guests are these?'

Shimrod pointed; the gryphs turned to discover a troop of eight baboons wearing red trousers and round red hats making free with their repast. Some stood at one side of the table, others opposite, while three stood on the table itself.

Vus and Vuwas roared in full outrage, and ran to chase off the baboons, but they were not so easily discouraged, and hopped with agility here and there, walking in the pickled salmon, and throwing food at the gryphs. Shimrod took advantage of the disturbance to cross the forecourt, and so arrived at the tall iron door. He was admitted and made his way to the great hall.

As before, a fire blazed in the fireplace. The glass globe hanging from the ceiling glowed sullen green. Murgen was not in evidence.

Shimrod seated himself beside the fire and waited. After a moment, he turned his head and glanced up at the suspended globe. Two black eyes glittered at him through the green murk. Shimrod turned his gaze back to the fire.

Murgen entered the room and joined Shimrod at the table. 'You seem a bit dispirited,' said Murgen. 'How went events at Ys?'

'Well enough, in certain respects.' Shimrod told of what had transpired at the Sunset Inn and at Melancthe's villa. 'I learned little that we did not already suspect, except the fact of Torqual's involvement.'

'It is important and signifies a conspiracy! Remember, he first came to Melancthe to learn her commands.'

'But on the second occasion he ignored her commands and forced her to his will.'

'It is perhaps cynical to note that he did not need to force very hard.'

Shimrod stared into the fire. 'What do you know of Torqual?'

'Not a great deal. He was born a Ska nobleman who became a renegade, and is now an outlaw living by plunder, blood and terror. His ambitions may well extend farther.'

'Why do you say that?'

'Is that not implied by his conduct? King Casmir wants him to incite revolt among the Ulfish barons; Torqual takes Casmir's money and goes his own way, with no real advantage to Casmir. If Aillas loses control of the mountains, Torqual will hope to become the ruler, and who knows what then? North and South Ulfland? Godelia? East Dahaut?'

'Luckily, it is an unlikely prospect.'

Murgen stared into the fire. 'Torqual is a man without mercy. It would be a pleasure to hang him in a bottle alongside Tamurello. Alas! I cannot violate my own law — unless he gives me cause. This cause may well be forthcoming.'

'How so?'

'The propulsion to this affair, so I tell myself, can only be Desmei. Where has she taken herself? She is either using some unexpected semblance or hiding where she cannot be discovered. Her hopes flourish and fester! She has revenged herself sweetly upon Tamurello, but not upon the race of men; she is not yet sated.'

'Perhaps she lives passive inside Melancthe, waiting and watching.'

Murgen shook his head. 'She would be constricted and far too vulnerable, since I would know at once. On the other hand, Melancthe, or a construct just like her, may be the vessel Desmei ultimately plans to fill.'

'Tragic that a thing so beautiful must be put to such humiliating uses!' said Shimrod. He sat back in his chair. 'Still, it is nothing to me.'

'Just so,' said Murgen. 'Now, for a space, I must put this matter aside. Other affairs press at my attention. The star Achernar is rife with odd activity, especially in the far outer tracts. Meanwhile Joald stirs in the depths. I must discover if a linkage exists.'

'In that case, what of me?'

Murgen rubbed his chin. 'I will set out a monitor. If Torqual uses magic we will interfere. If he is only a bandit, no matter how cruel, King Aillas and his armies must take him in charge.'

'I would favor more direct action.'

'No doubt; still our goal is minimal involvement! The Edict is a fragile force; if we are discovered in violation, its inhibition may dissolve into smoke.'

'One last word! Your devils are as horrid as ever! They might well frighten a timid person. You must definitely teach them a more polite etiquette.'

'I will see to it.'

6

I

At the end of summer, with the smell of autumn in the air, the royal family departed Sarris for Castle Haidion. There was no unanimity of feeling regarding the event. King Casmir left the informal style of life at Sarris with reluctance. Queen Sollace, on the other hand, could hardly wait to put the rustic deficiencies of Sarris behind her. Cassander cared little one way or the other; boon companions, flirtatious maidens, merry entertainments were as accessible at Haidion as at Sarris; perhaps more so. Princess Madouc, like King Casmir, departed Sarris with reluctance. She hinted to Lady Desdea, not once but several times, that conditions at Sarris suited her well, and that she would prefer not to return to Haidion at all. Lady Desdea paid no heed and Madouc's desires came to naught. Willy-nilly, sullen and bored, Madouc was instructed into the royal carriage for the long ride back to Lyonesse Town. In a brave if hollow voice, Madouc stated her intention to ride Tyfer instead. She pointed out that everyone's convenience would thereby be served. Those riding in the carriage would enjoy more space, while Tyfer would benefit from the exercise. Lady Desdea heard the proposal with eyebrows high in cold amazement. 'That is impossible, of course! It would be considered conduct most boisterous; the act of a hoyden! The folk of the countryside would stare in wonder – those who did not laugh outright – to see you trotting so proudly through the dust!'

'I had no plans to ride in the dust! I would just as lief ride in the van, ahead of the dust.'

'And what a sight you would be, leading the cavalcade on your intrepid steed Tyfer! I am surprised that you do not choose to wear mail and carry a banner on high, like a prodrome of old!'

'I had nothing like this in mind; I only – '

Lady Desdea held up her hand. 'Say no more! For once you must conduct yourself with dignity, and ride properly with Her Majesty. Your maidens will be allowed to sit beside you in the carriage, for your amusement.'

'That is why I want to ride Tyfer.'

'Impossible.'

So went the arrangements. Despite Madouc's dissatisfaction, the carriage departed Sarris with Madouc sitting across from Queen Sollace, with Devonet and Chlodys on the seat to her left.

In due course the party arrived at Castle Haidion, and the ordinary routines of life were resumed. Madouc was housed as before in her old chambers, though suddenly they had become cramped and constricted, or so it seemed. 'Odd!' thought Madouc. 'In a single summer I have aged an entire era, and of course I have become far wiser. I wonder . . .' She put her hands to her chest, to feel two small pads of softness she had not previously noticed. She felt them again. They were definite. 'Hm,' said Madouc. 'I hope I do not grow to look like Chlodys.'

The autumn passed, and then the winter. For Madouc the most noteworthy event was the retirement of Lady Desdea, on the plea of backache, nervous cramp and general malaise. Spiteful tongues whispered that Madouc's perverse antics and general intractability had at last conquered Lady Desdea and had made her ill. Indeed, during the late winter, Lady Desdea turned lemon-yellow, began to swell in the middle, and presently died of the dropsy.

Her successor was a noblewoman younger and more flexible: Lady Lavelle, third daughter to the Duke of Wysceog.

Lady Lavelle, having taken note of past attempts to educate the obstreperous princess, changed tactics and dealt casually with Madouc. She took for granted – at least ostensibly – that Madouc, keen to her own advantage, would wish to learn the tricks, ploys and stratagems which would allow her to negotiate court protocol with the least inconvenience. Of course, as a prerequisite, Madouc must learn the conventions which she would be learning to avoid. So, despite herself and half-aware of Lady Lavelle's tactics, Madouc assimilated a smattering of court procedure and certain pretty little skills of genteel coquetry.

A series of storms brought howling winds and driving rains to Lyonesse Town, and Madouc was pent inside Haidion. After a month the storm abated, and the town was washed in a sudden flood of pale sunlight. After such long confinement Madouc felt impelled to go out and wander in the open air. With no better destination at hand, she decided to revisit the hidden garden where Suldrun had pined away her life.

Assuring herself that she went unseen Madouc hastened up the cloistered walk. Through the tunnel in Zoltra Bright-star's Wall, then the rotting old portal, Madouc stepped into the garden.

At the top of the vale she stopped to look and listen. She saw no living creature and heard no sound save the far muffled rush of the surf. Odd! thought Madouc. In the wan winter sunlight the garden seemed less melancholy than as she remembered it.

Madouc wandered down the trail to the beach. The surf, driven by the storms, reared high to crash heavily down upon the shingle. Madouc turned away to look up the vale. Suldrun's conduct seemed more incomprehensible than ever. According to Cassander she could not bring herself to face the dangers and hardships of life on the road. But what then? For a clever person, determined to survive, the dangers could be minimized and perhaps avoided. But Suldrun, timid and apathetic, had preferred to languish in the hidden garden and so at last she had died.

'As for me,' Madouc told herself, 'I would have been over the fence in a trice! After that, I would pretend to be a boy and also a leper. I would feign sores on my face, to disgust anyone who came near me, and those who were not disgusted, I would stab with a knife! Had I been Suldrun, I would be alive today!'

Madouc soberly started up the path. There were lessons to be learned from those tragic events of the past. First, Suldrun had hoped for King Casmir's mercy, which had not been forthcoming. The significance was clear. A princess of Lyonesse must marry as Casmir desired or else incur his merciless displeasure. Madouc grimaced. The correspondence between Suldrun's case and her own was much too close for comfort. Still, displeasure or not, King Casmir must be persuaded not to involve her in his schemes of empire.

Madouc left the garden, and returned down the way to the castle. Out over the Lir a bank of black clouds was approaching fast, and even as Madouc approached the castle, a damp gust of wind struck at her, whipping the skirt around her legs. The day grew dark and the new storm arrived with thunder, lightning and rain. Madouc wondered if winter would ever end.

A week passed and another, and at last the sun drove shafts of light down through the clouds. The next day dawned sparkling clear.

King Casmir, himself oppressed by the bad weather,

decided to take the air with Queen Sollace, and in the process show themselves to the folk of Lyonesse Town. He ordered out the ceremonial carriage, which presently pulled up in front of the castle. The royal family took their places: King Casmir and Queen Sollace facing forward; Prince Cassander and Princess Madouc stiffly opposite.

The procession set off: a herald holding high the royal arms, consisting of a black Tree of Life on a white field, with a dozen scarlet pomegranates hanging from the branches. Next rode three men-at-arms in chain corselets and iron helmets, holding halberds high, followed by the open carriage with its royal cargo. Another three men-at-arms, riding abreast, brought up the rear.

The procession moved down the Sfer Arct – slowly, so that the townspeople might rush out to stare and point and raise an occasional cheer.

At the foot of the Sfer Arct, the procession turned to the right and continued around the Chale to the site of the new cathedral. Here the carriage halted and the royal party alighted, so that they might inspect the progress of construction. Almost at once they were approached by Father Umphred.

The meeting was not accidental. Father Umphred and Queen Sollace had calculated at length how best to engage King Casmir's interest in the cathedral. Father Umphred, in pursuance of their plans, now bustled importantly forward and proposed a tour of the half-finished construction.

King Casmir gave him a curt response. 'I can see well enough from here.'

'As Your Majesty desires! Still, the full scope of "Sollace Sanctissima" might be more pleasurably apparent upon closer view.'

King Casmir glanced across the site. 'Your sect is not numerous. The structure is far too large for its purpose.'

'We earnestly believe to the contrary,' said Father Umphred cheerfully. 'In any event, is not magnificence and grandeur more suitable for the "Sollace Sanctissima" than some makeshift little chapel of sticks and mud?'

'I am impressed by neither one nor the other,' said King Casmir. 'I have heard that in Rome and Ravenna the churches are crammed so full with gold ornaments and jeweled gewgaws that they lack space for aught else. Be assured that never a penny from the Royal Exchequer of Lyonesse will be spent on such bedizenry.'

Father Umphred forced a laugh. 'Your Majesty, I submit that the cathedral will enrich the city, rather than the reverse. By this same token, a splendid cathedral will do the same, only faster.' Father Umphred gave a delicate cough. 'You must remember that at Rome and Ravenna the gold came not from those who built the cathedrals but those who came to worship.'

'Ha!' King Casmir was interested despite his prejudices. 'And how is this miracle accomplished?'

'There is no mystery. The worshippers hope to attract the favorable attention of Divinity by making a financial contribution.' Father Umphred turned out his hands. 'Who knows? The belief may be well-founded! No one has proved otherwise.'

'Hmf.'

'One thing is certain! Every pilgrim arriving at Lyonesse Town will depart enriched in spirit, though poorer in worldly goods.'

King Casmir appraised the unfinished cathedral as if with a new vision. 'How do you hope to attract wealthy and munificent pilgrims?'

'Some will come to worship and to participate in the rites. Others will sit in the hush of the great nave for hours, as if steeping themselves in a holy suffusion. Others will come to marvel at our relics, to feel the awe of their presence. These relics are of signal importance, and attract pilgrims from far and wide with great efficacy.'

'"Relics"? What relics are these? To my knowledge we have none.'

'It is an interesting subject,' said Father Umphred. 'Relics are of many sorts, and might be classified into several categories. The first and most precious are those directly associated with the Lord Jesus Christ. In the second rank and very excellent we find objects associated with one or another of the Holy Apostles. In the third rank, often most precious and most rare, are relics from antiquity: for instance, the stone with which David slew Goliath, or one of Shadrach's sandals, with scorch-marks on the sole. In the fourth rank, and still very fine, are objects associated with one or another of the saints. There are also what I shall call incidental relics, interesting because of association rather than holy essence. For instance, a claw of the bear which devoured Saint Candolphus, or a bangle from the arm of the prostitute Jesus defended before the temple, or a desiccated ear from one of the Gadarene swine. Unfortunately, many of the best and most wonderful relics have vanished, or were never collected. On the other hand, articles of guaranteed quality sometimes appear and are even offered for sale. One must take care, of course, when making such purchases.'

King Casmir pulled at his beard. 'How can you know that any of the relics are genuine?'

Father Umphred pursed his lips. 'If a false item were placed in sanctified surroundings, a divine lightning-bolt would strike down to destroy the factitious article and also the perpetrator of the hoax, or so I have been told. Further, the debased heretic would languish forever in the deepest pits of Hell! This is well-known and is our safeguard and our surety!'

'Hmmf. Does this divine lightning-bolt descend often?'

'I have no knowledge as to the number of such cases.'

'So how do you propose to acquire your relics?'

'By various means. Some will come as gifts; we will despatch agents to seek out others. The most cherished relic of all is the Holy Grail, which the Savior used at his Last Supper, and which also was used by Joseph of Arimathea to catch the blood from the divine wounds. Later he brought it to Glastonbury Abbey in Britain; thence it was taken to a sacred island on Lough Corrib in Ireland. Thence it was brought to the Elder Isles to preserve it safe from the pagans, but its present whereabouts is unknown.'

'That is an interesting tale,' said King Casmir. 'You would be well-advised to seek this "Grail" for your display.'

'We can only hope and dream! If the Grail came into our possession, we would instantly become the proudest church of Christendom.'

Queen Sollace could not control a small cry of excitement. She turned her great moist eyes upon King Casmir. 'My lord, is it not clear? We must have the best and most excellent relics; nothing else will suffice!'

King Casmir gave a stony shrug. 'Do as you like, so long as you make no draft upon the royal exchequer. That is my unswerving resolve.'

'But is it not clear? Any small sums paid out now will be returned a hundred times over! And all will go for the greater glory of our wonderful cathedral!'

'Precisely so!' Father Umphred used his richest tones. 'As always, dear lady, you have uttered the wise and incisive comment!'

'Let us go back to the carriage,' said King Casmir. 'I have seen all I care to see and heard rather more.'

II

The months of the year went their way and winter became spring. The period was enlivened by a variety of events. Prince Cassander became involved in an untidy scandal and was sent off to Fort Mael, close under the Blaloc border, to cool his heels and to reflect upon his misdeeds.

From South Ulfland came news of Torqual. He had led out his band on a foray against the isolated and apparently undefended Framm Keep, only to encounter an ambush laid by troops of the Ulfish army. In the skirmish Torqual lost the greater part of his band and was lucky to have escaped with his life.

Another event, of moment to Madouc herself, was the betrothal of her agreeable and apparently casual preceptress Lady Lavelle. Preparations for the wedding to Sir Garstang of Twanbow Hall necessitated her departure from Haidion and return to Pridart Place.

Madouc's new preceptress was Lady Vosse, spinster daughter to Casmir's second cousin Lord Vix of Wildmay Fourtower, near Slute Skeme. Unkind rumor suggested that Lady Vosse had been fathered by a vagabond Goth during one of Lord Vix's absences from Wildmay Fourtower; whatever the truth of the case, Lady Vosse in no way resembled her three younger sisters, who were slender, dark of hair, gentle of disposition and sufficiently well-favored to attract husbands for themselves. Lady Vosse, in contrast, was tall, iron-gray of hair, heavy of bone, with a square granitic face, gray eyes staring from under iron-gray eyebrows and a disposition deficient in those easy casual qualities which had commended Lady Lavelle to Madouc.

Three days after the departure of Lady Lavelle, Queen Sollace summoned Madouc to her chambers. 'Step forward, Madouc! This is Lady Vosse, who is to assume the duties which I fear were somewhat scamped by Lady Lavelle. Your instruction will henceforth be supervised by Lady Vosse.'

Madouc glanced sidelong at Lady Vosse. 'Please, Your Majesty, I feel that such supervision is no longer needed.'

'I would be happy if it were so. In any case Lady Vosse will ensure that you are proficient in the proper categories. Like myself, she will be satisfied only with excellence, and you must dedicate all your energies to this end!'

Lady Vosse said: 'Lady Lavelle, so I am told, was lax in her standards, and failed to drive home the exactitude of each lesson. The victim of such laxity, sadly enough, is Princess Madouc, who fell into the habit of frittering away her time.'

Queen Sollace said: 'I am pleased to hear these words of dedication! Madouc has never taken kindly to precision, or discipline. I am sure, Lady Vosse, that you will remedy this lack.'

'I will do my best.' Lady Vosse turned to Madouc. 'Princess, I demand no miracles! You need only do your best!'

'Just so,' said Queen Sollace. 'Madouc, do you understand this new principle?'

Madouc said bravely: 'Let me ask this. Am I the royal princess?'

'Well, yes, of course.'

'In that case, Lady Vosse must obey my royal commands and teach me what I wish to learn.'

'Ha hah!' said Queen Sollace. 'Your arguments are valid to a certain point, but you are still too inexperienced to know what is best for you. Lady Vosse is most wise in this regard, and will direct your education.'

'But Your Highness, if you please! This might be the wrong education! Must I learn to be like Lady Vosse!'

Lady Vosse spoke in a measured voice: 'You will learn what I choose to teach! You will learn it well! And you will be the better for it!'

Queen Sollace waved her hand. 'That is all, Madouc. You may go. There is no more to be said on the subject.'

Almost at once Madouc's conduct gave Lady Vosse cause for complaint. 'I intend to waste neither time nor soft words with you. Let us have an understanding: either obey my instructions exactly and without quibble, or I shall go on the instant to Queen Sollace and ask her permission to beat you properly.'

'That would be incorrect conduct,' Madouc pointed out.

'It would happen in private and no one would know, save you and me. Further, no one would care – save you and me. I advise you: beware! The privilege may well be allowed to me, and I would welcome it, since your contumacity is as offensive as your smirking insolence!'

Madouc spoke primly: 'These remarks are outrageous, and I forbid you to enter my presence again until you apologize! Also, I demand that you bathe more often, since you smell of goat, or something similar. You are dismissed for the day.'

Lady Vosse stared at Madouc with a slack jaw. She turned on her heel and departed the room. An hour later Madouc was summoned to the chambers of Queen Sollace, where she went slack-footed and heavy with foreboding. She found Queen Sollace sitting in an upholstered chair while Ermelgart brushed her hair. To one side stood Father Umphred, reading from a book of psalms. To the other side, silent and still on a bench, sat Lady Vosse.

Queen Sollace spoke in a peevish voice: 'Madouc, I am displeased with you. Lady Vosse has described your insolence and your insubordination. Both would seem to be studied and deliberate! What have you to say for yourself?'

'Lady Vosse is not a nice person.'

Queen Sollace gave an incredulous laugh. 'Even were your opinion correct, what is the consequence, so long as she does her duty?'

Madouc essayed a cheerful rejoinder. 'It is she who is guilty of insolence to me, a royal princess! She must apologize at this moment, or I will order her treated to a good whisking. Father Umphred may wield the whisk, for all of me, so long as he strikes strong, often and true to the mark.'

'Tchah!' cried Lady Vosse in shock. 'What nonsense the child does prattle! Is she mad?'

Father Umphred could not restrain a fruity chuckle. Lady Vosse turned him an icy gray glance, and Father Umphred abruptly fell silent.

Queen Sollace spoke sternly: 'Madouc, your wild talk has amazed us all! Remember! Lady Vosse acts in my stead; when you disobey her, you disobey me! Apparently you will not allow your hair to be properly coiffed nor will you abandon those rude garments which you are wearing at this instant. Faugh! They are suitable for a peasant boy, but not a dainty royal princess!'

'Agreed!' said Lady Vosse. 'She is no longer a young child, but a budding maiden, and now must observe the proprieties.'

Madouc blew out her cheeks. 'I do not like my hair pulled up so high that my eyes bulge. As for my clothes, I wear what is sensible! Why wear a fine gown to the stables only to drag the hem in manure?'

Queen Sollace spoke sharply: 'In that case, you must avoid the stables! Do you see me roistering about among the horses, or Lady Vosse sitting familiarly by the dung-heap? Of course not! We observe the gentilities of rank and place! As for your hair, Lady Vosse correctly wants to coif it in a fashionable style, and teach you courtly demeanor, so that the young gallants will not think you a freak when they meet you at a ball or a charade.'

'They will not think me a freak, because I will not be present, either at ball or charade.'

Queen Sollace stared fixedly at Madouc. 'You will be on hand if you are so instructed. Soon there will be serious talk of betrothal, and you must appear to advantage. Always remember: you are Princess Madouc of Lyonesse and so you must seem.'

'Precisely so!' said Madouc. 'I am Princess Madouc, of high rank and authority! I have ordered a whisking for Lady Vosse. Let us see to it at this very moment!'

'Yes,' said Queen Sollace grimly. 'I shall see to it. Ermelgart, from the besom pluck me five long withes; let them be both stout and supple.'

Ermelgart hastened to obey.

'Yes, these will do nicely,' said Queen Sollace. 'Now then, let us proceed to the whisking! Madouc! Come hither!'

'What for?'

Queen Sollace swished the whisk back and forth. 'I am not keen for this sort of thing; it sets me in a sweat. Still, a task worth doing is worth doing well. Come hither, and remove your lower garments.'

Madouc spoke in quavering tones: 'I would feel foolish doing as you suggest. It is far more sensible to stand as far as possible from you and your whisk.'

'Do you defy me?' bellowed Queen Sollace. She heaved herself to her feet. 'I shall put this whisk to good use!' Throwing back her robe with a sweep of her heavy white arm, Sollace marched forward. Father Umphred, book of psalms dangling from his fingers, stood beaming: Lady Vosse sat straight and stern. Madouc looked right and left

210

in despair. Once again injustice seemed ascendant, with everyone eager to crush her pride!

Madouc licked her lips, worked her fingers and uttered a soft hiss. Queen Sollace stood limp-kneed and quivering, mouth agape, arms shaking, fingers twitching so that the whisk dropped away, while her teeth chattered like pebbles shaken in a box. Father Umphred, still wearing his benign smile, uttered a gurgling squeak, then, chattering like an angry squirrel, he hunched low, stamping and kicking as if performing a Celtic jig. Ermelgart and Lady Vosse, both off to the side, were jarred and shaken, but evinced only a desultory chattering and grinding of the teeth.

Madouc placidly turned and started from the room, only to encounter the bulk of King Casmir. He halted in the doorway. 'What is amiss? Why is everyone so wild and so strange?'

Father Umphred spoke plaintively: 'Sire, Princess Madouc has learned witch-tricks; she knows a sleight to set us into a fit of confusion, so that our teeth rattle and our brains reel like spinning hoops.'

Queen Sollace spoke in a plangent croak: 'Father Umphred states the truth! Madouc hisses, or sings a whistling song – I was too unnerved to notice – and instantly our bones turned to jelly, and all our teeth rang and clattered and resounded again and again!'

King Casmir looked down at Madouc. 'What is the truth of this?'

Madouc said pensively: 'I believe that Queen Sollace took bad advice and started to beat me, then was deterred by her own true kindness. It was Lady Vosse for whom I ordered the whisking; I hope that you will see to it now.'

'A farrago of nonsense!' blurted Lady Vosse. 'This mad little imp hissed and we were all forced to chatter and jump!'

'Well then, Madouc?' demanded King Casmir.

'It is nothing of consequence.' Madouc tried to edge around Casmir's bulk, so that she might gain to the door. 'Sire, excuse me, if you please.'

'I do not so please! Certainly not until matters are clarified for my understanding! What is this "hissing" that you do?'

'It is a small knack, Your Highness: no more.'

'"A small knack" then,' cried Queen Sollace. 'My teeth still wamble and pulse! If you recall, Lady Desdea complained of similar events at Sarris!'

Casmir frowned down at Madouc. 'Where did you learn this trick?'

Madouc said bravely: 'Sire, best for everyone's comfort if we regard the matter as my personal secret.'

Casmir looked down in astonishment. 'Impudence again? Condescension from a foxen fluff of a girl! Ermelgart, bring me the whisk.'

Madouc tried to dodge and dart through the doorway, but King Casmir seized her and bent her over his leg. When she tried to hiss, he clapped his hand to her mouth, then thrust a kerchief between her teeth. Taking the whisk from Ermelgart, he struck six majestic strokes, so that the withes whistled through the air.

King Casmir released his grip. Madouc slowly righted herself, tears of humiliation and rage coursing down her cheeks. King Casmir asked in a heavily sardonic voice: 'And what do you think of that, Miss Sly-boots?'

Madouc stood holding both hands to her smarting haunches. 'I think that I will ask my mother for some new tricks.'

Casmir opened his mouth, then suddenly became still. After a tense moment he said: 'Your mother is dead.'

Madouc in her fury thought only to detach herself in

utter totality from both Casmir and Sollace. 'My mother was not Suldrun, and you know this full well.'

'What are you saying?' roared Casmir, standing back. 'Is this more impudence?'

Madouc sniffed and decided to say no more.

Casmir blustered on: 'If I say your mother is dead, she is dead! Do you want another beating?'

'My mother is the fairy Twisk,' said Madouc. 'Beat me as you like; it changes nothing. As for my father, he remains a mystery, and I still lack a pedigree.'

'Hm hah,' said Casmir, thinking over this and that. 'Quite so. A pedigree is something everyone should have.'

'I am happy that you agree, since one of these days I intend to search out my own.'

'Unnecessary!' declared Casmir bluffly. 'You are Princess Madouc and your pedigree or its lack need never be called into question.'

'A fine long pedigree is better than its lack.'

'Just so.' Casmir looked around the chamber, to find all eyes fixed upon him. He signalled to Madouc. 'Come.'

King Casmir led the way to his private sitting room. He pointed to a sofa. 'Be seated.'

Madouc perched herself gingerly upon the cushions, to the best possible easement of her pain, watching King Casmir warily all the while.

King Casmir paced up the length of the room, then back. Madouc's parentage was irrelevant; so long as no one knew the facts. Princess Madouc could be used to cement a valuable alliance. Madouc the changeling waif lacked all value in this regard. Casmir stopped short in his tracks. 'You suspect, then, that Suldrun was not your mother?'

'My mother is Twisk. She is alive and she is a fairy.'

'I will be frank,' said Casmir. 'Indeed we knew you for a changeling, but you were so bonny a baby that we could

213

not put you aside. We took you to our hearts as "Princess Madouc". That is how it is today. You enjoy all the privileges of true royalty, and of course the obligations, as well.' Casmir's voice changed a degree or two in timbre, and he watched Madouc covertly. 'Unless, of course, Suldrun's true-born son came forward to claim his birthright. What do you know of him?'

Madouc wriggled to lessen the throbbing of her scantily padded buttocks. 'I asked about my pedigree, but to no avail.'

'You did not learn the fate of your counterpart – the changeling who would be Suldrun's son, and just your own age?'

With great effort Madouc quelled a gleeful laugh. A year in the fairy shee meant time far longer in the outside world – perhaps seven years, or eight, or nine; no exact correspondence could be made. Casmir had no inkling of the case. 'He is nothing to me,' said Madouc. 'Perhaps he still haunts the shee. He may well be dead; the Forest of Tantrevalles is a perilous place.'

King Casmir asked sharply: 'Why are you smiling?'

'It is a wince of pain,' said Madouc. 'Do you not remember? You struck me six vicious blows. I remember well.'

With narrowed eyes King Casmir asked: 'And what do you mean by that?'

Madouc looked up, blue eyes innocent. 'I use no special meaning other than the words themselves. Is that not the way you talk?'

King Casmir frowned. 'Now then! Let us not maunder and gloom over past grievances! Many happy times lie ahead. To be a princess of Lyonesse is an excellent thing!'

'I hope that you will explain this to Lady Vosse, so that she will obey my orders or, better, return to Wildmay Fourtowers.'

214

King Casmir cleared his throat. 'As to that, who knows? Queen Sollace perhaps has a preference. Aha, then, harrumph. Naturally we cannot flaunt our secrets far and wide, for the vulgar interest. Away would fly your chances for a grand marriage! Therefore, we will bury these facts deep in obscurity. I will speak to Ermelgart, the priest and Lady Vosse; they will not gossip. And as always, you are the charming Princess Madouc, full and whole, whom we all love so well.'

'I feel sick,' said Madouc. 'I think I will go now.' She rose to her feet and went to the door. Here she paused to look back over her shoulder, to find King Casmir watching her with a brooding expression, legs apart, arms behind his heavy torso.

Madouc said softly: 'Please do not forget; I want no more of Lady Vosse; she has proved herself a disgrace and a failure.'

King Casmir only grunted: a sound signifying almost anything. Madouc turned and left the room.

III

Spring became summer, but this year there would be no removal to Sarris. The decision had been dictated by affairs of state, King Casmir having become involved in a dangerous game which must be controlled with precision and finesse.

The game had been initiated by a sudden turmoil in the Kingdom of Blaloc. Casmir hoped to manipulate events to his advantage, so blandly that neither King Audry nor King Aillas could reasonably make protest.

The troubles in Blaloc stemmed from a debility suffered by King Milo. After long dedication to the joys of tankard, tun and beaker, he had at last succumbed to swollen joints, gout and bloat of the liver, and now lay in the dark, apparently moribund, speaking only in grunts. For nourishment the doctors allowed him only raw egg beaten into buttermilk and an occasional oyster, but the regimen seemed to have little beneficial effect.

Of King Milo's three sons, only the youngest, Prince Brezante, had survived, and was now heir-apparent to the throne. Brezante lacked force of character and for a variety of reasons was unpopular with many of the grandees. Others, loyal to King Milo and the House of Valeu, gave Brezante lukewarm support. As King Milo continued to decline, the factions became ever more definite in their postures and there was ominous talk of civil strife.

King Milo's authority dwindled by the day, in step with his health, and dukes of the outer provinces ruled their fiefs like independent monarchs.

From these troubled circumstances King Casmir hoped to work profit for himself. He contrived a series of small but irking provocations between his own border barons and those dissident dukes whose lands were convenient for the exercise. Every day some small new foray was made into Blaloc from the remote corners of Lyonesse. Sooner or later, so Casmir hoped, one or another of the hot-headed Blaloc dukes, jealous of his prerogatives, would be prompted into a retaliation – whereupon Casmir, on the pretext of maintaining order, keeping the peace and supporting the rule of King Milo, could despatch an overwhelming force from the nearby Fort Mael and gain control over Blaloc. Then, responding to the prayers of those factions opposed to Prince Brezante, King Casmir would graciously accede to assuming the crown of Blaloc, thereby joining Blaloc to Lyonesse. And neither King Audry of Dahaut nor King Aillas of Troicinet could accuse him of extraordinary conduct.

Days passed, and weeks, with King Casmir playing a most delicate and cautious game. The dissident dukes of Blaloc, while infuriated by the raids from Lyonesse, sensed the dangers of reprisal, and bided their time. At Twissamy, Prince Brezante, recently wed to a young princess from the Kingdom of Bor in South Wales, detached himself from his matrimonial duties long enough to notice that all was not well across the land. Noblemen loyal to King Milo inveighed upon him, until at last he sent off despatches to King Audry and King Aillas, alerting them to the peculiar rash of forays, raids and provocations current along the Lyonesse border.

King Audry's response was couched in general terms. He suggested that King Milo and Prince Brezante might have misinterpreted a few untoward but probably insignificant incidents. He counseled Prince Brezante to discretion. 'Above all, we must be suspicious of sudden guesses or presumptions – "jumps into the dark" is my own style of expressing the case. These sudden acts are often bootless and perfervid. Every falling acorn should not send us forth to complain that the sky is falling. This principle of strong and even statesmanship is my personal preference, and I endorse it to you, in the hope that you may find it equally useful. In any case, be assured of our benevolent good wishes.'

King Aillas responded differently. He sailed from Domreis with a flotilla of nine warships on what he announced to be 'naval maneuvers'. As if on sudden impulse he paid an unscheduled visit to Lyonesse Town aboard the *Sangranada*, a galleass of three masts.

With the *Sangranada* standing offshore, Aillas sent a boat into the harbor with a despatch for King Casmir, requesting permission to enter the harbor. His visit, he stated, since it was fortuitous, would be informal and devoid of ceremony; still he hoped to exchange views with King Casmir on matters of mutual interest.

Permission to enter the harbor was at once forthcoming; the *Sangranada* eased through the harbor entrance and was warped alongside the dock. The remainder of the flotilla lay offshore, anchoring in the open roadstead.

With a small entourage Aillas and Dhrun disembarked from the *Sangranada*. King Casmir awaited them in his state carriage; the group rode up the Sfer Arct to Castle Haidion.

Along the way Casmir expressed concern for the ships anchored out along the roadstead. 'So long as the wind is light and offshore or from the west, there is no danger. But should the wind shift, your ships must instantly put to sea.'

'Our stay will be short for that reason,' said Aillas. 'Still, the weather should hold for a day or two.'

'It is a pity you must leave so soon,' said Casmir politely. 'Perhaps there will be time to arrange a tournament of jousting. You and Prince Dhrun might even care to participate.'

'Not I,' said Aillas. 'The sport consists of taking hard knocks and bruises, then falling from one's horse. I have no taste for it.'

'And Dhrun?'

'I am far more apt with the diabolo.'

'As you like,' said King Casmir. 'Our entertainment, then, will be quite informal.'

'That suits me very well,' said Aillas. As always, when he spoke with King Casmir, he marveled at his own capacity for dissimulation, since in all the world there was no one he hated more than Casmir. 'Still, since the winds have kindly blown us to your shores, we might spend a profitable hour or two discussing the way of the world.'

King Casmir assented. 'So it shall be.'

Aillas and Dhrun were conducted to chambers in the East Tower, where they bathed, changed their garments, then went to dine with the royal family. For the occasion Casmir chose to use the Green Hall, so-called for the panels of green-stained willow and the great rug, gray-green with a scattering of red flowers.

Aillas and Dhrun, arriving in the Green Hall, found the royal family already on hand. No other guests were present; the dinner evidently was to be completely informal. King Casmir stood by the fireplace, cracking walnuts, eating the meats and hurling the shells into the fire. Sollace sat placidly nearby, statuesque as always, her coils of blonde hair confined in a net of pearls. Madouc stood to the side, staring into the fire, her expression remote and her thoughts apparently far away. She had allowed herself to be dressed in a dark blue frock with a white frill at the neck; a white ribbon bound her hair, so that the copper-auburn curls lay in ordered locks, framing her face to advantage. Dame Etarre, who supervised Madouc's wardrobe (Madouc would not allow Lady Vosse into her chambers), had reported to Queen Sollace: 'For once she has allowed herself to seem something other than a wild thing.'

Lady Vosse, who stood nearby, grunted. 'Her moods are unfathomable.'

'I refuse to speculate,' said Queen Sollace with a sniff. 'Thank you, Dame Etarre; you may go.' Dame Etarre bowed and left the chamber. Queen Sollace went on to say: 'What with her highly dubious background – this, of course, we are not allowed to discuss – her volatility should come as no surprise.'

'The situation is extraordinary,' said Lady Vosse heavily. 'Still, the king's orders are clear and it is not for me to doubt their wisdom.'

'There is no mystery involved,' said Queen Sollace. 'We

hope to marry her to advantage. Meanwhile, we must bear with her quirks.'

Sitting in the Green Hall, Queen Sollace gave Madouc a covert appraisal. She would never be a real beauty, thought Sollace, though admittedly she exerted a certain jaunty appeal. There was simply not enough of her in the places where it mattered, nor was there any promise that such endowments would ever be hers. A pity, thought Sollace comfortably. Ripeness and amplitude were the first and most essential ingredients of true comeliness. Men liked to grasp something substantial when in a mood to do so: this was Queen Sollace's experience.

Upon the arrival of Aillas and Dhrun, the party took their places at the table: King Casmir at one end, King Aillas opposite, Queen Sollace to one side, Dhrun and Madouc to the other.

The dinner, as Casmir had promised, was a relatively simple repast: salmon poached in wine, a peasant stew of woodcock, onions and barley; boiled sheep's head with parsley and currants; ducks roasted with a stuffing of olives and turnips; a haunch of venison served with red sauce; a dessert of cheeses, pickled tongue, pears and apples.

Madouc sat pensively, taking only a fragment of fowl, a swallow of wine and a few grapes from the centerpiece. To Dhrun's attempts at conversation, Madouc responded without spontaneity, so that Dhrun became puzzled – unless, he speculated, this might be her ordinary conduct in the presence of the king and queen.

The meal came to its conclusion. For a period the party sat sipping that sweet soft wine known as Fialorosa, served in the squat traditional goblets of purple glass, twisted and warped into engaging shapes so that no two were alike. At last, King Casmir signaled his intention to retire, the party rose from their chairs, bade each other goodnight and went off to their respective chambers.

In the morning, Aillas and Dhrun breakfasted at leisure in a small sunny morning parlor adjoining their chambers. Presently Sir Mungo the High Seneschal appeared with the message that King Casmir would be pleased to confer with King Aillas at his convenience – immediately, if he felt so inclined. Aillas acquiesced to the proposal and Sir Mungo conducted him to the king's sitting room, where Casmir rose to meet him.

'Will you sit?' asked Casmir. He indicated a chair. Aillas bowed and seated himself; Casmir settled into a similar chair nearby. At Casmir's sign, Sir Mungo retired.

'This is not only a pleasant occasion,' said Aillas. 'It also allows us an opportunity to exchange views. We are not often in communication.'

Casmir assented. 'Yet, the world remains in its place. Our deficiency has caused no grand cataclysm.'

'Still, the world changes and one year is never like the next. With communication between us, and coordination of our policies, we would, at the very least, avoid the risk of surprising one another.'

King Casmir gave an affable wave of the hand. 'It is a persuasive idea, if over elaborate. Life in Lyonesse moves at a hum-drum pace.'

'Just so. It is amazing how some small or hum-drum episode, trivial in itself, can cause an important event.'

King Casmir asked cautiously: 'Are you referring to any specific event?'

'Nothing in particular. Last month I learned that King Sigismondo the Goth intended to land a war party on the north shore of Wysrod, where he would take up lands and defy King Audry. He was deterred only because his advisers assured him that he would instantly be engaged by the full might of Troicinet, as well as the Daut armies, and would face certain disaster. Sigismondo drew back, and is now considering an expedition against the Kingdom of Kharesm.'

Casmir thoughtfully stroked his beard. 'I heard nothing of this.'

'Odd,' said Aillas. 'Your agents are notoriously efficient.'

'You are not alone in fearing surprises,' said Casmir with a sour smile.

'Extraordinary that you should say so! Last night my mind was active and I lay awake formulating plans by the dozen. One of these I wish to submit to you. In effect, and to use your words, it would remove the component of fear from surprises.'

Casmir asked skeptically: 'What sort of proposal might this be?'

'I suggest quick consultation in the event of emergency, such as a Gothic incursion, or any other breach of the peace, with an eye to coordinated response.'

'Ha hm,' said Casmir. 'Your scheme might well be cumbersome.'

Aillas gave a polite laugh. 'I hope that I have not exaggerated the scope of my ideas. They are not much different from the goals which I established last year. The Elder Isles are at peace; we must ensure, you and I, that this peace persists. Last year my envoys offered defensive alliances to every realm of the Elder Isles. Both King Kestrel of Pomperol and King Milo of Blaloc accepted our guarantees; we will therefore defend them against attack. King Milo, so I am told, is ill and also must contend with his disloyal dukes. For this reason the flotilla now at anchor in the roadstead, will immediately make sail for Blaloc, in order to indicate our confidence in King Milo, and give pause to his enemies. I will show no mercy to

222

anyone who tries to subvert his rule or its orderly transition. Blaloc must remain independent.'

Casmir for a space had no comment to make. Then he said: 'Such solitary excursions might be misunderstood.'

'I am concerned on just this account. Hence I would be happy to gain your endorsement for the program, in which case there would be no mistakes, and King Milo's enemies would be defeated out of hand.'

King Casmir smiled a quizzical smile. 'They might argue that their cause is just.'

'More likely they hope to curry favor with some speculative new regime, which could only result in trouble. There is no need for any but a legitimate succession to the throne.'

'Unfortunately, Prince Brezante is something of a "weak reed" and is not everywhere popular. Hence the disturbances inside Blaloc.'

'Prince Brezante is adequate to the needs of Blaloc, which are not demanding. Naturally we would prefer King Milo's full recovery.'

'His prospects are poor. Now he takes only a single quail egg poached in buttermilk for his meal. But are we not straying from the subject? What is your proposal?'

'I will point out the obvious, that our two realms are the most powerful of the Elder Isles. I propose that we issue a joint protocol guaranteeing territorial integrity everywhere throughout the Elder Isles. The effects of such a doctrine would be profound.'

King Casmir's face had become a stony mask. 'Your goals do you credit, but certain of your assumptions may be unrealistic.'

'I make only one assumption of any importance,' said Aillas. 'I assume that you are as dedicated to peace as I am. There is no other possibility save the reverse: that you are not dedicated to peace, which is of course absurd.'

King Casmir showed a small sardonic smile. 'All very well, but would not your doctrine be considered somewhat vague, or even naïve?'

'I think not,' said Aillas. 'The central idea is clear enough. A potential aggressor would be deterred for fear of certain defeat, along with punishment and an end to his dynasty.'

'I will certainly give your proposal careful consideration,' said King Casmir woodenly.

'I expect no more,' said Aillas.

IV

While Aillas expounded his implausible schemes to King Casmir, Dhrun and Madouc went out upon the front terrace and stood leaning against the balustrade. Below them was the quadrangle known as the 'King's Parade' and, beyond, all of Lyonesse Town. Today, despite Lady Vosse's disapproval, Madouc wore her ordinary garments: a knee-length frock of oatmeal-colored nubble-cloth, belted at the waist. A band of plaited blue cord bound her curls, with a tassel dangling beside her left ear; she wore sandals on her bare feet.

Dhrun found the tassel intriguing and was moved to comment: 'You wear that tassel with remarkable flair.'

Madouc pretended indifference and made a flippant gesture. 'It is nothing much: a caprice, no more.'

'It is a distinctly jaunty caprice, with more than a hint of fairy panache. Your mother Twisk might well wear that tassel with pride.'

Madouc gave her head a doubtful shake. 'When I saw her she wore neither tassels nor ties, and her hair floated like a blue fog.' Madouc considered a moment. 'Of course,

I am not well acquainted with fairy fashions. There is not much fairy stuff left in me.'

Dhrun inspected her from head to toe. 'I would not be too sure on that account.'

Madouc shrugged. 'Remember: I never lived among the fairies; I have eaten no fairy bread, nor drunk fairy wine. The fairy stuff – '

'It is called "soma". It is true that the "soma" drains away, leaving only human dross behind.'

Madouc looked reflectively out over the town. 'All taken with all, I do not like to think of myself as "human dross".'

'Of course not! Never would I consider you such!'

'I am pleased to hear your good opinion,' said Madouc modestly.

'You knew it before,' said Dhrun. 'Also, if I may say so, I am relieved to see you in good spirits. Last night you were almost morose. I wondered if you were bored with the company.'

'Was my mood so apparent?'

'You seemed, at the very least, subdued.'

'Still, I was not bored.'

'Why were you unhappy?'

Once again Madouc looked out over the vista. 'Must I explain the truth?'

'I will take my chances,' said Dhrun. 'I can only hope that your remarks are not too corrosive. Tell me the truth.'

'I am the one who takes chances,' said Madouc. 'But I am reckless and I know no better. The truth is this: I was so pleased to see you that I became sick and miserable.'

'Remarkable!' said Dhrun. 'And when I leave, sorrow will cause you to sing and dance for sheer merriment.'

Madouc said dolefully: 'You are laughing at me.'

'No. Not really.'

'Then why are you smiling?'

'I think there is more fairy stuff in you than you suspect.'

Madouc gave a thoughtful nod, as if Dhrun had addressed certain of her own suspicions. 'You lived long at Thripsey Shee; you yourself should be charged with fairy stuff.'

'Sometimes I fear as much. A human child too long at the shee becomes addled and moonstruck. Thereafter he is good for nothing but to play wild music on the pipes. When he starts up a jig, the folk can never leave off dancing; they must hop and skip till their shoes wear out.'

Madouc gave Dhrun a wondering examination. 'You do not seem moonstruck to me – though I am no proper judge. By chance, do you play the pipes?'

Dhrun nodded. 'For a time I piped tunes for a troupe of dancing cats. That was long ago. It would not be considered dignified now.'

'When you played, did people dance without restraint? If so, I would like you to play, as if by casual impulse, for the king and queen and Lady Vosse. Sir Mungo also might be helped by a few capers, and also Zerling the executioner.'

'I did not bring my pipes,' said Dhrun. 'The fairy waft is draining away, and my temperament has become somewhat dull. Perhaps I am not moonstruck after all.'

'Do you often think of the shee?'

'Occasionally. But the memories are blurred, as if I were recalling a dream.'

'Do you remember my mother Twisk?'

'Not well; in fact, not at all. I remember King Throbius and Queen Bossum, and also an imp named Falael who was jealous of me. I remember festivals in the moonlight and sitting in the grass making flower chains.'

'Would you like to visit the shee again?'

Dhrun gave his head an emphatic shake. 'They would

think I had come for favors and play me a dozen wicked tricks.'

'The shee is not far away?'

'It is north of Little Saffield on Old Street. A lane leads to Tawn Timble and Glymwode and on into the forest, and so to Thripsey Shee on Madling Meadow.'

'It should not be too hard to find.'

Dhrun spoke in surprise: 'Surely you are not planning to visit the shee yourself?'

Madouc gave an evasive response. 'I have no immediate plans.'

'I would advise against any plans whatever, indefinite or otherwise. The roads are dangerous. The forest is strange. Fairies are not to be trusted.'

Madouc seemed unconcerned. 'My mother would protect me from harm.'

'Do not be too sure! If she were cross and the day had gone badly, she might give you a badger's face or a long blue nose, for no reason whatever.'

Madouc said positively: 'My mother would never harm her own dear daughter!'

'Why would you want to go in the first place? They would not receive you nicely.'

'I care nothing for that. I want only to learn news of my father, and what might be his name and his estate, and where he now lives: perhaps at some fine castle overlooking the sea!'

'What does your mother say to this?'

'She pretends to remember nothing. I believe that she has not told me everything she knows.'

Dhrun was dubious. 'Why should she hide the information? Unless your father was a scapegrace and a vagabond, of whom she is ashamed.'

'Hm,' said Madouc. 'I had not thought of that. But it is hardly likely – or so I hope.'

From the castle came King Casmir and Aillas, both showing faces of conventional impassivity.

Aillas spoke to Dhrun: 'The wind seems to be shifting toward the south, and we had best gain sea room before conditions worsen.'

'It is a pity we must go so soon,' said Dhrun.

'True! Still, that is the way of it. I have invited King Casmir, along with Queen Sollace and the princess, to spend a week with us at Watershade later this summer.'

'That would be a pleasant occasion!' said Dhrun. 'Watershade would be at its best! I hope that Your Majesty will decide to visit us. It is not too irksome a trip!'

'It would be my great pleasure, if the press of affairs permits,' said King Casmir. 'I see that the carriage awaits; I will make my farewells here and now.'

'That is quite in order,' said Aillas. 'Goodbye, Madouc.' He kissed her cheek.

'Goodbye! I am sorry that you are going so soon!'

Dhrun bent to kiss Madouc's cheek, and said, 'Goodbye. We will see you again before long, perhaps at Watershade!'

'I hope so.'

Dhrun turned away and followed Aillas down the stone steps to the road, where the carriage awaited them.

V

King Casmir stood by the window of his private parlor, legs apart, hands clasped behind his back. The Troice flotilla had departed and was gone beyond the eastern headlands; the Lir stretched blank and wide before him. Casmir muttered soft words under his breath and turned away from the window. Hands still clasped behind his back, Casmir paced back and forth across the room, slow step after slow step, head bent forward so that his beard brushed his chest.

Queen Sollace entered the parlor. She halted and stood watching King Casmir's ponderous travels. Casmir darted her an ice-blue glance sidewise from under his eyebrows, and continued to pace in silence.

With nostrils haughtily pinched, Queen Sollace marched across the room to the couch and seated herself.

King Casmir at last halted. He spoke, as much to himself as to Sollace, 'It cannot be brushed aside. Once again my progress is checked and my great effort thwarted – by the same agency and for the same reasons. The facts are blunt. I must accept them.'

'Indeed?' asked Sollace. 'What are these ugly facts which cause you such distress?'

'They concern my plans for Blaloc,' grumbled Casmir. 'I cannot intervene without bringing Aillas and his Troice warships down around my ears. Thereupon that fat jackal Audry would be sure to turn on me, and I cannot withstand so many blows from so many directions.'

'Perhaps you should adopt a different plan,' said Queen Sollace brightly. 'Or you might make do with no plan at all.'

'Ha!' barked Casmir. 'So it might seem! King Aillas talks softly and with great politeness; he has the uncomfortable skill of calling one a false-hearted black-guard, a liar, a cheat and a villain, but making it seem a fulsome compliment.'

Queen Sollace shook her head in bewilderment. 'I am surprised! I thought King Aillas and Prince Dhrun had come to pay a courtesy call.'

'That was not his only reason: I assure you of that!'

Queen Sollace sighed. 'King Aillas has achieved his own great successes; why cannot he be more tolerant of your hopes and dreams? There must be an element of jealousy at work.'

Casmir nodded curtly. 'There is no love lost between us, that is fact. Still, he only acts as he must. He knows my ultimate goal as well as I know it myself!'

'But it is a glorious goal!' bleated Queen Sollace. 'To unite the Elder Isles once again, as of old: that is a noble dream! It would surely give impetus to our holy faith! Think! One day Father Umphred might be Archbishop over all the Elder Isles!'

King Casmir spoke in disgust: 'Once again you have been listening to that clabber-faced priest. He has cozened you into your cathedral; let that suffice.'

Queen Sollace raised her moist gaze to the ceiling. She spoke in long-suffering tones: 'No matter what else, please realize that my prayers are dedicated to your success. You must surely win in the end!'

'I wish it were so easy.' King Casmir flung himself heavily into a chair. 'All is not lost. I am checked in Blaloc, but there are always two ways around the barn!'

'Your meaning escapes me.'

'I will give new instructions to my agents. There will be no more disorder. When King Milo dies, Brezante will be king. We will give him Madouc in marriage, and by this means join our houses.'

Queen Sollace made an objection. 'Brezante is already wed! He married Glodwyn of Bor!'

'She was frail, young and sickly, and she died in childbirth. Brezante is notably uxorious, and he will be quite ready for new nuptials.'

Queen Sollace said mournfully: 'Poor little Glodwyn! She was barely more than a child, it is said she never gave over her homesickness.'

Casmir shrugged. 'Still and all, it might well work to our advantage. King Milo is as good as dead. Brezante is a bit dull, a factor favorable to our cause. We must make occasion for his visit.'

Sollace said doubtfully: 'Brezante is not altogether gallant, nor is he handsome, or even dashing. His penchant for young maidens is notorious.'

'Bah! Old or young, what of that? The business is all cut from the same cloth! Kings are above small-minded scandal.'

Queen Sollace sniffed. 'And queens as well, no doubt!'

Casmir, staring thoughtfully across the room, ignored the remark.

'One matter further,' said Sollace. 'I refer to Madouc. She is difficult in matters of this sort.'

'She will obey because she must,' said Casmir. 'It is I who am king, not Madouc.'

'Aha! But it is Madouc who is Madouc!'

'We cannot make bread without flour. Scrawny redheaded little whelp she may be: still she must yield to my command.'

'She is not ugly,' said Queen Sollace. 'Her time has come, and she is developing – slowly, of course, and with little to show for the effort. She will never boast a fashionable figure, such as mine.'

'It will be enough to affect Brezante.' He slapped his hands decisively on the arms of the chair. 'I am prepared to act with expedition.'

'Your policy is no doubt wise,' said Queen Sollace. 'Still —'

'Still what?'

'Nothing of consequence.'

King Casmir acted without delay. Three couriers rode off from Haidion into the evening: the first to Fort Mael, ordering a return to routine conditions; the second to a high-placed agent in Twissamy; the third to King Milo, wishing him health, deploring the ruffians who flouted

231

royal authority, and inviting King Milo and Prince Brezante to Haidion for a gala visit. Or Prince Brezante alone, if King Milo's health made such a visit impractical.

A few days later the couriers returned. From Fort Mael and the agent in Twissamy came simple acknowledgments that his orders had been received and would be acted upon. From King Milo came a dispatch of greater interest. King Milo thanked King Casmir for his kindly wishes and fraternal support. Next he announced his return to jovial good health and described how the change had come about. In a passage of some length he described the circumstances. It seemed that one day, just prior to his dinner, a sudden desperate spasm came upon him. Instead of his usual regimen: one quail egg and half a gill of buttermilk, he commanded a joint of roast beef with horseradish and suet pudding, a suckling pig sizzling on the spit surrounded by roast cinnamon apples, a pot of pigeon stew and three gallons of good red wine. For his supper he took a more moderate repast of four roast fowl, a pork and onion pie, a salmon and a number of sausages, along with sufficient wine to assist in digestion. After a night's sound sleep, he breakfasted on fried flounder, three dozen oysters, a raisin cake, a cassoulet of broad beans and ham for a savory, and a tankard or two of a particularly fine white wine. It was this return to a sound and wholesome diet, declared King Milo, which had renewed his strength; he now felt as good as new, if not better. Therefore, wrote King Milo, he and the recently bereaved Prince Brezante would be delighted to accept King Casmir's invitation. Neither he nor Brezante would be reluctant to discuss the topic at which King Casmir had hinted. He endorsed King Casmir's suggestion that an era of friendlier relations between their two realms was about to be initiated.

Madouc learned of the projected visit from several

sources, but it remained for Devonet to explain the occasion in detail. 'You will find Prince Brezante very attentive,' said Devonet airily. 'He may wish to take you somewhere alone, perhaps to his rooms, for a game of "sly" or "fiddle-de-doodle"; in this case you must be on your guard. Brezante is partial to young maidens. He may even suggest a marriage contract! In any case you should not succumb to his blandishments, since some men become bored with easy conquests.'

Madouc said stiffly: 'You need not fear on that account. I am interested neither in Prince Brezante nor his blandishments.'

Devonet paid no heed. 'Think of it! Is it not exciting? Someday you might be Queen Madouc of Blaloc!'

'I think not.'

Devonet spoke reasonably: 'I agree that Brezante is not the most comely of men; indeed, he is fleshy and squat, with a round belly and a big nose. Still, what of that? He is a royal prince, and you are to be envied, or so I suppose.'

'You are talking sheer foolishness. I have not the slightest interest in Prince Brezante, nor he in me.'

'Do not be too sure of that! You are much like his previous spouse. She was a young princess from Wales: a little wisp of a thing, naïve and innocent.'

Chlodys joined the conversation with eager zest. 'They say that she cried constantly from both homesickness and distress! I believe that eventually she went out of her mind, poor thing. Prince Brezante was troubled not at all and bedded with her nightly, until at last she died in childbirth.'

'It is a sad story,' said Madouc.

'Exactly! The little princess is dead and Prince Brezante is heartsick. You must do your best to console him.'

'He will surely want to kiss you,' said Chlodys with a

giggle. 'If so, you must kiss him nicely in return; that is the way one wins a husband. Am I not right, Devonet?'

'That is one of the ways, certainly.'

Madouc spoke with disdain: 'Sometimes I marvel at the ideas which seep through your minds!'

'Ah well,' sighed Devonet. 'It is less disgraceful to think than to do.'

'Although not so much fun,' added Chlodys.

'Either of you, or both, are welcome to Prince Brezante,' said Madouc. 'He will surely find you more interesting than I.'

Later in the day King Casmir met Madouc in the gallery. He was about to pass her by, eyes averted, in his usual style; instead, he stopped in his tracks. 'Madouc, I want a word with you.'

'Yes, Your Highness.'

'Come with me.' King Casmir led the way into a nearby council chamber, with Madouc lagging reluctantly six paces behind.

Casmir, smiling the smallest of grim smiles, waited by the door until Madouc entered, then closed the door and went to stand by the table. 'Sit.'

Madouc seated herself primly in a chair across the table from Casmir.

'I must now instruct you,' said Casmir ponderously: 'Listen with care and heed me well. Certain events of importance are in the offing. King Milo of Blaloc will presently be our guest, in company with Queen Caudabil and Prince Brezante. I intend to propose a contract of betrothal between you and Prince Brezante. The marriage will be joined at an appropriate time, possibly in three years. It will be an important marriage, in that it will consolidate a strong alliance with Blaloc, to counter Pomperol's tendency toward Dahaut. These are affairs of state which you will not understand, but you must believe that they are of the highest priority.'

Madouc tried to think of something to say, which would delicately convey her feelings and yet not enrage King Casmir. Several times she started to speak, then thought better of her remarks, and closed her mouth. At last she said, rather lamely: 'Prince Brezante may not favor such a match.'

'I suspect otherwise. King Milo has already expressed interest in the arrangement. Almost certainly an announcement will be made during the royal visit. It is a good match for you, and you may consider yourself lucky. Now then, attend! Lady Vosse will instruct you in the proprieties which must be observed. I expect total decorum from you on this occasion. You may not indulge in any of your famous vapors or tantrums, at risk of my extreme displeasure. Is this quite clear?'

Madouc answered in a tremulous voice: 'Yes, Your Highness, I understand your words.' She drew a deep breath. 'But they fly wide of the mark. It is best that you should know this now.'

King Casmir started to speak, using a dangerous voice, but Madouc was quick to anticipate him. 'In ordinary matters I would hope to obey you, but remember: my marriage is far more important to me than it is to you.'

King Casmir bent slowly forward. Over the years dozens of frightened wretches had seen such an expression on his face before being dragged away to torment in the dungeons under the Peinhador.

Casmir spoke from deep in his throat: 'So you think to thwart my volition?'

Madouc spoke more carefully than ever. 'There are circumstances, Your Highness, which make the plan impossible!'

'What circumstances are these?'

'First, I despise Prince Brezante. If he is so anxious to marry, let him betroth himself to Lady Vosse or Chlodys. Second, if you will recall, I am born of halfling mother and an unknown father. I know nothing of my pedigree; for practical purposes it is lacking; for this reason, my maidens call me "bastard", which I cannot deny. If King Milo knew of this, he would consider the betrothal a mockery, and an insult to his house.'

King Casmir blinked and stood silent. Madouc rose to her feet and stood demurely leaning on the table. 'Therefore, Your Highness, the betrothal is not possible. You must make other plans, which do not include me.'

'Bah!' muttered Casmir. 'All these circumstances are small fish in a big pan. Neither Milo nor Brezante need know of them! After all, who would tell them?'

'The task would fall to me,' said Madouc. 'It would be my duty.'

'That is sheer blather!'

Madouc hurried on, her tongue almost tripping over itself. 'Not so, Your Highness! I merely use the faith and candor I have learned from your noble example! Decent respect for the honor of both royal houses would compel me to admit my condition, no matter what the consequences!'

King Casmir spoke out harshly: 'It means nothing; I assure you of this! To talk of honor is frivol and foolishness! If it is a pedigree you need, the heralds will contrive something suitable and I will fix it upon you by ordinance!'

Madouc smilingly shook her head. 'Bad cheese stinks, no matter how thin it is sliced. Such a pedigree would be a laughable deceit. Folk would call you a "black-hearted monster", as false as a stoat, ready for any lie or duplicity. Everyone would sneer and joke; I would be doubly ridiculed, and doubly demeaned, for allowing such a brazen falsity! They would further call you a – '

Casmir made a brusque gesture. 'Stop! That is enough!'

Madouc said meekly: 'I was only explaining why my true and very own pedigree is essential to me.'

King Casmir's patience was wearing thin. 'This is folly, and quite beside the point! I do not propose to be thwarted by such paltriness! Now then – '

Madouc cried out plaintively: 'The facts cannot be denied, Your Highness! I lack all pedigree.'

'Then construct yourself a pedigree, or find one that you deem proper, and it shall be fixed upon you by fiat! Only be quick! Ask Spargoy the Chief Herald for help.'

'I would prefer the help of someone else.'

'Whoever you like! Fact or fancy, it is all one; I am indifferent to your whims. Only be quick!'

'Just so, Your Majesty. I will do as you command.'

Casmir's attention was caught by a bland overtone in Madouc's response: why had she become so docile? 'In the meantime, I will initiate discussions in regard to the betrothal. This must proceed!'

Madouc gave a poignant little cry of protest. 'Your Highness, have I not just explained that this cannot be?'

Casmir's torso seemed to swell. Madouc moved a slow step around the table, to put its maximum diameter between her and King Casmir. She cried out: 'Nothing has changed, Your Highness! I will search everywhere for my pedigree, but even should I discover the King of Byzantium for my sire, Prince Brezante remains as obnoxious as ever. If he speaks a single word to me, I shall declare myself an orphan bastard whom King Casmir wishes to foist off on him. If he is not deterred I will show him the "Imp-spring Tinkle-toe", so that he leaps six feet into the air.'

King Casmir's cheeks had become pink and his eyes bulged blue from his face. He took three strides around the table, in order that he might seize Madouc and beat her well. Madouc warily darted off an equal distance around the table. Casmir lumbered in pursuit, but Madouc ran nimbly to keep the table always between them.

Casmir at last halted, breathing hard both from passion and exertion. Madouc said breathlessly: 'You must excuse me for evading you, Your Highness, but I do not care to be beaten again.'

'I will call the footmen,' said Casmir. 'They will take you to a dark room, and I will beat you at my leisure and perhaps do else to you. No one defies me and escapes unscathed.' He took a slow step around the table, staring fixedly at Madouc as if trying to fascinate her into immobility.

Madouc sidled aside, and spoke tremulously: 'I beg you not to do such things, Your Highness! You will notice that I have not used my fairy magic upon you, which would be disrespectful. I command not only the Sissleway and the Tinkle-toe but also – ' Madouc groped for inspiration, which was not slow in coming – 'an irksome spell called "Insect's Arrayance", to be used only on persons who threaten me!'

'Oh?' asked King Casmir in a gentle voice. 'Tell me of this spell!' And he took a slow step around the table.

Madouc hurriedly skipped aside. 'When I am compelled to afflict some vile cur of a villain, insects swarm upon him from all directions! By day and by night they come, high and low, down from the sky, up from the soil!'

'That is an unnerving prospect.'

'True, Your Highness! Please do not creep around the table, as you frighten me and I might blurt out the "Arrayance" by mistake!'

'Indeed? Tell me more of this marvellous spell.'

'First come the fleas! They jump through the vile cur's golden beard, also his hair; they swarm in his rich garments till he tears his skin for scratching!'

'Irksome! Stand quietly, and tell me more!' King Casmir made a sudden movement; Madouc jumped around the table and spoke in desperate haste: 'When he sleeps large spiders crawl across his face! Weevils burrow into his skin and drop from his nose! He finds beetles in his soup and roaches in his porridge! Blow-flies crawl into his mouth and lay eggs in his ears; when he walks out he is beleaguered by gnats and moths and darting grasshoppers; wasps and bumble-bees sting him at random!'

King Casmir stood scowling. 'And you control this awful spell?'

'Oh yes indeed! There is worse to come! Should the villain fall to the ground, he is instantly overcome by a seethe of ants. Naturally, I would use this spell only to protect myself!'

'Of course!' King Casmir smiled a small hard smile. 'But do you truly command a spell of such power? I suspect not.'

'In all candor, I have forgotten one or two of the syllables,' said Madouc bravely. 'However they come readily enough from my mother's tongue. I can call her at need, and she will transform my enemies into toads, moles or salamanders, as I dictate, and this you must believe, since it is truth!'

King Casmir stared at Madouc a long moment. He made an abrupt gesture signifying a dozen emotions. 'Go. Remove yourself from my sight.'

Madouc performed a dainty little curtsey. 'I am grateful for Your Majesty's kind clemency.' She slipped gingerly past Casmir; then, with a sly glance back over her shoulder, ran quickly from the room.

VI

King Casmir walked with a slow and ponderous tread along the gallery, up the stairs and, after a moment's pause, along the corridor to the queen's sitting room. The footman standing at attention thrust the door wide; King Casmir marched into the room. Discovering Queen Sollace in earnest colloquy with Father Umphred, King Casmir stopped short and stood glowering. Queen and priest turned to look at him, their voices instantly hushed. Father Umphred performed a smiling bow. Casmir, ignoring the salute, marched across the room to the window, where he stood in morose contemplation of the vista.

After a respectful pause, Queen Sollace and Father Umphred resumed their conversation: at first in muted tones so as not to intrude upon King Casmir's cogitations; then, as he seemed neither to heed nor to hear, in their ordinary voices. As usual, they discussed the new cathedral. The two were agreed that all appurtenances and furnishings should be of the richest and most superb quality; only the best could be considered suitable.

'The focus of all – one might say, the "inspirational node" – is the altar,' declared Father Umphred. 'It is where all eyes look and the source from which rings out the Holy Word! We must ensure that it equals or transcends any other of Christendom!'

'I am of like mind,' said Queen Sollace. 'How fortunate we are! It is an opportunity vouchsafed to very few!'

'Exactly so, dear lady!' Father Umphred turned a sideglance toward the bulky figure at the window, but King Casmir seemed absorbed in his own thoughts. 'I have prepared certain drawings; unfortunately I neglected to bring them with me.'

Queen Sollace gave a cry of disappointment. 'Describe them, if you will! I would be interested to hear!'

Father Umphred bowed. 'I envision an altar of rare wood supported by fluted columns of pink Cappadocian marble. To either side candelabra of seven sconces shall stand, stately and tall, like transfigured luciferous angels! Such will be their effect! Eventually they shall be wrought of pure gold; for the nonce we will use articles of gold leaf on plaster.'

'We will do what needs to be done!'

'Below the altar is stationed the pyx, on a table of fine wood carved with a frieze depicting the twelve archangels. The pyx shall be a vessel of silver, inlaid with carbuncles, lapis and jade; it shall rest on a cloth embroidered with sacred signs, in simulation of that holy cloth known as the "Tasthapes". Behind the altar, the wall will be divided into twelve panels, each enamelled in designs of pure color to represent a scene of portent, for the joy of the beholder and the glory of the faith.'

Queen Sollace spoke fervently: 'I can see it now, as if in a vision! The concept moves me deeply!'

Father Umphred, after another quick glance toward the window, said: 'My dear lady, you are obviously sensitive to spiritual influences, and far beyond the ordinary! But let us consider how best to order our holy relics. The question is this: should we provide a particular reliquarium – let us say, to the side of the vestibule? Or perhaps a more general display in one of the transepts, or both, should we acquire several of these sacred objects?'

Queen Sollace said wistfully, 'As of now, with nothing to display, we can make no serious plans.'

Father Umphred made a gesture of reproach. 'Have

faith, dear lady! It has sustained you in the past! These objects exist, and we will procure them.'

'But can you be certain of this?'

'With faith and perseverance, we will find them, wherever they may be! Some remain to be discovered; others have been cherished and lost, and need finding again. I cite you the Cross of Saint Elric, who was cooked and eaten by the ogre Magre, one limb at a time. To fortify himself during the ordeal, he fashioned a crucifix from his two discarded tibia. This crucifix was at one time a treasure of Saint Bac's Monastery at Dun Cruighre; where is it now? Who knows?'

'Then how would we find it?'

'Through careful and dedicated search. I cite also the Talisman of Saint Uldine, who worked to convert Phogastus, troll of Black Meira Tarn. Her efforts were extended; indeed, she bore Phogastus four implings[1], each with a round bloodstone in the place of a third eye. The four stones were detached and set into a talisman, now immured somewhere among the crypts at Whanish Isle. This is also an object of mighty force; still it could be succored by a person staunch and intrepid. In Galicia, on the Pico Alto, is a monastery founded by the heretic Bishop Sangiblas. The monks preserve in their crypts one of the nails which pinned the feet of Our Savior. I could cite other such relics. Those which are not lost are revered and guarded with care. They might be difficult to obtain.'

Queen Sollace spoke decisively: 'No good thing comes without hardship. That is the lesson of life!'

'How true!' intoned Father Umphred. 'Your Highness has succinctly clarified a whole heron's nest of untidy ambiguities!'

---

[1] Saint Uldine's children were Ignaldus, Drathe, Alleia and Bazille. Each survived to pursue his or her destiny. The chronicles relating to these events may someday be made public.

Queen Sollace asked: 'Was there not some talk of the Grail? I refer to that sacred utensil used by the Savior at his last supper, and with which Joseph of Arimathea caught blood from the divine wounds. What are the tidings of this sanctified vessel?'

Father Umphred pursed his lips. 'The reports are not exact. We know that it was brought to Glastonbury Abbey by Joseph of Arimathea, then carried to Ireland and housed in a chapel on the islet Inchagoill in Lough Corrib; thence it was brought to the Elder Isles by Saint Porroig through fear of the pagans, and now it is deemed to be in secret custody: a mysterious place to be dared only by the most gallant or the most foolhardy!'

King Casmir had been listening to the conversation with half an ear. Now he turned, to stand with his back to the window, his face showing cynical amusement. Queen Sollace turned him an inquiring look, but King Casmir seemed to have nothing to say. She turned back to Father Umphred.

'If only we could assemble a brotherhood of noble paladins, devoted to the service of their queen! I would send them forth on a quest of glory, with all honor for him who succeeded in the enterprise!'

'It is an excellent scheme, Your Highness! It fires the imagination!'

'And then, should we secure the Grail, I would feel that my life's effort had been well spent!'

'It is undoubtedly the finest relic of all.'

'Surely we must obtain it for our own! The glory of our cathedral would resound across all Christendom.'

'Quite true, my dear lady! The vessel is a very good relic, very fine indeed. Pilgrims would come from afar to marvel, to pray, to bless the saintly queen who ordained the great church!'

King Casmir could tolerate no more. He took a step

forward. 'I have heard enough foolish prattle!' He jerked his thumb toward the priest. 'Go! I wish to speak with the queen!'

'Just so, Your Highness!' Father Umphred gathered up his gown and took his portly figure briskly from the parlor. He turned aside at once, into a dressing room adjacent to the parlor. After a quick look over his shoulder, he stepped into a closet and removed a small plug in the wall which allowed him to hear all that went on.

Casmir's voice came from near at hand. ' – the facts, and they cannot be disputed. Madouc is a changeling; her mother a fairy; her father is some nameless rogue of the forest. She flatly refuses a connection with Brezante, and I see no practical way to enforce my wishes.'

Sollace spoke with emotion: 'That is insolence at the extreme! You have already invited King Milo and his queen, and Prince Brezante as well, to Haidion!'

'Unfortunately true. It will do no harm to entertain them; still, it is a vexation.'

'I am indignant! The little hussy should not be allowed her victory!'

King Casmir grimaced and shrugged. 'Were she of ordinary blood, she would be grieving at this very moment. But her mother is a fairy, and I dare not test her spells. That is simple practicality.'

Queen Sollace spoke hopefully: 'If she were baptized and instructed in holy matters – '

King Casmir cut her short. 'We tried that before. The scheme is inept.'

'I suppose that you are right; still – but no matter.'

Casmir pounded his fist into the palm of his hand. 'I am cursed with problems! They swarm at me in a plague, each more dismal than the others, save only for the most carking of all, which gnaws at me night and day!'

'Which problem is that?'

'Can you not imagine? It is the mystery of Suldrun's child.'

Queen Sollace gave Casmir an uncomprehending stare. 'Is it such a desperate problem? I have long put the matter from my head.'

'Do you not remember the case? Suldrun's first-born son was taken and we were given a bratling.'

'Of course I remember; what of that?'

'The mystery remains! Who is the other child? He is the subject of Persilian's rote[2]; still I know neither his name nor where he bides. He will sit rightfully at Cairbra an Meadhan and rule from Evandig. That is Persilian's prophecy.'

'The rote by now may have waned.'

'Such predictions never wane, until they are fulfilled – or somehow circumvented! If I knew the child's name, I could work some sort of ploy and safeguard the realm.'

'There are no clues to the case?'

'None. He was born a boy, and now he will be the same age as Madouc. That is all I know; I would pay dearly to learn the rest!'

'The time is long past,' said Sollace. 'There is no one now to remember. Why not solicit a new and better rote?'

Casmir gave a sad sick chortle. 'It is not so easy to befuddle the Norns.' He went to sit on the couch. 'Now,

[2] The rote of Persilian went thus:

> Suldrun's son shall undertake
> Before his life is gone
> To sit his right and proper place
> at Cairbra an Meadhan.
> If so he sits and so he thrives
> Then he shall make his own
> The Table Round, to Casmir's woe,
> And Evandig the Throne.

despite all, I must entertain King Milo. He will be expecting a betrothal. How shall I explain that Madouc scorns his mooncalf of a son?'

Queen Sollace gave a throaty exclamation. 'I have the answer! Madouc can still serve to advantage – perhaps even better than before!'

'How so?'

'You heard us discuss our need for holy relics. Let us proclaim that whoever goes forth on a quest and returns with an authenticated relic, then he can expect a rich reward! Should he bring back the Holy Grail itself, he can demand a great boon from the king, even to the hand of the Princess Madouc herself!'

Casmir started to ridicule the idea, then closed his mouth. There was, so he reflected, nothing inherently wrong with the proposal. If pilgrims brought gold; if relics brought pilgrims; if Madouc – even indirectly – brought relics – then the concept was sound. Casmir rose to his feet. 'I have no objections to the plan.'

Queen Sollace said dubiously: 'We may only be postponing the problem!'

'How so?'

'Assume that some gallant knight brought hither the Holy Grail and asked the boon of the Princess Madouc's hand in marriage, and the boon was granted, but Madouc proved intractable, as well she might. What then?'

'I will give away the little shrew. She may choose either matrimony or servitude; it is all one to me; the problem at this point leaves our hands.'

Sollace clapped her hands together. 'So are solved all our problems!'

'Not all of them.' Casmir rose to his feet and departed the chamber.

The next day, on the landing of the great staircase, King Casmir was accosted by Father Umphred. 'Your Highness,

I beg the favor of a few words with you, on a matter of importance.'

Casmir looked the priest up and down. 'What is it now?'

Father Umphred glanced to right and left to make sure that they would not be overheard. 'Sire, during my tenure at Haidion as spiritual counsellor to Her Majesty, and what with my other duties, I have become privy to many events of greater or lesser importance. Such is the nature of my position.'

Casmir gave a sour grunt. 'As to this I have no doubt. You know more about my affairs than I do myself.'

Father Umphred laughed politely. 'Recently I have been given to understand that you are interested in Suldrun's first-born child.'

King Casmir said sharply: 'What of it?'

'I might be able to discover the name of this child, and his present domicile.'

'How would you do this?'

'I cannot be sure at this exact moment. But there is more to the case than the information alone.'

'Aha. You want something.'

'I will not deny it. My great ambition is the Archbishopric of the Lyonesse Diocese. If I were to convert the King of Lyonesse to Christianity, there would be strong argument for my elevation to this post at the next Synod of Cardinals at Rome.'

Casmir scowled. 'In short, if I become a Christian, you will tell me the name of Suldrun's child.'

Father Umphred nodded and smiled. 'In its ultimate essence, this is the case.'

Casmir spoke in a voice ominously flat. 'You are a sly devil. Have you ever been stretched on the rack?'

'No, Your Highness.'

'You are bold to the edge of insouciance! Were it not that Queen Sollace would never again give me peace, you would tell your tale without conditions, amidst gasps and squeals.'

Father Umphred showed a sickly smile. 'I intend no boldness and certainly no disrespect; indeed I hoped that Your Highness might take pleasure in my offer.'

'Again: you are lucky that Queen Sollace is your sponsor! What is involved in conversion?'

'Simple baptism, and you must recite a few words of the litany.'

'Ha hmm. It is no great thing.' King Casmir considered, then spoke in a harsh voice: 'Nothing will be changed, by so much as an iota! Do not presume upon your success! You will control none of the church monies; all funds must be paid into and out of the royal exchequer, with not a farthing for the popes of Rome!'

Father Umphred bleated a protest. 'Your Highness, this makes for unwieldy administration!'

'It also makes for honest archbishops. Further, I will tolerate no swarms of itinerant monks, coming like flies on the waft of carrion, to feast and make merry on public funds. Such vagabonds will be whipped and seized into servitude, that they may do useful work.'

'Your Highness!' cried Father Umphred aghast. 'Some of these wandering priests are holy men of the first rank! They carry the Gospel to wild places of the world!'

'Let them wander on without pausing: to Tormous or Skorne or High Tartary, so long as I never see the bulge of their paunches nor the shine of their pates!'

Father Umphred heaved a sigh. 'I am forced to agree; we will do what we can.'

'Rejoice, priest!' said Casmir grimly. 'Today your luck is good! You have gained your bargain and eased your fat limbs away from the rack. Tell me now your information!'

'It must be verified,' said Father Umphred smoothly. 'I shall have it ready tomorrow, after the ceremony.'

King Casmir turned and strode off to his chambers.

The following day at noon Casmir repaired to the queen's small chapel. He stood silent while Father Umphred sprinkled him with holy water and recited phrases in unctuous Latin. Next, to Father Umphred's prompting, he mumbled a Paternoster and a few phrases of litany. Thereupon, Father Umphred seized up a cross and advanced upon Casmir, the cross held high. 'Down upon your knees, Brother Casmir! In humility and the full transports of your joy kiss the cross and dedicate your life to worshipful deeds and the glory of the Church!'

King Casmir spoke evenly: 'Priest, guard your tongue! I brook no fools in my presence.' He looked around the chapel and made a peremptory gesture to those who had attended the ceremony. 'Leave us!'

The chapel was empty except for Casmir, the priest, and Queen Sollace, whom Casmir now addressed. 'My dear queen, it might be well if, for the nonce, you also took yourself apart.'

Queen Sollace vented a large sniff. Rigid with resentful dignity, she marched from the chapel.

King Casmir turned to the priest. 'Now then! Tell me what you know! If it is either false or foolish, you will languish long in the dark.'

'Your Highness, here is the truth! Long ago a young prince was washed up the beach, half-drowned, at the foot of Suldrun's garden. His name was Aillas, who is now King of Troicinet and elsewhere. Suldrun bore him a son: he who was taken to the Forest of Tantrevalles for safety. There the son, whose name was Dhrun, was changed by the fairies for Madouc. Aillas was consigned to the oubliette but escaped by some means beyond my knowledge. Now he hates you passionately. His son, Prince Dhrun, holds you in no more affection.'

Casmir listened slack-jawed. The information was far

more surprising than he had expected. He muttered: 'How is this possible? The son should be of an age with Madouc!'

'The child Dhrun bided a year in the fairy shee, as reckoned in human time. But this year equalled seven years or more of halfling time! So is resolved the paradox.'

Casmir made a series of soft grunting sounds. 'Do you have proof of what you say?'

'I have no proof.'

Casmir did not press the point. There were facts in his possession which had long puzzled him: why, for instance, had Ehirme, Suldrun's one-time servitor, been spirited away to Troicinet with all her family and there endowed with a rich estate? Even more baffling was a fact which had caused a thousand marvelling conjectures: how could Aillas be so near in age to his son Dhrun? Now, all was explained.

The facts were just and true. Casmir said in a heavy voice: 'Speak nothing of this, into any ears whatever! It must be known only to me!'

'Your Highness has spoken and I will obey!'

'Go.'

Father Umphred hurried importantly from the chapel. Casmir stood gazing unseeingly toward the cross on the wall, which meant no more to him now than yesterday. He spoke to himself: 'Aillas hates me well!' Then, in a voice even more soft: 'And it is Dhrun who will sit at Cairbra an Meadhan – before his death. So be it! He shall so sit and he will rule from the throne Evandig, if it is only to send a page boy off for a kerchief. But so, before his death, shall he sit and so shall he rule.'

VII

Evening came to Haidion Castle. King Casmir, sitting alone in the Great Hall of the Old Tower, took an austere supper of cold beef and ale.

Upon finishing his meal, he swung about, to sit gazing into the fire.

He sent his memory back across the years. Images fleeted and flickered: Suldrun as a golden-haired child; Suldrun as he had last seen her: woebegone but still defiant. Presently he glimpsed the haggard youth he had dropped with such bleak fury into the oubliette. Time blurred the drawn white face, but now it wore the semblance of a young Aillas. So it had been! How Aillas must hate him! What yearnings for sweet revenge must control the mind of Aillas!

Casmir gave a soft dismal grunt. Recent events must now be considered from a new perspective. Aillas, by assuming sovereignty over North and South Ulfland, had thwarted Casmir in his goals, and had only just done so again in connection with Blaloc. What artful dissimulation Aillas and Dhrun had used during their visit! How blandly they had urged pacts of peace, all the while despising him and conspiring for his doom!

Casmir pulled himself up in his chair. It was now time for counterblows, harsh and definite, though still controlled, as always, by prudence; Casmir was not one to indulge in rash acts which might react against his own best interests. At the same time, he must discover a method by which the prophecy of Persilian could be voided and its meaning vitiated.

Casmir sat ruminating, weighing his options and reckoning the value of each. Clearly, if Aillas were dead, Casmir's interests must be advanced. In such a case, Dhrun would become king. At this juncture, so Casmir reasoned, a colloquy at Avallon could easily be arranged, on one pretext or another. Dhrun would be seated at Cairbra an Meadhan and somehow persuaded to issue an order from the throne Evandig. The rest would be routine: a movement in the shadows, a glint of steel, a sad cry, a body on the floor – and Casmir would pursue his goals free of fear and almost unopposed.

The plan was straight forward and logical, and needed only implementation.

First: the death of Aillas must be effectuated, but within the constraints of prudence. Assassination of a king was always chancy, and a bungled attempt usually left a clear trail to the instigator, which would not be advantageous.

A name entered Casmir's mind as if by its own force.

Torqual.

Casmir pondered at some length. Torqual's qualifications were superb, but he was not easily controlled. In fact, he was not to be controlled at all. Torqual often seemed as much enemy as ally, and barely troubled to maintain a cynical pretense of cooperation.

With regret, Casmir put aside the name 'Torqual'. Almost immediately another name entered his mind, and this time Casmir leaned back in his seat, nodding thoughtfully to himself and feeling no misgivings whatever.

The name was 'Sir Cory of Falonges'[3], and it referred

---

[3] NOTE: The honorific 'Sir' is here used to designate persons born to noble estate, without reference to their place in the exactly graduated hierarchy. The contemporary language uses a multiplicity of titles and honorifics to specify each subtle distinction; these would be impractical to render in the present chronicle.

Hence 'Sir Cory' is designated by the same honorific as his father, the landed baron 'Sir Claunay', and his brother, 'Sir Camwyd', even though their absolute ranks are greatly at variance.

to a man more or less of Torqual's stripe. Sir Cory's willing cooperation, however, could be taken for granted, since he now crouched deep in a dungeon under the Peinhador awaiting the stroke of Zerling's axe. By acceding to King Casmir's wishes, Sir Cory, so it seemed, had everything to gain and nothing to lose.

Casmir signalled to the footman who stood by the door. 'Fetch me Sir Erls.'

Sir Erls, Chancellor of State and one of Casmir's most trusted advisers, shortly entered the hall: a small sharp-eyed sharp-featured person of middle age, with fine silver hair and pale ivory skin. Casmir had no great liking for the fastidious Sir Erls. However, Sir Erls served him with punctilious efficiency, and Casmir ignored all else.

Casmir indicated a chair; Sir Erls, after a stiff bow, seated himself. Casmir asked: 'What do you know of Sir Cory, who rests in the Peinhador?'

Sir Erls spoke with instant facility, as if he had expected the question. 'Cory is second son to Sir Claunay of Falonges, now dead. The first son, Sir Camwyd, took the estate, which is to the north of Western Province in the Troagh, close under the Ulf border. Cory could not adapt to the plight of the second son, and tried to murder Sir Camwyd. During the night a dog howled; Sir Camwyd was wakeful and the deed was aborted. Cory became a fugitive, then an outlaw. He ranged the Troagh and conducted ambushes along Old Street. He was captured by Duke Ambryl, who would have hanged him out of hand had not Cory identified himself as one of Your Majesty's secret agents. Ambryl stayed his hand and sent Cory here for your own disposition. He is said to be a person of good address, if a black-hearted scoundrel, ripe for Zerling's axe. That is the sum of my knowledge.'

'Perhaps Sir Cory used a premonition after all,' said Casmir. 'Have him brought here at once.'

'As Your Majesty commands.' Sir Erls' voice was carefully toneless. He left the hall.

In due course a pair of jailers brought Cory of Falonges into the hall, with chains at his wrists and a rope around his neck.

Casmir inspected Cory with cool interest. Cory was of middle stature, strong and agile, with a stocky torso, long sinewy arms and legs. His complexion was sallow, his hair dark, his features heavy and hard. He wore the garments in which he had been captured; originally of good quality, they were now torn and bedraggled and stank abominably of the dungeon. Nevertheless he returned King Casmir's inspection with incurious composure: alive and alert but resigned to his fate.

The jailers tied one end of the rope to a table-leg, so that Cory might not spring unexpectedly upon King Casmir, then, at Casmir's nod, they retired from the hall.

Casmir spoke in an even voice: 'You informed Duke Ambryl that you worked in my secret service.'

Cory gave a nod of the head. 'So I did, Your Highness.'

'Was not that a bold remark to make?'

'Under the circumstances, I prefer to think it an inspiration of the moment. It illuminates my resourceful intelligence and indicates my desire to put myself and my skills at your service.'

Casmir smiled his cold smile. 'You had not previously made these ambitions clear.'

'True, Sire! I have postponed the act too long, and now you discover me in shackles, to my shame.'

'Shame for your crimes, or shame for your failure?'

'I can only say, Sire, that I am not accustomed to failure.'

'Ha! That, at least, is a quality which I admire. Now then, as to employment in my service: it may be a game you shall play in earnest.'

'Willingly, Sire, since the work would seem to reprieve me from dungeon and axe.'

'That is the case,' said Casmir. 'You are evidently both clever and unscrupulous; these are qualities which I often find valuable. If you succeed in the work I am about to propose, you shall not only have earned your amnesty but also a substantial reward.'

Sir Cory bowed. 'Your Majesty, without hesitation I commit myself to your mission.'

Casmir nodded. 'Let us be clear at the outset. If you betray me, I will hunt you down with all my resources and bring you back to the Peinhador.'

Again Sir Cory bowed. 'Sire, as a realist I would expect nothing else. Tell me only what I must do.'

'The deed is simple enough. You must kill King Aillas of Troicinet, Dascinet and the Ulflands. He is now at sea with his navy, but you will presently find him at Doun Darric, in South Ulfland. I must not be implicated in the work.'

Cory compressed his lips and his eyes glittered in the torchlight. 'It is a delicate task, but not beyond my skill.'

'That is all for tonight. Tomorrow we will speak again. Guards!'

The jailers entered the room. 'Take Sir Cory back to the Peinhador; allow him to bathe, provide him fresh garments, feed him as he chooses and house him securely on the first level.'

'As you wish, Sire. Come along, dog's-body.'

Cory spoke haughtily: 'Henceforth, address me as "Sir Cory", or beware my displeasure!'

The jailer gave a sharp tug on the rope. 'Whatever your name, be quick about it; we are not as clement as His Majesty.'

Late in the afternoon of the next day King Casmir once again interviewed Sir Cory, this time in the Room of

Sighs, above the armoury. Sir Cory was now dressed decently and came unshackled.

King Casmir sat at his usual place, with the beechwood flagon and the beechwood wine-cup ready at hand. He motioned Sir Cory to a bench.

'I have made certain arrangements,' said Casmir. 'On the table is a purse, containing twenty florins of silver. Fit yourself out as a merchant of medicinal ointments, with a horse, a pack-animal and suitable stock-in-trade. Fare north along the Sfer Arct to Dazleby, proceed to Nolsby Sevan, then north along the Ulf Passway. You will negotiate the Gates of Cerberus and Kaul Bocach the fortress; continue six miles beyond to a wayside inn showing the sign of the Dancing Pig. There you will find four men awaiting you: blackguards as deep-dyed as yourself if not worse. They were destined to join Torqual's band, but first they will assist you in your endeavor. You shall use them as you think best.'

Casmir looked at a list, then spoke with distaste. 'This is an unusual group! Each would seem to exceed all the others combined for sheer villainy. First, I cite you Izmael the Hun, from the woods of Tartary. Next is Kegan the Celt, who is as thin as a ferret and no less avid for blood. Next: Este the Sweet, with curling golden hair and a limpid smile. He is Roman and claims kinship with the house of Ovid the poet. He carries a frail bow, like a toy, and shoots arrows which seem little more than slivers, but he can put out a man's eye at a far distance. Last is Galgus the Black, who carries four knives at his belt. Such are your paladins.'

'They would seem, rather, creatures out of a nightmare,' said Cory. 'Will they do my bidding?'

Casmir smiled. 'So I hope. They fear Torqual, certainly. He may be the only man alive who daunts them. For this

256

reason you must act in Torqual's name. There is a secondary benefit; when you are successful, as I hope, Torqual will be blamed for the deed and not I.'

'How will Torqual regard this project?'

'He will make no objection. I reiterate: my name must never be used. Is all clear to you?'

'Except as to a single point: am I required to work under Torqual's orders?'

'Only if it eases your task.'

Cory pulled thoughtfully at his long chin. He asked: 'May I speak with full candor?'

'So far we have done little else. Speak!'

'I have heard rumors that your secret agents seldom survive to enjoy the fruits of their toil. How am I guaranteed that I will live to enjoy my success?'

'I can answer only in these terms,' said Casmir. 'If you have served me capably once, I may well desire that you serve me again, which you will not be able to do if you are dead. Secondly, if you distrust the arrangements, you have the option of returning to the Peinhador.'

Cory smiled and rose to his feet. 'Your arguments are cogent.'

7

I

On Lally Meadow, well within the Forest of Tantrevalles, was the manse Trilda: a structure of timber and stone situated where Lillery Rill emerged from the forest on its way to join the Sweet Yellow River at the far end of the meadow.

Trilda, now almost a hundred years old, had been constructed to the order of the magician Hilario, whose previous residence had been Sheur Tower, on an islet off the north coast of Dahaut: a place too rude, cold and cramped for Hilario, a person of discriminating tastes. With great care he drew up his plans, specifying each detail with precision and reviewing at length the relationship between each part and the whole. To perform the work of construction, he hired a troop of goblin carpenters, who declared themselves to be highly qualified craftsmen. Hilario started to discuss the plans with Shylick the master carpenter, but Shylick took the plans from Hilario, glanced through them, and seemed to assimilate everything at a glance, and Hilario was much impressed by his perspicacity.

The carpenters set to work immediately; with remarkable zeal they dug, delved, hewed and sawed, hammered and pounded, fretted, fitted, and spun long shavings from their bodges[1], so that, to Hilario's astonishment, the work

---

[1] bodge: an outdoor lathe powered by a line running from a springy overhead tree-branch to a treadle which turns the spindles of the lathe.

was finished overnight, complete to a black iron weather-cock on the chimney.

As the first red rays of sunlight entered Lally Meadow, Shylick, the master carpenter, wiped the sweat from his forehead and, with a grand flourish, presented his reckoning to Hilario, and requested immediate payment, since the troop had urgent business elsewhere.

Hilario, however, was a man of cautious temperament, and was not to be influenced by Shylick's engaging mannerisms. He commended Shylick for his briskness and efficiency, but insisted upon inspecting the premises before paying off the account. Shylick protested, to no avail, and with poor grace accompanied Hilario as he made his inspection.

Almost at once Hilario discovered several mistakes in the work, and evidence of over-hasty or even slipshod methods. The contract called for masonry of 'sound, substantial blocks of fieldstone'; the blocks inspected by Hilario proved to be simulations prepared from enchanted cow droppings. Checking further, Hilario found that the 'stout timbers of well-seasoned oak' described in his specifications were in fact dried milk-weed stalks of little strength, disguised by another crafty enchantment.

Hilario indignantly pointed out these deficiencies to Shylick and demanded that the work be done properly, to exact standards. Shylick, now glum and out of sorts, did his best to evade the extra toil. He argued that total precision was impossible and unknown to the cosmos. He claimed that a reasonable and realistic person accepted a degree of latitude in the interpretation of his contract, since this looseness was inherent in the communicative process.

Hilaro remained inflexible and Shylick became ever more excited, striking at the floor with his tall green hat, and his arguments ever more abstruse. He stated that, since the distinction between 'seeming' and 'substance' was in any case no more than a philosophical nicety, almost anything was equivalent to almost anything else. Hilario said gravely: 'In that case, I will pay off my account with this bit of straw.'

'No,' said Shylick. 'That is not quite the same thing.' He went on to assert that, if only for the sake of simplicity, Hilario should pay the account and contentedly take up residence in his new abode.

Hilario would not be persuaded. He termed Shylick's arguments pure sophistry, from beginning to end. 'The manse presents a fine appearance, granted,' said Hilario. 'But enchantments of this sort are fugitive and tend to erode!'

'Not always!'

'Often enough! With the first good rain the entire jackleg contraption might collapse around my ears, perhaps in the middle of the night while I lay sleeping. You must do the work over, from start to finish, using standard materials and approved methods of construction.'

The carpenters grumbled but Hilario had his way and work commenced again. For three days and nights the goblins toiled and this time, from petulance or perhaps sheer perversity, they did the work twice as well as was needful, using rosewood, madura and choice walnut burl for the paneling; rhodocrosite, pink porphyry and malachite in the place of marble: all the while glaring sidewise at Hilario as if daring him to find fault.

At last the work was finished and Hilario paid off his account with two hundred and twelve cockleshells and a feast of pickled fish, fresh-baked bread, new cheese, nuts and honey, a tub of strong pear cider and another of mulberry wine; and the transaction ended on a note of good-fellowship and mutual esteem.

Hilario took up residence and lived many years at

Trilda, eventually dying of inexplicable causes out on Lally Meadow – perhaps the victim of a lightning bolt. Though, according to rumor, he had excited the resentment of the wizard Tamurello. In any case, nothing could be proved.

The manse remained empty for a number of years, until one day Shimrod, during his wanderings, came upon the lonely structure and decided to make it his own home. He added a wing for his workroom, planted flowers at the front and an orchard at the back, and Trilda was soon as charming as ever.

To maintain Trilda, to dust, mop and tidy, to polish the glass, wax the wood, weed the gardens and tend the fires, Shimrod engaged a family of merrihews (sometimes known as tree trolls) recently arrived in the neighborhood. These were small shy creatures who worked only when Shimrod's back was turned, so that he seldom noticed them except as a flicker of movement from the side of his eye.

The years went by, after the established cycle. Shimrod lived at Trilda for the most part in solitude, with only his work to distract him. Few folk came to Lally Meadow; perhaps an occasional woodcutter or mushroom-gatherer; and Shimrod entertained virtually no one. At the other end of the meadow was Tuddifot Shee: to the casual eye an outcropping of black trap, stained on the north side with lichen. From time to time Shimrod watched the fairies at their revels, but always from afar. Already he had learned that the society of fairies could lead to turmoils of bittersweet frustration.

Recently, at Murgen's behest, Shimrod had undertaken a monumental task: the analysis and classification of material confiscated from the wizard Tamurello and brought to Trilda as a disorganized clutter. Tamurello had been a magician of great scope and eclectic experience; he

261

had collected from near and far a great number of objects and magical adjuncts: some trivial, others quivering with force.

Shimrod's first task, in connection with this wonderful miscellaneity, was to make a cursory survey of documents, tracts, formularies and records. These were presented in many shapes, sizes and conditions. There were books old and new, scrolls from times beyond memory, illuminated parchments; portfolios of drawings, plans, maps and charts; cloth panels stamped with block characters, papers inscribed in odd-colored inks to languages even more arcane.

Shimrod sorted these articles into piles for future study, and began to examine the machines, tools, utensils, enhancers and assorted other artifacts. Many showed no obvious utility, and Shimrod frequently puzzled as to their purpose or, in reverse, their lack of purpose. For a month he had been studying such a contrivance: an assembly of seven disks of transparent material, rolling around the periphery of a circular tablet of black onyx. The disks swam with soft colors, and showed pulsing black spots of emptiness, forming and dying apparently at random.

Shimrod could conceive no practical purpose for the device. A clock? A toy? A curio? So complicated a machine, he reasoned, must have been constructed with a definite purpose in mind, though this purpose quite escaped his understanding.

One day as he sat watching the disks, a chime issued from a large bulging mirror hanging on the end wall.

Shimrod rose to his feet and approached the mirror, to find himself looking into the great hall at Swer Smod. Murgen stood by the table. He acknowledged Shimrod's attention with a nod and spoke without preliminaries.

'I have a complicated task to lay before you. It might well involve you in personal danger. Still, it is of great importance and must be accomplished. Since I cannot take time to do this work, it falls upon your shoulders.'

'That is the reason for my being,' said Shimrod. 'What is the task?'

'In the main, it is a continuation of your previous work at Ys. You now must pursue your investigations in greater detail. Specifically, you must learn the facts in regard to Desmei.'

'You have no theories?'

'I have guesses by the dozen; facts none. The best possibilities are very few; in fact, as I reckon it, they number two only.'

'And they are?'

'We start with this supposition. When Desmei created Melancthe and Carfilhiot she dissolved herself totally as a dramatic demonstration of spite toward the race of men. The qualification here is that no one would truly care: Tamurello least of all. As a more likely case, she chose to alter her state, that she might bide her time, and take revenge when the opportunity arose. With that as your premise, you are to discover the node of green taint which is Desmei – or whatever semblance she is using. Where is her hiding place? What is her scheme? I suspect that her agents are Melancthe and Torqual; if so, they will lead you to Desmei.'

'So then – how should I proceed?'

'First, alter your semblance, and definitely; Melancthe perceived you through the last. Then travel to the high moors of Ulfland. Under Mount Sobh in Glen Dagach is High Coram; there you will find Melancthe and Torqual.'

'And when I find Desmei?'

'Destroy her – unless first she destroys you.'

'That is a contingency I would regret.'

'Then you must arm yourself well. You cannot use

263

sandestin magic; she would sniff you out on the instant, since the green comes from demonland.'

'In that case, I am vulnerable to demon magic.'

'Not altogether. Hold out your hand.'

Shimrod did so, and at once found in his palm a pair of small black bloodstone spheres, each joined by a short chain to an earring.

'These are the hither projections of two Mang Seven efferents. They dislike all things from both Mel and Dadgath. Their names are Voner and Skel; you will find them useful. Now make your preparations, then I will give you further instructions.'

The mirror went blank; Shimrod saw only his own face. He turned away and considered his workbench, with its burden of oddments and mysteries. He watched the whirl of the seven careening disks and gave a soft grunt of vexation. He should have put a question to Murgen.

The time was early afternoon. Shimrod went out into his garden. High in the sky tumbles of cloud dreamed in the sunlight. Never had Lally Meadow seemed more tranquil. Shimrod turned his mind to Glen Dagach, where tranquility would certainly be unknown. But there was no help for it. What needed doing must be done.

Now he must fit himself into a semblance suited to the place and circumstances. With his usual magic denied to him, he must rely upon physical skills and weaponry. Some of these were native to him; others he must now absorb.

He considered his new semblance. It must be strong, durable, quick, competent, yet not conspicuous in the environment of the high moors.

Shimrod returned to his workroom, where he formulated an entity which more than fulfilled the requirements: a man tall, spare of physique, with a body which seemed to be based upon leather, sinew and bone. The head was narrow, with a keen hollow-cheeked face, glittering yellow eyes, a cruel underslung cleft of a mouth, and an axe-blade nose. Ringlets of coarse dull brown hair curled close to his scalp; his skin, weathered and sun-beaten, showed the same color. To the lobes of the small ears Shimrod hung the efferents Voner and Skel. At once he heard their voices; they seemed to be discussing the weather in places beyond his acquaintance: ' – almost a record cycle for interstitials, at least along the upper miasma,' said Skel. 'However, just past the kickfield of the Living Dead the modules have not yet shifted phase.'

'I know little of Carpiskovy,' said Voner. 'It is said to be very fine and I am surprised to hear of conditions so insipid.'

'Margaunt is worse, and by the hour! I found a delicate bang-green along the flitterway.'

'"Delicate", you say!'

'No less! The gray-pines are on regular duty, and there is never a tweak from the rubants.'

Shimrod spoke. 'Gentlemen, I am your supervisor. My name is Shimrod; however in this phase, I will use the name Travec the Dacian. Be on the alert for plans made against either Shimrod or Travec. I am pleased that you will be associated with me, since our business is of great importance. Now, for the moment I must ask you to keep silent, since I must assimilate much information into my mind.'

Skel said: 'You have made a poor beginning, Shimrod or Travec, whatever your name. Our conversation is on a high level. You would do well to listen.'

Shimrod spoke sternly: 'I have a limited mind. I insist upon obedience. Let us be clear on this at once; otherwise I must consult Murgen.'

'Bah!' said Voner. 'Just our luck! In Shimrod we discover another of these short-tail snatch-after martinets!'

'Silence, if you please!'

'Just so, if so it must be,' said Voner. 'Skel, I will speak with you later, when Shimrod is less testy.'

'By all means! The time cannot pass too swiftly, as they say in this eccentric universe.'

The efferents became silent save for occasional groans and mutters. Shimrod, meanwhile, formulated a biography for Travec and stocked his mind with pertinent information. Next, he established safeguards to protect Trilda from interlopers during his absence. An ironic circumstance if while he searched the moors for Desmei, she came to Trilda and plundered his workroom of all its precious adjuncts!

Shimrod's preparations at last were complete. He went to the mirror and made himself known to Murgen. 'I am ready to depart on my mission.'

Murgen inspected the unfamiliar image which confronted him. 'The semblance is adequate, if somewhat larger in impact than necessary. Still, who knows? It might prove useful. Now then: go six miles past Kaul Bocach on the Ulf Passway. Here you will find the Inn of the Dancing Pig.'

'I know this inn.'

'You will discover four cutthroats on the premises. They are awaiting orders from King Casmir. Let it be known that King Casmir has sent you to join the group, and that a certain Cory of Falonges will shortly arrive to serve as their leader on a special mission.'

'So far all is clear.'

'You should have no difficulty in attaching yourself to Cory's band. His orders are to assassinate King Aillas and, if possible, to capture Prince Dhrun.

'Cory will lead this company to Glen Dagach. Here, depending upon circumstances, you might transfer from Cory's band to that of Torqual. But move quietly and excite no one. At the moment Desmei feels no suspicion. Do not blunder and drive her into far hiding.'

Shimrod nodded. 'And thereafter: what of Cory?'

'He becomes inconsequential.'

The mirror went blank.

II

Travec the Dacian rode a hammer-headed dun horse north along the Great Ulf Passway. To the right of his saddle a lacquered box contained a short compound bow and two dozen arrows; at his left side hung a long scimitar, somewhat narrow-bladed, in a leather scabbard. He wore a black cloth shirt, loose trousers and knee-length black boots. A cloak, a chainmail shirt and a conical iron helmet were tied in a roll behind the saddle.

He rode slouched forward, eyes flickering constantly from side to side. Weapons, garments, and general mien identified Travec as a vagabond warrior or perhaps something worse. The folk he met along the way gave him a wide berth and saw him pass with relief.

Travec had ridden almost six miles beyond the fortress Kaul Bocach. On the left rose the mighty Teach tac Teach; to the right the Forest of Tantrevalles bordered the road, approaching sometimes so closely that branches shaded away the sky. Ahead, a small wayside inn showed the sign of the Dancing Pig.

Travec drew up his horse; at once a querulous question came from one of the black bloodstone globes at his ear: 'Travec, why do you halt your horse?'

'Because the Inn of the Dancing Pig is close ahead.'

'Surely that is a matter of no concern.'

Not for the first time Travec reflected upon Murgen's

hints that the efferents might not be the easiest of companions. During the whole of the journey, to while away the tedium, they had conversed in soft voices, creating an undertone of sound which Travec ignored to the best of his ability. Now he said: 'Listen well! I am about to instruct you.'

'That is unnecessary,' said Voner. 'Your instructions are beside the mark.'

'How so?'

'Is it not clear? Murgen gave orders that we were to serve Shimrod. You name your name "Travec". The disparity must be obvious, even to you.'

Travec uttered a grim laugh. 'One moment, if you please! "Travec" is merely a name: an item of verbiage. I am in every essential aspect Shimrod. You must serve me to your best capacity. If you make a single objection, I will complain to Murgen, who will then chastise you without mercy.'

Skel spoke in unctuous tones: 'All is explained. You need fear nothing; we are on full alert.'

Voner said: 'Still, if only for a review, list once again the contingencies against which we must guard.'

'First, warn me of all imminent danger, including but not limited to ambush, poison in my wine, weapons pointed in my direction that are intended to injure or kill me; also rock-slides, avalanches, pit-falls, snares, traps of all kinds, and any other sort of device or activity which might annoy, thwart, hurt, imprison, kill or debilitate me. In short, ensure my safety and good health. If you are at all doubtful as to my meaning, act always in the manner which will provide me the maximum satisfaction. Is that clear?'

Voner asked: 'What of doses, or double- or triple-doses of aphrodisiac?'

'All such dosages will ultimately be to my detriment.

They are included in the full category. If you have doubts, consult me.'

'As you like.'

'Second – '

'Is there more?'

Travec paid no heed. 'Second, notify me when you sense the green fume of Mel. We will then try to locate the source and destroy the node.'

'That is sensible enough.'

'Third, do not reveal yourselves to the demons of Mel, or Dadgath, or elsewhere. They might flee before we are able to kill them.'

'Just as you wish.'

'Fourth, be on the lookout for the witch Desmei, in any of her phases. She might even use another name, but do not be confused! Report any suspicious circumstance at once.'

'We will do our best.'

Travec once more set his horse into motion, and proceeded along the road, while the efferents discussed the terms of Travec's instructions, which they seemed to find perplexing, so that Travec wondered if the efferents had grasped the full sense of his requirements.

Travec, approaching the inn, discovered it to be a rather ramshackle structure, built of rough timber and roofed with thatch so old that grass grew from the straw. At one side was a shed where the landlord brewed his ale; at the back the inn joined into the barn. Beyond, three small children worked in an acreage planted to oats and pot-herbs. Travec turned into the yard, dismounted and tied his horse to a rail. Nearby two men sat on a bench: Izmael the Hun and Kegan the Celt, both of whom had watched Travec's arrival with keen interest.

Travec spoke to Izmael in his own language: 'Well then,

creature born of outrage: what do you here, so far from home?'

'Hoy, dog-eater! I attend to my own affairs.'

'They may be mine as well, so treat me kindly, even though I have lopped the heads from a hundred of your kinsmen.'

'What is done is done; after all, I raped your mother and all your sisters.'

'And no doubt your own mother as well, on horseback.' Travec nodded toward the other man on the bench. 'Who is this gaunt shadow of a dead scorpion?'

'He calls himself Kegan; he is a Celt from Godelia. He would as soon cut your throat as spit.'

Travec nodded and reverted to the language of the country. 'I have been sent to meet a certain Cory of Falonges. Where is he to be found?'

'He has not yet arrived. We thought you might be Cory. What do you know of the venture?'

'I was assured of profit and danger, no more.' Travec went into the inn, and found the landlord, who agreed to provide lodging, in the form of a straw pallet in the loft over the barn, which Travec accepted without enthusiasm. The landlord sent a boy to take care of the dun horse; Travec brought his bundle of belongings into the inn, and commanded a pint of ale from the landlord, which he took to a table by the wall.

Nearby sat another two men. Este the Roman, slender with delicate features and hazel eyes, carved a bit of wood into the likeness of a harpy. Galgus the Black from Dahaut amused himself rolling dice across the table, from one hand to the other. He showed the startling white skin and lusterless black hair of an arsenic-eater; his face was sad and saturnine. The two were presently joined by Izmael and Kegan the Celt. Izmael muttered a few words, and all turned to look toward Travec, who ignored the attention.

270

Kegan began to play at dice with Galgus, wagering small coins, and presently the whole group became involved in the game. Travec watched with somber attention, wondering as to the outcome of the situation. The group, lacking a leader, was unstable, with each man jealous of his reputation. After a few minutes Izmael the Hun called over to Travec. 'Come! Why do you not join the sport? Dacians are notorious for their insensate gambling!'

'True, to my regret,' said Travec. 'But I did not wish to join the game without an invitation.'

'You may consider yourself invited. Gentlemen, this is Travec the Dacian, who is here on business similar to our own. Travec, you see here Este the Sweet, who claims to be the last true Roman. His weapon is a bow so small and fragile that it seems a toy, while his arrows are little more than slivers; still, he can sling them away with great speed and put out a man's eye at fifty yards without rising from his chair. Next is Galgus, who is Daut and clever with knives. Yonder sits Kegan from Godelia; he favors a set of curious weapons, among others, the steel whip. I myself am a poor lost dove; I survive the ferocities of life only through the pity and forbearance of my fellows.'

'You are a notable group,' said Travec. 'I am privileged to be associated with you. Does anyone know the details of our mission?'

Galgus said: 'I can guess, since Casmir is at the bottom of it. But enough talk; let us roll the dice. Travec, do you understand the game?'

'Not altogether, but I will learn quickly enough.'

'Then what about money?'

'No problem there! I carry ten gold pieces paid over to me by King Casmir.'

'That should suffice! Very well; I will roll the dice. Everyone must wager, then I either call out my number or "odd" or "even", and so goes the game.'

Travec played for a period, and won modestly. Then Galgus began to use false dice, which he substituted with great cleverness when it came his time to throw, and Travec lost his ten gold pieces. 'I will play no more,' said Travec. 'Else I might find myself without a horse.'

The sun had long since dropped behind the mountains. As the sky began to grow dark the landlord served a supper of lentils and bread. Even as the five men finished their meal, a newcomer arrived at the inn, riding a fine black horse. He dismounted, tied his horse to the rail and strode into the inn: a dark-haired man of middle stature, long and sinewy of arm and leg, with a hard harsh face. He spoke to the landlord: 'Take care of my horse and provide me the best your house can offer, since I have ridden far this day.' He turned and surveyed the five men, then approached their table. 'I am Cory of Falonges; I am here on orders from an eminent person of whom you know. It is my business to command you on a venture. I expected four men; I find five.'

'I am Travec the Dacian. King Casmir sent me to join your troop, along with a bag of ten gold pieces which you were to pay out to the other four men. However, this afternoon I gamed at dice. To my regret I lost all ten gold pieces, so that the men must go without their pay.'

'What!' cried Izmael in consternation. 'You gambled with my money?'

Cory of Falonges looked at Travec wonderingly. 'How do you explain your behavior?'

Travec shrugged. 'I was pressed to join the game and Casmir's money was the first to hand. After all, I am a Dacian and accept all challenges.'

Este looked accusingly at Galgus. 'The money you have won is rightfully mine!'

'Not necessarily!' cried Galgus. 'Your remark is based

272

on a hypothesis. Also, let me ask this: if Travec had won, would you now reimburse me my losses?'

Cory spoke decisively: 'Galgus in this case is not at fault; Travec is to blame.'

Travec, seeing how the tide was running, said: 'You are all making much of nothing. I have five gold pieces of my own, which I will put up for wager.'

Galgus asked: 'You wish to gamble further?'

'Why not? I am a Dacian! But we will play a new game!' Travec put the earthenware bean-pot on the floor and indicated a crack running across the floor some fifteen feet from the pot. 'Each man in turn will stand behind the crack and toss a gold-piece toward the pot. The man whose coin goes into the pot collects all the coins which have gone astray.'

'And if two or more men succeed?' asked Este.

'They share the booty. Come then, who will play? Galgus, you are adept and a good judge of distances; you shall go first.'

Somewhat dubiously Galgus put his toe to the crack and tossed a coin; it struck the side of the pot and rattled away.

'Too bad,' said Travec. 'You will not win this round. Who will go next? Este?'

Este tossed, then Izmael and Kegan; all their coins went wide of the opening, though it seemed as if their aim was true and that only at the last instant did some influence nudge the coins aside. Travec threw last, and his coin rattled clean and true into the pot. 'In this case I am lucky,' said Travec. He collected his winnings. 'Come; who will be first? Galgus again?'

Once more Galgus stepped to the crack and with the most subtle touch, tossed his coin, but it sailed entirely over the pot as if it had wings. Este's coin seemed to dip for a moment into the opening, then career away. Izmael and Kegan likewise failed in their attempts, but as before Travec's coin rang into the pot as if drawn there by a will of its own.

Travec collected his winnings. He counted out ten gold pieces and gave them to Cory. 'Let there be no further complaint!' He turned to his fellows. 'Shall we toss another round?'

'Not I,' said Este. 'My arm is sore from so much exercise.'

'Nor I,' said Kegan. 'I am confused by the erratic flight of my coins. They dart and veer like barn-swallows; they shy away from the pot as if it were a hole into Hell!'

Kegan went to look into the pot. A black arm reached up from within and tweaked his nose. He gave a startled cry and dropped the pot, which broke into a hundred pieces. None had observed the incident and his explanations met with skepticism. Travec said: 'The landlord's ale is strong! No doubt you felt its influence!'

The landlord now came forward. 'Why did you break my valuable pot? I demand payment!'

'It is your pot which tonight cost me dear!' roared Kegan. 'I will pay not so much as a falsified farthing, unless you recompense me my loss!'

Cory stepped forward. 'Landlord, be calm! I am the leader of this company and I will pay the cost of your pot. Be good enough to bring us more ale, then leave us in peace.'

With a sullen shrug the landlord retreated and in due course returned with mugs of ale. Meanwhile, Cory had turned to appraise Travec. 'You are deft with your coin-tossing. What other skills can you demonstrate?'

Travec showed a flicker of a smile. 'Upon whom?'

'I stand aloof, in judgment,' said Cory.

Travec looked around the group. 'Izmael, your nerves

are strong; otherwise the deeds you have done would have made you mad.'

'That may well be true.'

'Stand here, then, at this spot.'

'Tell me first what you have in mind. If you intend to cut off my scalp-lock, I must respectfully refuse.'

'Be calm! With as much amity as may be possible between Dacian and Hun, we will demonstrate the niceties of combat as we know it on the steppes.'

'As you like.' Izmael slouched to the stipulated place.

Cory turned to Travec. He asked sharply: 'What sort of foolery is this? You carry neither bludgeon nor mace; there is no blade at your belt nor none in your boot!'

Travec, paying no heed, spoke to Izmael. 'You are waiting in ambush. Make ready your knife, and strike as I walk past.'

'As you like.'

Travec walked past Izmael the Hun. There was a flurry of movement, almost too fast to follow. Travec flung out his arm; a knife appeared miraculously in his hand; the pommel was pressed against Izmael's corded neck, with the blade gleaming in the lamp-light. Izmael's arm was knocked aside; his knife clattered to the stone floor. At the same time he raised his leg, a horrid double-pronged blade protruding from the toe of his soft felt shoe. He kicked at Travec's crotch; Travec dropped his other hand and caught Izmael's ankle, and Izmael was forced to hop backward toward the fireplace; had Travec stepped forward and thrust, Izmael would have fallen backward into the blaze.

Travec, however, released Izmael's ankle and resumed his seat. Izmael stolidly picked up his knife and returned to his own place. 'So go events on the steppe,' said Izmael without rancor.

275

Este the Sweet spoke in silky tones: 'That is deft knife-work, and even Galgus, who reckons himself supreme, will agree to this. Am I right, Galgus?'

All eyes turned to Galgus, who sat brooding, his pallid face pinched into a dyspeptic mask. 'It is easy to be deft when one has a knife in his sleeve,' said Galgus. 'As to the thrown knife, that is an art superb at which I excel.'

Este asked: 'What of it, Travec? Can you throw the knife?'

'By Dacian standards I am considered moderately skilful. Which of us is the better man? There is no way of proving without one or the other or both taking a knife in the throat, so let us not force a comparison.'

'Ah, but there is a way,' said Galgus. 'I have seen it used often at a trial among champions. Landlord, bring us a length of thin cord.'

Grudgingly the landlord tendered a hank of string. 'You must now pay me a silver bit, which will also compensate me for my pot.'

Cory contemptuously tossed him a coin. 'Take this and cease your whining! Avarice ill becomes a landlord; these folk, as a class, should be generous, decent and open-handed.'

'None such exist,' growled the landlord. 'All answering that description have become wandering paupers.'

Galgus meanwhile had tied the cord across the face of a horizontal six-foot baulk at the far end of the room. At the center he suspended a beef knuckle-bone upon which the dogs had been chewing, then returned to where his comrades stood watching.

'Now then,' said Galgus. 'We stand at this crack, facing away from the string. At the signal, we turn and throw our knives. Travec aims at the string two feet to the right of the bone, I aim at a point two feet to the left. Should we both strike the string, one knife will cut an instant

276

sooner than the other, and the bone will swing somewhat away from vertical before it falls and thus give a clear indication of which knife struck first – that is, if either of us has the competence to hit the mark in the first place.'

'I can only try my best,' said Travec. 'First I must find a knife to throw, as I would not wish to use my sleeve-knife for such rough work.' He looked about the room. 'I will try this old cheese-knife; it will serve as well as any.'

'What?' exclaimed Galgus. 'The blade is a trifle of pot-metal, or lead, or some other base substance; it is barely able to gnaw through an ounce of cheese!'

'Still, it must do, since I have no other. Este, you must referee the drop. Find the exact verticality, so that we may detect to the width of a spider-leg who is the better man.'

'Very well.' After several tests, Este marked a spot on the floor. 'Here is the point of determination! Kegan, you come here as well; we will crouch and watch the spot, and if the bone drops we will validate each other's decision.'

Kegan and Este went to kneel under the knuckle-bone. 'We are ready.'

Galgus and Travec took their places by the crack, backs turned to the wooden baulk. Cory said: 'I will rap my knuckles on the table with this cadence: one – two – three – four – five. At the fifth rap, you must turn and throw. Are you ready?'

'Ready!' said Galgus.

'Ready!' said Travec.

'Attention, then! I will start the count!' Cory rapped his knuckles upon the table. Rap. Rap. Rap. Rap. Rap. Galgus with the speed of a striking snake swung about; metal flashed through the air; the blade struck home in the wood. But the bone never wavered; the blade had entered the baulk at the target point but with its blade flat and parallel to the cord. Travec, who had turned in a leisurely manner, said: 'That is not bad; but let me see if I cannot do better with this old cheese-biter.' He hefted the wooden handle, slung it sidewise. The knife wavered through the air, slashed the cord; the bone fell to the side. Este and Kegan rose to their feet. 'It appears that on this occasion Travec must be declared the winner of the trial.'

Galgus, muttering under his breath, went to retrieve his knife. Cory said abruptly: 'Enough of these trials and tests; clearly you all are competent at slitting throats and drowning old women. Whether you can achieve more strenuous acts remains to be seen. Now then: seat yourselves, and give me all your attention, and I will tell you what I expect of you. Landlord, bring us ale, then step from the room, as we wish to make private conversation.'

Cory waited until the landlord had obeyed his instructions, then, placing one foot on a bench, he spoke in a voice of command. 'At this moment we are a disparate group, with nothing in common but our mutual villainy and our greed. These are poor bonds, no doubt, but they must serve, since we have no other. It is important that we work as one; our mission will collapse into disaster for all of us unless we act with discipline.'

Kegan called out: 'What is this mission? This is what we need to know!'

'I cannot tell you the details at this time. I can describe it as dangerous, dastardly and in the interests of King Casmir – but you know this already, and perhaps you can guess what is wanted of us. Still, I prefer to avoid an exact definition of our goal until we have proceeded somewhat further. But this I can tell you: if we succeed, we gain great rewards, and will never need to rob or plunder again, save for recreation.'

Este asked: 'All very well, but what are these rewards? A few more gold pieces?'

'Not so. As for myself, I will be restored to the Barony

of Falonges. Each of you may expect the rank and estate of a knight, in a district of your own choosing. Such, at least, is my understanding.'

'Well then, what next?' asked Este.

'The program is simple: you need only obey my orders.'

'That is, perhaps, a trifle too simple. After all, we are not fresh recruits.'

'The details are these: tomorrow we set off across the mountains to a place of rendezvous with others of our ilk. There we shall take advice and perfect our plans. At last we shall act, and if we do our work with decision, we are done.'

Galgus said sardonically: 'Nothing could be more expeditious, as you explain it.'

Cory paid him no heed. 'Listen now to me. My demands are few. I ask neither love, nor flattery, nor special favors. I require discipline and obedience to my commands, in exactitude. There must be no hesitant questions, nor arguments, nor murmuring doubts. You are as horrid a band of brutes as ever haunted a nightmare – but I am more vicious than all five together – if my orders are disobeyed. So then – here and now! Anyone who finds the program beyond his scope may take his leave; it is now or never! Travec, do you accept my regulations?'

'I am a Black Eagle of the Carpathians! No man is my master!'

'During this venture, I am your master. Accept this fact, or go your own way.'

'If all the others agree, I will abide by your regulations.'

'Este?'

'I accept the conditions. After all, someone must lead.'

'Exactly so. Izmael?'

'I will abide by the rule.'

'Kegan?'

279

'Ha! If I must, I must, though the ghosts of my ancestors cry out at the indignity.'

'Galgus?'

'I submit to your leadership.'

'Travec the Dacian: once more to you?'

'You shall be the leader. I will not dispute your rule.'

'That is still ambiguous. Once and for all, will you or will you not obey my command?'

Travec said stonily: 'I will obey.'

III

An hour after daybreak Cory of Falonges and his dreadful company departed the Inn of the Dancing Pig. Tern, the landlord's oldest son, served as their guide and led a pair of pack-horses. He had stated that the journey would require two days only, barring untoward incident and provided that the Atlantic gales held off the full force of their blowing.

The column rode north, past the defile which led under Tac Tor into the Vale of Evander and beyond, then turned into a trail which led up a steep gulch. Back and forth wound the trail, among tumbled rocks, alder thickets, brambles and brakes of thistle, with a small river gushing and gurgling always near at hand. After a mile, the trail left the river to climb the hillside, traversing back, forth, back, forth, to emerge at last on the upper face of a spur.

The company rested for a space, then continued: up the hump of the spur, across barrens of scree, through dells shaded under cedars and pines, along ridges with windy spaces to either side, then once more back against the base mass of the Teach tac Teach, to climb by laborious slants and switch-backs, to come out at last upon the high moors, to find the sun already behind the western cloud-banks. In the shelter of thirteen tall dolmens, the company made camp for the night.

In the morning, the sun rose red in the east, while a wind from the west sent low clouds streaming across the moor. The company of adventurers huddled close around the fire, each thinking his own thoughts and toasting bacon on a spit, while porridge bubbled in the pot. The horses were brought up and saddled; the party, bending low to the chill wind, set off across the moor. Crags of the Teach tac Teach, rearing high, one after the other in lonely isolation, dwindled away to right and left. Ahead rose Mount Sobh.

The trail had now disappeared; the company rode across the open moor, around the flanks of Mount Sobh, down through a stand of stunted pines to where a sudden panorama burst open before them: ridges and slopes, dark valleys choked with conifers, then the low moors and a nondescript murk, where vision could no longer penetrate the distance.

From somewhere a trail had once again appeared, slanting down the slope and into a forest of pines and cedars.

Something white glimmered ahead. The company, approaching, discovered the skull of an elk nailed to the trunk of a pine tree. At this point Tern pulled up his horse.

Cory rode up beside him. 'What now?'

'I go no farther,' said Tern. 'Behind the tree hangs a brass horn; blow three blasts and wait.'

Cory paid him in silver coins. 'You have guided us well; good luck to you.'

Tern turned about and departed, leading his two pack-horses.

Cory surveyed his company. 'Este of Rome! You are

281

accounted a musician of sorts! Find the horn and send three good blasts ringing down the valley!'

Este dismounted and approached the tree, where he found a brass horn of three coils hanging on a peg. He put it to his lips and blew three sweet strong tones which seemed to echo on and on.

Ten minutes passed. Travec sat his dun hammer-headed horse to the side, apart from the others. He muttered: 'Voner! Skel! Do you hear me?'

'Naturally we hear you, quite as well as need be.'

'Are you aware of this place?'

'It is a great up-fold in the mother-stuff of the world. A scurf of vegetation shades the sky. Three furtive scoundrels peer at us from the shadows.'

'What of the green seep from Mel?'

'Nothing of consequence,' said Voner. 'A wisp from yonder declivity, no more.'

'Not enough to excite our interest,' said Skel.

Travec said: 'Still, after this, alert me to any green taint whatever, since it might indicate a node of green.'

'Just as you say. Should we make ourselves known and destroy yonder stuff?'

'Not yet. We must learn more of where and how it arises.'

'As you like.'

Behind Travec spoke a rasping voice; turning, Travec looked into the face of Kegan the Celt. 'How gratifying must be the comfort of these intimate conversations with yourself!'

'I repeat my lucky slogans; what of that?'

'Nothing whatever,' said Kegan. 'I have foolish quirks of my own. I can never kill a woman without first uttering a prayer to the goddess Quincubile.'

'That is only sensible. I see that Este's blasts have brought response.'

From the forest came a yellow-haired yellow-bearded man, tall and massive, wearing a tricorn iron helmet, a chain shirt and black leather trousers. At his girdle hung three swords, of varying length. He called out to Cory in a great windy voice: 'Name your names and explain why you have sounded the horn.'

'I am Cory of Falonges; I have been sent by a person of high rank to take counsel with Torqual. This is my company; the names will mean nothing to you.'

'Does Torqual know of your coming?'

'I cannot say. It is possible.'

'Follow behind me. Do not stray off the trail by so much as two yards measurement.'

The company rode single-file along a narrow track which led first through a dense forest, then along a barren mountainside, then up a gorge to a small stony flat, thence up a narrow spine of rock, with a steep declivity at either side, to come out at last upon a small meadow hard under a cliff. An ancient fortress, half in ruins commanded the approach. 'You stand on Neep Meadow, and there is High Coram Keep,' said the blond outlaw. 'You may dismount and either stand to wait, or rest upon yonder benches. I will tell Torqual of your coming.' He disappeared into the tumbled recesses of the old castle.

Travec dismounted with the others and looked about the meadow. Under the cliff several dozen rude huts had been laid up of stone and sod: here, presumably, were housed Torqual's followers. Within the huts Travec glimpsed a number of bedraggled women and several children playing in the dirt. To the side an oven for the baking of bread had been built of rough bricks, which apparently had been formed of meadow clay fired on the spot in open fires.

Travec went to look down Glen Dagach, which dropped

steeply to open at last upon the lower moors. He spoke under his breath: 'Voner! Skel! What of the green?'

'I notice a suffusion centered in the castle,' said Voner.

Skel added: 'A tendril leads elsewhere.'

'Can you see its source?'

'No.'

'Are there other nodes of green?'

'There is such a node in Swer Smod; no others are obvious.'

From the castle came Torqual, wearing the black garments of a Ska nobleman. He approached the newcomers. Cory stepped forward. 'Torqual, I am Cory of Falonges.'

'I know your reputation. You have scoured the Troagh like a ravening wolf, or so it is said. Who are these others?'

Cory made an indifferent gesture. 'They are talented villains, and each is unique. That one is Kegan the Celt. That is Este the Sweet, who might be the Roman he claims to be. There stands Travec the Dacian; there Galgus the Daut, and that misshapen wad of pure evil yonder is Izmael the Hun. They know two motivations only: fear and avarice.'

'That is all they need to know,' said Torqual. 'Any other I distrust. What is your errand?'

Cory took Torqual aside. Travec went to sit on the bench. He whispered: 'Voner! Skel! Torqual and Cory speak together; bring me their conversation, but to my ears alone, so that no one will know that I listen.'

Skel said: 'It is boring and inconsequential chatter; they talk of this and that.'

'Still, I wish to hear.'

'Whatever you like.'

Into Travec's ear came Torqual's voice: ' . . . sent no funds for my account?'

'Fifteen gold coins only,' spoke Cory. 'Travec also

284

brought funds from Casmir: ten gold crowns, but said they were for the company. Perhaps they were intended for you. Here! Take the lot!'

'It is a pittance!' said Torqual in disgust. 'This is Casmir's careful scheme: he thinks to divert me from my own plans so that I should work in accordance with his.'

'Does he know your plans?'

'Perhaps he guesses.' Torqual turned and looked off down Glen Dagach. 'I have made no great secret of them.'

'Out of curiosity, then, what might be your plans?'

Torqual said tonelessly: 'I will take command of these mountains, through devastation and terror. Then I will conquer both Ulflands, North and South. I will rally the Ska once more to war. First we take Godelia, then Dahaut, and next all the Elder Isles. Then we attack the world. There never shall be such a conquest nor so wide an empire! That is my scheme. But now I must grovel to Casmir for men and weapons to take me through these arduous first times.'

Cory spoke in a subdued voice. 'Your plan has, if nothing else, the merit of grandeur.'

Torqual said indifferently: 'It is something which can be done. Hence, it must be done.'

'The odds would seem to be against you.'

'Such odds are difficult to compute. They can fluctuate overnight. Aillas is my foremost and worst enemy. He would seem formidable, with his army and his navy, but he is insensitive; he ignores Ulfish rancor against his Troice regime. The barons grudge him their every submission; many would revolt at a moment's notice.'

'And you would lead them?'

'It is necessary. Left to themselves they are a proud and quarrelsome rabble; they grumble because Aillas has checked their feuds! Ha! When at last I lead them they will know the meaning of Ska discipline! Compared to me, Aillas will seem an angel of mercy!'

Cory gave a non-committal grunt. 'My assignment is to assassinate Aillas. I command five murderers who will work for the joy of it – though all hope to be paid.'

'That is a joke,' said Torqual. 'Casmir rewards his faithful servants with the twist of a noose. He bestows few boons after the deed is done.'

Cory nodded. 'If I am as successful as I hope, I can control Casmir nicely by holding Prince Dhrun as a captive. For the moment, at least, our interests run parallel. I hope, therefore, that you will give me counsel and cooperation.'

Torqual brooded for a moment, then asked: 'How do you propose to act?'

'I am a careful man. I will spy out Aillas' movements. I will learn where he eats, sleeps and rides his horse; whether he uses a paramour or enjoys solitude, and the same for Dhrun. When I discover a pattern or an opportunity, I shall do my work.'

'That is a methodical plan,' said Torqual. 'Still, it will require much time and effort, and might well provoke suspicion. I can suggest a more immediate opportunity.'

'I will be glad to hear it.'

'Tomorrow I set off on a rich expedition. The town Willow Wyngate is guarded by Green Willow Castle. Lord Minch, his sons and his knights, have journeyed to Doun Darric; there they will greet King Aillas who has only just returned from abroad. The way is not far: only twenty miles and they think the castle secure in their absence. They are wrong; we will take Green Willow Castle and loot the town as well. Now then! Aillas and Lord Minch will be notified that Green Willow is under attack; they will instantly ride to its relief. This may be your opportunity, since the route provides scope for ambush. A single arrow and Aillas is dead.'

'What of Prince Dhrun?'

'This is the charm of the situation. Dhrun fell from a horse and broke a rib; he will stay at Doun Darric. If you ride at speed from your ambush, you may be able to take Dhrun as well.'

'It is a bold thought.'

'I will assign you a scout. He will show you where to lay your ambush and then lead you to Doun Darric. He knows also where Dhrun is lodged.'

Cory pulled at his chin. 'If all goes well, both of us profit – to our mutual benefit and perhaps to our continued association.'

Torqual nodded. 'So it may be. We depart tomorrow afternoon, so that we may attack Green Willow at dawn.' He looked at the sky. 'Clouds are sweeping in from the sea and soon rain will be blowing across Neep Meadow. You may bring your men into the keep to sleep by the fireplace.'

Cory returned to where his company waited. He said weightily: 'I now will explain our venture. We are to put an arrow into King Aillas.'

Este said with a small smile: 'This news is no surprise.'

Galgus said gruffly: 'What is the plan? We expect to take risks, but we are alive today because we season daring with caution.'

'Well spoken,' said Travec. 'I am not eager to die along these dank moors.'

'If anything, I am even less eager than you,' said Cory. 'The plan bodes well. We strike in stealth from ambush, then flee like wild birds to escape our punishment.'

'That is sensible procedure,' said Izmael. 'On the steppe it is our native custom.'

'At this moment you may put up the horses and bring your gear into the castle, where we will sleep by the fireplace. There I will explain further details of the plan.'

Travec took his hammer-headed horse to the stables, and lingered a moment after the others were gone. He whispered: 'Skel! You must carry a message!'

'Cannot it be delayed? Both Voner and I are fatigued with all this moil. We were planning to spend an hour or so tracing out illusions.'

'You must wait until after your task is done. Go instantly to the town Doun Darric, which lies northwest of this place. Seek out King Aillas, and without delay give him the following message . . .'

IV

During the late afternoon veils of rain drifted up Glen Dagach, and presently slanted into Old Neep Meadow. Cory and his company gathered in the great hall of the ancient castle, where flames roared high in the fireplace to cast a ruddy light around the room. They were served a supper of bread, cheese, a pot of venison stew and a leather sack of tart red wine.

After the meal the group became restless. Galgus brought out his dice, but no one cared to gamble. Kegan, from sheer boredom, looked into a dusty chamber under the old staircase, where he noticed, beneath the detritus of uncounted years, a cupboard of desiccated wood. He scraped away the trash and opened the warped doors, but in the dim light saw only empty shelves. As he turned away, his eye fell upon a shape at the back of the lowest shelf. He reached down and extricated an oblong box. The box was large and heavy, and joined of dense cedar heartwood.

Kegan carried the box out to the table in front of the fireplace and while his comrades looked on, he pried open the lid. Everyone peered down at the object inside: a carefully carved fabrication of soapstone slabs and other pieces, stained black, and decorated with a hundred elaborations carved from onyx, jet and agate. Cory came to look. 'It is a little catafalque, in the ancient style – a miniature, or a model, or perhaps a toy.' He reached to lift it from the box, but Kegan seized his arm. 'Stop! It may be a bewitchment, or a cursed object! Let no one touch the thing!'

Torqual came into the hall, followed by a slender dark-haired woman of extreme beauty.

Cory called Torqual's attention to the miniature catafalque. 'What do you know of this? Kegan found it under the staircase.'

Torqual frowned down into the box. 'It means nothing to me.'

Este said: 'In some fashionable house of Rome this object might well be used as a high-style salt cellar.'

'It may be a shrine to someone's favorite cat,' suggested Galgus the Daut. 'In Falu Ffail, King Audry clothes his spaniels in trousers of purple velvet.'

'Put it aside,' said Torqual brusquely. 'Such things are best not disturbed.' He turned to the woman. 'Melancthe, this is Cory of Falonges and these are his associates. I have forgotten their names, but this is a Hun, that a Roman, that a Celt, over there a Daut, and that creature, half hawk, half wolf, declares himself a Dacian. What is your opinion of the group? Do not be afraid to speak your mind; they are devoid of illusions.'

'They do not concern me.' Melancthe went to sit alone at the end of the table where she stared into the fire.

Travec whispered: 'Voner! What do you see?'

'There is green in the woman. A tendril touches her; it darts so swift and sudden that I cannot trace it.'

'What does that mean? Is she a node of force?'

289

'She is a shell.'

Travec watched her a moment. She raised her head, looked around the room with brows knit. Travec averted his eyes. He whispered: 'What then? Did she sense my presence?'

'She is uneasy, but she does not know why. Do not stare at her.'

'Why not?' muttered Travec. 'Everyone else is doing so. She is the world's most beautiful woman.'

'I do not understand such things.'

Presently Melancthe left the room. Torqual and Cory conferred apart for half an hour, then Torqual departed as well.

'What now?' demanded Galgus. 'It is too early to sleep and the wine is vile. Who will game at dice?'

Este had gone to look into the cedar box. He said, 'Rather, who will raise the cover on this toy catafalque to see what lies within?'

'Not I,' said Galgus.

'Do not touch the thing,' said Izmael the Hun. 'You will bring a curse down upon the company.'

'Not so,' said Este. 'It is clearly a macabre joke in the form of a jewel box and may well be brimming with sapphires and emeralds.'

Kegan's interest was aroused. 'That is reasonable. Maybe I will take one little peek, just to make sure.'

Galgus looked toward Travec: 'And what are you saying to yourself this time, Travec?'

'I chant my spell against death-magic,' said Travec.

'Ah bah, it is nothing! Go to it, Kegan! A glimpse only; no harm can come of it!'

With one long yellow thumb-nail Kegan lifted the soapstone lid. He bent his head, so that his thin crooked nose almost entered the crack, and peered within. Then slowly he drew back and lowered the lid.

Cory demanded: 'Well then, Kegan! Do not keep us in suspense! What did you see?'

'Nothing.'

'So why all the drama?'

'It is a fine toy,' said Kegan. 'I will carry it upon my horse and take it away, as my little keepsake.'

Cory gave him a wondering stare. 'As you like.'

At noon of the following day the two companies departed Neep Meadow and rode down Glen Dagach. Where glen opened upon low moor, the parties separated. Cory, the five in his company, and the guide: a sallow sly-eyed stripling named Idis struck off to the northwest to arrange their ambush. Torqual, with his thirty-five warriors, continued westward toward Willow Wyngate. For two hours they waited in the shelter of a forest, then at dusk continued along the road: down over the low moors and into the valley of the river Wirl.

The company rode at a carefully regulated pace, so that, just as the first light of dawn brought substance to the land, the troop entered the park surrounding Castle Green Willow and rode along the stately entry drive, between parallel lines of poplar trees.

The troop rounded a bend, to halt in consternation. A dozen knights, mounted on chargers, blocked the road, lances at the ready.

The knights charged. The bandits turned in confusion to flee, but a similar group of knights blocked the road to the rear. And now, from behind the poplars, stepped archers, to pour volley after volley into the screaming outlaws. Torqual on the instant turned his horse to the side, burst through a gap in the poplars and crouching low, galloped like a madman across the countryside. Sir Minch, who commanded the troop, sent off ten men in pursuit, with orders to track Torqual to the ends of the world, if necessary. Those few outlaws who still survived he condemned to death on the spot, to save the toil of as many hangings. Swords were raised; swords fell; heads rolled, and Torqual's troop and his dreams of empire were at the same time dissolved.

The ten warriors pursued Torqual up Glen Dagach, where he rolled rocks down upon them, killing two. When the others arrived upon Old Neep Meadow, they found only the serving women and a few small children. Torqual and Melancthe had already fled by secret ways up toward the high moors and the chasms at the back of Mount Sobh. At this time there was no point in further pursuit, even though Mount Sobh was not yet the ends of the world.

V

At Lyonesse Town all was in flux, what with King Milo, Queen Caudabil, and Prince Brezante due to arrive for a three-day visit, and a festival suddenly ordained in their honor.

The festival had been conceived by King Casmir, after his hopes for an advantageous betrothal had gone glimmering. His enthusiasm for the visit had cooled, and he was especially reluctant to entertain his guests at a succession of long, bibulous banquets where King Milo, a noteworthy trencherman, and Queen Caudabil, only slightly less redoubtable, regaled themselves upon course after course of fine viands and great quantities of Castle Haidion's best wines. King Casmir therefore proclaimed a festival at which there would be all manner of sports, games and competitions in honor of the royal visitors: the high kick, the broad vault, foot races, wrestling, throwing the stone, sparring with padded staves on a plank over a mud pit, which would also be used at tug-of-war trials. There would be dancing of jigs, lilts and rounds to music; bull-baiting, an archery contest and jousting with buffed lances. The program was arranged so that King Milo and Queen Caudabil were constantly occupied, listening to panegyrics, judging contests, awarding prizes and applauding winners, consoling losers and granting awards. To all of these events, King Milo and Queen Caudabil, as royal sponsors, must give their keen attention, leaving no time for long and lavish feasts, at which King Milo might test his prodigious capacity for wine. The two instead must hurriedly nourish themselves at collations of cold ham, bread and cheese, with flagons of stout ale to wash down the hearty and inexpensive fare.

King Casmir was pleased with his stratagem. He would be spared endless hours of utter boredom; further, the festival would demonstrate his benevolence and royal jocundity. There was no way he could avoid the welcoming banquet, nor the farewell feast – though the first might be truncated on the pretext of allowing the royal family time to recover from the rigors of the journey. Perhaps the second as well, reflected Casmir, on similar grounds.

Preparations for the festival were at once put into effect, in order that gray old Lyonesse Town might be transformed into a setting for antic frivolity. Bunting was draped and banners raised around the periphery of the King's Parade, and a platform erected for the convenience of the royal families. At the side of the quadrangle, beside the Sfer Arct, a rack would support two great tuns of ale which each morning would be broached for those who wished to salute either King Milo, or King Casmir, or both.

Along the Sfer Arct booths came into existence, for the sale of sausages, fried fish, pork buns, tarts and pastries. Each booth was required to drape its visible sections with gay cloths and ribbons, and shops along the avenue were enjoined to do likewise.

At the appointed hour King Milo, Queen Caudabil and Prince Brezante arrived at Castle Haidion. In the van rode six knights in gleaming dress armor, with black and ocher pennons flying from their lances. Another six knights, similarly accoutered, brought up the rear. In a lumbering unsprung vehicle, more wagon than carriage, King Milo and Queen Caudabil sat on a wide upholstered couch, under a green canopy hung with a hundred decorative tassels. Both Milo and Caudabil were portly, white-haired, round and florid of face, and seemed more like canny old peasants on the way to market than the rulers of an ancient realm. To the side rode Prince Brezante on an enormous bay gelding with a peculiarly large high rump. Perched on this great animal, Brezante, who was plump and pear-shaped, made no gallant first impression. His nose hung from a narrow back-sloping forehead, to droop over his full mouth; his eyes were large, round and unblinking; his black hair was sparse, both on his scalp and at his chin where he entertained a small indecisive beard. Despite all, Brezante fancied himself a cavalier of romantic appeal and took great pains with his garments. He wore a doublet of russet fustian, with sleeves of puff-pleated black and red stuff. A jaunty red forester's cap sat aslant his head, with a raven's wing for a panache.

The column came down the Sfer Arct. A dozen heralds in scarlet tabards and tight yellow hose stood six to each side of the way. As the carriage passed, they tilted their clarions to the sky and sounded a welcoming fanfare.

The carriage turned from the Sfer Arct, into the King's Parade and halted before Castle Haidion. King Casmir, Queen Sollace and Princess Madouc stood waiting on the terrace. King Casmir raised his arm in amiable greeting;

King Milo responded in kind, as did Prince Brezante, after a glance toward Madouc, and so the royal visit began.

At the evening banquet, Madouc's protests went unheeded and she was required to sit with Prince Brezante at her left and Damar, Duke of Lalanq, to her right. During the meal, Madouc sat staring straight ahead at the fruit centerpiece, seemingly unaware of Brezante, who never gave off peering at her with his round black eyes. Madouc spoke little, responding to Brezante's facetious sallies with absent-minded monosyllables, to such effect that Brezante at last lapsed into scowls and sulks, to which Madouc was serenely indifferent. From the corner of her eye she noticed that both King Casmir and Queen Sollace pointedly ignored her conduct; apparently they had accepted her point of view, and now, so she hoped, she would be left in peace.

Madouc's triumph was of short duration. On the next morning, the two royal families went down to the pavilion on the King's Parade, that they might witness the beginning of the competitions. Once again Madouc's explanations that she preferred not to join the party went for naught. Lady Vosse, speaking on explicit behalf of Queen Sollace, declared that Madouc must participate in the ceremonies, and without fail. Scowling and fretting, Madouc marched to the pavilion and plumped herself down beside Queen Caudabil, in the chair intended for King Milo, so that Milo sat at Caudabil's other side and Brezante was forced to take himself to the far end of the platform, beside King Casmir. Again Madouc was pleased, if somewhat mystified, by the lack of response from King Casmir and Queen Sollace to her self-willed conduct. What was in the wind, to cause them such portentous restraint?

The answer to her question was not long in coming. Almost as soon as the royal party had been seated,

Spargoy the Chief Herald, stepped to the front of the platform, to face the crowds which filled the quadrangle. A pair of young heralds sounded that fanfare known as 'Call to Attention!', and the folk in the King's Parade became silent.

Spargoy unrolled a scroll. 'I do accurately read and recite the words of that proclamation issued on this day by His Royal Majesty, King Casmir. Let all give full heed to the import of these words. I now begin.' Spargoy opened the scroll and read.

'"I, King Casmir, Monarch of Lyonesse, its several territories and provinces, declare in this fashion:

'"At Lyonesse Town rises an edifice of exalted condition: the new Cathedral of Sollace Sanctissima, destined to become far-famed for the richness of its appurtenances. That it may best fulfill its function, the premises must be endowed with those articles deemed holy and worshipful in themselves: namely those rare and precious relics, or other objects associated with past exemplars of the Christian faith.

'"We are told that these relics are worthy of our acquisition; hence, we are now prepared to offer our royal gratitude to such persons who endow us with good and holy relics, that we may make our new cathedral preeminent among all others.

'"Our gratitude is contingent upon truth and authenticity. A factitious object will excite not only our royal displeasure, but will incur the frightful processes of divine wrath! So let all who are tempted to knavery: beware!

'"Especially joyful to our hearts will be the Cross of Saint Elric, the Talisman of Saint Uldine, the Sacred Nail, and – most cherished of all – that chalice known as the Holy Grail. The rewards shall match the worth of the relic; whosoever brings us the Holy Grail may ask of us any boon his heart desires, up to and including the most precious treasure of the kingdom: the hand of the Princess Madouc in marriage. In the absence of the Grail, whoever brings us the relic otherwise most holy and sublime, he may demand of us as he likes, including the hand of our beautiful and gracious Princess Madouc in marriage, after an appropriate and seemly betrothal.

'"I address this proclamation to all who have ears to hear and strength to pursue the quest! From every land, from high to low; none shall be dismissed by reason of place, age or rank. Let all persons of bravery and enterprise go forth to seek the Grail, or such other holy objects accessible to acquisition, for the glory of the Cathedral of Sollace Sanctissima!

'"So say I, King Casmir of Lyonesse; let my words resound in all ears!"'

The clarions sounded; Sir Spargoy rolled up the scroll and retired.

Madouc heard the proclamation with astonishment. What new nonsense was this? Must her name and physical attributes, or their lack, now be bandied about the land, and discussed by every starveling knight, addle-pate, mooncalf, varlet and cock-a-hoop bravo of the realm and elsewhere? The scope of the edict left her speechless. She sat stiff and still, conscious nonetheless of the many eyes which scrutinized her. A scandal and an outrage! thought Madouc. Why had she not been consulted?

Sir Spargoy meanwhile had gone on to introduce King Milo and Queen Caudabil, whom he described as patron and patroness of the festival, the judges of all competitions and the sponsors of all prizes. At this information, both King Milo and Queen Caudabil stirred uneasily in their seats.

The competitions began. King Casmir watched a few moments, then unobtrusively departed the pavilion by the stairs which led up to the terrace, followed a moment later by Prince Brezante. Madouc, observing that no attention was being paid to her, did the same. Arriving upon the terrace, she found Brezante leaning on the balustrade, looking down at the activity in the Parade.

Brezante by this time had learned of Madouc's refusal to consider his suit. He spoke to her in a voice subtly mocking: 'Well then, Princess! It seems that you will be married after all! I here and now congratulate this still unknown champion, whoever he may be! You will live henceforth in delicious suspense. Eh, then? Am I correct?'

Madouc replied in a soft voice: 'Sir, your ideas are incorrect in every possible respect.'

Brezante drew back with eyebrows raised high. 'Still, are you not excited that so many persons, both noble knights and callow squires, will go forth on quests that they may claim you in wedlock?'

'If anything, I am saddened that so many folk will strive in vain.'

Prince Brezante asked in perplexity: 'What does that remark mean?'

'It means what I say it means.'

'Ha,' muttered Brezante. 'Somewhere I detect an ambiguity.'

Madouc shrugged and turned away. Making sure that Brezante did not follow, she circled the front of the castle to the beginning of the cloistered walk and there turned aside into the orangery. In a far corner she secluded herself and sprawled out in the sunlight, chewing on grass.

At last she sat up. It was hard to think so many thoughts and reach so many decisions at the same time.

First things first. She hoisted herself to her feet and brushed the grass from her gown. Returning into the castle, she took herself to the queen's parlor.

Sollace had also excused herself from the platform, pleading urgent consultations. She had gone to her parlor,

298

where she had fallen into a doze. Upon Madouc's entrance, she looked about, blinking out from among the cushions. 'What is it now?'

'Your Majesty, I am disturbed by the king's proclamation.'

Queen Sollace was still somewhat torpid and her thoughts came sluggishly. 'I fail to grasp your concern. Every cathedral of note is famous for the excellence of its relics.'

'So it may be. Still, I hope that you will intercede with the king, so that my hand in marriage is not one of the boons which might be conferred. I would not like to be traded away for somebody's old shoe, or a tooth, or some such oddment.'

Sollace said stiffly: 'I am powerless to effect such changes. The king has carefully considered his policy.'

Madouc scowled. 'At the very least, I should have been consulted. I am not interested in marriage. It seems in certain ways both vulgar and untidy.'

Queen Sollace posited herself higher among the cushions. 'As you must know, I am married to His Majesty the King. Do you consider me "vulgar and untidy"?'

Madouc pursed her lips. 'I can only speculate that, as a queen, you are exempt from such judgments. That would be my best guess.'

Queen Sollace, half-amused, sank back into the cushions. 'In due course you will understand these matters with greater lucidity.'

'All this to the side,' cried Madouc, 'it is unthinkable that I should marry some witling, merely because he brings you a nail! For all we know he has just found it behind the stable.'

'Most unlikely! The criminal would not dare a divine fulmination. I am told by Father Umphred that a special level in Hell is set apart for those who falsify relics. In any case, it is a chance we must take.'

'Bah!' muttered Madouc. 'The plan is absurd.'

The queen again raised herself up. 'I failed to hear your remark.'

'It was of no consequence.'

The queen gave a stately nod. 'In any case, you must obey the king's ordinance, and to the exact degree.'

'Yes, Your Highness!' said Madouc with sudden energy. 'I shall do precisely that! Please excuse me; at this very instant I must make my preparations.'

Madouc curtsied, turned and left the chamber. Sollace looked after her in wonder. 'What does she mean by "preparations"? Marriage is not so imminent as all that. How, in any event, would she think to prepare herself?'

VI

Maduoc ran at a brisk half-trot along the main gallery: past statues of ancient heroes, urns taller than herself, alcoves furnished with ornate tables and tall-backed chairs. At intervals, men-at-arms in the scarlet and gold livery of Haidion stood with halberds at parade-rest. Only their eyes moved to follow Madouc as she passed them by.

At a pair of tall narrow doors Madouc stopped short. She hesitated, then, pushing open one of the doors, peered through the gap into a long dim chamber illuminated by a single narrow window in the far wall. This was the castle library. A shaft of light slanted down across a table; here sat Kerce the librarian, a man of advanced years though still tall and erect, with a gentle mouth and a dreamer's forehead in a face otherwise austere. Madouc knew little of Kerce save that he was said to be the son of an Irish druithine, and a poet in his own right.

After a single side-glance toward the door, Kerce continued with his work. Madouc came slowly into the room. The air carried an aromatic reek, of old wood, wax, lavender oil, the soft sweet fusk of well-tanned leather. Tables to left and right supported librams two or three feet on a side and three inches thick, bound in limp leather or sometimes heavy black felt. Shelves were crammed with scrolls, parchments in cedar boxes, papers tied in bundles, books clamped between carefully-tooled boards of beechwood.

Madouc approached Kerce, step by demure step. At last he straightened in his chair, turned his head to watch her approach, and not without a trace of dubious speculation, for Madouc's repute had penetrated even the far fastnesses of the library.

Madouc stopped beside the table, and looked down at the manuscript upon which Kerce had been working. She asked: 'What are you doing?'

Kerce looked critically down at the parchment. 'Two hundred years ago some nameless lout covered over this page with a paste of powdered chalk mixed with sour milk and seaweed gum. Then he attempted to indite the Morning Ode of Merosthenes, addressed to the nymph Laloe, upon his discovery of her one summer dawn plucking pomegranates in his orchard. The lout copied without care and his characters, as you see, are like bird-droppings. I expunge his scrawl and dissolve his vile compost, but delicately, since below there may be as many as five other layers of ever older and ever more enthralling mysteries. Or, to my sorrow, I might find more ineptitude. Still, I must examine each in turn. Who knows? I might uncover one of Jirolamo's lost cantos. So there you have it: I am an explorer of ancient mysteries; such is my profession and my great adventure.'

Madouc examined the manuscript with new interest. 'I had no idea you lived so exciting a life!'

Kerce spoke gravely: 'I am intrepid and I defy every challenge! I scratch at this surface with the delicacy of a surgeon cutting the carbuncle of an angry king! But my hand is deft and my tools are true! See them, loyal comrades all: my stout badger-tail brush, my faithful oil of limpet, my obsidian edge and dangerous bone needles, my trusty range-wood rubsticks! They are all paladins who have served me well! Together we have made far voyages and visited unknown lands!'

'And always you return safe and sound!'

Kerce turned her a quizzical glance, one eyebrow arched high, the other in a crooked twist. 'I wonder what you mean by that.'

Madouc laughed. 'You are the second today to ask me such a question.'

'And what was your response?'

'I told him that my words meant what I said they meant.'

'You have odd quirks in your mind for one so young.' Kerce turned in his seat and gave her his full attention. 'And what brings you here? Is it caprice, or the work of Destiny?'

Madouc said soberly: 'I have a question which I hope you will answer.'

'Ask away; I will lay out all my lore for your inspection.'

'There has been much talk of relics here at Haidion. I have become curious about what they call the "Holy Grail". Is there indeed such a thing? If so, what does it look like, and where might it be found?'

'Of the "Holy Grail" I can tell you only a few bare facts,' said Kerce. 'While I know of a hundred religions, I give credence to none. The "Grail" is reputedly the chalice used by Jesus Christos when last he dined with his disciples. The chalice came into the hands of Joseph of Arimathea, who, so it is said, caught blood in the chalice from the wounds of the crucified Christ. Subsequently, Joseph wandered across the world and at last visited Ireland, where he left the Grail on Isle Inchagoill in Lough Corrib north of Galway. A band of heathen Celts threatened the island chapel, and a monk named Father Sisembert brought the chalice to the Elder Isles, and from this point onward the stories go at variance. According to one account the chalice is buried in crypts on Weamish Isle. Another reports that as Father Sisembert passed through the Forest of Tantrevalles, he met a dreadful ogre, who put him to evil uses, claiming that Father Sisembert had neglected courtesy. One of the ogre's three heads drank Sisimbert's blood; another ate his liver: the third head suffered from toothache and, lacking appetite, made dice of Sisimbert's knuckles. But perhaps that is only a story to be told around the fire on stormy nights.'

'And who would know the truth?'

Kerce made a pensive gesture. 'Who can say? Perhaps in the end it is all no more than legend. Many knights of chivalry have sought the Grail across the length and breadth of Christendom, and many have wandered the Elder Isles on the quest. Some departed forlorn; others died in combat or suffered bewitchment; others disappeared and have been seen no more. In truth, it seems mortal peril to seek the Grail!'

'Why should that be – unless somewhere it is guarded with great jealousy?'

'As to that, I cannot say. And never forget that in the end, the quest may only be the pursuit of an ideal dream!'

'Do you believe so?'

'I have no beliefs in this regard, nor in many another. Why are you concerned?'

'Queen Sollace wants to grace her new cathedral with the Holy Grail. She has gone so far as to offer me in marriage to whomever brings her this object! My own wishes, needless to say, were not consulted.'

Kerce gave a dry chuckle. 'I begin to understand your interest!'

'If I myself found the Grail, then I would be safe from such an annoyance.'

'So it would seem – still, the Grail may no longer exist.'

'If such is the case, a false Grail might be offered the queen. She would not know the difference.'

'But I would,' said Kerce. 'The ploy would not succeed; I can assure you of this!'

Madouc looked at him sidewise. 'How can you be so sure?'

Kerce compressed his lips, as if he had said more than he might have wished. 'It is a secret. I will share it with you, if you hold it tightly to yourself.'

'I promise.'

Kerce rose to his feet and went to a cupboard. He removed a portfolio, extracted a drawing which he brought to the table. Madouc saw depicted a footed pale blue chalice eight inches tall, with handles at either side, slightly irregular. A dark blue band encircled the top rim; the base showed a ring of the same dark blue color.

'This is a drawing of the Grail. It was sent from Ireland to the monastery on Weamish Isle long ago, and rescued from the Goths by one of the monks. It is a true depiction, exact even to this nick in the base, and the differing length of the handles.' Kerce returned drawing and portfolio to the cupboard. 'Now you know what there is to be known of the Grail. I prefer to keep the drawing secret, for several reasons.'

'I will keep silent,' said Madouc. 'Unless the queen tries to marry me to someone who brings her a false Grail; then, if all else fails – '

Kerce waved his hand. 'Say no more. I will make a true and accurate copy of the drawing, which may be used for attestation, if any such is needed.'

Madouc departed the library; then, taking pains to go unobserved, she went around to the stables. Sir Pom-pom was nowhere in evidence. Madouc looked in on Tyfer and rubbed his nose, then returned to the castle.

At noon Madouc dined in the Small Refectory with her six maids-in-waiting. Today they were unusually voluble, for there was much to discuss. King Casmir's proclamation, however, came to dominate the conversation. Elissia remarked, perhaps with sincerity, that Madouc must now be considered a famous person, whose name would resound down centuries to come. 'Think of it!' sighed Elissia. 'Here is the sheer stuff of glamor! Legends will tell how handsome knights from far and near dared fire, ice, dragon and troll; how they fought crazed Celt and fierce Goth, all for love of the beautiful red-haired princess!'

Madouc offered a small correction. 'My hair is not precisely red. It is a most unusual color, as of copper alloyed with gold.'

Chlodys said: 'Nevertheless, for purposes of the legend, you will be considered red-haired and beautiful, with no regard whatever for the truth.'

Devonet made a thoughtful comment. 'As of now, we cannot be absolutely sure that this legend will come to pass.'

'How so?' asked Ydraint.

'Much depends upon circumstances. Assume that some valiant and handsome knight brings the Holy Grail to Queen Sollace. King Casmir asks as to what boon the brave knight desires. At this point events hang in the balance. If he decides that he is disinclined for marriage, he might ask the king for a fine horse or a pair of good hunting dogs – which of course provides small scope for a legend.'

Chlodys said sagaciously: 'It is a chancy situation.'

Felice spoke. 'Another matter! It is the best relic which wins the boon! So that after great efforts and far quests, the best relic brought to the queen might be, let us say, a hair from the tail of the lion who ate Saint Milicia in the Roman arena. Poor stuff, of course, but Madouc must still marry the lummox who submits such an article.'

Madouc tossed her head. 'I am not so pliable as you might like to think.'

Devonet spoke with grave concern. 'I will counsel you! Be meek, modest and patient! Yield gracefully to the king's commands! It is not only your duty; it is also the way of prudence. That is my reasoned advice.'

Madouc listened with no great attention. 'Naturally, you must do as you think proper.'

'One word more! The king has declared that if you cark or pout, or attempt to avoid his fiat, he will simply give you off into servitude!'

Chlodys turned to Madouc, who sat stolidly eating raisin pudding. 'And what do you say to that?'

'Nothing.'

'But what will you do?'

'You shall see.'

VII

On the second day of the festival King Milo and Queen Caudabil were aroused early from their beds and allowed only a quick breakfast of curds and groats so that they might be on hand to call out the start to the tug-of-war between the members of the Fishmonger's Guild and the Stonemason's Guild.

Madouc was also up early, before Lady Vosse could communicate the wishes of Queen Sollace.

Madouc went directly out to the stables. This fine bright morning she found Sir Pom-pom forking manure from the stalls into a barrow. 'Sir Pom-pom!' called Madouc. 'Step outside, if you please, where the air is less thick.'

'You must wait your turn,' said Sir Pom-pom. 'The barrow is full and I must wheel it out to the dung-heap. Then I will be able to give you a moment or two.'

Madouc compressed her lips but waited in silence until Sir Pom-pom, with measured deliberation, put aside the barrow and came out into the stable yard. 'Whatever your whims, you may no longer count upon me for their fulfillment,' said Sir Pom-pom.

Madouc spoke severely: 'Your conduct seems surly and gruff! I would not like to think you a boor. Why do you speak so brusquely?'

Sir Pom-pom gave a bark of curt laughter. 'Hah! It is simple enough. Have you not heard the king's proclamation?'

'I have indeed.'

'I have heard it as well. Tomorrow I relinquish my post as royal stable attendant and lackey to the princess. On the following day I will seize time by the forelock and go

307

in search of the "Holy Grail", or any other relic I can lay my hands upon. It may well be the opportunity of my lifetime.'

Madouc gave a slow nod. 'I understand your ambition. But is it not sad that you must give up your good and secure employment to go out chasing a will-o'-the-wisp? To me it seems an act of reckless folly.'

'So it may be,' said Sir Pom-pom doggedly. 'Still, such chances for fame and fortune come rarely. One must grasp them as they pass.'

'Quite so. Still, I might help you have the best of both worlds were you to moderate your churlish behavior.'

Sir Pom-pom looked around in cautious interest. 'How so and to what degree?'

'You must swear to hold secret what I am about to tell you.'

'Hm. Will this secret involve me in trouble?'

'I think not.'

'Very well. I will hold my tongue. I have done so before and I suppose I can do so again.'

'Listen then! The king has ordered me to go forth in search of my pedigree, and without delay. Admittedly he was in a state of exasperation when he spoke, but his orders were explicit, and included the service of a suitable escort. Therefore, I command that you serve me in this capacity. If you obey, you will retain your employment and still be able to seek the Holy Grail.'

Sir Pom-pom squinted off into the sunlight. 'The proposition, on the surface, seems reasonable. Still, what if our quests lead in different directions?'

Madouc brushed aside the objection. 'Why borrow trouble? Obviously we cannot anticipate every quirk of Fate before we have even made our preparations.'

Sir Pom-pom put on a stubborn frown. 'I still feel that we should agree on a plan.'

'Tush,' said Madouc. 'More than likely, the question will never arise. If so, we shall deal with it then and there.'

'All this to the side,' growled Sir Pom-pom, 'I would feel easier if I had definite orders from the mouth of the king himself.'

Madouc gave her head a decisive shake. 'I have been granted leave to go, with no restrictions; that is enough. I do not want to re-open the discussion and risk some foolish qualification.'

Sir Pom-pom turned a dubious glance over his shoulder. 'It is true that I have long-standing orders to attend you wherever you ride, and they have never been revoked. If I choose to retain my employment, the king has charged me to follow where you go, and serve you as best I may. When do you wish to depart?'

'Tomorrow morning.'

'Impossible! It is already late in the day; I will not be able to make the preparations!'

'Very well. We will leave on the morning of the day after tomorrow, half an hour before dawn. Have Tyfer saddled and ready, and also a horse for yourself.'

'Now then,' said Sir Pom-pom, 'we must think clearly in this regard. Even though you claim that His Majesty has given you leave to go off on this venture, is it possible that he might have spoken in haste, or that he might change his mind?'

'Anything is possible,' said Madouc haughtily. 'I cannot trouble myself with every swing of the weather-cock.'

'What if he suddenly discovers that his beloved Madouc is missing and sends off his knights and his heralds to bring her back? They would have an easy time of it if you were mounted on the dappled pony Tyfer, with the costly saddle and fringed reins. No, Princess! We must ride as might the children of peasants; our horses must attract no attention;

otherwise we may well be home and in disgrace long before we arrive even so far as Frogmarsh.'

Madouc tried to argue that Tyfer, with his dappled coat, was of a sort to blend among the shadows of a landscape and was hence inconspicuous, but Sir Pom-pom would hear nothing of it. 'I will select the proper mounts; you need think no more on the subject.'

'If that is how it must be, so shall it be,' said Madouc. 'Still, you must pack the saddle-bags well, with bread, cheese, dried fish, raisins, olives and wine. You will obtain these victuals from the royal pantry, which you will enter by crawling through the back window, as you well know through long experience. Bring weapons, or at least a knife to cut cheese and an axe to hew wood. Do you have any questions?'

'What of money? We cannot go skiting the countryside over without good silver coins.'

'I will carry three gold pieces in my wallet. This should amply suffice for our needs.'

'So it should, were we able to spend them.'

'The gold is good round gold, soft and yellow, even though it derived from Shimrod.'

'Of that I have no doubt, but how will you spend such gold? To buy a wisp of hay for the horses? Or a plate of beans for our own nourishment? Who would give us back our proper exchange? They might well take us for thieves and clap us into the nearest dungeon.'

Madouc looked off across the stable yard. 'I had not considered along these lines. What must be done?'

Sir Pom-pom made a wise signal. 'Luckily, I know how to deal with the problem. Fetch here your three gold pieces, as soon as possible.'

'Oh?' Madouc raised her eyebrows in puzzlement. 'What then?'

'It so happens that I need a pair of boots, stout and

310

proper, flared at the knee after the new mode, each with a suitable buckle. I will purchase the boots, which are needful for the journey, and I will pay with a gold piece. The cobbler must provide the exchange in silver and copper, which then we may use for our expenses.'

Madouc glanced at the buskins currently worn by Sir Pom-pom. 'You seem adequately shod.'

'Still, we ride abroad, and must maintain our dignity!'

'What is the cost of these elegant new boots?'

'A silver florin!' blurted Sir Pom-pom in scorn. 'Is it really so much when one demands both style and quality?'

Madouc heaved a sigh. 'I suppose not. What of the other two gold pieces?'

'Have no fear! I will contrive a plan which will serve our purposes! But you must bring me the gold at once, that I may start negotiations!'

'As you wish, but work to good effect! We must leave Haidion before something happens to change our plans!'

Sir Pom-pom, still dubious in regard to the venture, looked around the stable yard. 'Where will be our first destination?'

'First we go to Thripsey Shee.'

Sir Pom-pom drew back in shock and disapproval. 'That is sheer folly! The fairies will give us donkey's ears and turn our feet backwards! This is what befell my grandmother's cousin.'

'Sir Pom-pom, name me the name of my mother.'

'The Princess Suldrun was your mother. That is what we are told, though I, personally, cannot vouch for the case.'

'You are wise not to do so, since my mother is the fairy Twisk who lives at Thripsey Shee.'

Sir Pom-pom gaped at Madouc in wonderment. 'Surely you are not serious!'

'I am serious indeed. I met my mother when last we

ventured into the forest. Remember how I cured your aches and pains? I used a fairy balm.'

'This news is hard to believe,' grumbled Sir Pom-pom. 'Though, for a fact, you are a strange little creature.'

'Believe or disbelieve as you like; we still go first to Thripsey Shee, and there I will take council with my mother.'

Sir Pom-pom scratched his chin. 'I wonder if this mother of yours would know aught of the Holy Grail.'

'It is possible.'

'So be it!' declared Sir Pom-pom with sudden energy. 'I am not one to ignore the call of Destiny!'

'Brave words, Sir Pom-pom! I am of a like mind.'

Sir Pom-pom turned Madouc a sly and waggish grin. 'If I win the boon, I will then be entitled to wed the royal princess!'

Madouc pursed her lips against a smile. 'I do not know about that. But surely you would be received at court, where you could choose a spouse from among my maids-in-waiting.'

'First I must possess myself of the Grail,' said Sir Pom-pom. 'Then I will make my own choice. But as of this moment, fetch the gold, and I will see to my business.'

Madouc ran at speed to her chambers. She brought out the three gold coins from a secret place under her bed and took them to the stables. Sir Pom-pom hefted their weight, examined them on both sides, bit upon them and at last was satisfied. 'Now I must run down into town for my boots. When you make ready, dress as a peasant. You can not safely go abroad as the proud Princess Madouc.'

'Very well! I will meet you at the appointed time. Take care not to get caught in the pantry!'

As Madouc returned to her chambers she was accosted by Lady Vosse, who spoke in sharp tones: 'Where have you been? Are you devoid of all sense of duty?'

Madouc looked up in wonder, mouth innocently adroop. 'What have I done this time?'

'Surely you remember! I instructed you myself! You must remain in attendance upon our guests! That is proper etiquette. It is also the wish of the queen.'

'It is the queen who invited these folk here, not I,' grumbled Madouc. 'Go rouse the queen from her own bed.'

Lady Vosse stood back, momentarily at a loss for words. Then, rallying, she subjected Madouc to an examination, nose drawn up in distaste. 'Your gown is soiled and you reek of horse! I might have known that you were at the stables! Quick then! To your chamber and into something fresh: perhaps your new blue frock. Come now, on the run! There is no time to waste!'

Ten minutes later Madouc and Lady Vosse arrived on the platform, where King Milo and Queen Caudabil were observing the stone-throw competition, though with little attention.

As noon approached, stewards began to set out a collation of cold beef and cheese on a trestle at the back of the platform, so that King Milo and Queen Caudabil could enjoy the sports with no interruption for a fullscale repast. Taking note of these preparations, Milo and Caudabil conferred in low voices, then Milo suddenly clutched his side and set up a hollow groaning.

Queen Caudabil called out to Sir Mungo the Seneschal: 'Alas! King Milo has suffered a seizure! It is his old complaint! We will be unable to enjoy any more games and competitions! He must retire at once to our quarters for rest and proper treatment!'

Once in their chambers, Queen Caudabil ordered in a repast of eight courses and a sufficiency of good wine, which she declared was the best possible tonic for King Milo.

During the middle afternoon Prince Brezante took a message to King Casmir, to the effect that King Milo felt well enough to join King Casmir at the evening banquet, and so it was, with King Casmir and Queen Sollace sitting at table with the now merry Milo and Caudabil until well into the evening.

In the morning King Milo was unable to rise early for fear of a new attack, so that King Casmir and Queen Sollace sat as judges at the foot-races. Meanwhile King Milo and Queen Caudabil took hearty breakfasts and were so improved that they declared themselves ready to sit at a noon banquet of ordinary or even festive proportions, while Sir Mungo and other officials of the court supervised the competitions.

Late in the afternoon all the games and competitions were concluded and it only remained for the champions to be awarded their prizes. The two royal families assembled at one side of the platform; at the other gathered those who had gained victory in the various sports, each now wearing a laurel wreath and showing self-conscious grins to the crowds in the quadrangle.

At last all was in readiness. Madouc found herself seated beside Brezante, whose efforts at conversation were desultory.

Four under-heralds blew a fanfare, and Sir Mungo stepped to the front of the platform. 'This is an auspicious day! Our royal guests from Blaloc regrettably must make their departure tomorrow, but we hope that they have enjoyed to the fullest the superb demonstrations of speed, stamina and skill which our men of Lyonesse have demonstrated over the last three days! I will announce the champions and in each case King Milo will bestow the prize, so well-deserved, so proudly achieved, and so long to be cherished! And now without further ado – ' Sir Mungo raised his hand high in a dramatic gesture. He looked all around, up the Sfer Arct, and his voice went dead in his throat. Slowly his hand sank so that, with a trembling finger, it pointed.

Down the Sfer Arct came a strange conveyance: a large black catafalque borne on the shoulders of four running corpses, which at one time had used the names Izmael the Hun, Este the Sweet, Galgus of Dahaut and Kegan the Celt. On top of the catafalque stood a fifth corpse: the sallow young scout Idis, who now wielded a whip and slashed at the four running cadavers, urging them to their best efforts.

Nearer came the corpses carrying their elaborate burden. With wild sweeps of the whip Idis guided them into the King's Parade, while the affrighted crowds drew back.

In front of the platform the runners tottered and collapsed. The catafalque fell to the stone flags and broke open; out rolled another corpse: Cory of Falonges.

VIII

The royal family of Blaloc took a last breakfast at Haidion in company with King Casmir and Queen Sollace. It was a somber occasion. The two queens made polite conversation, but the two kings had little to say, and Prince Brezante sat moodily silent. Princess Madouc had not appeared for breakfast but no one troubled to inquire in regard to her absence.

After breakfast, with the sun now halfway up the sky, King Milo, Queen Caudabil and Prince Brezante exchanged final compliments with King Casmir and Queen Sollace and took their leave. King Casmir and Queen

Sollace stepped out upon the terrace to watch the column depart.

Lady Vosse came from the castle and approached King Casmir. 'Your Highness, I noticed the absence of Princess Madouc at the leave-taking and went to inquire the reason for her lassitude. In her chamber I found there this missive, which, as you see, is addressed to you.'

King Casmir, frowning in automatic displeasure, broke the seal and unfolded the parchment. He read:

'Your Royal Highness, my best respects!

In accordance with your commands I have set out to discover the name and condition of my father, and also the details of my pedigree. Your instructions were definite; I have commanded for myself the services of an escort. As soon as my goals have been achieved, I will return. I informed Queen Sollace of my intention to obey Your Majesty's orders in this matter. I depart immediately.

Madouc'

King Casmir looked blankly at Queen Sollace. 'Madouc has gone.'

'"Gone"? Where?'

'Somewhere – to seek her pedigree, so she says.' Casmir slowly read the note aloud.

'So that is what the little vixen meant!' cried Sollace. 'And now – what is to be done?'

'I must consider. Perhaps nothing.'

8

I

An hour before dawn, with the castle silent, Madouc climbed from her bed. For a moment she stood indecisive, hugging herself and shivering to the cool air which played around her thin shanks. She went to the window; it seemed as if the day might be fair; still, at this dim hour the world seemed cheerless and unsympathetic. Doubts slid into Madouc's mind; could it be she was making a foolish dreadful mistake?

Madouc shivered and hopped away from the window. Standing by her bed, she considered. Nothing had changed. She scowled and set her mouth into a firm line. Decisions had been made; they were irrevocable.

Madouc quickly dressed in a peasant boy's knee-length smock, bast stockings, ankle-boots, and a loose cloth cap pulled low to hide her curls. Taking up a small bundle of extra belongings, she left her chambers, stole along the dim corridor, descended the stairs and went from the castle by a back way, out into the pre-dawn stillness. She stopped to look and listen, but no one was abroad. So far, so good. She set off around the castle toward the stables.

At the edge of the service yard she paused in the shadows; only the most discerning eye could have identified this thin and furtive peasant boy as 'Princess Madouc'.

In the kitchen scullions and fire-boys were astir; maids would soon be going out to the buttery. At the moment the service yard was empty; Madouc darted across the open space and so made her way unchallenged to the stables. Here Sir Pom-pom awaited her with a pair of horses saddled and ready. Madouc examined the horses without enthusiasm. To one side a sway-backed bay mare of advanced age, with one wall-eye and a tail woefully lacking in hair; to the other, a gray gelding almost as old, fat in the barrel and thin in the shank. Sir Pom-pom had achieved well his stated purpose of avoiding prideful ostentation.

Madouc's saddle had been fitted on the bay mare; the gray gelding was evidently Sir Pom-pom's chosen steed. Sir Pom-pom himself wore not his usual garments, but a smart doublet of good blue cloth, a blue cap with a jaunty red feather, and a pair of glossy new boots, flaring modishly high past the knees and boasting pewter buckles at the insteps.

'Your garments are stylish,' said Madouc. 'You would seem almost dapper were it not that you still show the face of Sir Pom-pom.'

Sir Pom-pom scowled. 'My face cannot be changed.'

'Were not those garments costly?'

Sir Pom-pom gave a brisk jerk of the hand. 'It is all relative. Have you not heard the saying: "When Need is on the march, Expense must step aside"?'

Madouc put on a sour face. 'Whoever made up this nonsense was either a spendthrift or a fool.'

'Not so! The saying is apt! To change over the gold pieces, I bought needful articles! One does not go forth on an important quest looking the hobbledehoy.'

'I see. Where is the balance of the money?'

'I carry it in my wallet, for safe-keeping.'

Madouc extended her hand. 'Give it here, Sir Pom-pom, on the instant!'

Sir Pom-pom sullenly reached in his pouch, brought out coins, which he handed over to Madouc. She reckoned up the sum, then looked back to Sir Pom-pom. 'Surely there is more money than this!'

'Possibly so, but I hold it for security.'

'That is unnecessary. You may give me the full total of the exchange.'

Sir Pom-pom tossed over his wallet. 'Take as you will.'

Madouc opened it and counted the coins. 'This surely is not all?'

'Bah!' grumbled Sir Pom-pom. 'Perhaps I still carry a few odd pieces in my pocket.'

'Give them here: every last farthing!'

Sir Pom-pom said with dignity: 'I will retain one silver florin and three copper pennies, for incidental expense.' He passed over further coins. Madouc poured all into her pouch, and returned the wallet to Sir Pom-pom. 'We shall have an accounting later,' said Madouc. 'You have not heard the last of this, Sir Pom-pom.'

'Bah,' muttered Sir Pom-pom. 'It is no great matter. Let us be on our way. The bay mare shall be your steed. Her name is Juno.'

Madouc gave a sniff of disdain. 'Her belly sags low! Will she support my weight?'

Sir Pom-pom smiled grimly. 'Remember, you are no longer a prideful princess! You are a vagabond.'

'I am a prideful vagabond. Keep this in mind, if you will.'

Sir Pom-pom shrugged. 'Juno has a kindly gait. She neither jibs nor shies, though she will take a fence no more. My own horse is Fustis. He was at one time a war-charger of note; he responds best to a firm seat and a strong hand.' Sir Pom-pom swaggered in his new boots over to Fustis; in a single brave bound he vaulted into the saddle. Madouc mounted Juno more deliberately, and the two set off up the Sfer Arct, into the hilly region north of Lyonesse Town.

319

Two hours along the way they arrived at the village Swally Water and here came upon a crossroad. Madouc read the sign. 'To the east is the village Fring; we shall travel this lane to Fring and there veer north, and so come into Old Street.'

'It is a longer route, by some miles,' noted Sir Pom-pom.

'Perhaps so, but by keeping to the back lanes we will tend to avoid anyone sent out to impede our journey.'

Sir Pom-pom grunted. 'I thought that His Majesty had ratified your quest, and with all his heart-felt blessings.'

'That is how I interpret his commands,' said Madouc. 'Still, I prefer to take nothing for granted.'

Sir Pom-pom gave the remark careful thought, then said, somewhat glumly: 'I hope that I find the Holy Grail before we need to test your interpretation.'

Madouc deigned no reply.

At noon the two passed through Fring and, finding no lane leading northeast, continued eastward across a pleasant country-side of farms and meadows. Presently they arrived at the town Abatty Dell where a fair was in progress. At Sir Pom-pom's urging, they dismounted, tethered their horses to a rail at the front of the inn, and went to watch the clowns and jugglers performing in the square. Sir Pom-pom gave a cry of amazement. 'Look yonder! That man in the red hat just now thrust a blazing torch down his throat! Look! He does so again! It is a marvel! His gut must be iron, from top to bottom!'

'An unusual talent, indeed,' said Madouc.

Sir Pom-pom's attention was caught by another performance. 'See there! It is finesse, full and true! Aha, did you see? That was a goodly thrust!'

Madouc, turning to look, saw a man and a woman lying on their backs about fifteen feet apart. With thrusts of their feet they propelled a small child back and forth through the air between them, lofting the child higher and ever higher with each passage. The child, under-sized, and wearing only a ragged breech-clout, jerked and twisted desperately in mid-air so that he might alight buttocks-first on the coiled legs of the target-individual. This person, after catching the child with dexterous feet, thrust out legs to propel him back through space the way he had come.

Upon conclusion of the display the man cried out: 'Mikelaus will now accept your gratuities!' The child ran among the spectators holding out his cap for coins.

'Ha hah!' exclaimed Sir Pom-pom. 'That trick deserves a farthing!' He reached in one of his side-pockets and brought forth a copper coin which he dropped into the soiled cap extended by Mikelaus. Madouc watched with raised eyebrows.

The three performers went on to another feat. The man placed a flat board two feet long on top of an eight-foot pole; the woman lifted Mikelaus so that he crouched on the board. The man thrust the pole high, with Mikelaus precariously balanced on top. The woman joined a second pole to the first; Mikelaus was raised even higher, the man controlling the swaying pole with sidling movements. The woman added a third extension to the pole; Mikelaus was raised twenty feet into the air. Gingerly he rose and stood on the board, atop the swaying pole. The woman sounded a flourish of tones on a set of pipes and Mikelaus chanted a song in a reedy rasping voice:

> Ecce voluspo
> Sorarsio normal
> Radne malengro.
>   Oh! Oh! Toomish!
>   Geltner givim.

(The woman blew a flourish on the pipes.)

Bowner buder diper
Eljus noop or bark
Esgracio delila.
　　Oh! Oh! Toomish!
　　Silvish givim.

(The woman blew a flourish on the pipes.)

Slova solypa
Trater no bulditch
Ki-yi-yi minkins.
　　Regular toomish.
　　Copriote givim.

The woman blew a final flourish and called out: 'Bravo, Mikelaus! Your song has moved us all and you well deserve a liberal reward! Now you may descend! So then: Ooops! Ah la la! And away!'

The man ran forward three short steps, heaved on the pole; Mikelaus hurtled through the air. The woman ran below with a net, but along the way she tripped over a dog and Mikelaus, consternation on his face, struck the ground head-first, to tumble over and over a distance of twenty feet.

The woman put a good face on the mistake. 'Next time we will surely do better! Now then, Mikelaus: To business!'

Mikelaus struggled to his feet and, removing his cap, limped back toward the spectators, pausing only to kick the dog.

'Hah!' said Sir Pom-pom. 'Another fine trick!'

'Come!' said Madouc. 'We have watched enough of this capering. It is time we were back on the road!'

'Not yet,' said Sir Pom-pom. 'The booths yonder look interesting; surely we can spare a moment or two.'

Madouc acceded to Sir Pom-pom's wishes, and they

322

walked around the square, inspecting the merchandise offered for sale.

At an ironmonger's booth, Sir Pom-pom paused to study a display of fancy cutlery. A group of damascene daggers in carved leather scabbards caught his eye and he went so far as to inquire prices. Finally, after cogitation, he settled upon one of the daggers and prepared to make the purchase. Madouc spoke in shocked wonder. 'May I ask what you are proposing to do?'

'Is it not clear?' blurted Sir Pom-pom. 'I badly need a dagger, of good quality and handsome workmanship. This article exactly fits my needs.'

'And how will you pay?'

Sir Pom-pom blinked up toward the sky. 'I have kept a small reserve for just such a case as this.'

'Before you buy so much as a nut to crack between your teeth, we must have an accounting. Show me your reserve.'

'This is an embarrassment!' stormed Sir Pom-pom. 'I am now held in contempt by the ironmonger!'

'No matter! Bring out this so-called "reserve".'

'Let us be reasonable! The money is safer with me! I am older than you and neither vague nor absent-minded. No cut-purse would dare approach me, especially if he saw a fine dagger at my belt. It is only prudent that I carry the money and plan the expenditures.'

'Your arguments are wise,' said Madouc. 'They fall short only because the money is mine.'

Sir Pom-pom angrily passed over a goodly handful of coins, both silver and copper. 'Take the money, then!'

Something in Sir Pom-pom's manner aroused Madouc's suspicions. She held out her hand. 'Give me the remainder.'

Sir Pom-pom grudgingly handed over further coins. 'Now then!' said Madouc. 'Is that all?'

Sir Pom-pom sourly showed her a silver florin and a few coppers. 'I retain only my reserve. This money at least will be safe.'

'And that is all?'

'That is all, and be damned to it.'

'You will not need that fancy dagger. In the first place, it is far too dear.'

'Not when purchased with your money.'

Madouc ignored the remark. 'Come! Let us be away!'

'I am hungry,' grumbled Sir Pom-pom. 'We could make our lunch on one of those pork pies. Also I want to watch the clowns. Look at them now! They throw Mikelaus high in the air and let him drop. No! At the last instant the man catches him in the net! It is most comical!'

'Come, Sir Pom-pom. You shall have your pork pie and then we will be on our way. Juno's only gait is a slow amble; we must ride long to ride far.'

Sir Pom-pom jerked peevishly at the bill of his new cap. 'The day is growing late! We should bide here overnight at one of the inns. Then we can enjoy the fair at our leisure.'

'The inns are surely full; we will go on.'

'That is folly! The next town is ten miles distant, we will never arrive before nightfall, and once again the inns may be full.'

'In that case, we shall sleep in the open, like true vagabonds.'

Sir Pom-pom had nothing more to say; the two departed Abatty Dell and proceeded on their way. As the sun dropped low in the west, they turned aside from the lane and rode a quarter-mile across a meadow to a little spinney beside a stream. Here Sir Pom-pom struck up a fire and tethered out the horses, while Madouc toasted bacon, which they ate for their supper along with bread and cheese.

Madouc had removed her hat. Sir Pom-pom studied her in the firelight. 'Somehow you look different! Now I see! You have cut your hair short.'

'How else would it fit under the cap?'

'You look more halfling now than ever.'

Madouc sat hugging her knees and looking into the fire. Somewhat wistfully she said: 'It is only appearance. With each passing day my human blood sings a louder song. That is always the way when one like myself leaves the shee and lives among men.'

'And if you had remained at the shee: what then?'

Madouc hugged her knees even more closely. 'I do not know what would have become of me. The fairies might have played tricks on me and shunned me because of my mixed blood.'

'Still, mortals die, and fairies dance and play forever.'

'Not so,' said Madouc. 'Fairies also die. Sometimes they sing sad songs by moonlight and pine away for sheer sorrow! Sometimes they drown themselves for love. Sometimes they are killed by raging bumble-bees or kidnapped and murdered by trolls who grind fairy-bones into a condiment to season their sauces and ragoûts.'

Sir Pom-pom yawned and stretched his legs toward the fire. 'It is not the life for me, after all.'

'Nor for me,' said Madouc. 'Already I am far too human!'

In the morning the sun rose bright into a cloudless sky, and the day became warm. Halfway through the morning they came to a river, and Madouc could not resist the temptation to bathe. She left Sir Pom-pom with the horses and scrambled down through the alders to the water's edge. Here she removed her clothes and plunged into the water, to dive and splash and enjoy the refreshing coolness. Chancing to look up the bank, she discovered Sir

Pom-pom peering down at her, his face framed by the foliage.

In a cross voice Madouc called out: 'What are you gaping at, Sir Pom-pom? Have you never seen a naked girl before?'

'Never a naked princess,' said Sir Pom-pom with a grin.

'That is sheer nonsense,' said Madouc in disgust. 'We are much alike, all of us. There is truly nothing noteworthy to see.'

'Still, I prefer it to looking at the back end of Juno.'

'Stare as you like,' said Madouc. 'I cannot be bothered with your foolishness.'

'It is not total foolishness, as you put it,' said Sir Pom-pom. 'I have a sound and practical reason for making a close inspection.'

'What is that?'

'Should I return with the Holy Grail, my boon might entitle me to wed the royal princess. Therefore I thought it sensible to discover just what advantages such a choice might entail. For a fact, I see nothing which arouses any great enthusiasm.'

Madouc struggled for words. At last she said: 'Since you seem to be idle, I suggest that you strike up a fire and boil us a soup for our noon meal.'

Sir Pom-pom drew his face back through the foliage. Madouc stepped from the water, dressed and returned to the road.

As the two sat in the shade of a great elm tree, eating their soup, they observed the approach of three persons on foot: a short plump man, a woman of similar proportions and an urchin, under-sized, pasty-gray of skin, seemingly all legs and head. As they drew close, Madouc recognized the three clowns who had performed at the Abatty Dell fair.

The three approached and halted. 'A very good day to

you both,' said the man, who had a round face, coarse black hair, a little bulb of a nose and bright protuberant black eyes.

'I echo this sentiment,' declared the woman, who like the man showed a round flexible face, black hair, round black eyes and a pink stub of a nose.

'Good day to you as well,' said Madouc.

The man glanced into the pot where simmered the soup. 'May we sit here in the shade and take a brief respite from our trudging?'

'The shade is free,' said Sir Pom-pom. 'Rest where you like.'

'Your words fall kindly on the ear!' said the woman gratefully. 'The way is long and I go with difficulty, and sometimes pain, by reason of my ailment.'

The three settled cross-legged in the shade. 'Allow me to make introductions,' said the man. 'I am Filemon, Master of Mirth. Here sits Dame Corcas, no less skilled in merry antics. And here, small but doughty, is our little Mikelaus. He is not altogether cheerful, and perhaps somewhat ill, since he has had no breakfast today. Am I right, poor Mikelaus, sad little tyke that you are?'

'Arum. Boskatch. Gaspa confaga.'

Sir Pom-pom blinked. 'What did he say?'

Filemon chuckled. 'Mikelaus has an odd way of speaking, which is not clear to everyone.'

Dame Corcas explained, with delicate precision: 'He inquired, quite clearly: "What is cooking in the pot?"'

'It is our meal,' said Sir Pom-pom. 'I have boiled up a soup of ham, onions and beans.'

Mikelaus spoke again: 'Vogenard. Fistilla.'

Filemon said reprovingly: 'Impossible, Mikelaus! It is not our food, no matter how much you crave sustenance.'

Dame Corcas said: 'Perhaps these kind folk might spare

him just a taste, to keep the spirit of life awake in his poor little soul.'

Madouc said: 'I suppose that is possible. Sir Pom-pom, serve a portion of soup to the creature.'

Sir Pom-pom glumly did as bidden. Dame Corcas reached to take the bowl. 'I must make sure that it is not too hot; otherwise Mikelaus will burn himself.' She spooned up a portion of the soup, along with a goodly chunk of ham and tested it. 'It is still far too hot for Mikelaus!'

Filemon scoffed at her caution. 'Probably not! Mikelaus has the gut of a salamander! Let me verify the temperature.' He took the bowl and raised it to his lips. 'That is excellent soup, but you are right; it is far too hot for Mikelaus.'

'There is little left in the bowl,' said Sir Pom-pom.

Mikelaus said: 'Gamkarch noop. Bosumelists.'

'You must not be greedy!' admonished Dame Corcas. 'This young gentleman will surely make up more soup if there is not enough.'

Madouc, seeing the way the wind blew, heaved a sigh. 'Very well, Sir Pom-pom. Serve around the soup. I cannot eat with these hungry creatures watching my every mouthful.'

Sir Pom-pom growled 'I made only enough for our needs.'

'No problem whatever!' declared Filemon with enthusiasm. 'When good comrades meet along the road, they share each with each, and all rejoice in mutual amplitude! I notice yonder a fine butt of ham, onions, bread, cheese, and unless my eyes deceive me, a bottle of wine! We shall have a true banquet, here along the road, to which each shall give of his best! Corcas, you must make yourself useful! Assist this young gentleman with the fine boots!'

Dame Corcas sprang to her feet and so swiftly that Sir

Pom-pom could hardly follow the movement of her hands, she had thrown great chunks of ham into the pot, along with half a dozen onions, and three handfuls of oaten flour. While Sir Pom-pom and Madouc watched in bemusement, Filemon had brought out the bottle of wine, and had tasted its contents.

Mikelaus said: 'Arum. Cangel.'

'Why not?' said Filemon. 'You are poor, miserable, and misshapen, and only two feet tall; still, why should you not enjoy a sip of wine from time to time, along with the rest of your merry comrades?' He passed the bottle to Mikelaus, who tilted it high into the air.

'Enough!' cried Dame Corcas. 'While I stand here stirring the pot, and smoke finding the sure way to my eyes, you two consume all the wine! Put the bottle aside! Entertain these two fine folk with your jolly antics.'

'Just one more swallow,' begged Filemon. 'It will lubricate my lips for the fife.'

He drank more wine, then brought a fife from his pocket. 'Now then, Mikelaus! You must earn your soup! Show us your best hornpipe!'

Filemon played a lively tune, of skirling runs and quick returns, with trills high and warbles low, while Mikelaus danced a wild jig of kicking legs and knees brought high, ending all with a forward and backward somersault.

'Good work, Mikelaus!' cried Dame Corcas. 'Perhaps our friends will favor you with a coin or two, as is the habit of the gentry!'

Sir Pom-pom growled: 'Be content that you devour our food and swill our wine.'

Filemon put on a face of moist reproach, his eyes large and round. 'We are comrades of the road: vagabonds of the same far horizons! Is it not share with one, share with all? Those are the rules of the gallant wayfarers!'

329

'If this is true, I prefer otherwise,' muttered Sir Pom-pom.

Dame Corcas emitted a sudden groan. 'Ah! How the pangs do bite! It is my ailment; I have over-exerted myself, as is my wont! Always I do too much for others! Filemon, my potion: where is it?'

'In your pouch, my dear, as always!'

'Ah indeed! I must limit my exertions, or I may well become ill!'

Sir Pom-pom said: 'We saw you at the fair. You were bounding about with great agility. Filemon threw Mikelaus high in the air, and you ran like the wind to catch him in the net.'

Mikelaus said: 'Gurgo arraska, selvo sorarsio!'

Dame Corcas said: 'Yes, it was a shameful failure, for which we can blame the dog.'

'Bismal darstid: mango ki-yi-yi.'

'Whatever the case,' said Dame Corcas, 'the trick takes much out of me! I suffer for days afterward, but our public demands the spectacle; they know us of yore and we cannot disappoint them!'

Filemon chuckled. 'There is a variation to the trick, wherein we pretend to be three incompetent lunatics and purposely let Mikelaus fall, though pretending to catch him, but failing through one or another of our comic antics.'

'Dasa miago lou-lou. Yi. Tinka.'

'Just so!' said Filemon. 'And the soup is now prepared to Dame Corcas' exacting standards. I serve you with our compliments! Eat hearty, one and all! Even you, Mikelaus, for once in your penurious little life, you shall sup your fill!'

'Arum.'

After the meal, Madouc and Sir Pom-pom prepared to continue on their way. Filemon called in a cheery voice:

'If we may, we will go in your company, and thus enliven the journey!'

'Of course we shall!' said Dame Corcas definitely. 'It would be sad indeed if we were to part company now, after such a jolly time together.'

'Then it is so decided, by popular vote!' declared Filemon.

'We shall go as a little group of boon companions,' declared Dame Corcas. 'Even though you two ride fine horses while we must walk – or in the case of poor raggle-taggle little Mikelaus, scurry and lope. Be brave, good Mikelaus! Someday the world will turn right for you, and give you a fine reward for all your generous deeds.'

'Yi arum bosko.'

The group set off down the lane: Sir Pom-pom riding first on gray Fustis, with Madouc next on Juno, at a gait sufficiently easy that Filemon and Dame Corcas, trudging behind, had no difficulty in keeping pace, and even Mikelaus, by dint of first running at full speed, then halting to catch his breath, remained only a few yards behind.

The lane wound up hill and down dale: between hedges of hawthorn or low fences of mossy field-stone; past vineyards and orchards, fields of barley and water-meadows sprinkled with flowers; into the shade of small forests, then once more out into the open sunlight.

All at once, after two hours of travel, Dame Corcas gave a choking cry and, clutching her chest, fell to her knees, where she remained, sobbing under her breath. Filemon instantly went to tend her. 'My dear Corcas, what is it this time? Another of your attacks?'

Dame Corcas at last managed to speak. 'I fear as much. Luckily, it does not seem truly severe, and I do not need my potion. Still, for a period I am obliged to rest. You and dear Mikelaus must go on to Biddle Bray without me, and make arrangements for the gala. When I am better, I will creep on alone, at my own pace, and eventually, if the Fates are kind, I will arrive in time to do my stint at the performance.'

'Unthinkable!' declared Filemon staunchly. 'Surely there is a better solution to the problem! Let us take the advice of our friends.' He addressed Sir Pom-pom. 'What is your opinion?'

'I would not wish to offer advice.'

Filemon struck his fist into the palm of his hand. 'I have it!' He turned to Madouc. 'Perhaps you, in your kindness, might allow Dame Corcas to ride in your place onward to Biddle Bray, which lies along the road at no great distance.'

'It would be most companionable and loyal,' cried Dame Corcas fervently. 'I fear that otherwise I might just lie here in the road all night, until my strength returns.'

Madouc glumly dismounted. 'I suppose it will do me no great harm to walk for a bit.'

'I thank you, from the bottom of my heart!' cried Dame Corcas. With surprising agility she stepped to Juno's side and swung herself into the saddle. 'Ah! I feel better already! Filemon, shall we sing a brave little song, to bolster our spirits?'

'Of course, my dear! What shall it be?'

'"The Song of the Three Merry Vagabonds", of course.'

'Very good.' Filemon clapped his hands to establish the cadence, then, in his gustful baritone mingled with Dame Corcas' piping soprano, the song was rendered:

> Our wants are many, our farthings few;
> And oft we sleep in the rain and dew!
> Our evening meal is a turnip stew;
> In spite of all we're a jolly crew!
>
> Refrain (as sung by Mikelaus):

Signo chaska yi yi yi
Varmous varmous oglethorpe.

Our argosies ride distant tides;
Out there somewhere our fortune hides.
Though pain seems what our life provides
Our dauntless doctrine still abides!

Refrain (as sung by Mikelaus):

Poxin mowgar yi yi yi
Vilish hoy kazinga.

The land is broad, the sky is vast!
We travel far, but not too fast.
The dogs bark loud as we walk past;
At night the owls fly off aghast.

Refrain (sung by Mikelaus):

Varmous toigal yi yi yi
Tinkish wombat nip.

So went the ballad for sixteen more verses, with Mikelaus in each case croaking a refrain from the road behind.

Other songs were sung, with such gusto that Madouc at
last called up to Dame Corcas: 'You seem to have
recovered your strength.'

'To some extent, my dear! But it is verging into the
afternoon, and now I must take my potion, to prevent a
new attack. I believe that I have the packet ready to
hand.' Dame Corcas searched her pouch, then gave a cry
of consternation. 'This is a dreadful discovery!'

'What now, my dear?' cried Filemon.

'I left my potion at the spot where we made our meal! I
remember distinctly tucking the packet into the crotch of
the elm tree.'

'That is most inconvenient! You must have your potion, if you are to survive the night!'

'There is only one solution!' said Dame Corcas decisively. 'I will ride back at speed for the potion. Meanwhile, you must continue to the old hut where once before we passed the night; it lies only a mile or so ahead. You may prepare us all nice beds of straw, and I will be back with you surely before the sun sets.'

'It seems the only way,' said Filemon. 'Ride at best speed; still, do not founder the horse, gallant beast though it may be!'

'I know how to get the most out of such an animal,' said Dame Corcas. 'I will see you anon!' She turned back down the road, and kicked up Juno first into a trot, then into a rambling gallop, and soon disappeared from view, while Madouc and Sir Pom-pom watched nonplused.

'Come then,' said Filemon. 'As Dame Corcas mentioned, there is a deserted hut a short distance ahead, which will provide us a kindly shelter for the night.'

The group continued, with Sir Pom-pom, on Fustis, leading the way. Twenty minutes later they came upon a desolate old crofter's hut, situated a few yards off the road in the shade of two sprawling oak trees.

'Here we are,' said Filemon. 'It is not a palace, but it is better than nothing, and clean straw is to be had in the rick.' He turned to Mikelaus who had been trying to engage his attention. 'What is it now, Mikelaus?'

'Fidix. Waskin. Bolosio.'

Filemon stared down at him in shock. 'Can it be true?'

'Arum. Fooner.'

'I cannot recall the act! Still I will search my wallet.' Almost at once Filemon discovered a packet tied in black cord. 'Mikelaus, you are right! I absent-mindedly took up Dame Corcas' potion and dropped it into my pouch! And now the poor creature will be in a dreadful state! She will never give up her search while the light persists, and the worry may bring on a severe attack; you will recall that episode at Cwimbry.'

'Arum.'

'There is no help for it! I must ride to find her, so that she will not be in an agony of despair. Luckily, the way is not long.' He turned to Sir Pom-pom. 'Sir, I must beg the use of your horse Fustis! I take the blame for the entire inconvenience! But Mikelaus will make himself handy during my short absence. Mikelaus, hear me now and hear me well! I do not want to learn of your shirking! Show this gentleman to the hay-rick, then gather sticks for a fire. Further, I entrust you with a jar of my special wax. I want you to polish this gentleman's boots, and polish them until they shine like glass. It is the very least you can do for our friends until I return with Dame Corcas!' He sprang into the saddle which Sir Pom-pom had only just vacated and galloped off down the road.

'Hoy!' called Sir Pom-pom after him. 'At least leave behind the saddlebags, that we may make our supper in your absence!'

But Filemon failed either to hear or to heed and was soon lost to sight.

Sir Pom-pom looked into the hut, then backed away. 'I believe that I will sleep out in the open, where the must is less intense.'

'I will do likewise, since the night promises to be fine,' said Madouc.

Sir Pom-pom and Mikelaus brought straw from an old rick and laid it down to make soft sweet-smelling beds. Then Sir Pom-pom struck up a fire, but without saddlebags they could only look glumly into the flames and wait with what patience they could muster for the return of Filemon and Dame Corcas with their horses.

The sun sank low and disappeared behind the far hills.

Sir Pom-pom went to look along the road but discovered neither sight nor sound of either Dame Corcas or Filemon.

He returned to the fire and pulled off his boots. Mikelaus at once took them aside and began to polish them, using Filemon's special wax. Sir Pom-pom spoke in surly tones: 'I do not care to sit up until midnight. I will now lie down to sleep, which is the best remedy for an empty stomach.'

'I believe I will do the same,' said Madouc. 'Mikelaus may well stay up to wait; he has the polishing of your boots to occupy his time.'

For a period Madouc lay awake watching the stars drift past overhead, but at last her eyelids became heavy and she fell asleep, and so the night passed.

In the morning Madouc and Sir Pom-pom arose from their beds of straw and looked about. There was no sign of either Filemon, Dame Corcas, or the horses. When they looked for Mikelaus, he also was not in evidence, nor were Sir Pom-pom's boots.

Madouc said: 'I am commencing to wonder about the honesty of Filemon and Dame Corcas.'

'Do not leave that impling Mikelaus out of your calculations,' said Sir Pom-pom through gritted teeth. 'It is clear that he has decamped with my new boots.'

Madouc drew a deep breath. 'I suppose it is futile to lament our loss. At Biddle Bray we will buy you stout buskins and a pair of good stockings. Until then you must go barefoot.'

II

Madouc and Sir Pom-pom trudged glumly into Biddle Bray; even the red feather in Sir Pom-pom's cap had taken on a disconsolate slant. At the Dog's Head Inn they ate pease porridge for breakfast, after which, at a cobbler's shop, Sir Pom-pom was fitted with a pair of buskins. When the cobbler called for his money, Sir Pom-pom pointed to Madouc. 'You must discuss the matter with her.'

Madouc stared at him in displeasure. 'How so?'

'Because you have insisted upon carrying the funds.'

'What of the silver florin and the three copper pennies?'

Sir Pom-pom's face became bleak. 'I placed these coins in my pouch, which I tied to the pommel of my saddle. Filemon jumped on Fustis and rode off like a whirlwind, and with him horse, pouch and money.'

Madouc, restraining comment, paid the cobbler. 'The past is past. Let us be on our way.'

The two adventurers departed Biddle Bray by Bidbottle Lane, which led north toward Modoiry, a village on Old Street. After a mile or two Sir Pom-pom recovered something of his bravado. He began to whistle and presently he said: 'You spoke correctly! The past is past; today is today! The road is open; the sun shines bright, and somewhere the Holy Grail awaits my coming!'

'So it may be,' said Madouc.

'Footing it is not so bad,' Pom-pom went on. 'I see many advantages. Fodder and drench no longer concern us nor the nuisances of tether, bridle, blanket and saddle. We can also put aside all fear of horse-thieves.'

'Whatever the case, horseback or afoot, it is no great distance to Thripsey Shee,' said Madouc.

'Even so, that need not be our first destination,' said Sir Pom-pom. 'I am anxious to search for the Holy Grail: first in the crypts on Weamish Isle, where I suspect we will find a secret compartment.'

Madouc responded with decision: 'First we fare to Thripsey Shee, and there we will take advice from my mother.'

Sir Pom-pom scowled and kicked at a pebble.

'It serves no purpose to pout and sulk,' said Madouc. 'We shall keep a vigilant watch to right and left as we go.'

Sir Pom-pom turned a sullen side-glance upon Madouc. 'Your cap is pulled low and rests on your ears and nose. I wonder how you can see the road in front of your feet, much less the landscape to right and left.'

'You watch the landscape and I will guide us to Thripsey Shee,' said Madouc. 'And now what I see ahead is a blackberry thicket heavy with fruit. It would be a shame to pass by without a taste.'

Sir Pom-pom pointed. 'Someone already works at the harvest. He may even be on guard against vagabonds such as ourselves.'

Madouc scrutinized the person to whom Sir Pom-pom had referred. 'I would take him for a kindly old gentleman out for a stroll, who has paused to pick a few berries into his hat. Still, I will ask as to the berries.'

Madouc approached the thicket, where a man of mature years, in costume characteristic of the lesser gentry, paused at his work. Weather and sun had browned his skin and bleached his hair; his features were undistinguished, though even and regular; the gaze of his gray eyes was mild, so that Madouc felt no hesitation in addressing him. 'Sir, are these berries under your control, or are they available to others?'

'I must answer both "yes" and "no". For berries already

picked and in my hat I feel an attachment. Those berries yet on the bush I place under no restriction whatever.'

'In that case I will pick a few berries on my account, as will Sir Pom-pom.'

'"Sir Pom-pom", is it? Since I mingle with the aristocracy, I must look to my manners.'

'I am not truly a knight,' said Sir Pom-pom modestly. 'It is only a manner of speaking.'

'Here among the bushes it matters little,' said the old man. 'Knight and commoner alike cry "Ay caray!" at the prick of a thorn, and the flavor is the same on both tongues. As for me, my name is Travante; my rank or its lack are equally irrelevant.' Travante looked down at Madouc, who picked from a branch nearby. 'Below that cap I seem to notice red curls, and also some extremely blue eyes.'

'My hair is more copper-gold than red.'

'So I see, upon closer attention. And what is your name?'

'I am Madouc.'

The three picked blackberries, then sat together by the side of the road and ate their harvest. Travante asked: 'Since you came from the south, you are faring to the north. Where are you bound?'

'First to Modoiry on Old Street,' said Madouc. 'Truth to tell, we are vagabonds of a sort, Sir Pom-pom and I, and each of us has a quest to fulfill.'

'I too am a vagabond,' said Travante. 'I too pursue a quest: one which is futile and forlorn, or so I have been told by those who remain at home. If I may, I will accompany you, at least for a space.'

'Do so and welcome,' said Madouc. 'What is the quest that takes you so far and wide?'

Travante looked off down the road, smiling. 'It is an extraordinary quest. I am searching for my lost youth.'

339

'Indeed!' said Madouc. 'How did you lose it?'

Travante held out his hands in a gesture of puzzlement. 'I cannot be sure. I had it one moment and the next time I thought to notice it was gone.'

Madouc glanced at Sir Pom-pom, who was staring dumbfounded at Travante. She said: 'I suppose you are sure of your facts.'

'Oh indeed! I remember it distinctly! Then it was as if I walked around the table and poof! I found myself an old man.'

'There must have been the usual and ordinary intervals in between?'

'Dreams, my dear. Figments, wisps, sometimes a nightmare. But what of you?'

'It is simple. I do not know my father. My mother is a fairy from Thripsey Shee. I am seeking my father and with him my pedigree.'

'And Sir Pom-pom: what does he seek?'

'Sir Pom-pom seeks the Holy Grail, in accordance with King Casmir's proclamation.'

'Ah! He is of religious persuasion?'

'Not so,' said Sir Pom-pom. 'If I bring the Holy Grail to Queen Sollace, she will grant me a boon. I might well choose to marry the Princess Madouc, though she is as high-handed and vain as the artful little frippet who sits beside you now.'

Travante glanced down at Madouc. 'Could she possibly be one and the same individual?'

Sir Pom-pom put on his most portentous frown. 'There are certain facts we do not want generally known. Still, I can say this: you have guessed a good guess.'

Madouc told Travante: 'Another fact is not generally known, especially to Sir Pom-pom. He must learn that his dreams of marriage and the boon have nothing to do with me.'

Sir Pom-pom said obstinately: 'I can only rely upon the assurances of Queen Sollace in this regard.'

'So long as I control the Imp-spring Tinkle-toe, I will have the last word in this matter,' said Madouc. She rose to her feet. 'It is time we were on our way.'

Travante said: 'Sir Pom-pom, I strongly suspect that you will never marry Madouc. I advise you to work toward a more accessible goal.'

'I will give the matter thought,' growled Sir Pom-pom.

The three set off to the north along Bidbottle Lane. 'We make a notable company,' declared Travante. 'I am as I am! Sir Pom-pom is strong and brave, while Madouc is clever and resourceful; also, with her copper-gold curls, her wry little face and her eyes of heart-break blue she is both quaint and vastly appealing.'

'She can also be a vixen, when it suits her mood,' said Sir Pom-pom.

III

Bidbottle Lane wound north across the countryside: up hill and down dale, into the shade of the Wanswold Oaks, out across Srimsour Downs. Overhead floated lazy white clouds; their shadows drifted across the landscape. The sun moved up the sky; as it reached the zenith, the three wayfarers arrived at Modoiry, where Bidbottle Lane met Old Street.

Madouc and Sir Pom-pom would proceed another three miles east to Little Saffield, then fare north beside the River Timble and on to the Forest of Tantrevalles. Travante intended to continue past Little Saffield to the Long Downs, that he might conduct his search among the dolmens of the Stollshot Circus.

As the three approached Little Saffield Madouc found herself increasingly disturbed by the prospect of parting with Travante, whose company she found both reassuring and amusing; further, his presence seemed to discourage Sir Pom-pom's occasional tendencies toward pomposity. Madouc finally suggested that Travante accompany them, at least as far as Thripsey Shee.

Travante reflected upon the proposal. Then, somewhat dubiously, he said: 'I know nothing of halflings; indeed, all my life I have been wary of them. Too many tales are told of their caprice and exaggerated conduct.'

'In this case there is nothing to fear,' said Madouc confidently. 'My mother is both gracious and beautiful! She will surely be delighted to see me, and my friends as well, though I admit this is less certain. Still, she might well advise you in regard to your quest.'

Sir Pom-pom asked plaintively: 'What of me? I also am engaged upon a quest.'

'Patience, Sir Pom-pom! Your wants are known!'

Travante came to a decision. 'Well then, why not? I will welcome any advice, since I have had precious little luck searching on my own.'

'Then you will come with us!'

'For just a bit, until you find me a bore.'

'I doubt if that will ever occur,' said Madouc. 'I enjoy your company, and I am sure that Sir Pom-pom does so as well.'

'Really?' Travante looked half-incredulously from one to the other. 'I consider myself drab and uninteresting.'

'I would never use those words,' said Madouc. 'I think of you as a dreamer, perhaps a trifle – let us say – impractical, but your ideas are never dull.'

'I am pleased to hear you say so. As I mentioned, I have no great opinion of myself.'

'Whyever not?'

'For the most ordinary of reasons: I excel in nothing. I am neither a philosopher, nor a geometer, nor yet a poet. Never have I destroyed a horde of savage enemies, nor built a noble monument, nor ventured to the far places of the world. I lack all grandeur.'

'You are not alone,' said Madouc. 'Few can claim such achievements.'

'That means naught to me! I am I; I answer to myself, with no heed for others. I am persuaded that a life-span should not be futile and empty! For this reason I seek my lost youth, and with such special zeal.'

'And if you were to find it, what would you do?'

'I would alter everything! I would become a person of enterprise; I would consider wasted the day that did not include the contriving of some wonderful plan, or the building of a fine object, or the righting of a wrong! So would pass each day, in marvellous deeds. Then each night I would gather my friends for an occasion which would be remembered forever! That is how life should be lived, to the best effort of one's powers! Now that I know the truth, the time is too late – unless I find what I seek.'

Madouc turned to Sir Pom-pom. 'Have you been paying heed? These are lessons which you should take to heart, if only so that someday you may avoid Travante's regrets.'

'It is a sound philosophy,' said Sir Pom-pom. 'I have occasionally thought along similar lines. However, while toiling at the royal stables I could not put such theories into effect. If I find the Holy Grail and earn a boon, I will take pains to live a more glorious life.'

The three had now arrived at Little Saffield. The time was halfway through the afternoon: too late to proceed farther. The three repaired to the Black Ox Inn, to find all rooms occupied. They were given a choice of straw pallets in the garret among the rats, or the loft above the barn, where they might sleep in the hay, which option they selected.

In the morning the three set off to the north up Timble Lane. They passed first through the village Tawn Timble, then the hamlet Glymwode, with the Forest of Tantrevalles a brooding dark line close ahead.

In a field they found a peasant digging turnips who gave directions to Thripsey Shee on Madling Meadow. 'It is not so far as the dog runs, but the lane winds and crooks, all the while taking you more deeply into the forest, meanwhile becoming no more than a track. You will come at last to a wood-cutter's hut; thereafter the track becomes a trace, but you must proceed farther still, until the forest breaks, and before you will be Madling Meadow.'

'That seems simple enough,' said Travante.

'So it is, but beware the fairies of the shee! Above all, do not loiter after dusk or the imps will do you a mischief. They put donkey's ears and a donkey's utensil on poor Fottern, all because he made water on the meadow.'

'We will surely be more mannerly,' said Madouc.

The three went forward; the forest loomed dark and quiet ahead. The lane, now a track, veered to the east, then turned to plunge into the forest. Branches arched overhead; foliage blocked out the sky; the open country was gone and lost to view.

The track led deep into the forest. The air became cool and carried a hundred herbal scents. In the forest all colors were altered. Greens were various; greens of moss and fern, of wort, mallow, dock and tree-leaves in the sunlight. The browns were heavy and rich; black-brown and umber of the oak tree bole; russet and tan of forest floor. In the coverts, where the trees grew close and the foliage hung heavy, the shadows were deep, and tinged with maroon, indigo, black-green.

The three passed the wood-cutter's hut; the track dwindled to a trail, winding between boles, across dim dells, over outcrops of black rock, finally a break in the trees and beyond: Madling Meadow. Madouc halted and told her companions. 'You two must wait here for a time, while I go to find my mother. This will cause the least disturbance.'

Sir Pom-pom spoke in dissatisfaction. 'That may not be the best idea! I want to put my questions as soon as possible – to strike while the iron is hot, so to speak!'

'That is not the way to deal with fairies,' said Madouc. 'If you try to guide them, or work them to your will, they only laugh and dodge and curvet off slantwise, and may refuse to speak at all.'

'At least I can ask politely if they know anything whatever of the Grail. If not, we are only wasting our time and should hasten on to Weamish Isle.'

'Be patient, Sir Pom-pom! Remember, we are dealing with fairies! You must control your anxieties until I discover how the land lies.'

Sir Pom-pom said stiffly: 'I am not a bumpkin, after all; I too know how to deal with fairies.'

Madouc became vexed. 'Remain here, or go back to Lyonesse Town and ask questions of your own mother!'

Sir Pom-pom muttered: 'I do not dare; she would laugh herself ill for my part in this expedition, then send me out for a bucket of moonbeams.' He went to settle himself on a fallen log, where he was joined by Travante. 'Be quick, if you please; and if chance allows, ask after the Holy Grail.'

'You might also allude to my quest,' said Travante, 'if a gap opens in the conversation.'

'I will do what I can.'

Madouc went warily to the edge of the forest, pausing only to remove her cap and fluff out her curls. She halted

345

in the shade of a wide-spreading beech tree, and looked out over the meadow: a roughly circular area three hundred yards in diameter. At the center rose a hummock to which a dwarfed and contorted oak clung with sprawling roots. Madouc scanned the meadow, but saw only flowers nodding in the breeze. Nothing could be heard but a soft murmur which might have been the sound of bees and singing insects; still Madouc knew that she was not alone, especially after a mischievous hand pinched first one cheek of her round little rump, then the other. A voice giggled; another whispered: 'Green apples, green apples!'

The first voice whispered: 'When will she learn?'

Madouc indignantly cried out: 'Trouble me not, by fairy law!'

The voices became scornful. 'Hoity-toity to boot, apart from all else!' sneered the first.

'She is a hard one to know!' said the other.

Madouc ignored the remarks. She looked up at the sky, and decided that the time was near upon noon. In a soft voice she called: 'Twisk! Twisk! Twisk!'

A moment passed. Out on the meadow, as if her eyes had come into focus, Madouc saw a hundred filmy shapes moving about their unfathomable affairs. Above the central hummock a wisp of fog swirled high into the air.

Madouc waited and watched, nerves tingling. Where was Twisk? One of the shapes strolled at a languid pace across the meadow, taking on substance as it came, finally to show the charming lineaments of the fairy Twisk. She wore a knee-length gown of near-impalpable gauze which enhanced the effect of her supple and fascinating contours. Today she had selected pale lavender as a suitable color for her hair; as before it floated in a soft cloud behind her head and around her face. Madouc scanned the face anxiously, hoping for indications of maternal benevolence. Twisk's expression was impassive.

346

'Mother!' cried Madouc. 'I am happy to see you again!'

Twisk halted and looked Madouc up and down. 'Your hair is a jackdaw's nest,' said Twisk. 'Where is the comb I gave you?'

Madouc said hurriedly: 'Some clowns from the fair stole my horse Juno, along with saddle, saddle-bag and comb.'

'Clowns and entertainers are an untrustworthy lot; this should be your lesson. In any case you must make yourself tidy, especially if you plan to join the merriment at our grand festival! As you can see, the frolics are already underway.'

'I know nothing of the festival, mother dear. I had not planned merriment.'

'Oh? It is to be a grand gala! Notice all the pretty arrangements!'

Madouc looked across the meadow and now everything had changed. The swirl of fog above the hummock had become a tall castle of twenty towers with long banderoles streaming from each spire. In front of the castle stanchions of twisted silver and iron were linked by festoons of flowers; they surrounded a long table heaped with delicacies and liquors in tall bottles.

The festival apparently had not yet started, although fairies were already promenading and dancing about the meadow in great high spirits – all save one, who sat perched on a post scratching himself with great industry.

'I seem to have arrived at a happy time,' said Madouc. 'What is the occasion?'

'We celebrate a notable event,' said Twisk. 'It is the emancipation of Falael from seven long years of itch; King Throbius so punished him for malice and mischief. The curse will soon have run its course; in the meantime Falael sits yonder on the post, scratching as earnestly as ever. And now, I will bid you farewell once again, and wish you a fortunate future.'

'Wait!' cried Madouc. 'Are you not pleased to see me, your own dear daughter?'

'Not altogether, if truth be told. Your birth was travail, most unsavory, and your presence reminds me of the entire revolting circumstance.'

Madouc pursed her lips. 'I will put it out of my mind if you will do the same.'

Twisk laughed: a gay tinkle. 'Well spoken! My mood is slightly alleviated! Why are you here?'

'It is the usual reason. I need a mother's advice.'

'Proper and normal! Describe your trouble! Surely it is not an affair of the heart!'

'No, Mother! I only want to find my father, so that I can finally define my pedigree.'

Twisk gave a plangent cry of displeasure. 'The topic lacks interest! I have long put the circumstance out of my mind! I remember nothing!'

'Surely you remember something!' cried Madouc.

Twisk made an offhand gesture. 'A moment of frivolity, a laugh, a kiss: why should anyone wish to catalogue these in terms of place, date, phase of the moon, details of nomenclature? Rest content with the knowledge that one such event was conducive to your being; that is enough.'

'For you, but not for me! I am intent upon my identity, which means the name of my father.'

Twisk gave a gurgle of mocking laughter. 'I can not even name my own father, let alone yours!'

'Still, my father brought you a lovely child; surely that impressed your memory!'

'Hmm. One would so imagine.' Twisk looked off across the meadow. 'You have tickled my recollection! The occasion, so I recall, was unique. I can tell you this – ' Twisk looked past Madouc into the forest. 'Who are these solemn vagrants? Their presence obtrudes upon the mood of the festival!'

Madouc turned to find that Sir Pom-pom had crept through the forest and now stood close at hand. Not far behind, but well back in the shadows, lurked Travante.

Madouc turned back to Twisk. 'These are my companions; they are also embarked upon serious quests. Sir Pom-pom seeks the Holy Grail; Travante searches for his youth, which was lost when he was not paying heed.'

Twisk said haughtily: 'Had you not avouched for them, they might have come to grief!'

Sir Pom-pom, despite Madouc's glare of annoyance, stepped forward. 'Dame Fairy of the Silver Eyes: allow me to put you a question, which is this: where should I seek the Holy Grail?'

'Determine its location and go to that spot; that is my wise advice.'

Travante spoke tentatively: 'If you could guide me to my lost youth, I would be most grateful.'

Twisk jumped high in the air, pirouetted, settled slowly to the ground. 'I am not an index of the world's worries. I know nothing either of Christian crockery nor truant time! And now: silence! King Throbius has appeared and will fix his amnesty upon Falael!'

Sir Pom-pom muttered: 'I see nothing but wisps and blurs.'

Travante whispered in amazement: 'Look again! All is coming clear! I see the castle, and a thousand colored delights!'

'Now I see the same!' whispered Sir Pom-pom in amazement.

'Hist! Not another sound!'

At the castle tall doors of pearl and opal swung apart; King Throbius stepped forward at a stately pace, a dozen round-faced imps hopping behind holding the hem of his long purple train. For the occasion he wore a crown of sixteen tall silver prongs, curving outward and terminating in sparkling points of white fire.

King Throbius advanced to the balustrade, and halted. He looked out over the meadow, where all was hushed, and even Falael desisted from his scratching long enough to look around in awe.

King Throbius held up his hand. 'Today marks a significant epoch in our lives, in that it celebrates the regeneration of one of our ilk! Falael, you have erred! You have contrived ills and wrongs by the dozen, and put many of these schemes into effect! For such offenses, you have been visited with a remedial condition which at the very least has occupied your attention and brought about a welcome cessation of mischief! Now then Falael! I ask you to address this company, and tell them of your redemption! Speak! Are you ready to have the "Curse of the Itch" removed?'

'I am ready!' cried Falael with fervor. 'In all aspects, up and down, right and left, in and out: I am ready.'

'Very well! I hereby – '

'One moment!' called Falael. 'I have one particularly vexing itch I wish to subdue before the curse is removed.' With great zeal Falael scratched an area along his belly. 'Now then, Your Majesty. I am ready!'

'Very good! I hereby lift the curse, and I hope, Falael, that the inconveniences of your punishment will have persuaded you to forbearance, kindliness and restraint, as well as a full terminus to your penchant for wicked tricks!'

'Absolutely, Your Majesty! All is changed! Henceforth I shall be known as Falael the Good!'

'That is a noble aspiration, which I endorse and applaud. See that you keep it always to the fore! Now then! Let the festival proceed! All must participate in Falael's joy! One last word! Yonder, so I notice, stand three wights from the world of men: two mortals and the beloved daughter of our own dear Twisk! In the spirit of festival we give them welcome; let there be neither molestation nor prank, no matter how amusing! Today jocundity is rife, and all shall share!'

King Throbius held up his hand in salute and returned into the castle.

Madouc had been politely listening to the remarks of King Throbius; when she turned back she found Twisk had started to saunter off across the meadow. Madouc called out in distress: 'Mother, where do you go?'

Twisk looked around in surprise. 'I go off to rejoice with the others! There will be dancing and a great drinking of fairy wine; you have been allowed to join us; will you do so?'

'No, mother! If I drank fairy wine, I would become giddy and who knows what might happen?'

'Well then, will you dance?'

Madouc smilingly shook her head. 'I have heard that those who dance with the fairies are never able to stop. I will neither drink wine nor dance, nor will Sir Pom-pom nor Travante.'

'As you like. In that case – '

'You were about to tell me of my father!'

Sir Pom-pom stepped forward. 'You might also specify how I am to find the location of the Holy Grail, that I may go to this spot and find it.'

Travante spoke more hesitantly: 'I would welcome even a hint in regard to my lost youth!'

'It is all a nuisance,' said Twisk fretfully. 'You must wait until another time.'

Madouc turned toward the castle and cried out: 'King Throbius! King Throbius! Where are you? Come here, if you please, and at once!'

Twisk jerked back in consternation. 'Why do you act so strangely? You lack all convention!'

A deep voice spoke; King Throbius himself stood at hand. 'Who calls my name with such unseemly shrieks, as if at the imminence of peril?'

Twisk spoke in a silken voice: 'Your Majesty, it was only an excess of girlish excitement; we are sorry you were disturbed.'

'Not so,' declared Madouc.

'I am puzzled,' said King Throbius. 'You were not excited or you were not sorry?'

'Neither, Your Highness.'

'Well then – what sent you into such frantic transports?'

'In truth, Your Highness, I wished to consult my mother in your presence, so that you might help her recollection when it faltered.'

King Throbius nodded sagely. 'And what memories did you wish to explore?'

'The identity of my father and the nature of my pedigree.'

King Throbius looked sternly at Twisk. 'As I recall, the episode was not altogether to your credit.'

'It went neither one way nor the other,' said Twisk, now crestfallen. 'It occurred as it occurred and that was the end to it.'

'And how went the details?' asked Madouc.

'It is not a tale for immature ears,' said King Throbius. 'But in this case we must make an exception. Twisk, will you tell the story, or must I assume the task?'

Twisk's response was sullen. 'The incidents are both ridiculous and embarrassing. They are nothing to blazon about, as if in pride, and I prefer to stand in detachment.'

'Then I will recount the episode. To begin with, I will point out that "embarrassment" is the other face of "vanity".'

'I have a profound admiration for myself,' said Twisk. 'Is this "vanity"? The point is debatable.'

'The term may or may not apply. I will now revert to a time some years in the past. Twisk, then as now, fancied herself a great beauty – as indeed she was and is. In her folly she teased and tormented Mangeon the troll, flaunting herself then leaping nimbly from his grasp, and taking gleeful pleasure in his expostulations. Mangeon finally became swollen with malice and decided to punish her for her tricks. One day, coming upon Twisk unaware, he seized her, dragged her up Wamble Way to Munkins Road, and chained her to Idilra Post which stands beside the crossroad. Mangeon then cast a spell, to hold the chains secure until Twisk had persuaded three wayfarers to engage her in erotic congress. Twisk will now elaborate upon the tale, if she is of a mind.'

'I am not so of a mind,' said Twisk crossly. 'Still, in the hope that my daughter Madouc may profit from my error, I will recount the circumstances.'

'Speak on,' said King Throbius.

'There is little to tell. The first to pass was the knight Sir Jaucinet of Castle Cloud in Dahaut. He was both courteous and sympathetic and would have persisted longer than was perhaps truly needful, but at last I dismissed him, since the time was close on dusk and I wished not to discourage other wayfarers. The second to pass was Nisby, a ploughboy on his way home from the field. He was most helpful, in a rude but vigorous fashion. He wasted no time since, so he explained, he expected bacon for his supper. I was desperate to be free before nightfall and was relieved to see him depart. Alas! I was to be disappointed! Dusk became evening; the moon rose full; it shone down from the sky as bright as an escutcheon of polished silver. Now along the road came a shadowy figure, cloaked in black, with a wide-brimmed hat shading his face from the moonlight, so that his features could not be discerned. He came at a slow gait, stopping every three paces, from watchfulness, or perhaps from mindless habit. I found him bereft of all appeal, and did not call out to him, that he might liberate me from the post. Nevertheless, he saw me by moonlight, and stopped short, to make an appraisal. Neither his posture nor his silence eased my misgivings; still, I could not depart by reason of the chain and its connection to Idilra Post, so I made a virtue of necessity and remained where I was. With slow and careful step the dark wayfarer approached and at last worked his will upon me. Where Nisby was abrupt and Sir Jaucinet elegant, the dark creature used a furious zeal lacking in all sentimentality, failing even to remove his hat. Neither did he speak his name, nor so much as comment upon the weather. My response, under the circumstances, was confined to cold disdain.

'Eventually the affair ran its course and I was free. The dark creature went off through the moonlight, his gait even slower and more thoughtful than before. I hastened back to Thripsey Shee.'

At this point, Queen Bossum, splendid in a gown of sapphire spangles and pale cobweb, came to join King Throbius, who turned to greet her with full gallantry.

Twisk continued her tale. 'In my term I was delivered of an infant, who brought me neither pleasure nor pride, by reason of her provenance. At the first opportunity and with little remorse I changed her for the infant Dhrun, and all the rest is known.'

Madouc made a sad sound. 'The case is even more confused than before! To whom will I look for my pedigree? To Nisby? To Sir Jaucinet? To the dark creature of the shadows? Must it be one of these?'

'I would think so,' said Twisk. 'Still, I guarantee nothing.'

'It is all most untidy,' said Madouc.

Twisk spoke with petulance: 'Then is then! Now is now,

and now is the festival! Vivacity tingles in the very air; see how the fairies dance and play! Notice Falael and the merry capers he is cutting! How he enjoys his liberation!'

Madouc turned to look. 'He is indeed very brisk. Still, dear mother, before you join the revelry, I need your further advice!'

'You shall have it and gladly! I advise that you depart Madling Meadow at this very instant! The day is waning, and soon the music will start. If you loiter you might be prompted to bide here all night long to your sorrow! Therefore I bid you farewell!'

King Throbius finished his gallant interchanges with Queen Bossum. He turned about in time to overhear Twisk's advice to Madouc, and was affected adversely. He called out: 'Twisk, I bid you stay!' He strode forward, and the twelve round-faced implets who carried his train were obliged to hop and run to keep pace.

King Throbius halted and made a stately gesture of admonition. 'Twisk, your conduct, on this day of joy, strikes a discord. At Thripsey Shee "faith", "truth" and "loyalty" are not just catch-words to be abandoned at the first inconvenience! You must dutifully assist your daughter, odd little crotchet though she may be!'

Twisk flung out her hands in despair. 'Sire, I have already gratified her needs to a surfeit! She arrived devoid of parents except for me, her mother; she may now select from any of three fathers, each with his distinctive pedigree. I could hardly have provided a greater choice and still retain my dignity.'

King Throbius nodded in measured approval. 'I commend your delicacy.'

'Thank you, Your Majesty! Now may I join the company?'

'Not yet! We are agreed to this extent: Madouc has an

amplitude of choice. Let us learn if she is pleasurably content.'

'Not at all!' cried Madouc. 'The case is worse than ever!'

'How so?'

'I have choices, but where do they lead? I shudder to think of the pedigree I might derive from the dark creature.'

'Aha! I believe that I understand your dilemma!' King Throbius turned to Twisk. 'Can you resolve this problem, or must I intervene?'

Twisk shrugged. 'My best efforts have evidently gone for naught. Madouc, His Highness has offered assistance; I suggest that you accept, after first inquiring what he wants in return. That is a mother's sage advice.'

King Throbius spoke severely: 'On this day of gladness, I will do what needs to be done, and demand nothing in return! Listen then, to my instructions! Bring hither to this spot your three putative fathers: Nisby, Sir Jaucinet, and the dark creature. Stand them together side by side; I will identify your father on the instant and discover the length of his pedigree!'

Madouc reflected for a moment. 'All very well, but what if the three refuse to come to Thripsey Shee?'

King Throbius reached to the ground and picked up a pebble. He touched it to his forehead, to his nose, to his chin, and finally to the point of his sharp fairy tongue. He handed the pebble to Madouc. 'Whomever you touch with this stone must follow where you lead, or stand at your command, until you touch him on the backside with this same stone and cry out: "Begone!" By this means you may induce the three to come with you.'

'Thank you, Your Highness! Only one detail remains.'

'What might that be?'

'Where shall I find these individuals?'

King Throbius frowned. 'That is a reasonable question. Twisk, what are your concepts in this regard?'

'Your Majesty, I know nothing for certain. Nisby came from the direction of the Dillydown; Sir Jaucinet mentioned Castle Cloud in Dahaut; as for the third I know nothing whatever.'

King Throbius signaled Twisk to the side. The two conferred for several minutes, then turned back to Madouc. 'The problem, as always, has a solution.'

'That is good news!' said Madouc. 'My dear mother Twisk has volunteered to make the search?'

King Throbius held up his hand to quell Twisk's instant outcry. 'The possibility was discussed, then abandoned. Our scheme is far more cunning! You shall not seek out these three individuals; instead, they shall come in search of you!'

Madouc's jaw dropped in bewilderment. 'I do not understand.'

'This is the plan. I shall disseminate to all quarters an information. Bosnip! Where is Bosnip?'

'Here I am, Sire!'

'Make an exact record of the following decree. Are you ready?'

Bosnip the Royal Scribe produced a sheet of mulberry paper, a vial of black-beetle ink, a long quill pen. 'Sire, I am ready!'

'This is the decree; write with your best flourishes:

"Can anyone forget the penalty visited upon the fairy Twisk, so proud and haughty, at Idilra Post? Now her equally beauteous daughter must also be chastened; is it not a pity? Like Twisk, she flaunted and teased, then ran off to hide. The penalty is just: like Twisk, she will be constrained to Idilra Post until liberated, as before, by some sympathetic passerby.

"So say I, Throbius, of Thripsey Shee, the King."'

357

Bosnip wrote with concentration, the tip of his black quill pen twitching back and forth at speed. King Throbius asked: 'You have transcribed these words?'

'Exactly, Sire!'

'That, then, shall be my decree,' said King Throbius. 'It shall be made known to all, save only the ogres Fuluot, Carabara, Gois and three-headed Throop. Nisby will hear, also Sir Jaucinet, and the dark creature as well, whatever his name and his nature.'

As Madouc listened to the decree, her mouth had drooped open in wonder. Finally, in a choked voice, she asked: 'Is this the crafty scheme, that I am to be chained to an iron post, and there subjected to unspeakable acts?'

King Throbius explained the details of his scheme in a patient if somewhat heavy voice: 'It is our theory that the three persons who liberated Twisk will wish to assist you in the same fashion. When they approach intent on their good offices, you need only touch them with the pebble to bring them under your control.'

Madouc discovered a flaw in the plan. 'Have you not noticed? I lack the attributes of my mother Twisk! Will any of the three be inclined even to approach the post? I see them coming in haste, taking note of me, stopping short, turning and running back the way they had come, careless if I were to be liberated or not.'

'The point is well taken,' said King Throbius. 'I will cast a glamor upon you, so that folk will be enthralled, and mistake you for a creature of allure.'

'Hmmf,' said Madouc. 'I suppose that will have to be the way of it.'

'The scheme is sound,' said Twisk.

Madouc was still not totally convinced. 'Might not our plans go awry in some unexpected way? Suppose the pebble lost its force, so that, willy-nilly, I was liberated even though I needed no such help?'

'It is a chance we must take,' said King Throbius. He stepped forward, fluttered his fingers over Madouc's head, muttered a cantrap of nineteen syllables, touched her chin, then stood back. 'The glamor is cast. To work its effect, pull at your left ear with the fingers of your right hand. To suspend the glamor, pull at your right ear with the fingers of your left hand.'

Madouc asked with interest: 'Shall I try it now?'

'As you like! You will notice the change only as it affects others; you yourself will not be altered.'

'For a test, then, I will try the spell.' Madouc tugged at her left ear with the fingers of her right hand, then turned to Sir Pom-pom and Travante. 'Can you notice a change?'

Sir Pom-pom drew a deep breath and seemed to clench his teeth. 'The change is definite.'

Travante made a wild, if controlled, gesture. 'I will describe the change. You are now a slender maiden, of perfect if not better conformation. Your eyes are as blue as the warm summer sea; they are melting and sympathetic, and look from a face tart and sweet, clever and wry, of a haunting fascination. Soft copper-gold curls swing past this face; the hair is scented with the perfume of lemon blossoms. Your form is enough to make a strong man weak. The glamor is effective.'

Madouc pulled at her right ear with the fingers of her left hand. 'Am I myself again?'

'Yes,' said Sir Pom-pom regretfully. 'You are as usual.'

Madouc heaved a sigh of relief. 'With the glamor upon me I feel somewhat conspicuous.'

King Throbius smiled. 'You must learn to ignore it, since, in your case, the glamor is no more than a reflection of the near future.' He looked up into the sky and signaled. Down flew a small green faylet with gauzy wings. King Throbius gave instructions: 'Gather your cousins, fly hither and yon, ensure that all creatures of the

359

neighborhood, save only three-headed Throop, Fuluot, Carabara, and Gois, learn the news of the decree which Bosnip will recite to you. Three especially must hear: Sir Jaucinet of Castle Cloud, the peasant Nisby, and the faceless creature who saunters abroad by moonlight wearing a broad-brimmed black hat.'

The faylet was gone. King Throbius gave Madouc a grave salute. 'I trust that our little scheme fulfills its purpose, without mistakes or inconvenience. In due course – ' A sudden tumult from across the meadow attracted his attention. He spoke in amazement. 'Can it be? Shemus and Womin, both officials of high degree, are at odds!'

King Throbius marched off across the meadow, so swiftly that the implets who carried his train were jerked from their feet and swept through the air.

King Throbius went to where a long table had been set with a variety of fine comestibles: ichors and wines in quaint glass bottles; pastries flavored with milkweed cream and the pollen of daffodil, buttercup and crocus; tarts of currants both black and red; candied crabapples; glacés and jellys; the crystallized nectars of sweet-briar, rose and violet. Beside the table an altercation had suddenly been transformed into a confusion of shouts, blows and curses. The parties at contention were Womin, Registrar of Rightnesses, and Shemus, Conductor of Rituals. Shemus had seized Womin's beard with one hand and was beating him over the head with a wooden mug, from which he had been drinking parsnip ale.

King Throbius spoke sharply: 'Why this sordid moil? It is shameful conduct on a day of such happiness!'

Shemus cried out in a passion: 'I would agree in all respects, Your Highness, had I not suffered an abominable affront from this rat-fanged old scavenger!'

'What are the facts? Describe your complaint!'

'Gladly! This degenerate registrar thought to work a

vulgar prank upon me! When I turned away for a moment, he dropped his foul stocking into my mug of parsnip ale.'

King Throbius turned to Womin. 'And what was your motive?'

'I had no motive!'

'None?'

'None! For this reason: I was not a party to the deed! The accusation is a canard! Yonder sits Falael, who witnessed the whole episode; he will attest to my innocence!'

King Throbius swung about. 'Well then, Falael: let us hear your testimony.'

'I was weaving a daisy chain,' said Falael. 'My attention was fixed upon my work; I saw nothing germane to the case.'

'Nonetheless, I am guiltless,' declared Womin. 'In view of my reputation, only a person with pot cheese for brains could think otherwise.'

'Not so!' stormed Shemus. 'If you are innocent, why are you wearing a single stocking? Why does the stocking I found in my ale show the same puce color as that on your leg?'

'It is a mystery!' stated Womin. 'Your Highness, hear me out! The party at fault is this ale-swilling old toad, who stands here fulminating like a mad thing! He struck me several stout blows, meanwhile drenching my stocking in his revolting tipple, into which he had undoubtedly snuffled and sniffed.'

Shemus jumped up and down in fury. 'That remark is a further provocation, worth at least two more blows!' Shemus would have chastised Womin further had not King Throbius stepped forward.

'Desist from this folly! Evidently a mistake has been made; let us carry the case no further!'

Womin and Shemus turned their backs on each other

and peace was restored. King Throbius returned across the meadow. He spoke to Madouc. 'I will bid you farewell, for the nonce. When you return with your three gentlemen-in-waiting, as we must call them, then we shall prove identities to your full satisfaction, and you will know your pedigree.'

Sir Pom-pom could no longer restrain his own urgencies. 'Please, Your Highness! I too need instruction! How shall I find the Holy Grail?'

King Throbius looked in puzzlement to Twisk. 'What might be the "Holy Grail"?'

'I have heard mention of the object, Your Highness. Long ago Sir Pellinore spoke of such an article. I believe it to be a cup, or something of the sort.'

'It is a chalice sacred to the Christians,' said Sir Pom-pom. 'I am anxious to find it, that I may earn a royal boon.'

King Throbius pulled at his beard. 'I know nothing of such an object; you must seek elsewhere for information.'

Travante also made bold to put a request: 'Perhaps Your Highness will instruct me as to where I might search for my lost youth.'

King Throbius again pulled at his beard. 'Was it mislaid or truly lost? Do you remember any of the pertinent circumstances?'

'Unfortunately not, Your Highness. I had it; I lost it; it was gone.'

King Throbius gave his head a dubious shake. 'After such long neglect, it might be almost anywhere. As you travel the roads, you must keep on the alert. I can tell you this: if you find it, be nimble indeed!' King Throbius reached high into the air and brought down a silver hoop two feet in diameter. 'If you find what you seek, capture it with this hoop. It was once the property of the nymph Atalanta, and is in itself a great curiosity.'

'I thank Your Highness.' Travante tucked the hoop carefully over his shoulder and inside his doublet.

King Throbius and Queen Bossum gave stately bows of farewell and strolled away across the meadow. Even as they went a new commotion broke out near the long table, again involving Womin. The activity consisted of screams, outcries and angry gesticulations. It appeared that someone, both cunning and deft, had purloined Womin's single remaining stocking and had affixed it to the crest of the chatelaine Batinka's elaborate coiffure, where it created a ridiculous and humiliating spectacle. Batinka, upon discovering the prank, had chided Womin and had tweaked his nose. The usually mild-mannered Womin, after taking Falael's quiet advice, had retaliated by pushing Batinka's face into a pudding. At this point King Throbius intervened. Batinka cited Womin's misdeeds which Womin denied, save for his use of the pudding. Once again he asserted that Falael could bear witness as to his blamelessness. King Throbius, as before, turned to Falael for the facts, but Falael, as before, claimed to have been preoccupied with his daisy chain, to the exclusion of all else.

King Throbius considered the case for a moment or two, then turned to Falael: 'Where is the daisy chain upon which you have been so diligently employed?'

Falael was taken aback by the unexpected request. He looked here and there and at last cried out: 'Aha! Here it is!'

'Indeed. You are certain?'

'Of course!'

'And you worked throughout the period of both episodes involving Womin, without so much as raising your eyes: so you have attested.'

'Then it must be so, since I am a stickler for accurate detail.'

363

'I count nine flowers to this chain. They are marigolds, not daisies. What do you say to that?'

Falael shifted his gaze here and there. 'I was paying no great heed, Your Highness.'

'Falael, the evidence suggests that you have been paltering with the truth, giving false testimony, performing mischievous pranks and attempting to deceive your king.'

'It is surely a mistake, Your Highness!' said Falael, his expression brimming with limpid innocence.

King Throbius was not deceived. In a grave voice, and despite Falael's reedy expostulations, he imposed a penalty of another seven years' itch. Falael dolefully went to sit on his post, and once more began to scratch his affected parts.

King Throbius called out: 'Let the festival proceed, though now we must consider it a celebration of hope, rather than accomplishment!'

Meanwhile Twisk had bidden Madouc and her company farewell. 'It has been a pleasure to have seen you again! Perhaps some day at another time – '

'But good mother Twisk!' cried Madouc. 'Have you forgotten? I shall soon return to Thripsey Shee!'

'True,' sighed Twisk, 'presuming that you avoid the dangers of the forest.'

'Are these then so terrible?'

'Sometimes the forest is sweet and clear,' said Twisk. 'Sometimes evil lurks behind every stump. Do not explore the morass which borders on Wamble Way; the long-necked heceptors will rise from the slime. In the gully nearby lives the troll Mangeon; avoid him as well. Do not fare west along Munkins Road; you would come to Castle Doldil, the seat of three-headed Throop the ogre. He has caged many a brave knight and devoured many more, perhaps including gallant Sir Pellinore.'

'And where shall we sleep by night?'

'Accept no hospitality! It will cost you dear! Take this kerchief.' Twisk gave Madouc a square of pink and white silk. 'At sundown place it upon the turf and call out "Aroisus!" It will become a pavilion for both safety and comfort. In the morning, call out: "Deplectus!" and the pavilion will again become a kerchief. And now – '

'Wait! Where is the way to Idilra Post?'

'You must cross the meadow and pass under the tall ash tree. As you go, pay no heed to the festival! Taste no wine; eat no fairy-cake; tap not so much as your toe to fairy music! Beside the ash tree Wamble Way leads to the north; after twelve miles, you will come to the crossing with Munkins Road, and here stands Idilra Post, where I suffered my many trials.'

Madouc spoke soothingly: 'It was, on the whole, a lucky occasion, since, as a consequence, I am here to gladden your heart!'

Twisk could not restrain a smile. 'At times you can be quite appealing, with your sad blue eyes and strange little face! Good-bye then, and take care!'

Madouc, Sir Pom-pom and Travante crossed Madling Meadow to the ash tree and set out to the north along Wamble Way. When the sun sank low, Madouc placed the kerchief upon the turf of a little glade beside the way and called out: "Aroisus!" At once the kerchief became a pavilion furnished with three soft beds and a table loaded with good food and flasks of wine and bitter ale.

During the night peculiar sounds could be heard from the forest, and on several occasions there was the pad of heavy footsteps along Wamble Way. On each occasion, the creature halted as it paused to inspect the pavilion, and then, after consideration, continued along the way and about its business.

IV

Morning sunlight slanted through the forest to lay bright red spatters on the pink and white silk of the pavilion. Madouc, Sir Pom-pom and Travanté arose from their beds. Outside the pavilion dew glistened on the turf; the forest was silent save for an occasional bird-call.

The three breakfasted at the bountiful table, then prepared to depart. Madouc called out "Deplectus!" and the pavilion collapsed to a pink and white kerchief which Madouc tucked into her wallet.

The three set off up Wamble Way, with both Sir Pom-pom and Travante keeping a careful lookout for the objects of their quest, as King Throbius had advised.

The lane skirted a tract of quaking black mud, inter-sected by rills of dark water. Tussocks of reed, burdock and saw-grass broke the surface, as well as an occasional clump of stunted willow or rotting alder. Bubbles rose up through the slime, and from one of the larger tussocks came a croaking voice, of unintelligible import. The three wayfarers only hastened their steps, and without untoward incident left the morass behind.

Wamble Way veered to avoid a steep-sided hillock with a crag of black basalt at the summit. A path paved with black cobbles led into a shadowy gulch. Beside the path a sign indited with characters of black and red, presented two quatrains of doggerel for the edification of passersby:

NOTICE!

> Let travellers heed! This message confides
> That Mangeon the Marvellous herein resides!
> When Mangeon is wrathful his enemies quail;
> But friends drink his health in beakers of ale.

366

His visage is handsome, his address is fine;
His touch causes damsels to sigh and repine.
They beg his caress; at his parting they weep,
And they murmur his name full oft as they sleep.

The three passed sign and cobblestone path without so much as a pause, and continued northward along Wamble Way.

With the sun halfway up the sky they arrived at the crossing with Munkins Road. Beside the intersection stood a massive iron post: almost a foot in diameter and eight feet tall.

Madouc surveyed the post with disfavor. 'Taken all with all, the situation is not to my liking. But it seems that I must carry out my part in the charade, misgivings or not.'

'Why else are you here?' growled Sir Pom-pom.

Madouc deigned no reply. 'I will now work the glamor upon myself!' She tweaked her left ear with the fingers of her right hand, then looked toward her companions. 'Has the spell taken effect?'

'Noticeably,' said Travante. 'You have become a maiden of fascinating appeal.'

Sir Pom-pom asked: 'How can you bind yourself to the post when we lack both chain and rope?'

'We will do without the binding,' said Madouc decisively. 'Should there be a question, I will make an excuse.'

Travante uttered a caution: 'Keep your magic stone ready at hand, and take care not to drop it!'

'That is good advice,' said Madouc. 'Go now and take yourselves well out of sight.'

Sir Pom-pom became difficult and wanted to hide nearby in the bushes, that he might see what went on, but Madouc would not listen. 'Leave at once! Do not show yourselves until I call! Furthermore, do not be peeking and peering, inasmuch as you might be seen!'

367

Sir Pom-pom demanded in sour tones: 'What will you be doing that requires such privacy?'

'That is none of your affair!'

'I am not so sure of that, especially were I to earn the royal boon.' Sir Pom-pom showed a sly grin. 'Even more especially since you control the glamor.'

'The boon will not include me; rest easy on that score! Now go, or I will touch you with the pebble and send you off in a stupor!'

Sir Pom-pom and Travante went off to the west along Munkins Road and around a bend. They discovered a little glade a few yards from the road and seated themselves on a log where they could not be seen by passersby.

Madouc stood alone at the crossroads. She looked in all directions and listened carefully. Nothing could be seen or heard. She went to Idilra Post and gingerly seated herself at its base.

Time went by: long minutes and hours. The sun reached its zenith, then slid past into the west. There were neither comings nor goings, save only for the furtive appearance of Sir Pom-pom, who came peering around the bend in Munkins Road that he might discover what, if anything, had taken place. Madouc sent him back the way he had come with a sharp rebuke.

Another hour passed. From the east came the faint sound of someone whistling. The tune was sprightly, yet somehow tentative as if the whistler were not completely confident or assured.

Madouc rose to her feet and waited. The whistling grew louder. Along Munkins Road came a young man, stocky and stalwart, with a broad placid face and a thatch of chestnut hair. His garments and soiled buskins identified him as a peasant well acquainted with both pasture and barn.

Arriving in the crossroads he halted and surveyed

368

Madouc with frank curiosity. At last he spoke: 'Maiden, are you pent here against your will? I see no chain!'

'It is a magic chain, and I may not win free until three persons undertake my release, and this by an unconventional method.'

'Indeed so? And what awful crime could have been committed by so lovely a creature?'

'I am guilty of three faults: frivolity, vanity and foolishness.'

The peasant spoke in puzzlement: 'Why should they bring so stern a penalty?'

'That is the way of the world,' said Madouc. 'A certain proud person wished to become over-amiable, but I derided him and pointed out his lack of appeal. He ordained my humiliation, so here I wait upon the charitable attention of three strangers.'

The young peasant came forward. 'How many have assisted you to date?'

'You are the first to pass.'

'As it happens, I am a man of compassion. Your plight has aroused my pity, and something else besides. If you will dispose yourself comfortably, we shall spend a merry interval, before I am obliged to return home to my cows and their milking.'

'Step a bit closer,' said Madouc. 'What is your name?'

'I am Nisby of Fobwiler Farm.'

'Just so,' said Madouc. 'Come just a bit closer.'

Nisby stepped bravely forward. Madouc touched the pebble to his chin. Nisby at once became rigid. 'Follow me,' said Madouc. She led him off the road, and behind a copse of bayberry trees. On the turf she laid the pink and white kerchief. 'Aroisus!'

The kerchief became a pavilion. 'Enter,' said Madouc. 'Sit down on the floor; make neither sound nor disturbance.'

Madouc returned to Idilra Post and seated herself as before. The hours passed slowly, and once again Sir Pom-pom could not restrain his curiosity; Madouc saw the shine of his face through a growth of mullein plants. Pretending not to notice, she hissed softly through her teeth and activated the Imp-spring Tinkle-toe. Up from the mullein leapt Sir Pom-pom, to bound a full three feet into the air. Madouc called out: 'What are you up to now, Sir Pom-pom, with your wild leaps? Did I not beg you to remain out of sight until I called?'

'I only wanted to make sure of your safety!' declared Sir Pom-pom in a surly voice. 'I did not intend to disturb you, no matter what you were up to; still, for some reason, I was forced to leap into the air.'

'Please do not trouble yourself again,' said Madouc. 'Go back to where you left Travante.'

Sir Pom-pom departed with poor grace, and again Madouc disposed herself to wait.

Fifteen minutes passed. A jingling sound reached her ears. She rose to her feet and stood waiting. Down Wamble Way from the north came a creature running on eight splayed legs. Its head was like that of a great seahorse, rearing high from a torso segmented of dark yellow plates. Astride the creature sat a faun with a crafty brown face, small horns, and lower limbs overgrown with coarse brown fur. From his saddle and bridle hung a hundred small bells, which jingled to the gait of his bizarre steed.

The faun brought the creature to a halt and stared at Madouc. 'Why do you sit so calmly by Idilra Post?'

'I am calm by nature.'

'It is as good a reason as any. What do you think of my noble mount?'

'I have never seen such a creature before.'

'Nor I, but it is docile enough. Will you ride at my

back? I am bound for the isle in Kallimanthos Pond, where the wild grapes hang in purple tumbles.'

'I must wait here.'

'As you wish.' The faun urged his steed into motion. He was soon out of sight, and his jingling gone from hearing.

The sun declined into the west. Madouc began to fret and wonder; she had no wish to sit by Idilra Post during the long hours of night.

From eastward along Munkins Road came the *rumpety-tump rumpety-tump* of galloping hooves. Just short of the crossroads the sound diminished as the horse slowed to a walk. A moment later a knight in half-armor, mounted on a fine bay horse, rode into view.

The knight drew up his horse. For a moment he studied Madouc, then dismounted and tied the horse to a tree. He lifted the helmet from his head and hung it to the saddle. Madouc saw a gentleman somewhat past his first youth, with lank yellow hair hanging beside a long mournful face. Heavy-lidded eyes drooped at the corners; long yellow mustaches dangled to either side of his mouth, creating an impression of amiable impracticality.

He turned to face Madouc and performed a courtly bow. 'Allow me to present myself. I am Sir Jaucinet of Castle Cloud, and a knight of full chivalry. May I inquire your name, your condition and why I find you in such dismal straits, standing as if in need of succor beside Idilra Post?'

'You may ask, certainly,' said Madouc. 'I would gladly answer in full were it not that dusk is coming on, and the sooner I am finished with my deplorable duty the better.'

'Well spoken!' declared Sir Jaucinet. 'I take it that I can be of assistance?'

'True. Be kind enough to approach. No; you need not remove your armor as of this particular instant.'

'Are you sure?' asked Sir Jaucinet doubtfully.

'Quite sure, if you will only come a few steps closer.'

'With pleasure! You are a most beautiful maiden; let me kiss you!'

'Sir Jaucinet, under different conditions I would consider you extremely forward, or even brisk. But still . . .'

Sir Jaucinet stepped close and in due course joined Nisby inside the pavilion.

Madouc resumed her vigil. The sun sank low, and once again Sir Pom-pom showed himself, now brazenly in the middle of the road. He called: 'How long must we dawdle here? Darkness approaches: I do not want to mingle with creatures of the night.'

'Come then,' said Madouc. 'Bring Travante; the two of you may sit in the pavilion.'

Sir Pom-pom and Travante hastened to follow the suggestion, and now it was discovered that the pavilion had added to itself another chamber, where Nisby and Sir Jaucinet sat in conditions of apathy.

The sun disappeared behind the trees. Madouc stretched her cramped muscles, walked three paces in all directions, looked up each road, but vision blurred in the gathering dusk and she discovered nothing.

Madouc went back to the post, and stood with uneasiness tweaking at her nerves.

Twilight shrouded the Forest of Tantrevalles. For a period Madouc watched the bats wheeling and darting overhead. As twilight waned the sky went dark, then brightened in the east as the moon rose into the sky.

Madouc shivered to a waft of cool air. She wondered if she truly wanted to stand by Idilra Post in the wan moonlight.

Probably not. She brooded over the reasons why she had come, and she thought of Nisby and Sir Jaucinet secure in the pavilion: two of the three. Madouc sighed and looked apprehensively in every direction. All color was gone, blanched by the moonlight. The roads were silver-gray; shadows were black.

The moon rose up the sky.

An owl drifted across the forest and was briefly silhouetted upon the face of the moon.

Madouc saw a shooting star.

From far off in the forest came an odd hooting sound.

The moving shadow Madouc had been expecting came along the road, advancing step by slow step. Fifteen feet from the post it halted. A black cloak muffled the body; a broad-brimmed hat shaded the face. Madouc shrank back against the post, tense and quiet.

The shadowed figure stood motionless. Madouc drew a slow breath. She peered, trying to discern a face under the hat. She saw nothing. The area was blank, as if she were looking into a void.

Madouc spoke, her voice tremulous: 'Who are you, dark shadow?'

The shape made no response.

Madouc tried again: 'Are you dumb? Why will you not speak?'

The shadow whispered: 'I have come to succor you from the post. Long ago I did the same for the wilful fairy Twisk, to her great content. You shall be allowed the same comfort. Remove your garments, that I may see your form in the moonlight.'

Madouc gripped the stone so tightly that she feared she might drop it, which would never do. She quavered: 'It is considered genteel for the gentleman to divest himself first.'

'That is not important,' whispered the dark shape. 'It is time to proceed.'

The creature sidled forward and reached to remove Madouc's gown. She thrust with the pebble into the blank countenance, but met only emptiness. In a panic she pressed the pebble at the groping hands, but the sleeves of the cloak thwarted her effort. The shadow brushed her arm aside and bore her to the ground; the pebble jarred loose and went rolling. Madouc gave a sad little cry, and for an instant lay limp; it was almost her ruin. But now, with a spasmodic effort, she squirmed free and groped for the pebble. The shadow seized her leg. 'Why this mettlesome agility? Calm yourself and lie quiet! Otherwise the process becomes exhausting.'

'One moment,' gasped Madouc. 'The process already goes too fast.'

'That to the side, let us continue.'

Madouc's fingers closed on the pebble. She thrust it against the black form and touched the creature in one of its parts. At once it went lax.

Madouc rose gratefully to her feet. She settled her gown and ran her fingers through her hair, then looked down at the listless shadow. 'Rise; follow me!'

She took the shambling figure to the side chamber of the pavilion where Nisby and Sir Jaucinet sat staring into vacancy. 'Enter; sit; do not move until I give the command.'

Madouc stood in the moonlight for a moment, looking out upon the crossroads. She told herself: 'I have succeeded, but now I am almost afraid to learn the truth. Sir Jaucinet seems the most noble, while the shadow is the most mysterious. There is little to be said for Nisby except his rustic simplicity.'

She thought of the glamor. 'It seems to make me more conspicuous than I like; for the nonce, I shall have done with it.' With the fingers of her left hand she tweaked the lobe of her right ear. 'Is it gone?' she wondered. 'I feel no change in myself.' When she entered the pavilion, the demeanor of both Sir Pom-pom and Travante assured her that the glamor had gone, which brought her a hurtful, if illogical, little twinge of something like regret.

V

In the morning Madouc, Sir Pom-pom and Travante breakfasted within the pavilion. It was thought best that neither Nisby nor Sir Jaucinet be aroused to take nourishment for which they might or might not feel appetite. The same considerations applied even more persuasively to the shadowy figure in the black cloak, who by day was as bizarre and incomprehensible as by night. Under the wide brim of his hat opened a void into which no one cared to look too closely.

After breakfast Madouc marshaled Nisby, Sir Jaucinet and the nameless shadow-thing out into the road. Sir Jaucinet's horse had broken loose during the night and was nowhere to be seen.

Madouc reduced the pavilion to a kerchief; the party set off to the south down Wamble Way, Sir Pom-pom and Travante taking the lead, Madouc coming after, followed by Nisby, then Sir Jaucinet, and finally the individual in the black cloak.

Shortly before noon, the group once again entered Madling Meadow, which, as before, seemed only a grassy expanse with a hummock at the center. Madouc called softly: 'Twisk! Twisk! Twisk!'

Mists and vapors confused their eyes, dissipating to reveal the fairy castle, with banners at every turret. The festival decorations celebrating Falael's rehabilitation were no longer in evidence; as for Falael, he had abandoned his post for the moment and sat under a birch tree to the edge of the meadow, using a twig to reach inaccessible areas of his back.

Twisk appeared beside Madouc, today wearing pale blue pantaloons riding low on her hips and a shirt of white diaphane. 'You have wasted no time,' said Twisk. She inspected Madouc's captives. 'How the sight of those three takes me back in memory! But there are changes! Nisby has become a man; Sir Jaucinet seems dedicated to wistful yearning.'

Madouc said: 'It is the effect of his plaintive eyes and the long droop of his mustaches.'

Twisk averted her eyes from the third member of the group. 'As for yonder odd creature, King Throbius shall judge. Come; we must interrupt his contemplations, but that is the way of it.'

The group trooped across the meadow to a place at the front of the castle. Fairies of the shee came from all directions: bounding, flitting, turning cartwheels and somersaults, to crowd close and babble questions; to pry, pinch and poke. From his place under the birch tree Falael came at a hop and a run, to mount his post the more readily to observe events.

At the main portal to the castle a pair of young heralds stood proudly on duty. They were splendid in livery of black and yellow diaper and carried clarions turned from fairy silver. At Twisk's behest they turned toward the castle and blew three brilliant fanfares of coruscating harmonies.

The heralds lowered their horns and wiped their mouths with the back of their hands, grinning all the while at Twisk.

A silence of expectation held the area, broken only by the giggles of three implets who were trying to tie small green frogs into Sir Jaucinet's mustaches. Twisk chided the implets and sent them away. Madouc went to remove the frogs but was interrupted by the appearance of King Throbius on a balcony, fifty feet above the meadow. In a stern voice he called to the heralds: 'What means this wanton summons? I was engrossed in meditation!'

One of the heralds called up to the balcony: 'It was Twisk! She ordered us to disturb your rest.'

The other herald corroborated the statement. 'She told us to blow a great blast that would startle you from your bed to the floor.'

Twisk gave an indifferent shrug. 'Blame me, if you like; however, I acted on the insistence of Madouc, whom you may remember.'

Madouc, with an injured glance toward Twisk, stepped forward. 'I am here!'

'So I see! What of that?'

'Do you not remember? I went to Idilra Post that I might learn the identity of my father!' She indicated the three individuals at her back. 'Here is Nisby the peasant, Sir Jaucinet the knight; also this mysterious shape of no category, nor yet any face.'

'I remember the case distinctly!' said King Throbius. He looked across the area with disapproval. 'Fairies! Why do you thrust and crush and press with such rude energy? One and all, stand back! Now then: Twisk! You must make a sure and careful inspection.'

'One glance was enough,' said Twisk.

'And your findings?'

'I recognize Nisby and Sir Jaucinet. As for the shadow, his face is invisible, which in itself is a significant index.'

'It is indeed unique. The case has aspects of interest.'

King Throbius stepped back from the balcony and a moment later came out upon the meadow. Again the fairies crowded about, to chortle and murmur, to mow and leer, until King Throbius issued orders so furious that his subjects shrank back abashed.

'Now then!' said King Throbius. 'We will proceed. Madouc, for you this must be a happy occasion! Soon you will be able to claim one of these three for your beloved father.'

Madouc dubiously considered the possibilities. 'Sir Jaucinet undoubtedly boasts the best pedigree; still I cannot believe that I am related to someone who looks like a sick sheep.'

'All will be made known,' said King Throbius confidently. He looked to right and left. 'Osfer! Where are you?'

'I have expected your call, Your Highness! I stand directly behind your royal back.'

'Come forward, Osfer, into the purview of my eyes. We must exercise your craft. Madouc's paternity is in question and we must definitely resolve the issue.'

Osfer stepped forward: a fairy of middle maturity, brown of skin and gnarled of limb, with eyes of amber and a nose which hooked almost to meet an upjutting chin. 'Sire, your orders?'

'Go to your workshop; return with dishes of Matronian nephrite, to the number of five; bring probers, nitsnips, and a gill of your Number Six Elixir.'

'Your Highness, I presumed to anticipate your commands, and I already have these items at hand.'

'Very good, Osfer. Order your varlets to bring hither a table; let it be spread with a cloth of gray murvaille.'

'The order has been effected, Sire. The table stands ready at your left hand.'

King Throbius turned to inspect the arrangements. 'Well done, Osfer. Now then: bring out your best extractor; we shall need fibrils of coming and going. When all is ready, we will contrive our matrices.'

'In minutes only, Your Highness! I move with the speed of flashing nymodes when urgency is the call!'

'Do so now! Madouc is hard-put to restrain her eagerness; it is as if she were dancing upon thorns.'

'A pathetic case, to be sure,' said Osfer. 'But soon indeed she will be able to embrace her father.'

In a subdued voice Madouc spoke to King Throbius: 'Enlighten me, Your Highness! How will you prove the case?'

'Be attentive; all will be made known. Twisk, why are you so exercised?'

'Osfer is molesting me!'

'Not so, Your Highness! You were about to order matrices; I had already started to apply the drain to Twisk.'

'Of course. Twisk, we must have three minims of your blood; be stoic.'

'I am loth to endure these martyrdoms! Is it truly needful?'

King Throbius made a meaningful sign. Hissing between her teeth Twisk gingerly allowed Osfer to ply his instruments. He took a quantity of blood from her slender wrist, which he then discharged into one of the nephrite dishes. By processes too swift for Madouc to follow, he used the blood to nurture a fragile construction of fibers and small blue, red and green plasms.

Osfer turned proudly to King Throbius. 'It is perfection in all respects! Each quirk and phase of Twisk's somewhat devious nature are open for inspection.'

'You have done well.' King Throbius turned to Madouc. 'Now it is your turn; from your blood Osfer will grow a matrix that is yours alone.'

Madouc cried out between clenched teeth. 'My turn has come and gone! He has already done his worst to me!'

Presently a matrix somewhat similar to that derived from Twisk appeared on a second plate.

'Next, let us try Sir Jaucinet!' said King Throbius. 'Soon we shall see who is father to whom!'

Osfer drew blood from Sir Jaucinet's nerveless arm and constructed the matrix peculiar to the lord of Castle Cloud.

King Throbius turned to Madouc. 'There you see three matrices, representing the innate fabric of yourself, your mother Twisk and this noble knight. By the most subtle means, Osfer will now subtract the influence of Twisk from your matrix, to create a new matrix. If your father is Sir Jaucinet, the new matrix will be identical to his, and you will know the truth of your paternity. Osfer, you may proceed.'

'Sire, I have completed the operation. Behold the two matrices!'

'I assume they are identical?' said King Throbius.

'Not at all, and in no particular!'

'Aha!' said King Throbius. 'So much for Sir Jaucinet; he may be excused. Liberate him from your thrall, Madouc; bid him be on his way.'

Madouc obeyed the instruction. Sir Jaucinet gave instant vent to peevish complaints, and demanded reasons for the many inconveniences to which he had been put.

'I can give you no easy response,' said Madouc. 'It is a long and detailed story.'

'What of the frogs in my mustache?' demanded Sir Jaucinet. 'Is their presence such a complicated affair?'

'Not altogether,' Madouc admitted. 'Still, King Throbius has ordered your departure, and you had best hurry, since the afternoon is waning and the way is long.'

Sir Jaucinet, his expression one of deep chagrin, turned on his heel. 'Wait!' called King Throbius. 'Osfer, apply the "Four-fold Spell" to speed good Sir Jaucinet on his journey.'

'Indeed, Sire, while he conferred with Madouc, I applied the "Six-fold Spell",' said Osfer.

'Good work, Osfer!' King Throbius spoke to Sir Jaucinet: 'As you march home, each of your strides will carry you six yards, and you will arrive at Castle Cloud well before you expected.'

Sir Jaucinet bowed stiffly; first to King Throbius and then to Osfer. For Madouc he spared only a glance of moist-eyed reproach; then he was gone, bounding across Madling Meadow on six-fold strides, and was soon lost to sight.

King Throbius turned to Osfer. 'Now then: let us deal with the peasant Nisby.'

'Sire, you will note on this dish the matrix of Nisby, which I have already taken the liberty of constructing.'

Madouc went to look. To her dismay, Nisby's matrix resembled hers not at all, and everyone agreed that her paternity surely resided elsewhere than with Nisby. Glumly Madouc liberated him from his nerveless apathy; Osfer applied the 'Six-fold Spell' and Nisby was sent on his way.

King Throbius addressed Madouc in a somber voice: 'My dear, I have taken your interest to heart, and I cannot say that I am pleased with our findings. You have been sired neither by Sir Jaucinet nor by Nisby; hence, we are left with this shadowy weirdling with vacancy for a face. The Third Statute of Logic, sometimes known as the "Law of Exclusion", forces me to declare him your father. You may liberate him and hold your reunion at whatever time and place suits your best convenience; no doubt you will have much to tell each other.'

Madouc cried out in a troubled voice: 'Your logic is naturally superb, but should we not also test this creature's matrix?'

King Throbius spoke to Osfer: 'What is your opinion?'

'I suggest a third matrix, if only to create a philosophical symmetry.'

King Throbius said: 'I am not opposed, though the test will be redundant. However, you may approach Madouc's father, draw three minims of blood and erect a matrix for all to see.'

Osfer gingerly approached the black-cloaked figure, then halted in bafflement.

King Throbius called out: 'Why do you delay? We are anxious to demonstrate Madouc's paternity!'

'I am in a quandary,' said Osfer. 'He wears cloak, boots and gloves; he lacks neck, face and scalp. In order to draw his blood, I must remove the cloak, and expose his person. Shall I proceed?'

'Proceed, by all means!' commanded King Throbius. 'Ordinarily we would respect his modesty, but delicacy must be put aside, along with the cloak. Madouc, you may avert your eyes if you wish.'

'I will see what needs to be seen,' said Madouc. She ignored Sir Pom-pom's disparaging snort. 'Continue with the work.'

Osfer, with little fingers extended, in the manner of a fastidious tailor, unclasped the buckle at the neck of the cloak, which then fell somewhat apart. Osfer looked into the gap and gave a startled exclamation. With a single sweep he drew the cloak aside, to reveal a squat gray-faced troll with a bottle nose, pendulous cheeks and eyes like small balls of black glass. His arms were long and knotted; his splayed legs were thrust into tall boots. Osfer cried out: 'It is Mangeon the troll!'

Twisk gave a thin wailing shriek of distress. 'Now I understand all! With what ignoble cunning he took his lewd revenge!'

Madouc quavered: 'Despite all logic, can this truly be my father?'

'We shall see!' said King Throbius. 'Osfer, build the matrix!'

'Sire, I have preceded your command! The matrix is already formed! You may examine it as you see fit, and compare it with that provided by Madouc.'

King Throbius peered down at the two matrices. He spoke in perplexity. 'How can it be? Does madness rule the world? Does the sun rise in the west? Is water wet and fire hot, or is it all in reverse? Logic has played us all false! This matrix is more at discord than both of the others together! I am baffled!'

Madouc could not restrain a yelp of happy relief. 'Sir Jaucinet is not my father. Nisby is not my father. This repulsive halfling is not my father. Who then is my father?'

King Throbius examined Twisk with a speculative eye. 'Can you clarify this puzzle?'

The dispirited Twisk could only shake her head. 'The time is long past. I cannot remember every trifle.'

'Still, one of these trifles produced Madouc.'

'So much is conceded,' said Twisk, 'but memories blend; faces merge. When I shut my eyes, I hear whispers: beguilements, adoration, sighs of love requited – but I find no name for these voices.'

King Throbius noticed Madouc's disconsolate face. He said: 'Do not despair! There remains yet another arrow in the quiver! But first I must deal with this odious troll.'

Twisk spoke with fervor. 'He deserves no mercy; he caused me great unease.'

King Throbius pulled at his beard. 'It is a complex situation, since I cannot decide which of our laws he has violated. His trickery was instigated in part by Twisk herself, but his response seems inordinately rude. Flirts through the ages have notoriously enjoyed immunity.' King Throbius paced back and forth, and the implets who carried his train were hard-put to carry out their duties.

383

Osfer meanwhile took Mangeon somewhat aside, along with several of his thaumaturgical instruments.

King Throbius came to a halt. He raised his hand in a majestic gesture. 'I have arrived at a judgment. Mangeon's conduct has been sordid and disreputable. Further, he has affronted the dignity of Thripsey Shee. The penalty must be consonant with the offense; still we must take note of contributory circumstances. We will therefore allow Mangeon tranquility and scope for remorse; we will urge him, whether he is so inclined or not, along the narrow path of restraint. Osfer, do you understand the nature of my indication, or must I spell it out in full detail?'

'Sire, I have understood you fully, and indeed I have already implemented your sentence, in full and final scope.'

'Osfer, you are a marvel of efficiency!' King Throbius turned to Madouc. 'You may now release Mangeon from his paralysis.'

Madouc touched Mangeon with the pebble. Instantly he gave vent to furious roaring complaint. 'I deplore the outrages committed upon my person! They represent an irresponsible philosophy!'

King Throbius spoke with dignity: 'You are free to depart; be happy on this account!'

'I am free, but to what purpose?' roared Mangeon. 'How now will I occupy the long hours of day and night? With poetry? By observing the flight of butterflies? Your judgment was incorrect!'

King Throbius made a peremptory gesture. 'I will hear no more! Be off to your ill-smelling hovel.'

Mangeon threw his arms into the air and ran off across the meadow, to disappear up Wamble Way.

King Throbius returned to Madouc. 'We must re-examine your case. Osfer, I suggest simulacra and the subtractive effect.'

'Exactly my opinion, Your Highness! I have prepared for the process.'

'Proceed, if you will.'

Osfer placed three silver plates upon the table. Twisk watched with a frown of foreboding. 'What is this new plan, and what does it entail?'

Osfer replied in soothing tones. 'It is the most elegant and subtle procedure of all! Soon you will look into the face of Madouc's father.'

Twisk frowned in annoyance. 'Why did you not work this sleight before and spare me the anguish of the blood-letting?'

'It is not so simple as we might like it to be. Step forward, if you will.'

'What? Not again! You shall have no more of my vital fluids! Do you wish me to become a wisp, a wraith, a desiccation?'

King Throbius called a sharp command and Twisk, writhing and moaning, at last allowed Osfer to draw off another three minims of her blood.

Osfer worked his thaumaturgy and up from the plate rose a simulacrum of Twisk's lovely head.

Next, Osfer signaled to Madouc. 'Come!'

Madouc cried out: 'I too am dangerously weak! If blood is needed, drain Sir Pom-pom, or even King Throbius himself.'

'That is an impractical suggestion,' said King Throbius. 'It is your blood which is needed! Quickly! We cannot waste all day!'

Madouc, scowling and wincing, allowed Osfer to draw three minims of her blood, from which Osfer contrived a second simulacrum.

'Now then!' said Osfer. 'We proceed as follows: Madouc is the sum of Twisk and an unknown father. Therefore, if we subtract the influence of Twisk from Madouc, what remains will depict the visage of Madouc's father, at least in general terms and perhaps blurred by discrepancies. So, stand back all, since I must work with a delicate touch!'

Osfer moved the two representations so that they faced each other, then arranged four panels of grass-cloth to form a screen around the two heads. 'I now adjure all to silence! Any distraction will alter the precision of my work!'

Osfer arranged his instruments, uttered eight staccato syllables, and clapped his hands. 'The spell has been effected.' Osfer removed the screens. One of the silver plates was empty. 'Twisk's image has been subtracted from that of Madouc. What remains is the likeness of Madouc's sire!'

Madouc stared at the residual face. With only half the substance, it was vague and colorless, as if formed of mist. The features seemed to represent a young man with irregular features in a rather gaunt long-jawed face and a suggestion of reckless optimism in his expression. His hair was cut in the Aquitanian style, and he wore a short modish beard at the chin. The face, though not ill-favored, lacked a patrician cast. Even in its blurred condition, the face affected Madouc with a rush of warm impulses.

Twisk was staring at the face in fascination. Madouc asked: 'What is his name?'

Twisk, now thoroughly out of sorts, made a capricious gesture and tossed her head. 'His name? It might be anyone. The features are indefinite; it is like looking through the fog.'

'Surely you recognize him?' cried Madouc. 'He even looks half-familiar to me.'

Twisk gave an airy shrug. 'Why should he not? You are seeing what is drawn from your own face.'

'Whatever the case, can you supply his name?'

Twisk said carelessly: 'I am truly bored with this business! I can barely distinguish a face in yonder puddle of murk; how can I give it a name?'

'But is he not familiar to you?'

'I might say "Yes" and I might say "No".'

King Throbius spoke gently: 'As Falael will attest, my patience knows a limit. Unless you care to sit on a post, scratching your lovely pelt with both hands, you will respond to questions quickly and accurately, without evasion or ambiguity. Am I clear on this?'

Twisk uttered a cry of poignant emotion. 'Alas! How I am wronged, when my only concern is truth!'

'Please make your elucidations less abstract.'

Twisk blinked. 'Excuse me, Your Highness, I am not certain of your command!'

'Speak more clearly!'

'Very well, but now I have forgotten the question.'

King Throbius spoke with a carefully controlled voice. 'Do you recognize the face?'

'Of course! How could I forget? He was a gallant knight of verve and a most fanciful habit of thought! My ordeal at Idilra Post followed hard upon the encounter and swept it clean from my mind.'

'Very well; so much is established. Name us now the name of this gallant knight.'

Twisk said regretfully. 'That is beyond my power.'

King Throbius surveyed her with raised eyebrows. 'Is your memory so vagrant?'

'Not at all, Sire! He used a name for himself, true, but we played at Romance, and this is a game where truth is a bagatelle. So we wanted it and so we played the game. I spoke my name as Lady Lis of the White Opals and he named himself Sir Pellinore, from the far shores of Aquitaine, and who knows? Perhaps it was so.'

'Most odd,' said King Throbius. 'Extraordinary, in all respects.'

Queen Bossum spoke. 'I ask Your Majesty this: do gentlemen always announce full name and title to their amourettes, no matter how sublime or poetic the occasion?'

'I accept this interpretation,' said King Throbius. 'For the nonce, we will know this knight as "Sir Pellinore".'

Madouc asked anxiously: 'How else did Sir Pellinore describe himself?'

'His references were always extravagant! He declared himself a wandering troubadour, dedicated to the ideals of chivalry. He asked if I knew of any caitiff knights in need of chastisement, and inquired in regard to damsels in need of deliverance. I mentioned the ogre Throop of the three heads, and I described the wicked deeds done by Throop to all the fair knights who had come seeking the Holy Grail. Sir Pellinore was horrified to hear my tales and swore enmity against Throop, but who knows? Sir Pellinore was surely more expert with the lute than the sword! Still, he knew no fear! At last we parted and went our ways, and I saw Sir Pellinore never again.'

'Where did he go?' asked Madouc. 'What happened to him afterward?'

'I hesitate to think,' said Twisk. 'He might have wandered north to Avallon or voyaged home to Aquitaine, but I suspect that his vow of hatred took him to Castle Doldil that he might revenge a thousand crimes upon Throop. If so, he failed, since Throop survives to this day! Sir Pellinore might have been boiled for soup or perhaps he languishes in a cage, so that with songs, lute and melody he enlivens Throop's evening repast.'

Madouc's mouth sagged open in dismay. 'Can it be possible?'

'Quite possible! Sir Pellinore played the lute with delicate grace, and his songs were so sweet as to bring tears from a bear.'

Madouc struggled to control her emotion. 'Why did you not try to rescue poor Sir Pellinore, whom you loved so well?'

Twisk fluffed out her lavender hair. 'My attention was engaged by other events, not the least being the affair at Idilra Post. One such as I lives from instant to instant, wringing every last drop of sklemik[1] from the adventure of life. So the hours and the days pass, and sometimes I can not remember which was which or what comes next.'

Madouc said without enthusiasm: 'Regardless of your faults or follies, you are my mother, and I must accept you as you are, lavender hair and all.'

'A dutiful daughter is not so bad either,' said Twisk. 'I am pleased to hear your compliments.'

---

[1] *sklemik*: Untranslatable: a fairy word signifying (1) passionate receptivity or involvement with each instant of life; (2) a kind of euphoria induced by close attention to unpredictable changes in the perceived surroundings as one instant metamorphoses into the next; a dedicated awareness to NOW; a sensitivity to the various elements of NOW. The concept of *sklemik* is relatively simple and quite bereft of mysticism or symbol.

9

I

King Throbius grew weary and decided to sit. With a gesture he brought a throne from the castle and caused it to be placed directly at his back. The implets who carried his train scurried frantically lest the throne pin the royal cloak to the turf, with consequences painful to themselves.

King Throbius settled himself upon the throne: a construction of ebony riveted with rosettes of black iron and pearl, surmounted by a fan of ostrich plumes. For a moment King Throbius sat upright, while the implets, working at speed, though with quarreling and bickering, arranged his train to its best display. He then leaned back to take his comfort.

Queen Bossum sauntered past on her way to the castle, where she would change to a costume suitable for the activities she had planned for the afternoon. She paused beside the throne and proffered a suggestion which King Throbius found persuasive. Queen Bossum continued to the castle and King Throbius summoned three of his officials: Triollet, the Lord High Steward; Mipps, Chief Victualler to the Royal Board; and Chaskervil, Keeper of the Bins.

The three responded with alacrity and listened in respectful silence while King Throbius issued his instructions. 'Today is auspicious,' said King Throbius in his roundest tones. 'We have discomfited the troll Mangeon, and minimized his predilection for certain wicked tricks. Mangeon will think twice before attempting new affronts!'

'It is a proud day!' declared Mipps.

'It is a day of triumph!' cried Triollet fervently.

'I concur with both my colleagues, in every respect!' stated Chaskervil.

'Just so,' said King Throbius. 'We shall signal the occasion with a small but superb banquet of twenty courses, to be served upon the castle terrace, thirty guests and five hundred flicker-lamps. Address yourselves to the perfection of this event!'

'It shall be done!' cried Triollet.

The three officials hurried off to implement the royal command. King Throbius relaxed into his throne. He surveyed the meadow, that he might observe his subjects and appraise their conduct. He took note of Madouc, where she stood by Osfer's table, sadly watching Sir Pellinore's face dissolve into mist.

'Hm,' said King Throbius to himself. He stepped down from his throne and with a stately tread approached the table. 'Madouc, I notice that your face shows little joy, even though your most ardent hope has been realized! You have learned the identity of your father, and your curiosity is gratified; am I not correct?'

Madouc gave her head a wistful shake. 'I must now discover whether he is alive or dead and, if alive, where he abides. My quest has become more difficult than ever!'

'Nevertheless, you should be clapping your pretty hands for joy! We have demonstrated that the troll Mangeon is not included among your forbears. This, by itself, should induce an almost delirious euphoria.'

Madouc managed the quiver of a smile. 'In this regard, Your Highness, I am happy beyond words!'

'Good!' King Throbius pulled at his beard and glanced around the meadow, to discover the whereabouts of Queen Bossum. At the moment she was nowhere in sight. King Throbius spoke in a somewhat lighter voice than before: 'Tonight we shall celebrate Mangeon's defeat! There will be a banquet both elegant and exclusive; only persons of special éclat will be present, all in full regalia. We will dine on the terrace under five hundred ghost-lanterns; the viands will be exquisite, equally so the wines! The feast will proceed until midnight, to be followed by a pavanne under the moon, to melodies of the utmost sweetness.'

'It sounds very fine,' said Madouc.

'That is our intent. Now then: Since you are visiting the shee in a special capacity, and have achieved a certain reputation, you will be allowed to attend the banquet.' King Throbius stood back, smiling and toying with his beard. 'You have heard the invitation; will you elect to be present?'

Madouc looked uneasily off across the meadow, uncertain how best to reply. She felt the king's gaze on her face; darting a side-glance she discovered an expression which surprised her. It was like that she had once glimpsed in the red-brown eyes of a fox. Madouc blinked; when she looked back, King Throbius was as bland and stately as ever.

Once again King Throbius asked: 'How say you? Will you attend the banquet? The queen's own seamstress shall provide your gown: perhaps a delicious trifle woven of dandelion fluff, or a flutter of spider-silk stained with pomegranate.'

Madouc shook her head. 'I thank Your Highness, but I am not ready for such a splendid affair. Your guests would be strange to me, with customs beyond my knowledge, and I might unwittingly give offense or make myself foolish.'

'Fairies are as tolerant as they are sympathetic,' said King Throbius.

'They are also known for their surprises. I fear all fairy

revelry; in the morning: who knows? I might find myself a withered crone forty years old! Many thanks, Your Highness! But I must decline the invitation.'

King Throbius, smiling his easy smile, made a sign of equanimity. 'You must act to your best desires. The day verges into afternoon. Yonder stands Twisk; go and say your goodbyes; then you may take your leave of Thripsey Shee.'

'One question, Sire, as to the magical adjuncts you have allowed me.'

'They are transient. The pebble already has lost its force. The glamor lingers more lovingly, but tomorrow you may pull all you like at your ear, to no avail. Go now and consult your fractious mother.'

Madouc approached Twisk, who pretended an interest in the sheen of her silver fingernails. 'Mother! I will soon be leaving Thripsey Shee.'

'A wise decision. I bid you farewell.'

'First, dear mother, you must tell me more of Sir Pellinore.'

'As you like,' said Twisk without enthusiasm. 'The sun is warm; let us sit in the shade of the beech tree.'

The two settled themselves cross-legged in the grass. Fairies one by one came to sit around them, that they might hear all that transpired and share in any new sensation. Sir Pom-pom also came slouching across the meadow, to stand leaning against the beech tree, where presently he was joined by Travante.

Twisk sat pensively chewing on a blade of grass. 'There is little to tell, beyond what you already know. Still, this is what happened.'

Twisk told the tale in a musing voice, as if she were remembering the events of a bitter-sweet dream. She admitted that she had been taunting Mangeon, mocking his hideous face and denouncing his crimes, which included a sly tactic of creeping up behind some careless fairy maiden, trapping her in a net and carrying her off to his dismal manse, where she must serve his evil purposes until she became bedraggled and he tired of her.

One day while Twisk wandered in the forest Mangeon crept up behind her and flung his net, but Twisk skipped clear and fled, pursued at a humping jumping run by Mangeon.

Twisk eluded him without difficulty, hiding behind a tree while Mangeon blundered past. Twisk laughed to herself and started back to Madling Meadow. Along the way she passed through a pretty glade, where she came upon Sir Pellinore sitting by a still pool, watching dragon-flies darting back and forth across the water, meanwhile plucking idle chords from his lute. Sir Pellinore carried only a short sword and no shield, but on a branch he had hung a black cloak embroidered with what Twisk took to be his arms: Three red roses on a blue field.

Twisk was favorably impressed by Sir Pellinore's appearance and stepped demurely forward. Sir Pellinore jumped to his feet and welcomed her with a nice blend of courtesy and candid admiration which pleased her to such an extent that she joined him by the pool, where they sat side by side on a fallen log. Twisk asked his name and why he ventured so deeply into the Forest of Tantrevalles.

After an instant of hesitation he said: 'You may know me as Sir Pellinore, a wandering knight of Aquitaine, in search of romantic adventure.'

'You are far from your native land,' said Twisk.

'For a vagabond, "here" is as good as "there",' said Sir Pellinore. 'Furthermore – who knows – I may well find my fortune in this secret old forest. I have already discovered the most beautiful creature ever to torment my imagination!'

Twisk smiled and looked at him through half-lowered

lashes. 'Your remarks are reassuring, but they come so easily that I wonder at their conviction. Can they really be sincere?'

'Were I made of stone I would still be convinced! Though my voice might be somewhat less melodious.'

Twisk laughed quietly and allowed her shoulder to brush that of Sir Pellinore. 'In regard to fortune, the ogre Gois has robbed, pillaged and preempted thirty tons of gold, which in his vanity he used to create a monumental statue of himself. The ogre Carabara owns a crow which speaks ten languages, foretells the weather and gambles with dice, winning large sums from everyone it encounters. The ogre Throop is master of a dozen treasures, including a tapestry which each day shows a different scene, a fire which burns without fuel and a bed of air upon which he rests in comfort. According to rumor, he took a chalice sacred to the Christians from a fugitive monk, and many brave knights, from all over Christendom, have attempted to wrest this article from Throop.'

'And how have they fared?'

'Not well. Some challenge Throop to combat; usually they are killed by a pair of goblin knights. Others who bring gifts are allowed into Castle Doldil, but to what effect? All end up either in Throop's great black soup kettle or in a cage, where they must amuse Throop and all three of his heads as they dine. Seek your fortune elsewhere; that is my advice.'

'I suspect that I have found the most marvelous fortune the world provides here in this very glade,' said Sir Pellinore.

'That is a graceful sentiment.'

Sir Pellinore clasped Twisk's slender hand. 'I would willingly enhance the occasion, were I not in awe of your fairy beauty, and also of your fairy magic.'

'Your fears are absurd,' said Twisk.

So for a time the two dallied in the glade, at last becoming languid.

Twisk tickled Sir Pellinore's ear with a blade of grass. 'And when you leave this glade, where will you go?'

'Perhaps north, perhaps south. Perhaps I will visit Throop in his den and avenge his murders, and also divest him of his wealth.'

Twisk cried out in sadness: 'You are both brave and gallant, but you would only share the fate of all the others!'

'Is there no way to baffle this evil creature?'

'You may gain time by a ruse, but in the end he will trick you.'

'What is the ruse!'

'Appear before Castle Doldil wih a gift. He then must offer you hospitality and return a host gift of the same value. He will offer food and drink, but you must take only what he gives and no more by so much as a crumb; or then, with a great roar, he will accuse you of theft and that will be your doom. Heed my advice, Sir Pellinore! Look elsewhere for both vengeance and fortune!'

'You are persuasive!' Sir Pellinore bent to kiss the beautiful face so close to his own, but Twisk, looking over his shoulder, saw the distorted visage of Mangeon the troll glaring through the foliage. She gave a startled cry, and told Sir Pellinore what she had seen, but when he jumped to his feet, sword in hand, Mangeon had disappeared.

Twisk and Sir Pellinore at last parted. Twisk returned to Thripsey Shee; as for Sir Pellinore, she could only hope that he had not taken himself to Castle Doldil, in accordance with his stated inclination. 'That,' said Twisk, 'is all I know of Sir Pellinore.'

'But where should I look to find him now?'

Twisk gave one of her airy shrugs. 'Who knows? Perhaps he set off to vanquish Throop; perhaps not. Only Throop will know the truth.'

'Would Throop remember after so long?'

'The shields of all his victim knights bedizen the walls of his hall; for recollection, Throop need only look along the ranked escutcheons. But he would tell you nothing unless you told him something of equal consequence in return.'

Madouc frowned. 'Might not he simply seize me and drop me into his soup kettle?'

'Indeed! If you made free with his property.' Twisk rose to her feet. 'My best advice is this: avoid Castle Doldil. Throop's three heads are equally merciless.'

'Still, I am anxious to learn the fate of Sir Pellinore.'

'Alas!' sighed Twisk. 'I can advise you no better! If through obstinate folly you risk the venture, remember what I told Sir Pellinore. First you must win past a pair of goblin knights mounted on griffins.'

'How shall I do this?'

Twisk spoke in irritation. 'Have I not taught you the Tinkle-toe? Apply it at triple-force. After you have thwarted the goblins and their nightmare steeds, you may request admission to Castle Doldil. Throop will admit you with pleasure. Greet each of the three heads in turn, as they are jealous of their status. On the left is Pism, in the center is Pasm, to the right is Posm. You must mention that you come as a guest and that you bring a host gift. Thereafter, take only what is freely given and not an iota more. If you obey this rule, Throop is powerless to do you harm, by reason of a spell long ago imposed upon him. If he offers you a grape, do not take the stem. If he allows you a dish of cold porridge, and you discover a weevil in the meal, put it carefully aside or inquire as to its best disposition. Take no gift for which you cannot make a proper return. If you give your host gift first, he must respond with a gift of equal value. Above all, attempt no theft from Throop, for his eyes see everywhere.'

Sir Pom-pom spoke: 'Does Throop for a fact hold the "Holy Grail" in custody?'

'Possibly. Many have lost their lives in the quest! So it may be.'

Travante put a question. 'What host gifts should we bring to Throop, to hold his rage in check?'

Twisk spoke in surprise. 'You too intend to risk your life?'

'Why not? Is it unthinkable that Throop keeps my lost youth locked away in his great chest, along with his other valuables?'

'It is not unthinkable, but not probable either,' said Twisk.

'No matter; I will search where I can: the most likely places first.'

Twisk asked, half-mocking: 'And what, of equal value, will you offer Throop in return?'

Travante considered. 'What I seek is beyond value. I must ponder carefully.'

Sir Pom-pom asked: 'What can I offer Throop that he might part with the "Holy Grail"?'

The fairies who had come to listen had lost interest and one by one had wandered away, until only three implets remained. After whispering together, they had become convulsed with mirth. Twisk turned to chide them. 'Why, suddenly, are you so merry?'

One of the implets ran forward and, half-giggling, half-whispering, spoke into her ear, and Twisk herself began to smile. She looked across the meadow; King Throbius and Queen Bossum still discussed the forthcoming banquet with their high officials. Twisk gave the implet instructions; all three scuttled around to the back of the castle. Twisk, meanwhile, instructed both Travante and Madouc in regard to the host gifts which they must offer Throop.

The implets returned, again by a devious route, now carrying a bundle wrapped in a tatter of purple silk. They came stealthily, keeping to the shadows of the forest, where they called to Twisk in soft voices. 'Come! Come! Come!'

Twisk spoke to the adventurers: 'Let us move into a secluded place. King Throbius is extremely generous, most especially when he knows nothing of his given gifts.'

Secure from observation, Twisk unwrapped the parcel, revealing a golden vessel studded with carnelians and opals. Three spouts projected from the top, pointing in three directions.

'This is a vessel of great utility,' said Twisk. 'The first spout pours mead, the second crisp ale and the third wine of good quality. The vessel has an unexpected adjunct, to prevent unauthorized use. When this onyx bead is pressed, the yield of all three spouts alters for the worse. The mead becomes a vile and vicious swill; the ale would seem to be brewed from mouse droppings; the wine has become a vinous acid, mingled with tincture of blister-beetles. To restore goodness to the drink, one must touch this garnet bead, and all is well. If the garnet bead is pressed during normal use, the three tipples take on a double excellence. The mead, so it is said, becomes a nectar of flowers saturated with sunlight. The ale takes on grandeur, while the wine is like the fabled elixir of life.'

Madouc inspected the vessel with awe. 'And if one were to press the garnet bead twice?'

'No one dares to contemplate these levels of perfection. They are reserved for the Sublime Entities.'

'And what if the onyx bead were pressed twice?'

'Dark ichor of mephalim, cacodyl and cadaverine: these are the fluids yielded by the spouts.'

'And thrice?' suggested Sir Pom-pom.

Twisk made an impatient motion. 'Such details need

not concern us. Throop will covet the vessel, and it will become your host gift. I can do no more save urge you to travel south, rather than north to Castle Doldil. And now: the afternoon is on the wane!' Twisk kissed Madouc, and said: 'You may keep the pink and white kerchief; it will provide you shelter. If you live, perhaps we shall meet again.'

II

Madouc and Travante wrapped the golden vessel in the purple silk cloth and slung it over Sir Pom-pom's sturdy shoulders. With no more ado, they circled Madling Meadow and set off up Wamble Way.

On this pleasant afternoon there were comings and goings along the road. The three had traveled only a mile when from far ahead sounded the shrilling of fairy trumpets, growing ever louder and more brilliant. Down the road came dashing a cavalcade of six fairy riders, wearing costumes of black silk and helmets of complex design. They rode black chargers of a strange sort: deep-chested, running low to the ground on taloned legs, their heads like black sheep skulls with flaring green eyes. Pell-mell the six fairy knights rode past, hunching low, black capes flapping, pale faces sardonic. The pounding of flailing feet receded; the shrilling of horns faded in the distance; the three wayfarers resumed their journey to the north.

Travante stopped short, then ran to peer into the forest. After a moment he turned away, shaking his head. 'Sometimes I think it follows me, close at hand, whether from loneliness or a necessity which I cannot understand. Often I think I glimpse it, but when I go to look, it is gone.'

Madouc peered into the forest. 'I could keep a better watch if I knew what to look for.'

'It is now a bit soiled, and somewhat tatterdemalion,' said Travante. 'Still, all taken with all, I would find it useful and a fine thing to own.'

'We will keep a sharp lookout,' said Madouc, and added pensively: 'I hope that I do not lose my youth in the same way.'

Travante shook his head. 'Never! You are far more responsible than I was at your age.'

Madouc gave a sad laugh. 'That is not my reputation! I also worry about Sir Pom-pom; he is heavier of mood than a boy his age should be. Perhaps it comes of working too long in the stables.'

'So it may be!' said Travante. 'The future will surely be full of surprises. Who knows what we might find should Throop throw open his great coffer?'

'Hardly likely! Even though Sir Pom-pom brings a fine host gift.'

'My gift is less ostentatious in its value, though Twisk insisted that it is quite suitable.'

'Mine is little better,' said Madouc. She pointed to Sir Pom-pom, twenty yards ahead. 'Notice how alert Sir Pom-pom has become! What could have aroused his interest?'

The object in question came into view: a sylph of superlative beauty riding sidewise on a white unicorn, one knee folded, one slim leg negligently dangling. She wore only the golden strands of her long hair, and guided the unicorn by little tugs on its mane. The two made a striking picture, and Sir Pom-pom, for one, was favorably impressed.

The sylph halted her white steed, and inspected the three travelers with wide-eyed curiosity. 'I bid you good afternoon,' she said. 'Where are you bound?'

'We are vagabonds, and each of us follows a dream,'

said Travante. 'At the moment our quests take us toward Castle Doldil.'

The sylph smiled a soft smile. 'What you find may not be what you seek.'

'We will carefully exchange courtesies with Sir Throop,' said Travante. 'Each of us brings a valuable host gift, and we expect a jovial welcome.'

The sylph gave her head a dubious shake. 'I have heard wails, groans, screams and plaintive moans from Castle Doldil, but never yet a jovial call.'

'Sir Throop's nature is perhaps over-serious,' said Travante.

'Sir Throop's nature is grim and his hospitality is precarious. Still, you undoubtedly know your own affairs best. Now I must ride on. The banquet starts when the fireflies come out, and I would not be late for the merriment.' She twitched at the unicorn's mane.

'One moment!' cried Sir Pom-pom. 'Must you go so soon?'

The sylph tugged at the mane; the unicorn bowed its head and pawed at the ground. 'What is your need?'

Madouc spoke. 'It is no great matter. Sir Pom-pom admires the play of light in your long golden hair.'

Sir Pom-pom compressed his lips. 'I might trade Holy Grail and all to ride with you to Thripsey Shee.'

Madouc spoke curtly: 'Control your admiration, Sir Pom-pom! This lady has better things to think about than your cold hands groping at her chest all the way to Madling Meadow.'

The sylph broke into a happy laugh. 'I must hurry! Goodbye, goodbye! For I know I shall never see you again!' She twitched at the white mane, and the unicorn paced off down Wamble Way.

'Come, Sir Pom-pom!' said Madouc. 'You need not stare quite so earnestly down the road.'

Travante said gravely: 'Sir Pom-pom is admiring the unicorn's fine white tail.'

'Hmf,' said Madouc.

Sir Pom-pom explained his interest. 'I only wondered how she keeps warm when the breeze blows cold and damp!'

'For a fact,' said Travante, 'I wondered much the same.'

'I looked closely,' said Sir Pom-pom. 'I saw no trace of goose pimples.'

'The topic lacks interest,' said Madouc. 'Shall we proceed?'

The three continued up Wamble Way. When the sun dropped behind the trees, Madouc selected an open area a few yards away from the road, placed down the pink and white kerchief and at the call of 'Aroisus' raised the pink-and-white-striped pavilion.

The three entered to discover, as before, three soft beds, a table laden with fine food, four bronze pedestals supporting four lamps. They dined at leisure, but somberly, with the thoughts of each fixed upon Castle Doldil and the ogre Throop's uncertain hospitality; and when they took to their beds, none slept easily.

In the morning the adventurers arose, took breakfast, struck the pavilion and set off to the north, presently arriving at Idilra Crossroads. To the right Munkins Road led eastward, at last to a junction with Icnield Way. To the left Munkins Road plunged ever deeper into the Forest of Tantrevalles.

The three travelers paused a few moments by Idilra Post, then, since there was no help for it, they turned to the left and with fatalistic steps set off along Munkins Road.

Halfway through the morning the three arrived at a clearing of goodly dimension, with a river running to one side. Beside the river stood the lowering mass of Castle

Doldil. They stopped to survey the gray stone keep and the sward in front where so many brave knights had come to grief. Madouc looked from Sir Pom-pom to Travante. 'Remember! Take nothing except that which is given! Throop will use all manner of wiles and we must be on the alert ten times over! Are we ready?'

'I am ready,' said Travante.

'I have come this far,' said Sir Pom-pom in a hollow voice. 'I would not turn back now.'

The three left the shelter of the forest and approached on the castle. At once the portcullis rattled up and two squat knights in black armor, with visors closed on their helmets and lances at the ready, galloped from the castle yard. They rode four-legged griffins with black-green scales; squat heads, half dragon, half wasp, and iron spikes in the place of winglets.

One of the knights cried out in a roaring voice: 'What insolent folly brings trespassers to these private lands? We give you challenge; no excuse will be heard! Which of you will dare to do us combat?'

'None of us,' said Madouc. 'We are innocent wanderers and we wish to pay our respects to the famous Sir Throop of the Three Heads.'

'That is all very well, but what do you bring with you, either for Sir Throop's profit or his amusement?'

'In the main, the vivacity of our conversation and the pleasure of our company.'

'That is not very much.'

'We also carry gifts for Sir Throop. Admittedly they are enriched more by our kind intentions than by their intrinsic worth.'

'The gifts, from your description, would seem to be mean and niggardly.'

'Even so, we want nothing in return.'

'Nothing?'

404

'Nothing.'

The goblin knights conferred in low mutters for a moment, then the foremost said: 'We have decided that you are no more than starveling rogues. We are often obliged to protect good Sir Throop from such as you. Prepare yourselves for combat! Who will joust the first course with us?'

'Not I,' said Madouc. 'I carry no lance.'

'Not I,' said Sir Pom-pom. 'I ride no horse.'

'Not I,' said Travante. 'I lack armor, helmet and shield.'

'Then we will exchange strong strokes of the sword, until one party or the other has been chopped into bits.'

'Have you not noticed,' asked Travante, 'we carry no swords?'

'As you prefer! We shall strike at each other with cudgels until blood and brains spatter this green meadow.'

Madouc, losing patience, directed the Imp-spring Tinkle-toe toward the first knight's fearsome mount. It gave a vibrant scream, leapt high, then, plunging and bucking, bounded this way and that, and at last fell into the river, where the knight, weighted down by his armor, sank quickly and was seen no more. The second knight raised a ferocious battle yell and lunged forward, lance leveled. Madouc directed the spell against the second griffin, which jumped and tossed with even greater agility, so that the goblin knight was pitched high in the air, to fall on his head and lay still.

'Now then,' said Madouc. 'Let us try our luck with Sir Throop's hospitality.'

The three passed under the open portcullis, into an ill-smelling courtyard, with a row of parapets fifty feet above. On a tall door of iron-bound timber hung a massive knocker in the shape of a hell hound's head. Exerting all his strength Sir Pom-pom lifted the knocker and let it fall.

A moment passed. Over the parapets leaned a great torso and three peering heads. The middle head called out in a rasping voice: 'Who performs this ruthless noise, which has disturbed my rest? Did not my minions give warning that at this time I take my comfort?'

Madouc responded as courteously as her quavering voice allowed. 'They saw us, Sir Throop, and ran away in terror.'

'That is extraordinary conduct! What sort of persons are you?'

'Innocent travelers, no more,' said Travante. 'Since we were passing, we thought it proper to pay our respects. Should you see fit to offer us hospitality, we bring host gifts, as is the custom in these parts.'

Pism, the head to the left, uttered a curse: 'Busta batasta! I keep but a single servant: my seneschal Naupt. He is old and frail; you must cause him no exasperation, nor put burdens upon his tired old shoulders! Nor may you pilfer my valuable goods, at risk of my extreme displeasure!'

'Have no fear on that score!' declared Travante. 'We are as honest as the day is long!'

'That is good to hear! See that your performance goes hand in hand with your boast.'

The heads drew back from the parapet. A moment later a great booming voice was raised in harsh command: 'Naupt, where are you! Ah, you torpid old viper, where do you hide? Show yourself on the instant or prepare for a purple beating!'

'I am here!' cried a voice. 'Ready as always to serve!'

'Bah batasta! Open the portal, admit the guests who wait without! Then go dig turnips for the great black kettle.'

'Shall I also cut leeks, Your Honor?'

'Cut leeks by the score; they will make a tasty relish for the soup! First, admit the guests.'

A moment later the tall portal swung ajar, with a creaking and groaning of the hinges. In the opening stood Naupt the seneschal: a creature mingled of troll, human man, and perhaps wefkin. In stature he exceeded Sir Pom-pom by an inch, though his corpulent torso surpassed that of Sir Pom-pom by double. Gray fustian breeches clung tight to his thin legs and knobby knees; a tight gray jacket dealt with his thin arms and sharp elbows in the same fashion. A few damp black locks hung over his forehead; round black eyes bulged to either side of a long twisted nose. His mouth was a gray rosebud over a tiny pointed chin, with heavy soft jowls sagging to either side.

'Enter,' said Naupt. 'What names shall I announce to Sir Throop?'

'I am the Princess Madouc. This is Sir Pom-pom of Castle Haidion, or at least its back-buildings; and this is Travante the Sage.'

'Very good, Your Honors! Come this way, if you will! Walk with delicate feet, that you do not unduly abrade the stone paving.'

Naupt, running on tip-toe at a half-trot, led the three down a dark high-ceilinged corridor smelling sour-sweet of decay. Moisture oozed from cracks in the stone; tufts of gray fungus grew where the detritus of ages had settled into cracks.

The corridor turned, the floor humped and settled; the corridor twisted again and opened into an enormous hall so high that the ceiling was lost in shadows. A balcony across the back wall supported a row of cages, now untenanted; along the walls hung a hundred shields, emblazoned with as many different emblems. Above each shield, a human skull wearing a knight's steel helmet looked from empty eye sockets across the hall.

Throop's furniture was crude, sparse and none too clean. A table of massive oak timbers stood in front of the fireplace, where burned a fire of eight logs. The table was flanked by a dozen chairs and another, three times ordinary size, at the head.

Naupt led the three into the center of the hall, then, hopping about on his thin legs, signaled the group to a halt. 'I will announce your arrival to Sir Throop. You are the Princess Madouc, you are Sir Pom-pom and you are Travante the Sage; am I correct?'

'You are almost correct,' said Madouc. 'That is Travante the Sage, and I am the Princess Madouc!'

'Ah! All is now explained! I will call Sir Throop; then I must make ready for Throop's evening meal. You may wait here. See that you take nothing that does not belong to you.'

'Naturally not!' said Travante. 'I am beginning to resent these imputations!'

'No matter, no matter. When the time comes you can never say that you were not warned.' Naupt scurried away on his thin little legs.

'The hall is cold,' grumbled Sir Pom-pom. 'Let us go stand by the fire.'

'By no means!' cried Madouc. 'Do you wish to become soup for Throop's supper? The logs which nourish the fire are not our property; we must avoid putting the warmth to our personal use.'

'It is a most delicate situation,' growled Sir Pom-pom. 'I wonder that we dare breathe the air.'

'That we may do, since the air is all-encompassing and not the property of Throop.'

'That is good news.' Sir Pom-pom turned his head. 'I hear steps approaching. Throop is on his way.'

Throop entered the hall. He lumbered five long paces forward and inspected his guests with the full attention of his three heads. Throop was large and bulky, standing ten feet in height, with the chest of a bull, great round arms and gnarled legs, each as thick as the trunk of a tree. The heads were round, heavy at the cheek-bone, with round white-gray eyes, snub noses, and purple heavy-lipped mouths. Each head wore a cocked hat of a different color: Pism's hat was green; Pasm's liver-colored; Posm's, a jaunty mustard-ocher.

The three heads completed their survey. Pasm, at the center, spoke: 'What is your purpose here, occupying space and taking shelter inside my castle Doldil?'

'We came to pay our respects, in the fashion dictated by courtesy,' said Madouc. 'Your invitation to enter gave us no choice but to occupy space and take shelter.'

'Bah batasta! That is a glib response. Why do you stand there like sticks?'

'We are anxious not to impose upon your good nature. Hence we await exact instructions.'

Throop marched to the head of the table and seated himself in the great chair. 'You may join me at the table.'

'Are we to sit on the chairs, Sir Throop, without regard for the wear we might cause?'

'Bah! You must be careful! The chairs are valuable antiques!'

'In that case, concern for you and your property would argue that we should stand.'

'You may sit.'

'In the warmth of the fire or otherwise?'

'As you choose.'

Madouc thought to detect a crafty ambiguity in the statement. She asked: 'Without indebtedness or penalty?'

All of Throop's heads scowled together. 'In your case I will make an exception and levy no charge for either fireheat or firelight.'

'Thank you, Sir Throop.' The three carefully seated themselves, and watched Throop in respectful silence.

Posm asked: 'Are you hungry?'

'Not particularly,' said Madouc. 'Since we are casual guests, we are anxious not to consume food you might have reserved for yourself, or Naupt.'

'You are gentility personified! Still, we shall see.' Pism twisted his burly neck and called past Pasm's ear: 'Naupt! Bring fruit! Let it be generous in scope!'

Naupt approached the table bearing a pewter tray piled high with mellow pears, peaches, cherries, grapes and plums. He offered the tray first to Throop. 'I will eat a pear,' said Pism. 'For me, a dozen of those luscious cherries,' said Pasm. 'Today I will devour a plum or two,' said Posm.

Naupt offered the tray to Madouc, who gave a smiling refusal. 'Thank you, but good manners force us to decline, since we have nothing to give in return.'

Posm, grinning widely, said: 'Each of you may taste one grape, free of obligation.'

Madouc shook her head. 'We might inadvertently break off the stem, or swallow a seed, and thus exceed the value of your gift, to our embarrassment.'

Pism scowled. 'Your manners are very good, but somewhat tiresome, since they delay our own meal.'

Posm said: 'All this to the side, was there not some talk of host gifts?'

'True!' said Madouc. 'As you can see, we are modest folk, and our host gifts, while of no large market value, come feelingly from the heart.'

Travante said: 'Such gifts, after all, are the best! They deserve a deeper regard than presentations of jewels or vials of rare perfume.'

'Batasta,' said Pism. 'Each has its place in the scheme of things. What, then, do you bring for our pleasure?'

'All in good time,' said Madouc. 'At the moment I thirst, and I wish to drink.'

'That can quickly be arranged!' declared Pism in great good humor. 'Posm, am I correct in this remark?'

'The sooner the better,' said Posm. 'The day draws on and we have not yet started the kettle.'

Pasm called: 'Naupt, remove the fruit; bring goblets on the run, that we may drink!'

Naupt scuttled off with the fruit and returned with a tray of goblets which he placed around the table. Madouc spoke politely to Throop 'These goblets are of good quality! Do you offer us their use freely and without obligation on our part?'

'We are not impractical theorists!' declared Pasm bluffly. 'In order to drink, one needs a proper receptacle, similar in shape to a goblet. Otherwise, the liquid, when poured, falls to the floor!'

'In short, you may use these goblets without charge,' stated Pism.

'Naupt, bring the elderberry wine!' called Posm. 'We wish to slake our thirsts!'

Madouc said: 'As we drink, you may also consider the guest gifts which it is incumbent upon you to offer in return. By the rules of gentility, such guest gifts should be of value equal to that of the host gift.'

Pasm roared: 'What foolish talk is this?'

Pism spoke with more restraint, and went so far as to wink at his brothers. 'There is no harm in such a discussion. Never forget our usual habit!'

'True!' said Posm with a chuckle. 'Naupt, have you prepared sufficient onions for the soup?'

'Yes, Your Honor.'

'Put them aside for the moment; there will be a short delay and the onions should not overcook.'

'Just so, Your Honor.'

'You may pour the elderberry wine which our guests have demanded for the slaking of their thirsts.'

'By no means!' said Madouc. 'We would never think to impose upon your generosity! Sir Pom-pom, set out your golden vessel. I will drink mead.'

Sir Pom-pom arranged the vessel and from the first spout poured mead for Madouc.

Travante said: 'I believe that I will drink good red wine today.'

Sir Pom-pom poured full Travante's goblet from the appropriate spout. 'As for myself, I will drink some fine cracking ale!'

From the last spout Sir Pom-pom poured foaming ale into his own goblet.

Throop's three heads watched the operation in wonder, then all muttered into each other's ears. Pasm said aloud: 'That is an excellent vessel!'

'So it is!' said Sir Pom-pom. 'And while we are on the subject, what do you know of the "Holy Grail"?'

All three heads instantly bent forward to stare at Sir Pom-pom. 'What is this?' demanded Pism. 'Did you put a question?'

'No!' cried Madouc. Of course not! Never! Not by so much as a breath! Nor an iota! You misheard Sir Pom-pom! He said that better than all else he enjoyed his ale!'

'Hmf. Too bad!' said Pasm.

'Information is valuable,' said Posm. 'We hold it dear!'

Pism said: 'Since you have been allowed free and liberal use of the goblets, perhaps you would allow us to taste the product of that remarkable vessel!'

'Certainly!' said Madouc. 'It is only good manners! How do your tastes incline?'

'I will drink mead,' said Pism.

'I will drink wine,' said Pasm.

'I will taste that smashing ale,' said Posm.

Naupt brought goblets which Sir Pom-pom filled from the vessel. Naupt then served to each of the heads its specified tipple.

'Excellent!' declared Pism.

'Tasty and of high quality!' said Pasm.

'Batasta!' cried Posm. 'I have not tasted such ale for many a year!'

Madouc said: 'Perhaps we should now offer our host gifts. Then you may offer your guest gifts in return and we will resume our journey.'

'Bah batasta!' growled Pasm. 'This talk of guest gifts scratches harshly on my ear.'

Pism once again winked a great white eye. 'Have you forgotten our little joke?'

Posm said: 'No matter! We must not cause our guests to wonder. Princess Madouc, so tender and sweet! What of your host gift?'

'My offering is valuable; it is recent news of your beloved brother, the ogre Higlauf! Last month he defeated a troop of sixteen strong knights under the Cliffs of Kholensk. The king of Muscovy intends to reward him with a carriage drawn by six white bears, with a flanking escort of twelve Persian peacocks. Higlauf wears a new cloak of red-fox fur and tall fur hats on all his heads. He is well, save for a fistula on his middle neck; his leg is also a trifle sore from the bite of a mad dog. He sends his fraternal regards and invites your visit to his castle at High Tromsk on the Udovna River. And this news, which I hope will bring you joy, is my host gift.'

All three heads blinked and sniffed in disparagement. 'Ah, bah,' said Posm. 'The gift is of little value. I do not care a fig whether Higlauf's leg hurts or not, nor do I envy him his bears.'

'I have done my best,' said Madouc. 'What of my guest gift?'

'It shall be an item of equal worth, and not an owl's whisker more.'

'As you like. You might give me news of my friend Sir Pellinore of Aquitaine, who passed this way some years ago.'

'Sir Pellinore of Aquitaine?' The three heads ruminated, and consulted among themselves. 'Pism, do you recall Sir Pellinore?'

'I am confusing him with Sir Priddelot, from Lombardy, who was so very tough. Posm, what of you?'

'I do not place the name. What were his arms?'

'Three red roses on a blue field.'

'I recall neither the name nor the arms. Many if not most, or even all, of the visitors to Castle Doldil lack all morality, and think either to steal or commit acts of treachery. These criminals are one and all punished and boiled into a nourishing soup, which is, in most cases, the most notable achievement of their otherwise futile lives. Their arms hang along the walls. Look, freely and without obligation: do you see the three red roses of your friend Sir Pellinore?'

'No,' said Madouc. 'Nothing of the sort is evident.'

Posm called: 'Naupt, where are you?'

'Here, Your Honor!'

'Look into the great register! Discover if we have entertained a certain "Sir Pellinore of Aquitaine".'

Naupt hopped from the hall, returning a few moments later. 'No such name is listed, either in the index, or in the memoranda of recipes. Sir Pellinore is not known to us.'

'Then that is the answer I must give, and it fully discharges the requirement. Now then, Travante the Sage: what have you brought as host gift?'

'It is an article of enormous value if used correctly; indeed, I have given my whole life to its acquisition! Sir Throop, for my host gift, I present you with my hard-won senility, my old age and the veneration which is its due. It is truly a valuable gift.'

Throop's three heads grimaced, and the great arms pulled at the three beards, one after the other. Posm said: 'How can you freely bestow a gift so valuable?'

'I do so out of regard for you, my host, in the hope that it brings you the same profit it has brought me. As for my guest gift, you can restore to me the callow and insipid condition of youth, since I lost my own somewhere along the way. If by chance my lost youth is stored in one of your attics, I will once again take it in charge, and it will serve well enough.'

Pism called out: 'Naupt, hither!'

'Yes, Your Honor?'

'You heard Travante's requirements; do we keep anything of that description stored among the castle lumber?'

'I am certain not, sir.'

Throop turned his three heads back upon Travante. 'In that case, you must keep your gift of senility, since I can make no responsive guest gift, and that shall be an end to the transaction. Now then, Sir Pom-pom: what have you to offer?'

'In truth, I have nothing whatever, save only my golden vessel.'

Posm said quickly: 'You need not apologize; that should be adequate.'

'I agree,' said Pasm. 'It is a gift of great utility, unlike the more abstract gifts of the Princess Madouc and Travante the Sage.'

'There is a single difficulty,' said Sir Pom-pom. 'I would no longer have a utensil from which to drink. If you were able to provide me a suitable replacement – just some ordinary or even antique chalice, of two handles, and I would prefer a blue color – then I might well use the vessel as a host gift.'

Pism called: 'Naupt? Where do you keep yourself? Are you asleep by the stove? You must do better in the future or it shall be the worse for you!'

'As always, I do my best, Your Honor!'

'Attend me! Sir Pom-pom needs a utensil from which to drink. Provide him with an article to his taste.'

'Very good, Your Honor! Sir Pom-pom, what are your needs?'

'Oh, just some rough old chalice, of two handles, pale blue in color.'

'I will inspect the closet, and perhaps I can discover a vessel to your taste.'

Naupt ran off and presently returned with a number of cups, mugs and a chalice or two. None suited Sir Pom-pom. Some were too wide, others too narrow; some too heavy, others an unsuitable color. Naupt ran back and forth until the table was covered with drinking utensils.

Throop became testy. Posm acted as spokesman. 'Surely, Sir Pom-pom, among this assortment is a vessel to meet your needs.'

'Not really. This one is too big. This one is too squat. This one is bedizened with unsuitable decorations.'

'Batasta, but you are fastidious in your drinking! We have no others to show you.'

'I might even accept something in the Irish style,' suggested Sir Pom-pom.

'Ah,' cried Naupt. 'Remember that strange old chalice we took long ago from the Irish monk? Perhaps that might be in Sir Pom-pom's style!'

'Just conceivably,' said Sir Pom-pom. 'Fetch it here and let me see it.'

'I wonder where I stored the old piece,' mused Naupt. 'I believe it is in the cupboard beside the entrance to the dungeons.'

Naupt ran off, to return with a dusty old double-handled cup, of fair size, pale blue in color.

Madouc noticed that the rim was marred by a small chipped place, and that it otherwise resembled the drawing she had seen in the library at Haidion. She said: 'If I were you, Sir Pom-pom, I would accept this old cup and not dither any longer, even though it is old and chipped, and of no value whatever.'

Sir Pom-pom took the chalice in trembling hands. 'I suppose it will serve me well enough.'

'Good,' said Pasm. 'This affair of gifts and giving is now at an end, and we must take up other matters.'

Posm called to Naupt: 'Have you prepared a bill of damages?'

'Not yet, Your Honor!'

'You must include charges for the time we have wasted with the Princess Madouc and Travante the Sage. Sir Pom-pom brought an article of value; both Madouc and Travante tried to befuddle us with talk and nonsense! They must pay the penalty for their deceit!'

Posm said: 'Put the onions into the pot and prepare the kitchen for our work.'

Madouc licked her lips nervously, and spoke in a faltering voice: 'You cannot be planning what I suspect you are planning!'

'Hah batasta!' declared Pism. 'Your suspicions may not fall short of the truth!'

'But we are your guests!'

'And no less savory for all of that, especially with our special seasoning, of ramp and horseradish.'

Pasm said: 'Before we proceed with our work, perhaps we should enjoy a draught or two from our golden vessel of plenty.'

'A good idea,' said Posm.

Sir Pom-pom rose to his feet. 'I will demonstrate the

best method of pouring. Naupt, bring tankards of large size! Pism, Pasm and Posm wish to drink deep of the stuff they love the best!'

'Just so,' said Pasm. 'Naupt, bring out the great pewter tankards, that we may enjoy our draughts!'

'Yes, Your Honor.'

Sir Pom-pom busied himself at the golden vessel. 'What then will each drink?'

Pism said: 'I will take mead, in plenitude!'

Pasm said: 'As before, I will drink red wine, in copious flow!'

Posm said: 'I crave more of that walloping ale, and let it not all be foam in the tankard!'

Sir Pom-pom poured from the three spouts, and Naupt carried the tankards to Throop of the Three Heads. 'I bid you, raise your tankards high and drink deep! An amplitude remains in the vessel.'

'Ha hah batasta!' cried Pasm. 'One and all: drink deep!'

Throop's two hands raised the three tankards, and poured the contents down the throats of Pism, Pasm and Posm all together.

Three seconds passed. Pism's great round face turned bright red and his eyes bulged three inches from his head, while his teeth clattered to the floor. Pasm's countenance seemed to vibrate and turn upside-down. Posm's face became as black as coal and red flames darted from his eyes. Throop rose to his feet, to stand swaying. Within his great belly sounded first a rumble, then a muffled explosion and Throop fell over backward, in a tumble of unrelated parts. Travante stepped forward and taking up Throop's massive sword, hacked the three heads free of the body. 'Naupt, where are you?'

'Here, sir!'

'Take up these three heads and throw them into the fire, at this instant, that they may be destroyed.'

'As you say, sir!' Naupt carried the heads to the fireplace and thrust them into the heart of the flames. 'Watch to make sure that they are utterly consumed!' said Travante. 'Now then: are prisoners pent in the dungeons?'

'No, Your Lordship! Throop ate them all, every one!'

'In that case there is nothing to delay our going.'

'To the contrary,' said Madouc in a faint voice. 'Sir Pom-pom, you evidently pushed the onyx bead, not once but twice?'

'Not twice,' said Sir Pom-pom. 'I pushed it a full five times, and once more for good measure. I notice that the vessel has collapsed into corroded fragments.'

'It has served its purpose well,' said Madouc. 'Naupt, we spare you your horrid little life, but you must alter your ways!'

'With pleasure and gratitude, Your Ladyship!'

'Henceforth you must devote your time to good works and a kindly hospitality toward wayfarers!'

'Just so! How glorious to be free of my thralldom!'

'Nothing more detains us,' said Madouc. 'Sir Pom-pom has found the object of his quest; I have learned that Sir Pellinore exists elsewhere; Travante is assured that his lost youth is not immured among the oddments and forgotten curios of Castle Doldil.'

'It is something, but not much,' sighed Travante. 'I must continue my search elsewhere.'

'Come!' said Madouc. 'On this instant let us depart! I am sickened by the air!'

III

The three travelers departed Castle Doldil at their best speed, giving a wide berth to the corpse of the goblin knight with the broken neck. They marched westward in silence along Munkins Road, which, according to Naupt would presently join the Great North-South Road. And many glances were turned backward, as if in expectation of something terrible coming in pursuit. But the way remained placid and the only sounds to be heard were of birds in the forest.

The three walked on, mile after mile, each preoccupied with his own concerns. At last Madouc spoke to Travante. 'I have derived some benefit, so I suppose, from this awful occasion. I can, at the very least, give a name to my father, and it would seem that he is alive. Therefore, I have not quested in vain. At Haidion I will make inquiries, and surely some grandee of Aquitaine will give me news of Sir Pellinore.'

'My quest has also been advanced,' said Travante, without great conviction. 'I can dismiss Castle Doldil from all future concerns. This is a small but positive gain.'

'It is surely better than nothing,' said Madouc. She called out to Sir Pom-pom, who walked ahead. 'What of you, Sir Pom-pom? You have found the "Holy Grail" and so you are successful in your quest!'

'I am dazed by events. I can hardly believe in my achievement!'

'It is real! You carry the Grail, and now may rely on the king's bounty.'

'I must give the matter serious thought.'

'Do not choose to wed the royal princess,' said Madouc.

'Some maidens sigh and fret; she uses both Sissle-way and Tinkle-toe with no remorse whatever.'

'I have already made a decision on that score,' said Sir Pom-pom shortly. 'I want no spouse so wilful and reckless as the royal princess.'

Travante said, smiling: 'Perhaps Madouc might become meek and submissive once she was married.'

'I, for one, would not take such a risk,' said Sir Pom-pom. 'Perhaps I shall marry Devonet, who is very pretty and remarkably dainty, though a trifle sharp of tongue. She berated me bitterly one day in regard to a loose surcingle. Still, failings such as hers can be cured by a beating or two.' Sir Pom-pom nodded slowly and reflectively. 'I must give the matter thought.'

For a time the road followed the river: beside pools shadowed under weeping-willows, along reaches where reeds trembled to the current. At a ledge of gray rock, the river swung south; the road rose at an incline, dropped in a swoop, then veered away under enormous elms, with foliage glowing all shades of green in the afternoon sunlight.

The sun declined and dusk approached. As shadows fell over the forest, the road entered a quiet glade, empty save for the ruins of an old stone cottage. Travante looked through the doorway to find a compost of dust and mouldering leaves, an ancient table and a cabinet, to which, by some miracle, the door still clung. Travante pulled open the door to find, almost invisible on a high shelf, a booklet of stiff parchment, the leaves bound between sheets of gray slate. He gave the booklet to Madouc. 'My eyes are no longer apt for reading. Words blur and squirm, and reveal none of their secrets. It was not so in the old days, before my youth slipped away.'

'You have suffered a serious loss,' said Madouc. 'As for

remedy, you can surely do no more than what you are doing.'

'That is my own feeling,' said Travante. 'I shall not be discouraged.'

Madouc looked around the glade. 'This seems a pleasant place to pass the night, especially since dusk will soon be dimming the road.'

'Agreed!' said Travante. 'I am ready to rest.'

'And I am ready to eat,' said Sir Pom-pom. 'Today we were offered no food except Throop's grape, which we declined. Now I am hungry.'

'Thanks to my kind mother, we shall both rest and dine,' said Madouc. She laid out the pink and white kerchief and cried: 'Aroisus!' and raised the pavilion. Entering, the travelers found the table laid as usual with a bounty of excellent comestibles: a roast of beef with suet pudding; fowl fresh from the spit and fish still sizzling from the pan; a ragoût of hare and another of pigeons; a great dish of mussels cooked with butter, garlic and herbs; a salad of cress; butter and bread, salt fish, pickled cucumbers, cheeses of three sorts, milk, wine, honey; fruit tarts, wild strawberries in clotted cream; and much else. The three refreshed themselves in basins of scented water, then dined to repletion.

In the light of the four bronze lamps Madouc examined the booklet taken from the cottage. 'It appears to be an almanac of sorts, or a collection of notes and advices. It was indited by a maiden who lived in the cottage. Here is her recipe for a fine complexion: "It is said that cream of almonds mixed with oil of poppy is very good, if applied faithfully, and also a lotion of sweet alyssum drowned in the milk of a white vixen (Alas! Where would a white vixen be found?), then ground with a few pinches of powdered chalk. As for me, I command none of these ingredients and might not use them were they at hand, since who would trouble to notice?" Hmm.' Madouc turned a page.

'Here is her instruction for training crows to speak. "First, find a young crow of alert disposition, jolly and able. You must treat it kindly, though you will clip its wings that it may not fly. For one month, add to its usual food a decoction of good valerian, into which you have seethed six hairs from the beard of a wise philosopher. At the end of the month you must say: 'Crow, my dear crow: hear me now! When I raise my finger you must speak! Let your words be clever and to the point! So you shall make for the joy of us both, since we may relieve each other of our loneliness. Crow, speak!'

'"I followed the instruction with every possible care, but my crows all remained mute, and my loneliness has never been abated".'

'Most odd,' mused Sir Pom-pom. 'I suspect that the "philosopher" from whose beard she plucked the six hairs was not truly wise, or possibly he deceived her with a display of false credentials.'

'Possibly true,' said Madouc.

'In such a lonely place, an innocent maiden might easily be deceived,' said Travante. 'Even by a philosopher.'

Madouc returned to the booklet. 'Here is another recipe. It is called "Infallible Means for Instilling Full Constancy and Amatory Love in One Whom You Love".'

'That should be interesting,' said Sir Pom-pom. 'Read the recipe, if you will, and with exact accuracy.'

Madouc read: '"When the dying moon wanders distrait and, moving low in the sky, rides the clouds like a ghostly boat, then is the time to prepare, for a vapor often condenses and seeps down the shining rind, to hang as a droplet from the lower horn. It slowly, slowly, swells and sags and falls, and if a person, running below, can catch the droplet in a silver basin, he will have gained an elixir

423

of many merits. For me there is scope for much dreaming here, since, if a drop of this syrup is mixed into a goblet of pale wine and, if two drink together from the goblet, a sweet love is infallibly induced between the two. So I have made my resolve. One night when the moon rides low I will run from this place with my basin and never pause until I stand below the horn of the moon, and there I will wait to catch the wonderful droplet".'

Travante asked: 'Are there further notations?'

'That is all to the recipe.'

'I wonder if the maiden did so run through the night, and whether, in the end, she caught her precious droplet!'

Madouc turned the parchment pages. 'There is nothing more; the rain has blurred what remains.'

Sir Pom-pom rubbed his chin. He glanced toward the sacred chalice, where it reposed on a cushion; then he rose to his feet and, going to the front of the pavilion, looked out across the glade. After a moment he returned to the table.

Travante asked: 'How goes the night, Sir Pom-pom?'

'The moon is near the full and the sky is clear.'

'Aha! Then there will be no seepage of moon syrup tonight!'

Madouc asked Sir Pom-pom: 'Were you planning to run through the forest carrying a basin at the ready?'

Sir Pom-pom responded with dignity: 'Why not? A drop or two of the moon elixir might someday come in useful.' He turned a quick glance toward Madouc. 'I am still uncertain as to the boon I will ask.'

'I thought that you had decided to become a baron and wed Devonet.'

'Espousing a royal princess might be more prestigious, if you take my meaning.'

Madouc laughed. 'I take your meaning, Sir Pom-pom,

and henceforth I will be wary of your pale wine, though you offer it by the gallon on your bended knee.'

'Bah!' muttered Sir Pom-pom. 'You are absolutely unreasonable.'

'No doubt,' sighed Madouc. 'You must make do with Devonet.'

'I will think on the matter.'

In the morning the three continued along Munkins Road, under great trees which filtered the morning sunlight. They traveled an hour, when suddenly Travante gave a startled cry. Madouc turned to find him staring into the forest.

'I saw it!' cried Travante. 'I am sure of it! Look yonder; see for yourself!' He pointed, and Madouc thought to see a flash of movement under the trees. Travante cried out: 'Hold! Do not go away! It is I, Travante!' He raced off into the forest, shouting: 'Do not flee from me now! I see you plain! Will you not slow your pace; why are you so fleet of foot?'

Madouc and Sir Pom-pom followed for a space, then stopped to listen, hoping that Travante would return, but the cries grew fainter and ever fainter and at last could be heard no more.

The two returned slowly to the road, pausing often to look and listen, but the forest had become still. In the road, they waited an hour, walking slowly back and forth, but at last they reluctantly set off into the west.

At noon they arrived at the Great North-South Road. The two turned south, Sir Pom-pom as usual in the lead.

Finally Sir Pom-pom halted in exasperation and looked over his shoulder. 'I have had enough forest! The open country lies ahead; why do you tarry and loiter?'

'It happens without my knowing,' said Madouc. 'The reason I suppose is this: each step brings me closer to

425

Haidion and I have decided that I am a better vagabond than princess.'

Sir Pom-pom gave a scornful grunt. 'As for me, I am bored with this constant trudging through the dust! The roads never end; they simply join into another road, so that a wanderer never comes to his journey's end.'

'That is the nature of the vagabond.'

'Bah! It is not for me! The scenery shifts with every ten steps; before one can start to enjoy the view it is gone!'

Madouc sighed. 'I understand your impatience! It is reasonable! You want to present the "Holy Grail" to the church and win grand honors for yourself.'

'The honors need not be so grand,' said Sir Pom-pom. 'I would like the rank of "baron" or "knight", a small estate with a manor house, stables, barn, stye, stock, poultry and hives, a patch of quiet woodland and a stream of good fishing.'

'So it may be,' said Madouc. 'As for me, if I did not want Spargoy the Chief Herald to identify Sir Pellinore, I might not go back to Haidion at all.'

'That is folly,' said Sir Pom-pom.

'So it may be,' said Madouc once again.

'In any event, since we have decided to return, let us not delay.'

IV

At Old Street Madouc and Sir Pom-pom turned west until they arrived at the village Frogmarsh and the road south, sometimes known as 'the Lower Way', which led to Lyonesse Town.

During the afternoon clouds began to loom in the west; toward evening trails of rain brushed the landscape. In a convenient meadow, behind a copse of olive trees, Madouc raised the pavilion, and the two rested warm and secure while the rain drummed on the fabric. For much of the night lightning flashed and thunder rumbled, but in the morning the clouds had broken and the sun rose bright to shine upon a world fresh and wet.

Madouc reduced the pavilion; the two continued down the road: into a region of pinnacles and gorges, between the twin crags Maegher and Yax, known as 'The Arqueers'; then out under the open sky once more and down a long rolling slope, with the Lir visible in the distance.

From behind came the rumble of galloping hooves. The two moved to the side of the road, and the riders passed by: three rakehelly young noblemen, with three equerries riding at their backs. Madouc looked up at the same moment Prince Cassander glanced aside and into her face. For a fleeting instant their eyes met, and in that time Cassander's face sagged into a mask of disbelief. With a flapping arm he waved his comrades to a halt, then wheeled his horse and trotted back, to learn whether or not his eyes had deceived him.

Cassander reined up his horse near Madouc and his expression changed to half-scornful half-pitying amusement. He looked Madouc up and down, darted a glinting blue glance at Sir Pom-pom, then gave a chuckle of incredulous laughter. 'Either I am hallucinating or this unkempt little ragamuffin lurking beside the ditch is the Princess Madouc! Sometimes known as Madouc of the Hundred Follies and the Fifty Crimes!'

Madouc said stiffly: 'You may put aside that tone of voice, since I am neither fool nor criminal, nor yet do I lurk.'

Cassander jumped down from his horse. The years had changed him, thought Madouc, and not for the better. His amiability had disappeared under a crust of vanity; his self-conscious airs made him seem pompous; with his highly-colored face, tight brassy curls, petulant mouth and hard blue eyes, he seemed a callow replica of his father. In measured tones he answered Madouc: 'Your condition lacks dignity; you bring ridicule upon us all.'

Madouc gave a stony shrug. 'If you do not like what you see, look elsewhere.'

Cassander threw back his head and laughed. 'Your appearance is not so bad, after all; in fact, travel seems to become you! But your deeds do a disservice to the royal house.'

'Ha!' said Madouc in scorn. 'Your own deeds are not above criticism. In fact, they are a scandal, as everyone knows.'

Cassander laughed again, if uneasily. His comrades joined the amusement. 'I am speaking of different deeds,' said Cassander. 'Shall I enumerate? Item: you created a furore of hysterical inquiries. Item: you instigated a thousand recriminations which were discharged willy-nilly in all directions. Item: you have nourished a volume of angers, carks, resentments and sore emotions beyond all estimate. Item: you have focused upon yourself a full spate of bitter reproaches, not to mention threats, judgments and curses. Item: – '

'Enough,' said Madouc. 'It seems that I am not popular at Haidion; you need not proceed. It is all beside the point, and you yourself speak from ignorance.'

'Just so. The fox in the poultry-run cannot be blamed for the cackling of the pullets.'

'Your jokes are too airy for my understanding.'

'No matter,' said Cassander. He jerked his thumb toward Sir Pom-pom. 'Is this not one of the stable boys?'

'What of that? King Casmir allowed me horses and an escort. Our horses were stolen, so now we go afoot.'

'For a royal princess a stable boy is not suitable escort.'

'I have no complaints. Sir Pom-pom, or Pymfyd, as you know him, has conducted himself well and our quests have been for the most part successful.'

Prince Cassander shook his head in wonder. 'And what were these marvelous quests, that His Majesty should approve them so readily?'

'Sir Pom-pom went in search of holy relics, in accordance with the king's proclamation. I went to establish my pedigree, by the king's own order.'

'Odd, most odd!' said Cassander. 'Perhaps the king was distracted and paid no heed; there is much on his mind. We will travel to Avallon in a day or so for a great colloquy, and His Majesty perhaps did not understand what was afoot. As to your pedigree, what have you learned, if anything?'

Madouc glanced haughtily at Cassander's grinning comrades. 'It is not a matter to be aired before underlings.'

The mirth of Cassander's friends froze on their faces.

'As you like,' said Cassander. He looked back to the three equerries. 'You, Parlitz, dismount and ride behind Ondel; the princess shall use your horse. You, my lad – ' he pointed to Sir Pom-pom ' – you may ride behind Wullam on the bay. Come now, promptly does it! We must be home by noon!'

Along the way Cassander rode by Madouc's side and tried to make conversation. 'How did you learn your pedigree?'

'I consulted my mother.'

'How did you find her?'

'We went to Madling Meadow, which is deep in the Forest of Tantrevalles.'

'Aha! Is that not dangerous?'

'Extremely, if one is careless.'

'Hmf! And did you encounter such dangers?'

'We did, for a fact.'

'And how did you evade them?'

'My mother has taught me a few trifles of fairy magic.'

'Tell me about this magic!'

'She does not like me to discuss such things. Still, some time I will tell you of our adventures. I am not in the mood to do so now.'

Cassander spoke austerely: 'You are a strange little creature! I wonder what will become of you!'

'Often I wonder the same.'

'Ha bah!' declared Cassander in his most positive manner. 'One thing is certain, if nothing else! Destiny frowns on unruly little itlings who expect everyone to dance whenever they play their tunes!'

'It is not quite so simple,' said Madouc, without any great interest.

Cassander fell silent, and so the party rode on toward Lyonesse Town. After a mile or two, Cassander spoke again. 'Do not expect a gala reception – if only because we depart for Avallon on the day after tomorrow.'

'I have been wondering about this journey. What is the occasion?'

'It is a grand colloquy called by King Audry at King Casmir's suggestion, and all the kings of the Elder Isles will be on hand.'

Madouc said: 'I return at a lucky time! If I had delayed two days longer, I would have been too late for the journey.' After a thoughtful pause she said: 'And the history of the Elder Isles might have veered in sudden new directions.'

'Eh? What is that you say?'

'It concerns a concept which you mentioned only moments ago.'

'I recall no such concept.'

'You mentioned "Destiny".'

'Oh, ah! So I did! I am still perplexed. What is the connection?'

'No matter. I spoke at random.'

Cassander said, with pointed politeness: 'I am obliged to mention once more that you are not in good odor at Haidion, and no one will be anxious to gratify you your desires.'

'To what effect?'

'It may be that you will not be asked to join the royal party.'

'We shall see.'

The group rode down the Sfer Arct, rounded the tree-covered bluff known as Skansea Vantage, and all of Lyonesse Town was spread wide before their eyes, with Castle Haidion bulking large in the foreground. Ten minutes later the troop turned into the King's Parade and halted in front of the castle. Cassander jumped to the ground and with a courtly flourish assisted Madouc to alight. 'Now we shall see,' said Cassander. 'Do not expect a warm reception and you will not be disappointed. The most charitable terms I have heard applied to you are: "recklessly insubordinate".'

'Those ideas are not correct, as I have already explained to you!'

Cassander gave a sardonic laugh. 'You must prepare to explain again, and with considerably more humility, or so I would suggest.'

Madouc made no comment. In a not unkindly voice Cassander said: 'Come! I will take you into the presence of the king and queen, and perhaps in some degree soften their shock.'

Madouc signaled to Sir Pom-pom. 'You must come too. We shall go in together.'

Cassander looked from one to the other. 'That is surely unnecessary!' He gestured toward Sir Pom-pom. 'Be off with you, boy; we need you no more. Get back to your duties as quickly and furtively as possible and make what peace you can with the stablemaster.'

'Not so!' said Madouc. 'Sir Pom-pom must remain in our company, for a most important reason, as you will presently discover.'

Cassander shrugged. 'Just as you like; let us go do what must be done.'

The three entered the castle. In the great gallery they came upon Sir Mungo the High Chamberlain. Cassander asked: 'Where are the king and queen to be found?'

'You will find them in the Green Parlor, Your Highness. They have just finished their repast, and now sit over cheese and wine.'

'Thank you, good Sir Mungo.' Cassander led the way to the Green Parlor, only to discover that King Casmir's place was empty. Queen Sollace sat with three of her favorites, all nibbling grapes from a wide wicker basket. Cassander stepped forward, and bowed politely: first to the queen, then to the other ladies, and the conversation stopped short. Cassander asked: 'Where, may I ask, is His Highness the King?'

Queen Sollace, still unaware of Madouc's presence, said: 'He has gone early to his Seat of Judgment, that he may perform his necessary acts of justice before we leave for Avallon.'

Cassander brought Madouc forward, and announced with rather forced facetiousness: 'I have here a pleasant surprise! Look who we found along the way!'

Queen Sollace stared at Madouc with mouth agape. The ladies-in-waiting made small hissing noises and titters of wonder and surprise. Queen Sollace closed her mouth with a snap. 'So the little recreant has decided to show herself again!'

Cassander said in a courtly voice: 'Your Highness, I

suggest that for the purposes of your consultation with the princess, privacy is appropriate.'

'Quite so,' said Sollace. 'Ladies, be good enough to leave us now.'

The ladies, with covert glances of curiosity toward Madouc and veiled annoyance for Cassander, departed the chamber.

Queen Sollace again turned her gaze upon Madouc. 'Now then, perhaps you will explain your truancy! It has been the source of our great concern. Tell us: where have you been hiding?'

'With all respect, Your Highness, I must state that you have been misinformed. I have not been hiding, nor have I performed any mischiefs. Indeed, I set forth on a quest which was sanctioned by His Majesty, the King, and I was expelled from your presence and from Haidion by your own words.'

Queen Sollace blinked. 'I remember none of this! You are formulating spiteful tales! The king was as nonplused as I!'

'Surely he will remember the circumstances! At his behest I went to learn the identity of my father and the condition of my pedigree. I have acted only within the scope allowed me by Your Majesties!'

Sollace's face became mulish. 'It is possible that one or the other made an absent-minded remark which you chose to twist to fit your own wishes. I deplore such tactics!'

'I am sorry to hear this, Your Majesty, especially since these tactics have worked to your great benefit!'

Once again Queen Sollace stared in wonder. 'Do I hear you aright?'

'Indeed you do, Your Highness! Prepare yourself for an announcement which will stupefy you with joy!'

'Ha!' said Sollace sourly. 'I cannot say that I am hopeful on this account.'

433

Prince Cassander, standing to the side and smiling in lofty amusement, said: 'We are listening with keen attention! Announce away!'

Madouc brought Sir Pom-pom forward. 'Your Highness, allow me to introduce Pymfyd, whom I have dubbed "Sir Pom-pom", by reason of his bravery in my service. Sir Pom-pom served as my loyal escort, and also went questing on your behalf. At Thripsey Shee we heard mention of the "Holy Grail", and immediately became attentive.'

Queen Sollace jerked herself erect. 'What? Can it be so? Say on and quickly! You speak the dearest words my ear could hear! Was the information at all circumstantial? Tell me in exact terms what you learned!'

'We heard a rumor that the Grail was guarded by the ogre Throop of the Three Heads, and that a hundred brave knights had died in the attempt to liberate it.'

'And where is it now! Speak! Tell me at once! I am beside myself with excitement!'

'Just so, Your Highness! Throop immured the Grail in a closet of his Castle Doldil, deep within the Forest of Tantrevalles.'

'That is absolutely important news! We must assemble an army of goodly knights and march on an expedition of succor! Cassander, go this instant to inform His Highness the King! All else is trivial.'

'Hear me out, Your Highness!' cried Madouc. 'I am not yet done! With advice from my mother Sir Pom-pom and I presented ourselves at Castle Doldil; and there, with bravery unsurpassed, Sir Pom-pom inflicted death upon Throop and won the Holy Grail, which he has carried back to Lyonesse Town wrapped in purple silk, and which he will now place before you. Sir Pom-pom, you may present the Holy Grail.'

'I cannot believe this!' cried Queen Sollace. 'I am in a state of entrancement, or ecstasy of the ninth order!'

Sir Pom-pom stepped forward and gravely removed the wrapping of purple silk from the chalice; on bended knee he placed the sacred object on the table before Queen Sollace. 'Your Majesty, I hereby offer you this Holy Grail! I hope that you will cherish it with joy, and also that you will grant me the boon of my desires as stated in the king's proclamation.'

Queen Sollace, her eyes fixed on the Grail, was numb to all else. 'Glory of glories! I marvel that this unction has been yielded to me! I am confounded by rapture! It is beyond belief; it is beyond all ordinary scope!'

Madouc said primly: 'Your Highness, I must call to your attention that you have Sir Pom-pom to thank for the presentation of this Grail!'

'Indeed this is so! He has done a magnificent service for the church, and on behalf of the church I render him my full and royal thanks! He shall be well rewarded! Cassander, at this moment give the lad a gold piece as an earnest of my favor!'

Cassander brought a gold coin from his pouch and pressed it into Sir Pom-pom's hand. 'Do not thank me; thank the queen for her generosity!'

Queen Sollace called out to the footman who stood immobile by the door. 'Bring Father Umphred here at once, that he may share our joy! Hurry, run on your fastest feet! Tell Father Umphred only that glorious news awaits him!'

Sir Mungo the High Chamberlain entered the parlor. 'Your Highness, I notified His Majesty in regard to the Princess Madouc. He wishes me to bring her and her companion to the Hall of Judgments.'

Queen Sollace made an absent-minded gesture. 'You have my permission to leave. Madouc, you too have worked for the Good, and in my great happiness I discharge you of blame for your transgressions! But in the future you must learn tractability!'

Sir Pom-pom spoke diffidently: 'Your Highness, what of the boon promised by the king? When should I make my wants known, and when will the boon be granted?'

Queen Sollace frowned somewhat impatiently. 'In due course any feasible arrangements will be considered. In the meantime, you already have what is best of all: which is to say, the knowledge of how well you have served our church and our faith!'

Sir Pom-pom stammered something incoherent, then bowed and backed away. Sir Mungo said: 'Princess Madouc, you may come with me at this time, along with your companion.'

Sir Mungo led the two by a side corridor into the ancient Old Hall, through a portal in a dank stone wall out upon a landing, from which a stone ramp descended past monumental stone columns to give into the solemn spaces of the Hall of Judgments.

On a low dais sat King Casmir, wearing the traditional vestments of judgment: a black robe with black gloves, a square of black velvet on his head with gold tassels dependent and a gold fillet above. He sat on a massive throne with a small table before him; to either side of the dais stood a pair of men-at-arms clad in shirts and breeches of black leather, relieved only by epaulettes and brassards of black iron. Helmets of iron and leather clasped their faces, lending them a sinister aspect. Those unfortunate individuals awaiting judgment sat on a bench to one side of the hall, in attitudes of gloom. Those who had already been tortured stared blankly into space, eyes as empty as knotholes.

Sir Mungo brought Madouc and Sir Pom-pom before

the king. 'Your Highness, I bring you the princess Madouc and her companion, as you have requested.'

King Casmir leaned back in his throne and, frowning, considered the two.

Madouc curtsied primly. 'I trust Your Majesty enjoys good health.'

King Casmir's face altered by not so much as a quiver. At last he spoke. 'It seems that Prince Cassander surprised you beside the road. Where have you been and what has been your mischief, to the disgrace of the royal house?'

Madouc spoke haughtily: 'Your Majesty has been shamefully misinformed! Far from being surprised by Prince Cassander, we were returning at best speed to Lyonesse Town. Prince Cassander and his friends overtook us along the way. We neither lurked; skulked, hid, fled, not in any way compromised our dignity. As for mischief and disgrace, Your Majesty again has been victimized by misinformation, since I did no more than obey your instructions.'

King Casmir leaned forward, the pink rising in his already florid face. 'I instructed you to skite off into the wilderness, taking neither proper escort nor proper protection?'

'Just so, Your Majesty! You ordered me to discover my pedigree as best I could, and not to trouble you with the details.'

King Casmir slowly swung his head so as to stare at Sir Pom-pom. 'You are the stable boy who supplied the horses?'

'Yes, Your Majesty.'

'Your folly in this respect verges upon criminal negligence. Do you think yourself a proper and adequate escort for a royal princess under such circumstances?'

'Yes, Your Majesty, since that has been my occupation. I have long served the princess faithfully and there has never been aught but approval for the quality of my service.'

King Casmir leaned back once again. In a slow cold voice he inquired: 'You perceive no more hazard in a long journey by night and day, through strange parts and dangerous wilderness, than an afternoon's outing in the meadows at Sarris?'

'Sire, there is a difference indeed. But you must know that, on the basis of your proclamation, I had already decided to go questing for holy relics.'

'That is not germane to the wrongfulness of your conduct.'

Madouc spoke out angrily: 'Your Majesty, I commanded him to this conduct; he is guilty only of obedience to my orders.'

'Ha hah! And if you had ordered him to set fire to Castle Haidion, so that it burned in roaring flames, and he did so: would that make him no more than a dutiful servant?'

'No, Your Majesty, but – '

'To fulfill his duty best he should have notified someone in authority of your demands, and requested official permission. I have heard enough. Bailiff, take this person behind the Peinhador for a flogging of seven strokes, for his better instruction in prudent conduct.'

Madouc cried out: 'Your Majesty, one moment! You are pronouncing sentence too roundly and too rapidly. Both Pymfyd and I went out on our separate quests, and both of us were successful. I learned the name of my father, while Pymfyd did you and the queen a notable service; he killed the ogre Throop and won away the Holy Grail which he only just now presented to Her Majesty. She is ecstatic with joy! By your proclamation, Sir Pompom has earned a boon!'

King Casmir smiled a small smile. 'Bailiff, reduce the

flogging to six strokes and allow this tow-headed gossoon the resumption of his post at the stable. That shall be his boon.'

'Come, sirrah!' said the bailiff. 'This way, come!' He led Sir Pom-pom from the hall.

Madouc looked at King Casmir aghast. 'But you gave me full permission to do what I did! You told me to take an escort, and always I had taken him before!'

King Casmir made a sharp gesture with his clenched right hand. 'Enough! You must understand meanings rather than words. You thought to trick me and the fault is yours.'

Madouc, looking into Casmir's eyes, saw new meanings and took new understandings, which caused her to flinch. She held her face composed, though now she hated Casmir with all her being.

King Casmir spoke: 'You learned the identity of your father, then. What is his name?'

'He is a certain Sir Pellinore of Aquitaine, Your Majesty.'

King Casmir considered. '"Sir Pellinore"? The name has a familiar ring. Somewhere I have encountered it; perhaps long ago.' He turned to the High Chamberlain. 'Bring me here Spargoy the Herald.'

Spargoy the Chief Herald presented himself. 'Sire, your wishes?'

'Who is Sir Pellinore of Aquitaine; where is his seat and what are his connections?'

'"Sir Pellinore", Sire? Someone has spoken in jest.'

'What do you mean by that?'

'"Sir Pellinore" is a creature of fancy! He exists only in the romantic fables of Aquitaine, where he does marvelous deeds and woos lovely maidens and travels far and wide on wonderful quests! But that is all there is to "Sir Pellinore".'

439

King Casmir looked at Madouc. 'Well, then? What now?'

'Nothing,' said Madouc. 'Have I your leave to go?'

'Go.'

V

Madouc went on laggard feet to her old chambers. She stood in the doorway looking to right and left, at objects and articles which at one time had brought her comfort. The rooms, which she had thought so large and airy, seemed barely adequate. She summoned a maid and ordered hot water for her bath. Using mild yellow soap imported from Andalusia, she scrubbed herself and her copper-gold curls, and rinsed in water scented with lavender. Looking through her wardrobe, she discovered that her old garments now fit her somewhat too snugly. Strange, thought Madouc; how quickly the time went by! She studied her legs; they were still taut and slender, but – was it her imagination? – they looked somehow different than she remembered them; and her breasts were at last perceptible, if anyone troubled to look.

Madouc gave a fatalistic sigh. The changes were coming faster than she might have liked. She finally found a costume which still fit her nicely; a loose skirt of pale blue homespun and a white blouse embroidered with blue flowers. She brushed out her curls and tied them back with a blue ribbon. Then she went to sit in her chair and look from the window.

There was much to reflect upon: so much that her mind whirled from place to place, with ideas darting in and out, never staying long enough to take full shape. She thought of Sir Pellinore, Twisk, King Casmir in his black robes, and poor Sir Pom-pom with his stricken face. Here she averted her mind for fear that she would become sick. Zerling, were he to apply the strokes, would surely do so without undue energy, to allow Sir Pom-pom the flesh and skin of his back.

Thoughts swirled around the edges of her attention like moths around a flame. One set of such thoughts was more persistent than the others and nagged at her notice, insisting on its importance. These thoughts were connected with the forthcoming visit of the royal family to Avallon. Madouc had not been invited to join the group, and half-suspected that neither Queen Sollace nor King Casmir would trouble to do so – even though Prince Cassander would be on hand, together with princes and princesses from other courts of the Elder Isles – including Prince Dhrun of Troicinet. And she would not be there! The idea brought her a queer little pang, of a sort she had never known before.

For a space Madouc sat looking from her window with the image of Dhrun before her mind. And she found herself yearning for his company. It was a sensation melancholy and hurtful, yet somehow pleasant, and so Madouc sat dreaming.

Another idea entered her mind: a notion at first casual and then gradually becoming harsh and grim and frightening as it took on dimension. At Falu Ffail were the Round Table Cairbra an Meadhan and Evandig, the ancient throne of the Palaemon kings. The first-born son of Suldrun – so went the rote of Persilian the Magic Mirror – would sit at Cairbra an Meadhan and rule from Evandig before his death. This rote, according to Twisk, had become King Casmir's torment and his preoccupation, so that his days were taken up with devious plots and his nights with schemes of murder.

At Falu Ffail King Casmir, the Round Table, the throne

Evandig and Prince Dhrun would be in close proximity. The situation could not have escaped the attention of King Casmir; indeed, according to Cassander, he had proposed the colloquy to King Audry.

Madouc jumped to her feet. She must be included in the party journeying to Avallon. If not, then she would once again take leave of Haidion, and this time she would never return.

Madouc found the queen in her private parlor, in company with Father Umphred. Madouc entered so unobtrusively that Queen Sollace seemed not to notice her coming. At the center of a table, on a golden platter, rested the sacred blue chalice. Queen Sollace sat rapt in contemplation of the fabulous vessel. At her side Father Umphred stood, plump arms clasped behind his back, also engrossed in a study of the Grail. Elsewhere around the chamber a number of the queen's intimates sat murmuring together, pitching their voices at a low level so as not to disturb the queen in her reverie.

Father Umphred noticed Madouc's arrival. Bending, he spoke into the queen's ear. Sollace raised her head and looked half blankly around the chamber. She saw Madouc and beckoned. 'Come hither, Princess! There is much we would know.'

Madouc advanced and performed a grave curtsey. 'I am at the disposal of Your Highness, of course, and I have much to tell. It will be, I am sure, to your great fascination.'

'Speak! We wish to hear all!'

'Your Highness, allow me a suggestion! The telling will dissolve boredom during the journey to Avallon. If I tell you bits and incidents piecemeal, you will not appreciate the scope of our adventure nor the desperate manner in which we won the Grail.'

'Ha, hm,' said Queen Sollace. 'I had not expected that

442

you would be attending us on the journey. But, now that I reflect, it seems quite appropriate. There will be a number of notables present at King Audry's court, and perhaps you will attract favorable attention.'

'In that case, Your Highness, I must immediately enlarge my wardrobe, since none of my old gowns are now suitable.'

'We will instantly take this matter in hand. Two nights and a day intervene before our departure; this should be time enough.' Queen Sollace signaled to one of her maids. 'Have the seamstresses set to work at once. I stipulate not only haste and creditable workmanship, but also color and style appropriate to Madouc's years and innocence. There need be no bedizenry of precious gems or yellow gold; such adjuncts would go unnoticed on this barely female slip of a kitkin.'

'As Your Highness commands! I suggest that the princess come with me now, that the work may be expedited!'

'Sensible and to the point! Madouc, you have my leave to go.'

VI

The dressmakers brought out their fabrics, and consulted among themselves as to the nature and scope of their undertaking. Madouc, still smarting from Queen Sollace's deprecatory instructions, listened with head cocked sidewise. At last she intervened. 'You are talking for naught! I want none of your sallow yellows or pasty ecrus or horse vomit greens, and you must reconsider your styles!'

Hulda, the senior seamstress, spoke with concern. 'How so, Your Highness? We are bound to sew what is genteel and suitable!'

443

'You are bound to sew what I will consent to wear; otherwise your work will be wasted.'

'Of course, Your Highness! We want you to be happy and at ease in your garments!'

'Then you must sew as I direct. I will not wear these blooming pantaloons or these bloodless bodices that you are discussing.'

'Ah, Your Highness, these are what young maidens of your age are wearing.'

'That is the least of my concerns.'

Hulda sighed. 'Ah well, then! How does Your Highness wish to be dressed?'

Madouc indicated a bolt of cornflower blue and another of nubbled white linen. 'Use this and this. And here: what is this?' She pulled from the case a somewhat scant bolt of dark red velvet, soft of texture, of color so deep as to verge upon black.

'That is a hue known as "Black Rose",' said Hulda in a dispirited voice. 'It is quite unsuitable for a person of your age, and also, it is little more than a scrap.'

Madouc paid no heed. 'This is a most beautiful stuff. Also, there seems to be just enough to wrap around my skin.'

Hulda said hurriedly: 'There is not enough cloth for a proper girl's gown, with such pleats, flounces, swags, and fullness, as style and modesty dictate.'

'Then I will have a gown without these decorations, because I am ravished by the color.'

Hulda attempted expostulation, but Madouc would not listen. She pointed out that time was limited and that the gown of 'Black Rose' velvet must be cut and sewed before all else, and so it was, despite Hulda's misgivings. 'Truly, the material is scanty! The gown will fit you more explicitly than your age would seem to necessitate.'

'That is as may be,' said Madouc. 'I believe the costume

444

will have great charm, and for some strange reason the color is in accord with my hair.'

'I must admit that the gown will probably become you,' said Hulda grudgingly. 'If in a manner somewhat premature.'

10

I

The sun rose into a dreary sky, with clouds driving in from the Lir portending storms and rain for the journey to Avallon. Ignoring the dismal prospect, King Casmir and Prince Cassander had ridden from Haidion before dawn, that they might visit Fort Mael along the way. At the castle Ronart Cinquelon, near Tatwillow, where Old Street met Icnield Way, they would rejoin the main party and continue the journey north.

In due course, Queen Sollace, languid and yawning, rose from her bed. She made her breakfast upon porridge and cream, a dozen dates stuffed with soft cheese, and a heartening dish of sweetbreads seethed in milk and cinnamon. During her meal, Sir Mungo, the High Seneschal, came to inform her that the royal carriages, escort, equipage, and all else awaited her convenience in the King's Parade.

Queen Sollace responded with a sad grimace. 'Do not remind me, good Sir Mungo! I anticipate only discomfort, bad smells and monotony; why could not the colloquy be called here at Haidion, if only for my sake?'

'As to that, Your Majesty, I cannot say.'

'Ah! What is, is! This I have learned with brutal emphasis over the years! So it is now and I must endure the nuisance with all good grace!'

Sir Mungo bowed. 'I will await Your Majesty in the Octagon.'

Sollace was dressed; her hair was coiled and coiffed; her

face and hands were refreshed with balm of almonds, and finally she was ready for the journey.

The carriages waited below the terrace, along the King's Parade. Queen Sollace came from the castle and crossed the terrace, pausing occasionally to address last minute instructions to Sir Mungo, who responded to each of her requirements with the same urbane equanimity.

Queen Sollace descended to the Parade and was assisted into the royal carriage. She settled herself into the cushions and a robe of baby fox fur was tucked across her lap.

Madouc then entered the carriage, followed by Lady Tryffyn and Lady Sipple, and last by a certain Damsel Kylas, who had lately been appointed to attend Madouc.

All was in readiness. Queen Sollace nodded to Sir Mungo, who stood back and signaled the heralds. They blew three 'Royal Retreat' fanfares, and the cortege moved off across the King's Parade.

The procession turned up the Sfer Arct, and the company settled itself for the journey. Madouc sat beside Queen Sollace. Facing her was Damsel Kylas, a maiden sixteen years old, of high principles and dedicated rectitude, though Madouc found her tiresome, lacking both charm and wit. Prompted either by vanity or by exaggerated sensitivity, Kylas suspected that all men, young and old, who passed nearby had come to ogle her and perhaps make improper advances. The conviction caused her to bridle and toss her head, whether the man looked in her direction or not. The habit puzzled Madouc, since her thin shoulders and large hips; saturnine face with its long nose, black protuberant eyes and bundles of wiry black curls hanging to each side, like panniers on a donkey, created no image of memorable beauty. It was Kylas' habit to stare with fixed and unblinking attention at an object of interest. Madouc, sitting opposite, was unable to evade the scrutiny. She thought to fight fire with fire, and for five minutes focused her gaze on the tip of Kylas' nose, without effect. Madouc became bored, and turned away in defeat.

The procession entered the Arqueers; at the same time the weather, which earlier had presaged so poorly, changed; clouds and mist dissolved; the sun shone bright upon the landscape. Queen Sollace said, somewhat complacently: 'This morning I prayed that the weather be kind to us, and make our journey safe and pleasant, and so it is.'

Lady Tryffyn, Lady Sipple and Kylas uttered appropriate sounds of wonder and gratification. Queen Sollace arranged a basket of honeyed figs conveniently to hand and spoke to Madouc. 'Now, my dear, you may recount all concerning the recovery of the Blessed Grail!'

Madouc looked around the carriage. Kylas stared with owlish intensity; the two court ladies, ostensibly sympathetic, could not mask their hunger for sensation, ultimately to become the precious stuff of gossip.

Madouc turned to Queen Sollace: 'Such information, Your Highness, is suited for your royal ears alone! There are secrets which should not be heard by the common folk.'

'Bah!' grunted Sollace. 'Lady Tryffyn and Lady Sipple are trusted intimates; they can hardly be described as "common folk"! Kylas is a baptized Christian; she has interest in naught but the Blessed Grail itself.'

'So it may be,' said Madouc. 'Still, I am constrained.'

'Nonsense! Proceed with your narrative!'

'I dare not, Your Highness! If you wish fully to understand my prudence, come with me, you and I together, deep into the Forest of Tantrevalles.'

'Alone? Without an escort? That is insanity.' Sollace pulled on the bell cord; the carriage halted and a liveried groom jumped down to look through the window. 'What are Your Majesty's needs?'

'These ladies will ride for a space in one of the other carriages. Narcissa, Dansy, Kylas: be good enough to oblige me in this regard. As Madouc indicates, there may be matter here unsuited for general dissemination.'

With poor grace the two ladies and Damsel Kylas moved to another carriage. Madouc quickly took the place vacated by Lady Sipple, across from Queen Sollace, and the procession once more set off up the Sfer Arct. 'Now then,' said Sollace, munching a fig and paying no heed to Madouc's move. 'You may proceed. In all candor, I prefer to hear your tale in privacy. Ignore no detail!'

Madouc saw no reason to conceal any aspect of her adventures. She told the tale to the best of her recollection, and succeeded in arousing the wonderment of Queen Sollace. At the end she eyed Madouc with something like awe. 'Amazing! When half of your blood derives from Faerie, do you not feel a longing to rejoin the shee?'

Madouc shook her head. 'Never. If I had remained at the shee, to eat fairy bread and drink fairy wine, then I would grow into something close to a fairy, except that mortality would come upon me more quickly. At this time, almost all fairies have taints of human blood in their veins; so they are known as halflings. In time, so it is said, the race will mingle into the ruck and the fairies will be gone. Among the human men and women, no one will realize that their quirks and oddities come from the fairy trace. As for me, I am largely mortal, and I cannot change. So I will live and die, as will my children, and soon the flow of Faerie will be forgotten.'

'Just so, and to the greater glory of the Faith!' stated Sollace. 'Father Umphred tells us that the folk of Forest Tantrevalles are devils and satanic imps, of lesser or greater venality. Along with heretics, pagans, atheists, impenitents and idolaters, all such folk are destined for the lowest pits of Hell!'

'I suspect that he is wrong,' said Madouc.

'Impossible! He is learned in doxology!'

'Other doctrines exist, and other learned men.'

'They are all heretical, and all false!' declared Queen Sollace. 'Logic compels this conviction! Listen now! Where would be the benefits for True Believers if everyone were to share alike in the glories of the hereafter? That is carrying generosity too far!'

Madouc was forced to admit the logic of the remark. 'Still, I have not studied the subject, and my opinions count for little.'

When at last Queen Sollace had discussed the affair to her satisfaction, she halted the cortege once again, and allowed Kylas and the Ladies Tryffyn and Sipple, all somewhat disgruntled, back into the carriage. Madouc slid over to the side of the seat. Lady Tryffyn and Kylas took their old places and Lady Sipple perforce occupied Madouc's original seat, opposite Kylas, to Madouc's great satisfaction.

Queen Sollace said: 'Princess Madouc was correct in her assumptions. She spoke of certain matters which clearly are best not made public.'

'It must be as Your Majesty asserts,' said Lady Tryffyn with a pursed mouth. 'It should be noted, however, that I, at least, am notorious for my discretion.'

Lady Sipple said with dignity: 'At Deep Daun Keep, where I maintain my household, we are haunted by three ghosts. They come by the dark of the moon to tell their woes. They have entrusted me with highly intimate details, without restraint.'

'So goes the world!' said Queen Sollace heavily. 'None of us is wise beyond all others. Even Madouc admits to this.'

Kylas spoke in her quiet, somewhat throaty, voice: 'I

am pleased to discover that the trait of modesty is included among Princess Madouc's many virtues.'

'Wrong, and wrong again,' said Madouc in a bored monotone. 'I have few virtues, and modesty is not one of them.'

'Ha hah!' said Queen Sollace. 'So it must be, since among all others Madouc knows herself best!'

II

While King Casmir and Prince Cassander visited the stronghold, Fort Mael, Queen Sollace, with her party, rested at Ronart Cinquelon, seat of Thauberet, Duke of Moncrif.

King Casmir and Cassander inspected the facilities at Fort Mael, reviewed troops, and in general were satisfied with what they saw. They departed the fortress during the early afternoon, and by dint of hard riding reached Ronart Cinquelon at dusk.

In the morning King Casmir discovered that Madouc was included among the company, coming upon her as she was about to climb into the carriage. Casmir stopped short in surprise and displeasure. Madouc performed a polite curtsey. 'Good morning, Your Majesty.'

For a moment Casmir seemed on the verge of uttering a harsh command, but he turned on his heel and strode away.

Madouc smiled thoughtfully and climbed into the carriage.

The party set off up Icnield Way. The cortege now included King Casmir, Prince Cassander, the carriage, a pair of royal equerries, an escort of six knights as well as a group of four men-at-arms who rode at the rear of the column and kept themselves apart from the others. Madouc thought them a singular group, quite deficient in military discipline, casual and almost disrespectful in their attitudes. Odd, thought Madouc. After a few miles King Casmir became annoyed with their conduct and sent Cassander back to have a word with them, after which they rode in better order.

On the third day after leaving Ronart Cinquelon the company arrived at Cogstone Head on the Cambermouth. A ferry propelled first in one direction then the other, by the ebb and flood of the tide, conveyed the company across the water to the northern shore. An hour later the party arrived at Avallon, the City of Tall Towers.

At the city gates the party was met by a detachment of King Audry's Elite Guards, splendid in uniforms of gray and green, with helmets of glistening silver. To the music of fifes, pipes and drums, the party from Lyonesse was escorted along a wide boulevard, through the formal gardens at the front of Falu Ffail, to the main portal. King Audry came forward to pronounce a stately welcome.

The royal party was then conducted to a set of chambers surrounding a garden courtyard in the east wing of the palace, with orange trees at the corners and a fountain at the center. Madouc's quarters were luxurious beyond any she had yet known. A heavy carpet of green plush covered the floor of her parlor; the furniture had been constructed to a light and graceful style, enameled white and upholstered with blue and green cushions. On two of the walls hung painted representations of nymphs at play in an Arcadian landscape; on the side table a blue majolica vase displayed a bouquet of mixed flowers. Madouc found the total effect both unusual and pleasing. Beside the parlor was a bedchamber, a bathroom with fixtures carved from pink porphyry, a dressing room with a large Byzantine mirror affixed to the wall and a variety of perfumes, oils and essences on the shelves of the cabinet.

Madouc discovered only a single disadvantage to the chambers: the fact that Kylas had been assigned quarters adjacent to her own, with a door opening into her parlor. For whatever reason, Kylas pursued her duties with full dedication, as if keeping a vigil. Wherever Madouc moved, the brilliant black gaze followed her.

Madouc finally sent Kylas on an errand. Waiting only until Kylas had disappeared from view, Madouc ran from the chambers and with all speed consonant with dignity departed the east wing.

She found herself in Falu Ffail's main gallery, which, like that of Haidion, ran the length of the palace. Arriving in the reception hall, she approached a portly young under-chamberlain, proud in his gray and green livery and loose flat cap of scarlet velvet, which he wore stylishly canted to the right so that it draped over his right ear. He took favorable note of the slender maiden with the copper-gold curls and sky-blue eyes and was pleased to inform her that neither King Aillas nor Prince Dhrun had arrived. 'Prince Dhrun will be here shortly; King Aillas has been delayed and may not arrive until tomorrow.'

'How so?' asked Madouc in puzzlement. 'Why do they not come together?'

'It is a complicated business. Prince Dhrun arrives aboard his ship the *Nementhe* on which he serves as first officer. King Aillas, so it appears, was been delayed at Domreis. His young queen is eight months heavy with child, and there was some question as to whether King Aillas would come at all. But we have had late report that he is on his way. Prince Dhrun, however, should be on hand at any moment; his vessel entered the Cambermouth this morning on the tide.'

Madouc turned to look about the hall. At the far end, an archway opened into an atrium illuminated by high glass skylights. To either side stood monumental statues, ranked in a pair of opposing rows.

The under-chamberlain observed the direction of Madouc's gaze. 'You are looking into the Court of Dead Gods. The statues are very old.'

'How is it known that these gods are dead? Or truly dead, for that matter?'

The under-chamberlain gave a whimsical shrug. 'I have never gone deeply into the subject. Perhaps when gods are no longer venerated, they fade, or dissipate. The statues yonder were worshipped by the ancient Evadnoi, who preceded the Pelasgians. In Troicinet Gaea is still reckoned the Great Goddess, and in the sea near Ys is a temple dedicated to Atalanta. Perhaps these gods are not dead after all. Would you like to see them more closely? I can spare a few moments, until the next party of dignitaries arrives.'

'Why not! Kylas will surely not come to seek me among the "Dead Gods".'

The under-chamberlain took Madouc into the Court of Dead Gods. 'See yonder! There stands Cron the Unknowable, across from his terrible spouse Hec, the Goddess of Fate. For a game they created the difference between "yes" and "no", then, once again becoming bored, they ordained the distinction between "something" and "nothing". When these diversions palled, they opened their hands and through their fingers let trickle matter, time, space and light, and at last they had created enough to hold their interest.'

'All very well,' said Madouc. 'But where did they learn this intricate lore?'

'Aha!' said the under-chamberlain wisely. 'That is where the mystery begins! When theologians are asked as to the source of Cron and Hec, they pull at their beards and change the subject. It is certainly beyond my understanding. We know for a fact only that Cron and Hec are father and mother to all the rest. There you see Atalanta, there Gaea; there is Fantares, there Aeris. These are the divinities of water, earth, fire and air. Apollo the Glorious is God of the Sun; Drethre the Beautiful is Goddess of the Moon. There you see Fluns, Lord of Battles; facing him is Palas, Goddess of the Harvest. Finally: Adace and Aronice stand in opposition, as well they might! For six months of each year Adace is the God of Pain, Cruelty and Evil, while Aronice is the Goddess of Love and Kindness. At the time of the equinoxes they change roles and for the next six months, Adace is the God of Bravery, Virtue and Clemency, while Aronice is the Goddess of Spite, Hatred and Treachery. For this reason they are known as "The Fickle Pair".'

'Ordinary folk change by the hour, or even by the minute,' said Madouc. 'By comparison, Adace and Aronice would seem to be steadfast. Still, I would not care to be a member of their household.'

'That is an astute observation,' said the under-chamberlain. He inspected her once again. 'Am I mistaken, or might you be the distinguished Princess Madouc of Lyonesse?'

'So I am known, at least for the moment.'

The under-chamberlain bowed. 'You may know me as Tibalt, with the rank of "esquire". I am happy to assist Your Highness! Please advise me if I may continue to be of service!'

Madouc asked: 'From sheer curiosity, where is the table Cairbra an Meadhan?'

Tibalt, with a brave flourish, pointed his finger. 'The portal yonder leads into the Hall of Heroes.'

Madouc said: 'You may conduct me to this hall, if you will.'

'With pleasure.'

A pair of men-at-arms, halberds at vertical rest, stood immobile by the portal; their eyes moved by not so much as a flicker at the approach of Madouc and Tibalt; the two passed unchallenged into the Hall of Heroes.

Tibalt said: 'This is the oldest part of Falu Ffail. No one knows who laid these great stones! You will have noticed that the chamber is circular and commands a diameter of thirty-three yards. And there is the Round Table: Cairbra an Meadhan!'

'So I see.'

'The total diameter is fourteen yards and eleven ells. The outer ring is five feet across, and is constructed of rock elm laid on oak timbers, leaving a central opening about eleven yards in diameter.'

Tibalt conducted Madouc around the table. 'Notice the bronze plaques: they name paladins of long past ages, and indicate their places at the table.'

Madouc bent to study one of the plaques. 'The characters are of archaic style, but legible. This one reads: "Here sits Sir Gahun of Hack, fierce as the north wind and relentless in battle".'

Tibalt was impressed. 'You are adept in the skill of reading! But then, that is the prerogative of a princess!'

'True enough,' said Madouc. 'Still, many common folk can do as well, if they apply themselves. I recommend the sleight to you; it is not so hard after the many peculiar shapes become familiar.'

'Your Highness has inspired me!' declared Tibalt. 'I will begin to master this skill at once. Now then!' Tibalt pointed across the chamber. 'There you see Evandig, the Throne of the Elder Kings. We stand in the presence of the mighty! It is said that once each year their ghosts gather in this hall to renew old friendships. And now what? Will you see more of this hall? It is a trifle gloomy, and used only at state occasions.'

'Will it be used during the present colloquy?'

'Definitely so!'

'Where will King Casmir sit, and where King Aillas and Prince Dhrun?'

'As to this, I am ignorant; it is in the province of the seneschal and the heralds. Will you see any more?'

'No, thank you.'

Tibalt led Madouc back through the portal and into the Court of Dead Gods. From the reception chamber came the sound of many voices.

Tibalt spoke in agitation: 'Excuse me, please; I am absent from my post! Someone has arrived and I would suspect it to be Prince Dhrun with his escort!'

Tibalt ran off with Madouc following close behind. She entered the reception hall to discover Prince Dhrun and three Troice dignitaries in the company of King Audry, along with the Princes Dorcas, Whemus and Jaswyn, and the two princesses, Cloire and Mahaeve. Madouc sidled through the press of courtiers, hoping to approach Dhrun, but without success; he and his company were led away by King Audry.

Madouc slowly returned to her own rooms. She found Kylas sitting stonily in the parlor.

Kylas spoke in clipped tones: 'When I returned from your errand, you were gone. Where did you go?'

'That is beside the point,' said Madouc. 'You must not trouble yourself with details of this nature.'

'It is my duty to attend you,' said Kylas stubbornly.

'When I require your assistance, I will notify you. As for now, you may retire to your own quarters.'

Kylas rose to her feet. 'I will be back presently. A maid has been assigned to your service and will help you dress for the evening banquet; the queen has suggested that I help you select a suitable gown from your wardrobe.'

'That is nonsense,' said Madouc. 'I need no advice. Do not return until I summon you.'

Kylas stalked from the room.

Madouc dressed early, and after only a moment's indecision chose the gown of 'Black Rose' velvet. She left early and alone for the Great Hall, where she hoped to find Dhrun before the start of the banquet.

Dhrun was not on hand. Prince Jaswyn, Audry's third son, a dark-haired youth fifteen years old, came forward and escorted her to a place at the table beside his own, with Prince Raven of Pomperol to her other side.

Dhrun at last appeared, and was conducted to a seat across the table and six places to the side. He had changed from his travel garments to an indigo blue doublet and white shirt: a simple costume which nicely set off his clear complexion and neat cap of dark blond hair. He noticed Madouc and waved his hand, but thereafter was held close in conversation by the Princess Cloire; and in the intervals when she relaxed her attention, by Queen Linnet of Pomperol.

The banquet proceeded, course by course; Madouc presently stopped eating or even tasting from the dishes tendered by the stewards. The four goblets before her contained two sorts of red wine, a soft white wine and a tart green wine; they were filled and refilled every time Madouc sipped, and she soon desisted, lest her head start to spin. Prince Jaswyn was an entertaining dinner companion, as was Prince Raven, youngest son to King Kestrel and brother to the egregious Bittern, who had not come to Avallon by reason of a rheum and an asthma. On several occasions Madouc discovered Queen Sollace's frosty gaze fixed upon her, but pretended not to notice.

King Audry at last rose to his feet, signaling the end of

the banquet. Soft music of lutes and rebecs at once began to issue from the adjacent ballroom. Madouc made hurried excuses to Prince Jaswyn and Prince Raven, slipped from her chair and ran to circle the table, so that she might approach Dhrun. She was first impeded by Prince Whemus, who wished to compliment her and to initiate a conversation. As quickly and politely as possible, Madouc detached herself but now, when she looked, Dhrun was nowhere to be seen. Ah, there he was, on the other side of the table! Madouc retraced her steps, only to meet Kylas, who brought an urgent message, which she transmitted with poorly suppressed satisfaction. 'Queen Sollace finds your gown unsatisfactory.'

'She is mistaken! You may tell her that I am quite satisfied with it.'

'It is the queen who is not satisfied. She thinks the gown unsuitable for a person of your years and lack of experience. She wishes that you and I repair to your chambers, where I am to help you select a gown more modest and youthful. Come; we must go at once.'

Madouc spoke tersely: 'I regret that the queen is displeased, but I am sure that you have misunderstood her instructions. She would hardly expect me to change clothes now. Excuse me, and do not approach me again.' Madouc tried to sidle past, but Kylas stood in her way. 'You have heard the queen's instructions! There has been no mistake!'

Madouc restrained her vexation with an effort. 'Explain to the queen that it would be most inconvenient for me to change clothes now, especially as this gown is quite suitable.'

'Not altogether.'

'In any event, stand aside; there is someone with whom I wish to speak!'

'Who might it be?'

'Really, Kylas! Your question serves no purpose!' Madouc dodged past, only to discover that Dhrun again was lost in the slow circulation of grandees and courtiers.

Madouc went to the side of the chamber. She looked right and left, searching from individual to individual. Overhead a thousand candle flames in five candelabra enriched a thousand colors in the flux of fabric below: rose-madder and saffron, steel-blue and moss-green; lemon-white, maroon, umber and rose-pink; also the twinkle of silver and the glow of gold, and everywhere the glitter of jewels. Faces swam in the candlelight like wan jellyfish in a luminous tide: faces of all kinds, each a symbol for the soul it concealed! But none, either to right or to left, was the face of Dhrun!

A voice spoke close by her ear. 'Why do you avoid me so? Am I now your hated enemy?'

Madouc whirled to find Dhrun standing beside her. 'Dhrun!' She barely restrained herself from an over-impulsive act. 'I have been looking everywhere for you! To no effect; wherever I went, you were gone; I was chasing a shadow!'

'You have found me at last, and I have found you, and I am amazed!'

Madouc looked up at him, smiling in sheer happiness. 'Tell me why!'

'You know why! If I told you more, I would be embarrassed!'

'Tell me anyway.'

'Very well. Long ago I knew that you would become beautiful – but I did not think it would happen so soon.'

Madouc laughed quietly. 'Are you embarrassed?'

Dhrun also laughed. 'You do not seem offended, or disturbed.'

'Then I will say something and perhaps I will be embarrassed.'

Dhrun took her two hands. 'I will listen, and I promise you I will take no offense.'

Madouc half-whispered: 'I am happy to hear what you said, since I care for no opinion other than yours.'

Dhrun spoke impulsively: 'If I dared, I would kiss you!'

Shyness overtook Madouc. 'Not now! Everyone would see!'

'True! But what of that?'

Madouc squeezed his hands. 'Listen now! I have something important to tell you, and you must heed me very carefully.'

'You have all my attention!'

Someone stood close by Madouc's shoulder. Madouc looked around and into Kylas' inquisitive black eyes.

Kylas asked: 'Are you coming to change your garments, as Her Highness wishes?'

'Not just now,' said Madouc. 'You may explain to Her Highness that Prince Dhrun and I are deep in consultation and he would think me eccentric if I suddenly ran off to change clothes.' She led Dhrun away, leaving Kylas staring after her.

Madouc said: 'Kylas is something of a trial. She watches my every move and reports to the queen, for what purpose I cannot imagine, since the queen has no notion of what I am about to tell you.'

'Tell me, then! What is so important?'

'Your life! I could not bear that you should lose it!'

'I feel much the same. Say on.'

'Do you know of Persilian the Magic Mirror?'

'I have heard the name from my father.'

King Audry approached the two and halted. He looked Madouc up and down. 'Who is this bright-haired little sylph? I noticed her at the table, deep in conversation with Prince Jaswyn.'

461

'Your Highness, allow me to introduce Princess Madouc of Lyonesse.'

King Audry raised his eyebrows and tugged at his fine mustache. 'Can this be the creature of whom we have heard such remarkable tales? I am astonished!'

Madouc said politely: 'The tales have surely been exaggerated, Your Highness.'

'All of them?'

'At times, perhaps, my conduct has lacked full meekness and sweet reason; on this account my reputation has suffered.'

King Audry shook his head and stroked his beard. 'A sad situation, to be sure! But there is still time for redemption!'

Madouc said demurely: 'Your Majesty has encouraged me to hope: I will not give way to despair!'

'It would be a pity if you did!' declared King Audry. 'Let us move into the ballroom, where the dancing will soon begin. What, may I ask, are your favorite steps?'

'I have none, Your Highness! I have never troubled to learn and I do not know one from the other.'

'Surely you can step the pavane?'

'Yes, Your Highness.'

'It is one of my own favorites, being at once grave, yet debonair, and susceptible to a thousand pretty intricacies, and that shall be the first of the dances.'

Prince Jaswyn, standing by, bowed before Madouc. 'May I have the honor of pacing the pavane with Your Highness?'

Madouc turned a quick sad glance toward Dhrun, then said: 'I will be pleased, Prince Jaswyn.'

The pavane came to an end. Prince Jaswyn conducted Madouc to the side of the room. She looked about for Dhrun; as before, he was not immediately visible, and Madouc clicked her tongue in exasperation. Why could he not remain in place? Did he not recognize the urgency of what she must tell him? Madouc looked in all directions, trying to see over the heads of the gallants and past the gowns of their ladies. At last she discovered Dhrun, in the company of Prince Cassander; the two were just entering the chamber. Madouc made hasty excuses to Prince Jaswyn. Marching across the room, she approached the two princes.

Cassander saw her come without pleasure. His greeting was lofty. 'Well then, Madouc! I should think that you would be in your element! Now is your chance to mingle with the society of Avallon!'

'I have already done so.'

'Then why are you not dancing, and gamboling about, and impressing the young folk with your wit?'

'I might ask the same of you.'

Cassander responded curtly. 'Tonight such entertainment fails to match my mood, nor that of Prince Dhrun. Such being the case – '

Madouc looked at Dhrun. 'You too are satiated and world-weary?'

'Perhaps not to the level described by Prince Cassander,' said Dhrun, grinning.

Cassander frowned. He told Madouc: 'Yonder stands Prince Raven of Pomperol. Why do you not discuss your theories with him?'

'Not just now. I also feel somewhat blasé. Where did you two go to avoid the demands of society?'

Cassander said coldly: 'We went elsewhere, to enjoy a few moments of quiet.'

'Cassander, you are resourceful! In revelry of this scale, where does one find privacy?'

'Here, there, one place or another,' said Cassander. 'It is all beside the point.'

'Still, I am curious.'

Dhrun said: 'Prince Cassander wished to visit the Hall of Heroes, so that he might honor an old tradition.'

'So now: the truth emerges!' said Madouc. 'Cassander is not so nonchalant as he pretends. What tradition did Cassander feel obliged to honor?'

Cassander spoke peevishly: 'It is only a whim, no more! Princes of royal blood who sit even a moment on the throne Evandig are assured of a long life and a fortunate reign: such is the legend.'

'That is a very obscure legend,' said Madouc. 'Dhrun, did you honor this tradition as well?'

Dhrun gave an uncomfortable laugh. 'Prince Cassander insisted that I share these benefits with him.'

'That was kind of Prince Cassander! And you sat at the Round Table as well?'

'For a moment or two.'

Madouc heaved a sigh. 'Well then, now that you have been soothed by the privacy, do you remember that you promised to dance with me?'

Dhrun looked puzzled for only an instant, then said: 'So I did! Prince Cassander, my excuses.'

Cassander gave his head a crisp nod. 'Dance away!'

Madouc took Dhrun not to the dance floor but to the shadows at the side of the hall. 'Think now,' she said. 'When you sat on the throne, did you speak?'

'Only to fulfill the terms of the tradition, as Cassander explained it to me. When he sat on the throne he uttered an order, that I should step forward a pace. I did the same in my turn.'

Madouc gave a fateful nod. 'So now you must fear for your life. You may die at any instant.'

'How so?'

'I have been trying to tell you of Persilian's prophecy. It guides every hour of your life!'

'What is the prophecy?'

'It goes to the effect that the first-born son of the Princess Suldrun – that is to say, you – will take his rightful place at Cairbra an Meadhan and rule from the throne Evandig before his death. You have now fulfilled the prophecy! You have sat at the table and you have given an order while sitting on Evandig, and now Casmir will put his assassins to work. You may be killed this very night!'

Dhrun was silent for several moments. 'I thought Cassander's conduct somewhat odd! Is he aware of the prophecy?'

'That is hard to guess. He is vain and foolish, but not altogether unkind. Still, he would obey King Casmir's orders, no matter where they led.'

'Even to murder?'

'He would obey orders. But he need not do so, since King Casmir brought others with all the needful skills.'

'It is a chilling thought! I will be on my guard! Three good knights of Troicinet are with me and they shall stay close by my side.'

'When does your father arrive?'

'Tomorrow, or so I believe. I will be glad to see him!'

'I as well.'

Dhrun looked down into Madouc's face. He bent his head and kissed her forehead. 'You did your best to spare me this peril. I thank you, my dear Madouc! You are as clever as you are pretty!'

'This is a most successful gown,' said Madouc. 'The color is called "Black Rose" and by some freak it goes nicely with my hair. The style also seems to enhance what I suppose I must call my posture. I wonder, I wonder!'

'What do you wonder?'

'You remember King Throbius, of course.'

'I remember him well. On the whole he was benign, if a trifle foolish.'

'Just so. For certain reasons, he laid a glamor upon me, which caused a great excitement and, to tell the truth, frightened me with its awful power. To relieve myself of the force, I was instructed to pull at my right ear with fingers of my left hand. Now I wonder if I pulled hard enough!'

'Hmm,' said Dhrun. 'It is difficult to say.'

'I could pull again, for the sake of honesty and reassurance. Still, if I instantly became a rag-tag starveling with my beautiful gown hanging limp, I would feel distress – especially if you drew away from me and took back all your compliments.'

'It might be best to let sleeping dogs lie,' said Dhrun. 'Still, I suspect that what we have here is you, in part and in full.'

'Once and for all I will make sure. That is the honorable course. Are you watching?'

'Very carefully.'

'Be prepared for the worst!' Madouc gave her right ear a tug with the fingers of her left hand. 'Do you notice a change?'

'Not a whit.'

'That is a relief. Let us go over yonder and sit on the couch and, if nothing else, I will tell you of my adventures in the Forest of Tantrevalles.'

III

The night passed without alarm or incident. The sun rose tangerine red in the east, and the day began. Madouc awoke early and lay for a few moments in her bed thinking. Then, abruptly, she jumped to the floor, summoned her maid, bathed in the pink porphyry tub, and dressed in a frock of soft blue linen with a white collar. The maid brushed her hair until the copper ringlets became disciplined and hung in shining curls, and were tied with a blue ribbon.

A knock sounded at the door. Madouc cocked her head to listen, then gave quick instructions to the maid. The knock sounded again, sharp and peremptory. The maid opened the door a slit, to find two black eyes gleaming at her from a sallow long-nosed face. The maid called out: 'Have you no respect for Her Highness? The princess receives no one so early! Go away!' She closed the door upon muffled expostulations: 'It is I, Damsel Kylas! I am a person of rank! Open the door that I may enter!'

Receiving no response, Kylas marched off to her own chambers, where she tried the door giving into Madouc's parlor, only to discover that the door was locked.

Kylas knocked, and called out: 'Open, if you please! It is I, Kylas!'

Instead of opening, Madouc was away: out the door, to the end of the garden courtyard, into the east gallery and out of sight.

Kylas knocked again. 'Open at once! I bring a message from Queen Sollace!'

The maid at last unlatched the door; Kylas stormed into the parlor. 'Madouc? Princess Madouc!' She went into the bedchamber, looking right and left, then into the dressing room. Finding no trace of her quarry, she called toward the bathroom: 'Princess Madouc! Are you within? Her Majesty insists that you attend on her at once, that she may instruct you for the day! Princess Madouc?' Kylas looked into the bathroom, then turned angrily upon the maid. 'Where is the princess?'

'She has already gone out, Your Ladyship.'

'I can see that for myself. But where?'

'As to that, I cannot say.'

Kylas gave a croak of annoyance and rushed away.

Madouc had taken herself to the Morning Saloon, as recommended the night before by Prince Jaswyn. This was a large room, pleasant and airy, with sunlight streaming through tall glass windows. A buffet, running the length of the room, supported a hundred dishes, platters, bowls and trenchers, offering foods of many sorts.

Madouc found King Audry and Prince Jaswyn already on hand, taking their breakfast together. Prince Jaswyn gallantly leapt to his feet and escorted Madouc to a place at his table.

'Breakfast is informal,' said King Audry. 'You may serve yourself or command the stewards, as you wish. I would not overlook either the ortolans or the woodcock; both are prime. I had an order out for hare and boar, but my huntsmen were unlucky, and today we must do without, nor will we eat venison, which, after all, is somewhat rich for breakfast, especially in a ragoût. Please do not think the worse of me for my paltry board; I am sure you are fed more adequately at Haidion.'

'I usually find enough to eat, one way or another,' said Madouc. 'I am not likely to make complaints, unless the porridge is burned.'

'The last cook to burn the porridge was flogged,' said King Audry. 'Since then, we have had no more difficulties.'

Madouc walked along the buffet, and served herself four plump ortolans, an omelet of morels and parsley, scones with butter and a bowl of strawberries and cream.

'What? No fish?' cried King Audry aghast. 'It is our fame and our pride! Steward! Bring the princess some salmon in wine sauce with new peas, and also a good taste of the lobster in saffron cream; also – why not? – a dozen each of the cockles and winkles, and do not spare the garlic butter.'

Madouc looked dubiously at the plates set in front of her. 'I fear that I would grow very fat indeed were I to dine with you regularly!'

'It is a delightful risk to take,' said King Audry. He turned at the approach of an official. 'Well then, Evian: what is your news?'

'The *Flor Velas* has been sighted in the Cambermouth, Your Majesty. King Aillas will be on hand shortly, unless he is set aback by an offshore wind.'

'How blows the wind at this time?'

'It veers, Your Majesty, from north to northwesterly, with a gust now and then from the west. The weathercocks are faithless.'

'That is not a favoring wind,' said King Audry. 'Still we must start our colloquy by the schedule; timely starts make for happy voyages. Am I not right, Princess?'

'That is my own opinion, Your Majesty. The ortolans are delicious.'

'Clever girl! Ah well, I had hoped that King Aillas would be present at the opening ceremonies, but we shall not delay, and he will miss nothing of substance, since we must proceed through a round or two of encomiums, salutes, noble breast-beating, laudatory allusions and the like. Until King Aillas arrives, Prince Dhrun shall listen with the ears of Troicinet, and speak the official Troice eulogies. He is over-young for such service, but it will be good training for him.'

Dhrun, with his three companions, came into the Morning Saloon. They approached King Audry's table. 'Good morning, Your Highness,' said Dhrun. 'Good morning to you, Prince Jaswyn, and to you as well, Princess.'

'No less to you,' said King Audry. 'Your father's ship has been sighted in the Cambermouth and he will be on hand shortly – certainly before the day is out.'

'That is good news.'

'Meanwhile, the colloquy begins on schedule! Until King Aillas arrives, you must act in his stead. Make ready, therefore, to deliver a resonant and inspirational oration!'

'That is bad news!'

King Audry chuckled. 'The acts of kingship are not all equally pleasurable.'

'I suspect this already, Your Highness, from observing my father.'

'Jaswyn has surely arrived at the same conclusion,' said King Audry. 'Am I right, Jaswin?'

'Absolutely, sir.'

King Audry gave a placid nod and returned to Dhrun. 'I keep you from your breakfast. Fortify yourself well!'

Madouc called out: 'King Audry recommends the ortolans and the woodcock. He also insisted that I eat cockles and winkles by the dozen.'

'I will heed your advice, as always,' said Dhrun. He and his comrades went off to the buffet. A moment later Prince Cassander entered the refectory, with his friend Sir Camrols.

Cassander halted and surveyed the room, then, approaching King Audry, paid his respects. 'King Casmir and Queen Sollace are taking breakfast in their chambers; they will appear at the Hall of Heroes at the appointed time.'

'The time is not far off,' said King Audry. 'The morning has gone apace!'

Cassander turned to Madouc. 'Queen Sollace wishes you to present yourself before her at once. I will warn you that she is not pleased with your flighty conduct, which verges upon rank insubordination.'

'The queen must postpone her censure, or – even better – put it aside altogether,' said Madouc. 'I am now taking breakfast with King Audry and Prince Jaswyn; it would be an act of unutterable rudeness if I were to jump up and depart. Further, Cassander, your own manners leave much to be desired. In the first place – '

Cassander, noting King Audry's amusement, became angry. 'Enough; in fact, more than enough! In regard to manners, it is you, not I, who will be sent packing back to Haidion before the hour is out.'

'Impossible!' said Madouc. 'King Audry has insisted that I be present at the colloquy, for my better education! I dare not disobey him!'

'Naturally not,' said King Audry in a genial voice. 'Come now, Prince Cassander, be gentle and easy, I beg of you! The world is not coming to an end because of Madouc's merry nature! Let her enjoy herself without reproach.'

Cassander bowed, coldly urbane. 'It shall be as Your Majesty wishes.' Cassander and Sir Camrols turned away and served themselves from the buffet.

Half an hour passed. Sir Tramador, High Chamberlain at Falu Ffail, appeared and spoke quietly to King Audry, who sighed and rose to his feet. 'In truth, I far prefer the Morning Saloon to the Hall of Heroes and, by the same token, the buffet to the Cairbra an Meadhan!'

Madouc suggested: 'Why not hold the Colloquy here instead of there? Whoever became bored with the speeches could devour an ortolan for diversion.'

'The concept is not inherently bad,' said King Audry. 'However, the schedule is firmly cast, and cannot be altered without extreme confusion. Prince Dhrun, are you coming?'

'I am ready, Your Majesty.'

In the corridor Dhrun waited for Madouc. 'I have become a person of importance – at least until my father arrives. I may be called upon to address the company. No one will listen, of course, which is just as well, since I have nothing to say.'

'It is simple. You must wish everyone a long reign and hope that the Goths invade elsewhere.'

'That should suffice. Also, it is possible my father will arrive before I am required to speak, whereupon I shall gratefully relinquish my place at the table.'

Madouc stopped short. Dhrun looked at her in wonder. 'What disturbs you now?'

'Last night, so you told me, you sat at the Round Table.'

'So I did.'

'But in all likelihood you did not sit in what will today be your "rightful place"! The prophecy is not yet satisfied! I will make sure that King Casmir is aware of this!'

Dhrun thought a moment. 'It makes no great difference, since I am now about to take this "rightful place".'

'But you must not! It is as much as your life is worth!'

Dhrun spoke in a hollow voice: 'I cannot refuse with honor!'

King Audry looked over his shoulder. 'Come along the two of you! There is no time for secrets! The colloquy is about to begin!'

'Yes, Your Highness,' said Dhrun. Madouc said nothing.

The two entered the Hall of Heroes, now illuminated by four iron candelabra suspended by iron chains over the Round Table. At each place a silver plate overlaid the ancient bronze plaque inlaid into the wood.

Around the Hall of Heroes stood the kings and queens of the Elder Isles, a fair number of princes and princesses and notables of high degree. King Audry mounted the low dais on which rested the throne Evandig. He addressed the company:

'At last we are here, in full force: the sovereigns of all the Elder Isles! We are come perhaps for many reasons, that we may explain our dearest hopes and aspirations; also, that each may extend to the others the fruits of his particular wisdom! It is truly a notable occasion: one which long will be memorialized by the historians! Reflect, each and every one! It has been many a long year since our land has known so full a convocation! Each realm is represented, save only Skaghane, where the folk still hold aloof from association. I point out as well that King Aillas is not yet on hand, but Prince Dhrun will speak with the voice of Troicinet, until such time as his father the king arrives.

'In regard to this colloquy and its happy portents, we must acknowledge the initiative of King Casmir! It is he who put forward the concept, asserting the need for broad and easy contact between the rulers of the separate states. I agree in all respects! The time is ripe for frank discussions, that we may define without hesitation our points at difference, and each, when necessary, make the compromises and adjustments decreed by simple fairness and justice.

'With so much said – and with so much more to be said – let us seat ourselves at the Cairbra an Meadhan. Heralds will conduct each to his place, which is marked by a silver plate indited in good round characters. Other persons will sit upon the couches arranged around the wall.'

King Audry stepped down from the dais and went to the Round Table, as did the other sovereigns and their councilors. Heralds in gray and green livery guided the dignitaries to their places, as indicated by the silver plate. One of the heralds came so to conduct Dhrun, but could not find the proper silver plate. He circled the table reading the names, but found none properly inscribed.

At one seat the silver plate was missing, and only the ancient bronze plaque inset into the black wood remained. The herald stopped at this place, where no one sat, read the bronze plaque, leaned forward incredulously and read again. He went to summon King Audry and led him to the empty place.

King Audry read, then read again. By this time the attention of everyone in the chamber was fixed upon him. Slowly he straightened, and spoke to the room at large. 'Sirs and ladies, the Cairbra an Meadhan is imbued with magic, and it has been at work. There is now no plate of silver at this place; it has disappeared. The bronze which over the centuries marked this place now reads: "HERE IS THE PLACE OF DHRUN, WHERE IN HIS GOOD AND FULL TIME HE SHALL SIT".'

Silence held the hall. King Audry spoke on. 'I cannot guess the meaning of this magic, nor the exact thrust of the words. A single point is clear: the table recognizes the presence of Prince Dhrun and has indicated his proper place! Prince Dhrun, you may sit.'

Dhrun came forward, step by reluctant step. Behind the chair he halted and spoke to King Audry: 'Sire, today I prefer not to sit! I will stand, if I may.'

King Audrey spoke in exasperation: 'You must sit! We are all waiting for you to take your rightful place.'

'Sire, I am not prepared to join your august deliberations at this time. It is more proper that I stand, pending the arrival of my father.'

King Casmir spoke in a voice which he tried to hold even but which grated with harshness. 'Come! Let us not waste any more time! Sit, Prince Dhrun! This is what we expect of you!'

'Quite so,' said King Audry. 'We do not wish to deliberate while staring at an empty seat. You must sit.'

Madouc could no longer restrain herself. She called out: 'Dhrun, do not sit! Today I will sit in your stead, and be your deputy!' She ran forward, and slipped into the place marked in Dhrun's name by the bronze plaque.

Dhrun stood close behind the chair. He spoke to King Audry: 'Your Majesty, so it shall be, by my choosing! Today Princess Madouc shall be my deputy and sit in my place, and, if necessary, speak with my voice. The formalities are thereby served, and the colloquy may properly begin.'

King Audry stood bewildered. 'This is strange conduct! I fail to understand what is going on!'

King Casmir roared: 'It is absurd! Madouc, get yourself hence, and quickly, or know my full and awful displeasure!'

'No, Your Majesty. I will sit here. Today is not the proper time for Dhrun to occupy his rightful place at Cairbra an Meadhan.'

King Casmir turned in a cold fury to King Audry: 'Your Majesty, I urge that you bring your footmen and remove this foolish maiden from the chair, so that Prince Dhrun may take his place! Otherwise, the colloquy cannot proceed with dignity!'

King Audry spoke in a troubled voice: 'Madouc, is this one of your famous caprices?'

'Your Majesty, I assure you to the contrary! I sit here only so that Prince Dhrun need not occupy this place today!'

'But Madouc! Notice the bronze plaque! It states that here is Dhrun's place!'

'"In his full and good time"! But not today!'

King Audry threw his arms out in a gesture of defeat. 'I see no great harm in the situation. The princess sits in the place by the will of Prince Dhrun.'

King Casmir spoke again. 'Madouc, once more I bid you depart the place of Prince Dhrun, that he may be seated.'

King Audry looked around the Round Table. Some faces were drawn into lines of displeasure, others were amused, others seemed to care little one way or another. He turned to King Casmir: 'Your Majesty, I tend to the opinion that no harm can be done by allowing the Princess Madouc to sit as she wishes.'

King Casmir said: 'With your permission, I will deal with the matter myself. Cassander, be good enough to escort Madouc to her chambers. If necessary, ask Sir Camrols for assistance.'

With a limpid gaze Madouc watched the approach of Cassander and the stalwart Sir Camrols of Corton Banwald. She made a small gesture and a hissing sound; Sir Camrols leapt high into the air, where he seemed to hang suspended a moment, his feet twisting rapidly one about the other. He alighted on his hands and knees, where he remained, staring at Madouc in bewilderment. Madouc looked at Cassander, and hissed again, as softly as before. Cassander performed a strange double-jointed jump, as if in two directions at once, and fell sprawling, to roll over and over.

Dhrun said: 'Prince Cassander and Sir Camrols have chosen to entertain us with their gymnastic feats, rather than molest the princess; I applaud their good judgment and we should let the matter end here.'

'I am of this opinion,' said King Audry. 'The princess evidently has good reason for her apparent caprice. Perhaps it will ultimately be made known to us; am I right, Princess?'

'It is certainly possible, Your Majesty.'

King Casmir spoke again: 'It is a farce! Here we sit dawdling, the sovereigns of important realms, while this insolent tippet monopolizes our attention!'

'It need not be,' said Dhrun reasonably. 'Let the business of the colloquy proceed!'

King Casmir pounded the table with his fist. 'I am

offended and outraged! I will not participate in the business until Prince Dhrun takes his rightful place!'

Madouc said in a clear voice: 'I see that I must explain my action and the reasons for King Casmir's outrage. Perhaps it is better, after all, that the facts be known. Listen then and I will tell you the information which came to me from my mother.

'Long ago King Casmir heard a prophecy from Persilian the Magic Mirror. He was told that the first-born son of Princess Suldrun would sit his rightful place at Cairbra an Meadhan and rule from the throne Evandig before his death. If this were so, King Casmir would never fulfill his yearning to conquer far and wide, and to rule the Elder Isles!

'King Casmir never knew the name of Suldrun's first and only son, and he lived in a state of anxiety. Only recently the priest Umphred revealed the truth to King Casmir and put the name "Dhrun" to Suldrun's son. Ever since Casmir has been scheming for a means to void the prophecy.

'For this reason he called for a colloquy here at Falu Ffail. He cares nothing for amity or peace; he intended only that Dhrun should fulfill the prophecy, so that Dhrun might then be murdered.

'Last night Prince Cassander persuaded Dhrun to sit on the throne Evandig and utter an order. Today Dhrun need only take his place at the Round Table to satisfy the terms of the prophecy; then he might safely be murdered, perhaps this very night. An arrow from the hedge or a knife from the shadows, and Dhrun is dead! Who would do the deed? There were four who rode north with us; I dare not call them villains and murderers for fear that I might do them a wrong, but they were neither knights nor soldiers.

'Now everyone knows what I know and my reasons for

denying Dhrun his place. Judge for yourselves if they are caprice; then let the colloquy proceed.'

Silence held the Hall of Heroes.

At last King Audry said uneasily: 'The colloquy is both shocked and somewhat addled by your revelations. We have heard a most unusual set of charges, which regretfully ring with the clear tone of authenticity. Still, King Casmir perhaps can refute these charges. What, then, do you say, Casmir of Lyonesse?'

'I say that this sly little whelp lies from her teeth, inward and outward, in all directions, with a vile contempt for truth, and an even viler relish for the taste of pure turpitude! Upon our return to Lyonesse Town, she will be instructed at length in the virtues of veracity.'

Madouc gave a jeering laugh. 'Do you think me insane? I am not returning to Lyonesse Town!'

'I think you insane indeed,' said Casmir carefully. 'Your tales are the ravings of lunacy! I know nothing of Persilian the Magic Mirror, nor yet his prophecy!'

A new voice spoke. 'Casmir, you lie, and you are the liar!' King Aillas came slowly into the Hall of Heroes. 'I myself, with my own hands, took Persilian the Magic Mirror from your secret place and buried it under the lime tree in Suldrun's garden. My only new knowledge is that concerning the priest Umphred, who had already caused Suldrun untold woe. Someday there shall be an accounting with Umphred the priest.'

King Casmir sat in silence, face flushed. King Audry said: 'I had hoped that this colloquy would induce a new sense of fellowship among the kings of the Elder Isles, and perhaps a reconciliation of all our old grievances, so that we could reduce our armies and abandon our forts and send our yeomen home, to till the soil for the greater prosperity of all. Perhaps I am idealistic in this hope.'

'Not altogether,' said Aillas. 'I will frankly admit that I

despise Casmir the man. I can never forget nor forgive his acts of cruelty. Still, I must deal with King Casmir of Lyonesse, and I will do so politely if it will further my policy. I will reiterate it here and now, since it is simple and all should understand it. We will not allow a strong aggressive country to attack a passive peaceful country. Explicitly, should Dahaut marshal a great force and attack Lyonesse, we would fight instantly on the side of Lyonesse. If Lyonesse foolishly chose to invade Dahaut, our forces would instantly march against Lyonesse. So long as peace reigns, we will uphold the peace. That is our national policy.'

King Kestrel of Pomperol said skeptically: 'All very well! Still, you took South Ulfland and then North Ulfland by conquest!'

'Not so! I am rightful King of South Ulfland through the laws of descent. The kingship of North Ulfland was fixed upon me by King Gax, as he lay dying, that I might repel the Ska. This I did, and the Ulflands are now free of their ancient fears!'

King Audry said dubiously: 'You hold lands in my western marches, and refuse to render them to me!'

'I conquered the fortress Poëlitetz from the Ska, which you could not do, and I hold it now because it forms the natural boundary between our countries. Poëlitetz indirectly serves to guard Dahaut itself.'

'Hmf,' said King Audry. 'I will not argue the point here; it is more or less a trivial concern. Let us work around the table, taking the opinions of each participant in turn.'

Each notable at the table had his say, for the most part pronouncing cautious amicability. At last it came to the place of Dhrun. Madouc cried out: 'Since I sit as the proxy of Prince Dhrun, I will in his name endorse the policies of King Aillas. Speaking for myself, Princess Madouc of Lyonesse, I decry the – '

King Casmir roared in sudden fury: 'Madouc, be silent! From this moment henceforth you are no longer princess at Haidion, or anywhere else! You are the nameless whelp of some prurient halfling and a hedgerow vagabond, without pedigree or known parentage! As such, you have no personal voice at this table of notables; be silent!'

King Audry cleared his throat. 'The point raised by King Casmir is well taken, even though his terms were immoderate. I rule that the maiden Madouc may no longer speak in her own voice at this colloquy, no matter how entertaining her observations.'

'Very well, Your Highness!' said Madouc. 'I will say no more.'

King Casmir spoke in a heavy voice: 'I see no point in prolonging this discussion, certainly not under conditions as they now exist.'

King Audry said unhappily: 'Today we have heard some divergent points of view, and indeed not a few sparks of contention! But perhaps these sores can be soothed and our differences reconciled at a later session – perhaps at the end of the afternoon, or even tomorrow. At this time, we shall have ordered our dispositions and resolved on the concessions which we all will choose to make, for the general weal.'

'"Concessions"?' demanded burly King Dartweg of Godelia. 'I have no concessions to make: to the contrary! I want Audry to chastise his Wardens of the March! We have no goodly forests in Godelia, and when our huntsmen venture into Dahaut to track down a fine stag, they are set upon by the damnable Daut patrols! There must be a cessation to this boorish practice!'

'That is quite unreasonable,' said King Audry coldly. 'I make a far more urgent complaint against you: to wit, your support of the Wysrod rebels, who give us no surcease!'

'They are good Celts,' declared King Dartweg. 'They are deserving of land, and Wysrod is their choice. Every honest man should lend his hand to help them. It is shameful that you, King Audry, bring this case out into the open!'

King Audry spoke angrily: 'My attempt to bring wise men together for a feast of logic and a banquet of reason has lured a number of lackwits and mooncalfs into our august presence, though protocol forbids me the naming of names! I have lost hope, faith and patience and I hereby declare the colloquy terminated.'

IV

The dignitaries and their ladies who had assembled in the Hall of Heroes filed slowly out: through the Court of Dead Gods, into the reception hall, where, with many a glance to right and left, they gathered in uncertain groups to discuss the morning's events in guarded voices. When the ladies spoke, they tended to focus their attention upon Madouc. Her behavior was analyzed from a dozen directions; terms such as 'brave', 'stubborn', 'theatrical', 'vain', 'madcap', 'intractable' were all used, as well as the word 'precocious'. While no one could exactly define the manner in which the word applied, all were in tacit accord that the word was appropriate.

As for Madouc herself, she went to sit unobtrusively to the side of the reception hall, in the company of Prince Jaswyn. For a time the two sat in silence, with Madouc gloomily wondering what to do with herself next.

Prince Jaswyn presently found his voice and put a tentative question, in regard to the mystery surrounding her birth. 'Your mother is truly a fairy?'

'Yes. She is Twisk of the Blue Hair.'

'Do you love her, and does she love you?'

Madouc shrugged. 'The word means something different to a fairy than it does to you – or to me.'

'I never noticed before, or thought to wonder, but now, when I look at you, the fairy phase is plain to see, as well as a certain jaunty carelessness which could only come from Faerie.'

Madouc smiled a wan smile, and looked off across the room to where Casmir stood talking with King Dartweg of Godelia. 'At the moment I feel anything but careless, and far from jaunty. My fairy blood runs thin; I have lived too long away from the shee, among human men and women.'

'And your father: is he man or fairy?'

'His name is "Sir Pellinore": so he spoke it to my mother, but both were in a fanciful mood. I have learned that "Sir Pellinore" is a creature of fable – a wandering knight who slays dragons, punishes caitiff knights by the dozen, and rescues beautiful maidens from horrid enchantments. He also plays the lute and sings sad songs, and speaks the language of the flowers.'

'And this brummagem "Sir Pellinore" beguiled your mother with false entitlements!'

'No,' said Madouc. 'This is not at all the way of it. He spoke in a mood of romance, and never suspected that I might some day wish to find him.' Looking across the hall, Madouc noticed the approach of Damsel Kylas. 'What do they want of me now?'

Prince Jaswyn chuckled. 'I am surprised that they so much as recognize your existence.'

'They will not forget me so soon,' said Madouc.

Kylas came to a halt and studied Madouc with care. After a moment she spoke. 'Strange things are being said about you.'

Madouc replied in a toneless voice. 'I am not interested. If that is all you came to tell me, you may go.'

Kylas ignored the remark. 'I bring word from the queen. She commands that you make ready for departure. We will be leaving shortly. You are to go to your chambers at once.'

Madouc laughed. 'I am no longer a princess of Lyonesse. I have no place in the queen's company.'

'Nevertheless, you have heard the queen's command. I will conduct you.'

'No need. I am not returning to Haidion.'

Kylas stared with mouth agape. 'Do you defy the queen's will, stark and outright?'

'Call it whatever you like.'

Kylas swung about and departed. A moment later, Madouc saw Queen Sollace march heavily to where King Casmir stood with King Dartweg. The queen spoke, fluttering her white fingers toward Madouc. King Casmir turned a single glance across the chamber; the impact of his eyes caused Madouc's stomach to knot. Casmir spoke a few terse words to Queen Sollace, then continued his conversation with King Dartweg.

Someone had come to stand by Madouc's side. She looked up, to discover Dhrun. He bowed before her with full formality. 'If Prince Jaswyn permits my intrusion, I would invite you to walk with me in the gardens for a period.'

Madouc looked to Prince Jaswyn, who politely rose to his feet. 'By all means! Our gardens are famous! You will find them refreshing after the turmoil of this morning!'

'Thank you, Jaswyn, for your courtesy,' said Dhrun.

Jaswyn moved away. Dhrun and Madouc went out into the gardens which surrounded Falu Ffail, and sauntered among the fountains, statues, flower beds, topiary and patches of green lawn. Dhrun said: 'I noticed the maiden Kylas speaking to you. What was her message?'

'She brought the queen's command! I was ordered to my chambers, to make ready for the return journey to Haidion.'

Dhrun laughed incredulously. 'And what did you say?'

'I said: "No!", of course. Kylas was amazed, and departed in shock. A few moments later I saw Queen Sollace complaining to the king. He looked at me, and I was very much frightened.'

Dhrun took her hand. 'You shall come to Troicinet. Are we agreed on this?'

'Yes. Especially since I have nowhere else to go. I doubt if ever I shall find my father, which perhaps is all for the best.'

Dhrun led the way to a bench; the two seated themselves. He asked: 'Why do you say that?'

'In truth, I am afraid of what I might find. When Sir Pellinore met my mother he was carefree and full of artful gaiety. Now, all is changed. The years have come and gone; perhaps he has become austere and aloof, or settled in his ways, or married to a woman of severe character, who has given him several unpleasant children. None would like me, or take me warmly into their family.'

'If you found this unfortunate man, it would be wise to approach him anonymously, and with great caution.'

'Even so, I would be forced to reveal myself in the end. No doubt he would insist that, willy-nilly, I join his sordid household, and I might be reluctant to do so.'

'It might not be so bad as you think.'

'Perhaps not. It might be worse, to my distress! I am not partial to folk who are grim and austere. I prefer fanciful folk who make me laugh.'

'Hmf,' said Dhrun. 'I would seem to be a failure – much

like poor miserable Sir Pellinore, with his virago of a spouse and his smelly children. I seldom see you laugh.'

'I am laughing now! Sometimes I smile quietly when you are not looking, or even when I am thinking of you.'

Dhrun turned his head and looked down into her face. He said: 'I pity the poor wretch you finally decide to marry; he will be in a constant state of nerves.'

'Not at all!' said Madouc airily. 'I would undertake to train him, and it should be easy enough, once he learned a few simple rules. He would be fed regularly, and I would sit with him if his manners were polite. He would not be allowed to snore, nor wipe his nose on his sleeve, nor sing loudly over his beer, nor keep dogs in the house. To gain my favor, he would learn to kneel nicely before me that he might tender me a red rose or perhaps a bouquet of violets, and then, with his best voice, beseech a touch of my fingers.'

'And then?'

'Much depends upon circumstances.'

'Hm,' said Dhrun. 'The spouse of your dreams, as you describe him, would seem idealistic and rather meek.'

'Not altogether and not always.'

'He would surely lead an interesting life.'

'I expect so. Of course I have not seriously considered the subject, except to decide whom I will marry when the time comes.'

Dhrun said, 'I also know whom I will marry. She has blue eyes, as soft as the sky and as deep as the sea, and red curls.'

'They are more of a copper-gold, are they not?'

'Quite so, and although she is still young, she grows prettier by the minute, and I do not know how long I will be able to resist the temptations which push at me.'

Madouc looked up at him. 'Would you like to kiss me now, just for practice?'

'Certainly.' Dhrun kissed her, and for a time they sat close together, with Madouc's head on Dhrun's shoulder. Dhrun presently asked, 'Now: are you still in fear of Casmir?'

Madouc sighed. 'Yes! I fear him greatly. Though for a time I had forgotten him.'

Dhrun rose to his feet. 'There is nothing he can do to you, unless you obey his orders.'

'I will not obey him: that would be folly.'

'There is no more to the colloquy, and my father does not want to embarrass King Audry by staying over. He wants to leave as soon as possible, perhaps within the hour, to catch the ebbtide.'

'I will need only a few minutes, to change from these pretty clothes, and bundle up a few other things.'

'Come, I will take you to your chambers.'

Dhrun escorted Madouc to the east wing and to her door. 'I will be back in ten minutes. Remember: allow no one to enter, except your maid.'

Ten minutes later, when Dhrun returned to Madouc's chambers, the maid reported that Madouc was gone, having departed only minutes before accompanied by three men-at-arms of Lyonesse.

Dhrun groaned. 'I told her to keep her door locked and to admit no one!'

'She followed your instructions, but they came from the chambers next door into the parlor! The Damsel Kylas opened the door to them!'

Dhrun ran back to the reception hall. King Casmir was no longer present, nor was King Audry, nor yet Aillas.

Dhrun made urgent inquiries and at last discovered Aillas in a small chamber to the side of the reception hall, in conversation with Audry.

Dhrun burst in upon them. 'Casmir has taken Madouc

away by force! She was to ride with us, but now she is gone!'

Aillas jumped to his feet, face taut with fury. 'Casmir went off five minutes ago! We must catch them before they cross the river! Audry, allow me eight fast horses at this very instant!'

'You shall have them, at best speed!'

Aillas sent messengers to the knights of his company, ordering their immediate presence at the front of the palace.

The horses were brought from the stables; Aillas, Dhrun and the six Troice knights of their escort mounted, wheeled and galloped off at a rush, south along the road to the Cambermouth ferry. Far ahead, the troop from Lyonesse could be seen, also riding at a pounding gallop.

Dhrun called over his shoulder to Aillas: 'We will never catch them! They will be aboard the ferry and gone!'

'How many ride in their company?'

'I cannot make it out. They are too far!'

'It looks to be a troop about like our own. Casmir will not choose to stand and fight.'

'Why should he fight when he can escape us on the ferry?'

'True.'

Dhrun cried out in fury: 'He will torment her, and take his revenge in some horrid fashion!'

Aillas gave a curt nod, but made no comment.

Far ahead, Casmir's party mounted the bluff which bordered the river, passed over the crest and was lost to view.

Five minutes later the Troice company rode to the edge of the scarp, where they could overlook the river. A hempen hawser led from a nearby stone buttress at a slant across the river to a similar buttress at Cogstone Head. The ferry, attached to the hawser by a bridle and a sheave rolling along the hawser, was propelled by reason of the slant of the hawser. When the tide ebbed the ferry was taken south; when the tide was at flood, the ferry was driven north across the river. A half-mile to the west, another hawser slanted in the opposite direction, so that with each change of the tide, the ferries crossed the Cambermouth in opposite directions.

The ferry conveying Casmir and his company was just now leaving the shore. His party had dismounted and were tying their horses to a rail. A slender still form wrapped in a brown cloak indicated the presence of Madouc. There seemed to be a bandage or a gag across her mouth.

Dhrun stared hopelessly at the ferry. Casmir looked back once, his face an impassive white mask. 'They have evaded us,' said Dhrun. 'By the time we can cross the river they will be to the other side of Pomperol.'

'Come!' said Aillas in sudden exultation. 'They have not evaded us yet.'

He rode pell-mell along the scarp to the buttress which anchored the hawser. He jumped to the ground and, drawing his sword, hacked at the taut cable. Strand by strand, twist by twist, the hawser was severed. The ferry tender, looking up from his hut, shouted a frantic protest, to which Aillas paid no heed. He hacked, sawed and cut; the cable sang, spun, as tension overtaxed the fibers. The hawser parted, the loose end snaking down the face of the scarp and into the water. The ferry, no longer impelled by the sidewise thrust of the current, drifted down the estuary toward the open sea. The hawser sang loosely through the sheave and at last pulled free altogether.

The ferry drifted quietly on the tide. Casmir and his party stood with sagging shoulders looking helplessly toward the shores.

'Come,' said Aillas. 'We will board the *Flor Velas*; it awaits our arrival.'

The company rode down the scarp to the harbor where the *Flor Velas*, a galleass eighty feet long with a square sail, a pair of lateen sails and fifty oars, rested at its mooring.

Aillas' party dismounted, put the horses into charge of the harbourmaster, and boarded the ship, Aillas giving the instant order to cast off.

Mooring lines were loosed from the bitts; the sails unfurled to catch a favorable north wind, and the vessel eased out into the estuary.

Half an hour later the *Flor Velas* drew close beside the ferry and made fast with grappling hooks. Aillas stood on the afterdeck with Dhrun; the two looked down with expressionless faces at Casmir's sour countenance. Cassander attempted a flippant salute to Dhrun and Aillas, which neither acknowledged, and Cassander haughtily turned his back.

From the mid-ships deck of the galleass a ladder was dropped to the deck of the ferry; four men-at-arms descended. Ignoring all others, they went to Madouc, pulled the bandage from her mouth and led her to the ladder. Dhrun came down from the afterdeck and helped her aboard.

The men-at-arms climbed back aboard the *Flor Velas*. Casmir, standing to the side, heavy legs spread apart, watched without expression.

No words had been spoken, either from galleass or from ferry. For a moment Aillas stood looking down at Casmir's party. He told Dhrun: 'If I were a truly wise king, here and now I would kill Casmir, and perhaps Cassander as well, and put an end to their line. Look at Casmir; he half expects it! He would have not a qualm in the world; indeed he would kill us both and rejoice in the act!' Aillas gave his head a jerk. 'I cannot do it. I may live to regret my weakness, but I cannot kill in cold blood.'

He gave a signal. The grappling hooks were jerked loose and brought aboard the galleass, which eased away from the ferry. Wind bellied the sails; wake bubbled astern and the galleass drove down the Cambermouth and toward the open sea.

From the Daut shore a pair of long-boats, each manned by a dozen oarsmen, put out after the ferry. They took it in tow and with help from the turning tide brought it back to the dock.

11

I

Upon returning to Castle Haidion, King Casmir went into virtual seclusion. He attended no court functions, received no visitors, granted no audiences. For the most part he kept to his private chambers, where he paced up and down the length of his parlor, pausing occasionally by the window to look out over the town and the gray-blue Lir beyond. Queen Sollace dined with him each night, but Casmir had little to say, so that more often than not Sollace lapsed into plaintive silence.

After four days of brooding, Casmir summoned Sir Baltasar, a trusted counsellor and envoy. Casmir gave Sir Baltasar careful instructions and sent him off on a secret mission to Godelia.

Upon the departure of Sir Baltasar, Casmir resumed many of his former routines, though his mood had changed. He had become terse, sharp in his commands, bitter in his judgments, and those who ran afoul either of Casmir or his justice now, more than ever, had cause for regret.

In due course Sir Baltasar returned, dusty and haggard from hard riding. He reported at once to King Casmir:

'I arrived at Dun Cruighre without incident. The town lacks all grace; you might well hesitate to stable your horses in the royal palace.

'King Dartweg would not receive me immediately. At first I thought his motives to be sheer Celtic perversity,

491

but later I learned that he was entertaining certain grandees from Ireland, and all were drunk. Finally he agreed to receive me, but even then he kept me standing to the side of his hall while he settled a dispute dealing with the breeding of a cow. The wrangling went on for an hour and was interrupted twice by dog fights. I tried to follow the litigation but found it beyond my understanding. The cow had been freshened by a prize bull without authorization and free of charge, by reason of a break in the fence; the cow owner not only refused to pay the stud fee, but beseeched a penalty for the illicit advantage taken of his cow by the amorous bull. King Dartweg was now gnawing a bone and drinking mead from a horn. He adjudicated the case in a manner I still find perplexing, but which must have been equitable, since it pleased no one.

'I was at last brought forward and presented to the king, who was quite drunk. He asked me my business; I said that I wished a private audience, that I might deliver the confidential messages entrusted to me by Your Highness. He waved high the bone upon which he was gnawing and declared that he saw no reason for "fiddle-faddle"; that I must speak out brave and bold like a good Celt. Stealth and furtive timidity were useless, he claimed; and secrecy was pointless, since everyone knew my business as well as I knew it myself; indeed, he could give me his answer without my so much as hinting of my mission; would that be suitable? He thought so, since it would expedite affairs and enlarge the time for tilting of the horn.

'I maintained as much dignity as was possible under the circumstances, and stated that protocol compelled me to request a private audience. He handed me a hornful of mead and told me to swallow all at a single draught, and this I managed to do, thereby gaining King Dartweg's favor, and allowing me to mutter my message into his ear.

'In the end I spoke with King Dartweg on three

occasions. Each time he sought to fill me full of strong mead, apparently hoping that I should become foolish and dance a jig, or babble my secrets. Needless to say, the attempt was fruitless, and in the end he began to find me a dull fellow, drunk or sober, and became surly. At our last meeting he blurted out his fixed and settled policies. In essence, he wants the fruits of victory with none of the risks. He will join our cause gladly, once we demonstrate that we have gained the upper hand over our enemies.'

'That is certainly a policy of caution,' said Casmir. 'He has everything to gain and nothing to lose.'

'He acknowledged as much, and said that it was in the best interests of his health, since only a program of this sort allowed him to sleep well of nights.

'I spoke of the need for a specific undertaking; he only waved his hand and said that you were not to worry on his account. He claimed that he would know the precise instant when the time was ripe and then he would be on hand in full force.'

King Casmir grunted. 'We are listening to the voice of an opportunistic braggart! What next?'

'From Dun Cruighre I journeyed by ship to Skaghane, where I met a dozen frustrations but gained no profit. The Ska are not only inscrutable and opaque in their conversation, but large in their manner. They neither want nor need alliances, and have a positive aversion for all folk but themselves. I broached the matter at hand, but they brushed it aside, giving neither "yes" nor "no", as if the matter were arrant nonsense. From Skaghane I bring back no news whatever.'

Casmir rose to his feet and began to pace back and forth. He spoke, more to himself than to Sir Baltasar: 'We are assured only of ourselves. Dartweg and his Celts in the end will serve us, out of greed. Pomperol and Blaloc will stand rigid, paralyzed by fear. I had hoped for

493

distraction, or even rebellion, among the Ulfs, but they merely crouch like sullen animals in their high glens. Torqual, despite my great expense, has done nothing. He and his witchwoman are fugitives; they maraud along the moors by night, and take cover by day. The peasants consider them ghouls. Sooner or later they will be brought to bay and slaughtered like wild beasts. No one will mourn them.'

II

Shimrod sat in his garden, somnolent in the shade of a bay tree. His garden was at its best. Pink hollyhocks stood like shy maidens in a row along the front of his manse; elsewhere blue delphiniums, daisies, marigolds, alyssum, verbena, wallflowers, and much else grew in casual clumps and clusters.

Shimrod sat with eyes half closed, letting his mind wander without restraint: through follies and fancies, along unfamiliar landscapes. He came to an engaging notion: if odors could be represented by color, then the scent of grass could be nothing else but fresh green. In the same way, the perfume of a rose must inevitably be rendered by velvet red, and the scent of heliotrope would be a ravishing lavender purple.

Shimrod conceived a dozen other such equivalences, and was surprised how often and how closely his colors, derived by induction, matched the natural and irrefutable color of the object from which the odor originated. It was a remarkable correspondence! Could it be ascribed to simple coincidence? Even the acrid tang of the daisy seemed perfectly consonant with the white, so prim and stark, of the flower itself!

Shimrod smiled, wondering whether similar transferences, involving the other senses, might exist. The mind was a marvelous instrument, thought Shimrod; when left to wander untended, it often arrived at curious destinations.

Shimrod watched a lark flying across the meadow. The scene was tranquil. Perhaps too tranquil, too serene, too quiet. It was easy to become melancholy thinking how quickly the days slipped past. What was lacking at Trilda was the sound of conviviality and happy voices.

Shimrod sat up in his chair. The work must be done, and sooner was better than later. He rose to his feet and after a last look around Lally Meadow went to his workroom.

The tables, once stacked high with a miscellany of articles, were now greatly reduced of their burden. Much of what remained was stubborn stuff, obscure, arcane, or intrinsically complex, or perhaps it had been rendered incomprehensible by Tamurello's eery tricks.

To one of the articles still under investigation Shimrod had given the name 'Lucanor', after the Druidic god of Primals[1].

---

[1] Lucanor's duties were three: he plotted the shape of the constellations and, when needful, altered the placement of the stars; he assigned to each thing of the world the secret name by which its existence was confirmed or denied; he regulated the cycle by which the end of the future merged into the beginning of the past. In Druidic depictions, Lucanor wore double-pointed shoes, with toes extending both forward and back. An iron circlet displaying seven golden disks clasped his head. Lucanor was a solitary god, who held himself aloof from the lesser gods of the Druidic pantheon, among whom he inspired awe and fear.

A Druidic myth relates how Lucanor, coming upon the other gods as they sat at the banquet table, found them drinking mead in grand style, to the effect that several were drunk, while others remained inexplicably sober; could some be slyly swilling down more than their share? The disparity led to bickering, and it seemed that a serious quarrel was brewing. Lucanor bade the group to serenity, stating that the controversy no doubt could be settled without recourse either to blows or to

'Lucanor', the magical artifice, or toy, consisted of seven transparent disks, a hand's breadth in diameter. They rolled around the edge of a circular tablet of black onyx, at varying speeds. The disks swam with soft colors, and occasionally showed pulsing black spots of emptiness, coming and going apparently at random.

Shimrod found the disks a source of perplexity. They moved independently of each other, or so it seemed, so that in their circuit of the tablet, one might pass another, and in turn be overtaken by still a third. At times two disks rolled in tandem, so that one was superimposed upon the other, as if an attraction held them together for a few instants. Then they would break apart and each would once more roll its own course. At rare intervals, even a third disk might arrive while two disks rolled together, and for a space the third disk also would linger, for a period perceptibly longer than if just two disks were together. Shimrod once or twice had observed what would seem to be a very rare chance, when four disks chanced to roll together around the tablet, and then they clung together for perhaps twenty seconds before parting company.

Shimrod had placed 'Lucanor' on a bench where it could catch the afternoon sunlight, and also where it most efficiently distracted him from his other work. Was 'Lucanor' a toy, or a complex curio, or an analog representing

---

bitterness. Then and there Lucanor formulated the concept of numbers and enumeration, which heretofore had not existed. The gods henceforth could tally with precision the number of horns each had consumed and, by this novel method, assure general equity and, further, explain why some were drunk and others not. 'The answer, once the new method is mastered, becomes simple!' explained Lucanor. 'It is that the drunken gods have taken a greater number of horns than the sober gods, and the mystery is resolved.' For this, the invention of mathematics, Lucanor was given great honor.

some larger process? He wondered if ever five of the seven disks might roll in unison, or six, or even all seven. He tried to calculate the probability of such concurrences, without success. The chances, while real, must be exceedingly remote, so he reflected.

At times, when a pair of disks rolled together, their black spots, or holes, might develop simultaneously and sometimes overlapped. On one occasion, when three disks rolled in unison, black spots grew on each of the three, and by some freak, they were superimposed. Shimrod squinted through the aligned holes as the disks rolled past; to his surprise he thought to see flickering lines of fire, like far lightning.

The black holes disappeared; the disks parted company, to roll their separate courses as before.

Shimrod stood back in contemplation of 'Lucanor'. The device undoubtedly served a serious purpose: but what? He could arrive at no sensible theory. Perhaps he should bring 'Lucanor' to the attention of Murgen. Shimrod temporized, since he would far prefer to resolve the puzzle himself. Three of Tamurello's ledgers remained to be deciphered; there might be a reference to 'Lucanor' in one or another of the tomes.

Shimrod returned to his work, but continued to watch the seven disks, causing him such distraction that at last he put a low-order sandestin on watch for unusual coincidences, and then took 'Lucanor' to a far corner of the workroom.

The days passed; Shimrod found no reference to 'Lucanor' in the ledgers, and gradually lost interest in the disks.

One morning, Shimrod took himself to his workroom as usual. Almost as soon as he passed through the door, the sandestin monitor called out an alarm: 'Shimrod! Attend your disks! Five roll together in congruence!'

Shimrod crossed the room on swift strides. He looked

497

down in something like awe. For a fact, five of the disks had joined to roll as one around the periphery of the tablet. Further, the disks showed no disposition to separate. And what was this? A sixth disk came rolling to overtake the five, and as Shimrod watched, it edged close, shuddered, merged into place with the others.

Shimrod watched in fascination, certain that he was witnessing an important event or, more likely, the representation of such an event. And now the seventh and last disk came to join the others, and the seven rolled as one. The single disk changed in color, to become marbled maroon and purple-black; it rolled lethargically, and showed no disposition to break apart. At the center a black spot grew dense and large. Shimrod bent to look through the hole; he saw what appeared to be a landscape of black objects outlined in golden fire.

Shimrod jerked away from 'Lucanor' and ran to his workbench. He struck a small silver gong and waited, looking into a round mirror.

Murgen failed to acknowledge the signal.

Shimrod struck the gong again, more sharply. Again: no effect.

Shimrod stood back, face drawn into lines of concern. Murgen occasionally went to walk on the parapets. Infrequently, he left Swer Smod, sometimes by reasons of urgency, sometimes for sheer frivolity. Usually he notified Shimrod of his movements.

Shimrod struck the gong a third time. The result was as before: silence.

Troubled and uneasy, Shimrod turned away, and went back to stare at 'Lucanor'.

III

Along the crest of the Teach tac Teach, from the Troagh in the south to the Gwyr Aig Rift in the north, a line of crags stood in a stern sequence, each more harsh and forbidding than the next. At about the center Mount Sobh raised a trapezoidal jut of granite high to split the passing clouds; Arra Kaw, next to the north, was if anything even more harsh and desolate.

Where the high moors broke against the base of Arra Kaw, five tall dolmens, the 'Sons of Arra Kaw', stood in a circle, enclosing an area forty feet in diameter. Where the westernmost stone gave a measure of protection against the wind, a rude hut had been built, of stones and sod. Clouds raced across the sky, passing in front of the sun to send shadows fleeting across the dun moors. Wind blew through gaps between the five Sons, creating a soft wailing sound which sometimes throbbed and fluttered to the changing force and direction of the wind.

Before the hut a small fire burned fitfully below an iron kettle which hung from a spindly tripod. Beside the fire stood Torqual, looking bleakly down into the blaze. Melancthe, impassive, if somewhat wan, and wrapped in a heavy brown cloak, knelt across from Torqual, stirring the contents of the kettle. She had cut her hair short and wore a soft leather casque which clasped her glossy dark curls close to her face.

Torqual thought to hear a calling voice. He jerked around, cocked his head to listen. He turned to Melancthe, who had raised her head. Torqual asked: 'Did you hear the call?'

'Perhaps.'

Torqual went to a gap between the Sons and peered out across the moors. Ten miles to the north the crag known as Tangue Fna reared even higher and more steeply than Arra Kaw. Between the two crags spread high moors, dappled by moving cloud shadows. Torqual saw a hawk, sliding eastward down the wind. As he watched, the hawk uttered a wild cry, almost inaudible.

Torqual allowed himself to relax, reluctantly, so it seemed, as if he were not averse that someone should dare attack him. He turned back toward the fire, and halted in frowning puzzlement. Melancthe, her face rapt, had risen to her feet and was walking slowly toward the hut. In the gloom behind the doorway Torqual was startled to observe the shape of a woman. Torqual stared. Was his mind playing him tricks? The shape seemed not only nude, but also distorted, insubstantial and illuminated as if by a dim green glow.

Melancthe, on stiff legs, stepped into the hut. Torqual started to follow, but halted by the fire to stand irresolute, wondering if he had seen correctly. He listened. For a moment the wind ceased its noise and he thought to hear from the hut the murmur of voices.

The situation could no longer be ignored. Torqual started for the hut, but before he could take three steps Melancthe emerged, walking with a firm step and carrying a short-handled implement formed of greenish-silver metal which Torqual had never seen before. He took it to be an ornamental hatchet, or a small halberd with a complex blade to one side and a four-inch spike to the other. A similar spike protruded from the tip.

Melancthe approached the fire, walking with a slow and measured tread, her face stern and somber. He watched her come with dour suspicion; this was not Melancthe as he knew her! Something untoward had occurred.

Torqual spoke curtly: 'Who is the woman in the hut?'

'There is no one there.'

'I heard voices and I saw a woman. Perhaps she was a witch, since she lacked both substance and clothing.'

'So it may be.'

'What is that weapon, or tool, you are carrying?'

Melancthe looked at the implement as if seeing it for the first time. 'It is a hatchet thing.'

Torqual held out his hand. 'Give it to me.'

Melancthe, smiling, shook her head. 'The touch of the blade would kill you.'

'You touch it and you are not dead.'

'I am inured to green magic.'

Torqual went on long strides to the hut. Melancthe watched impassively. Torqual looked into the gloom: right, left, up and down, but discovered nothing. He returned thoughtfully to the fire. 'The woman is gone. Why did you speak with her?'

'The whole story must wait. As of this instant, I can tell you this: an event of importance has occurred, for which plans have long been made. You and I must go now to do what needs to be done.'

Torqual said harshly: 'Speak in clear terms, if you please, and leave off your riddles!'

'Exactly so! You shall hear not riddles, but definite orders.' Melancthe's voice was heavy and strong; she stood with head thrown back, eyes showing a green glitter. 'Arm yourself and bring up the horses. We leave this place at once.'

Torqual glowered across the fire. He controlled his voice with an effort. 'I obey neither man nor woman. I go where I choose, and do only as I find needful.'

'The need has come.'

'Ha! The need is not mine.'

'The need is yours. You must honor the compact you made with Zagzig the shybalt.'

Torqual, taken aback, frowned across the fire. He said at last: 'That was long ago. The "compact", as you put it, was only loose talk over wine.'

'Not so! Zagzig offered the most beautiful woman alive, who would serve you as you wished and wherever you went, so long as you defended her and her interests in time of need. To this you agreed.'

'I see none of this need,' grumbled Torqual.

'I assure you that it exists.'

'Explain it, then!'

'You shall see for yourself. We ride to Swer Smod, to do what needs be done.'

Torqual stared in new astonishment. 'That is fateful folly! Even I fear Murgen; he is supreme!'

'Not now! A way has opened and someone else is supreme! But time is of the essence! We must act before the way closes! So come, while power is ours! Or do you prefer skulking your life away on these windy moors?'

Torqual turned on his heel. He left the area and saddled the horses and the two departed the Five Sons of Arra Kaw. At best speed they rode across the moor, at times out-racing the cloud shadows. Arriving at a trail, they veered to the east and followed the trail down the mountainside: back, forth, across tumbles of scree, down declivities and gullies, at last to come out upon the bulge of a bluff overlooking Swer Smod. They dismounted and clambered down the hillside afoot, halting in the shadows of the castle's outer walls.

Melancthe took the leather casque from her head and wrapped it around the head of the halberd-hatchet. She spoke, in a voice harsh as stone grinding on stone. 'Take the hatchet. I can carry it no farther. Do not touch the blade; it will suck out your life.'

Torqual gingerly took the black wood handle. 'What am I to do with it?'

'I will instruct you. Listen to my voice but, henceforth, do not look back, no matter what happens. Go now to the front portal. I will come behind. Do not look back.'

Torqual scowled, finding the venture ever less to his taste. He set off around the wall. Behind him he heard a soft sound: a sigh, a gasp, then Melancthe's footsteps.

At the front portal Torqual halted to survey the forecourt, where Vus and Vuwas, the devils who guarded the postern, had contrived a new entertainment to help while away the time. They had trained a number of cats to perform the function of war-chargers. The cats were caparisoned with gay cloths, fine saddles and a variety of noble emblems, that they might serve as proper steeds for knightly rats, themselves well-trained and clad in shining mail and gallant helmets. Their weapons were wooden swords and padded tourney lances; as the devils watched, placed wagers and cried out in excitement, the rat-knights spurred their cat-chargers and sent them springing down the lists in the effort to unseat each other.

Melancthe stepped through the portal; Torqual started to follow. A voice behind him said: 'Go easy and quiet; the devils are intent upon their game; we shall try to slip by unnoticed.'

Torqual stopped short. The voice said sharply: 'Do not turn! Melancthe will do what is needful; so she justifies her life!' Torqual saw that Melancthe was now as before: the pensive maiden he had first met in the white villa by the sea.

The voice said: 'Go now, and quietly. They will not notice.'

Torqual followed Melancthe; they went unseen along the side of the forecourt. At the last moment, the red devil Vuwas, his rat and cat having been defeated, swung away in disgust and so glimpsed the intruders. 'Hola!' he cried out. 'Who thinks to pass, on sly knees and long toes?

503

I smell evil at work!' He called his associate. 'Vus, come! We have work to do!'

Melancthe spoke in a metallic voice: 'Go back to your game, good devils! We are here to assist Murgen in his wizardry, and we are late, so let us pass!'

'That is the language of interlopers! Folk of virtue bring us gratuities! That is how we distinguish good from evil! You would seem to represent the latter category.'

'That is a mistake,' said Melancthe politely. 'Next time we will surely do better.' She turned to Torqual. 'Go at once; ask Murgen to step out and certify our quality. I will wait and watch the jousting.'

Torqual sidled away as Vus and Vuwas were momentarily distracted.

'Start a new course at the lists!' called Melancthe. 'I will place a wager. Which is the champion rat?'

'Just a minute!' cried Vus. 'What is that disgusting green shadow which dogs your back?'

'It is of no consequence,' said Torqual. He hastened his pace and so arrived at the tall iron door. The voice behind him said, 'Bare the edge of the hatchet and cut the hinges! Take care not to damage the point; it must serve another purpose!'

A cry of sudden anguish sounded from the forecourt. 'Do not look back!' grated the voice. Torqual had already turned. The devils, so he discovered, had fallen upon Melancthe, and were chasing her back and forth across the yard, kicking with taloned feet and striking out with great horny fists. Torqual stared, irresolute, half of a mind to interfere. The voice spoke harshly: 'Cut the hinges! Be quick!'

From the side of his eye Torqual glimpsed the distorted semblance of a woman, formed from a pale green gas. He jerked away, eyes starting from his head, stomach knotted in revulsion.

'Cut the hinges!' rasped the voice.

Torqual spoke in a fury: 'You impelled me this far by reason of my idle words with Zagzig! I will not deny them, since nothing remains of my honor save the sanctity of my word. But the compact concerned Melancthe, and now she is beyond need. I will not serve you; that again is my word, and you may rely upon it!'

'But you must,' said the voice. 'Do you want inducement? What do you crave? Power? You shall be king of Skaghane, if you choose, or all the Ulflands!'

'I want no such power.'

'Then I will drive you by pain, though it costs me dear in strength to do so, and you shall suffer sadly for my inconvenience.'

Torqual heard a thin hissing sound of great effort; he was gripped at the back of his head, behind his ears, by sharp pincer-like fingers; they pressed deep and the pain caused his sight to go dim and his mind to segment into irresolute parts. 'Cut the hinges with the edge of the hatchet; be careful of the point.'

Torqual drew the leather away from the curved green-silver blade and slashed at the iron hinges. They melted like butter under a hot knife; the door fell open.

'Enter!' said the voice, and the pincers applied new pressure. Torqual stumbled forward: into Swer Smod's entry hall. 'Ahead now! Down the gallery at best speed!'

With eyes starting from his head, Torqual went at a shambling run down the gallery and so arrived at the great hall.

'We are in time,' said the voice with satisfaction. 'Go forward.'

In the hall Torqual came upon a curious scene. Murgen sat stiff and still in his chair, gripped by six long thin arms, putty-gray in color, sparsely overgrown with coarse black hairs. The arms terminated in enormous hands, two of

505

which gripped Murgen's ankles; two more pinioned his wrists; the final two covered his face, leaving only his two gray eyes visible. The arms extended from a slit or a notch opening into another space directly behind Murgen's chair. The aperture admitted, along with the arms, a faint suffusion of green light.

The voice said: 'I now give you surcease from pain. Obey precisely, or it will return a hundredfold! My name is Desmei; I command great power. Do you hear?'

'I hear.'

'Do you notice a glass globe dangling from a chain?'

'I see it.'

'It contains green plasm and the skeleton of a weasel. You must climb upon a chair, cut the chain with the hatchet and with great care bring down the globe. With the point of the hatchet, you shall puncture the globe, allowing me to extract the plasm and therewith restore my full strength. I will seal the bubble once more, and compress and close Murgen into a similar bubble. Then I will have achieved my aims, and you shall be rewarded in such style as you deserve. I tell you this so that you may act with precision. Do I make myself clear?'

'You are clear.'

'Act then! Up with you! Cut the chain, using all delicacy.'

Torqual climbed upon a chair. His face was now on a level with the weasel-skeleton inside the glass globe. The beady black eyes stared into his own. Torqual raised the hatchet and, as if accidentally, slashed at the glass bubble, so that green plasm began to seep out. From below came a horrid scream of fury. 'You have broken the glass!'

Torqual cut the chain and allowed the globe to fall; striking the floor it broke into a dozen pieces, sending green plasm spurting in all directions. The weasel skeleton uncoiled painfully from its hunched position and scuttled

506

to hide under a chair. Desmei hurled herself to the floor and gathered as much of the green plasm as possible, and so began to assume physical form, showing first the outlines of internal organs, then a fixing of her contours. Back and forth she crawled, sucking up seepages of the green with her mouth and tongue.

A sibilant voice came to Torqual's ears: 'Take the hatchet! Stab her with the point! Do not hesitate, or we will all be in torment forever!'

Torqual seized the hatchet; a swift step took him to Desmei. She saw him coming and cried out in fear. 'Do not strike!' She rolled away and pulled herself to her feet. Torqual was after her, and followed her step by step, hatchet held before him, until Desmei backed into a wall and could retreat no further. 'Do not strike! I will be nothing! It is my death!'

Torqual thrust the point through Desmei's neck; her substance seemed to be sucked into the blade of the hatchet, which swelled in size as Desmei shrank and dissipated.

Desmei was gone. Torqual was left holding a heavy short-handled hatchet with a complicated blade of silver-green metal. He turned and brought the hatchet back to the table.

Tamurello the weasel skeleton had emerged from under the chair; he had grown in size until now he stood as tall as Torqual. From a cabinet, Tamurello brought out a board four feet long and two feet wide, on which rested the simulacrum of a strange gray creature, human in general configuration, with glistening gray skin, short hairy neck, heavy head with smeared features and the filmy eyes of a dead fish. A hundred gelatinous ribbons bound the creature to the board, restraining every twitch of movement.

Tamurello looked at Torqual. 'Can you name this thing, which is only an image of reality?'

'No.'

'I will tell you then. It is Joald, and Murgen has given his life to the restraint of this thing, despite the forces which try for its liberation. Before I kill Murgen, he shall watch me destroy his earnest effort, and he shall know that Joald arises. Murgen, do you hear me?'

Murgen made a throaty sound.

'Little time remains before the way closes and the arms draw back. But there is time enough for all, and first, I will liberate the monster. Torqual!'

'I am here.'

'Certain bonds hold Joald in check!'

'I see them.'

'Take your sword and cut the bonds, and I will sing the chant. Cut!'

From Murgen came a thin keening sound. Torqual, daunted, stood hesitant.

Tamurello croaked: 'Do my bidding; you will share with me my wealth and magical power; I swear it! Cut!'

Torqual came slowly forward. Tamurello began to chant monosyllables, of the most profound import. They tore the air and incited Torqual into half-hypnotic motion. His arm lifted; his blade gleamed on high. Down came the blade! The strand binding Joald's right wrist parted.

'Cut!' screamed Tamurello.

Torqual cut; the ribbons binding Joald's elbow parted with a hiss and snap! The arm pulsed and twisted.

'Cut!'

Torqual raised the sword and cut the strand at Joald's neck. Tamurello's chant reverberated through the castle, so that the stones sang and hissed.

'Cut! Cut! Cut!' screamed Tamurello. 'Murgen, oh

Murgen! Taste my triumph! Taste, and weep bitter tears, for the waste I shall do to your pretty things!'

Torqual cut the ribbon binding Joald's forehead, while Tamurello intoned the great spell: the most terrible chant yet heard in the world. Deep in the ocean Joald took sluggish cognizance of his loosened bonds. He strained against the remaining filaments; he heaved and kicked, and struck the submarine pillars which ultimately prevented the Teach tac Teach from sliding into the sea, and the land shuddered. Joald's enormous black right arm was free; he raised it high, groping and clutching with monstrous black fingers, that he might achieve the destruction of the Elder Isles. The arm broke the surface; sheets of green ocean cascaded down to churn up foam. By dint of an awful struggle Joald thrust the top of his head above the surface, where it became a sudden new island, with bony ridges cresting along the center; waves two hundred feet high surged away in all directions.

At Trilda, Shimrod struck the silver gong yet again, then turned away and went to a box hanging on the wall. He opened the front panels, spoke three words and applied his eye to a crystal lens. For a moment he stood rigid, then, stumbling back, he ran to his cabinet, buckled on his sword, pulled a cap down upon his head and went to stand on a disk of black stone. He uttered a spell of instant transfer and in a trice stood in the forecourt at the front of Swer Smod. Vus and Vuwas still toyed with the bloody rag that once had been Melancthe. At their behest the torn body jerked back and forth in a grisly jig, while they chortled and complimented the indefatigable vitality of the thing. They gave Shimrod a pair of quick suspicious glances, but thought to recognize him, and in any case were bored with their routine duties and so allowed him to pass without challenge.

Shimrod stepped through the broken doorway, and at

once felt the force of Tamurello's chant. He ran down the gallery and burst into the great hall. Murgen sat as before, constricted by the six arms from Xabiste. The weasel skeleton, as it chanted the great spell, seemed to be altering shape and taking on substance. Torqual, standing beside the table, took note of Shimrod's arrival. He stood glowering, sword raised on high.

Shimrod cried out: 'Torqual! Are you mad that you obey Tamurello?'

Torqual spoke in dull voice: 'I do what I choose to do.'

'Then you are worse than mad, and you must die.'

'It is you who shall die,' said Torqual in a voice of fate.

Shimrod came forward with drawn sword. He hacked down upon the weasel skeleton, and cleaved it to the fragile pelvis. The chant abruptly stopped, and Tamurello was a heap of twitching bone-splinters.

Torqual looked at the simulacrum of Joald, now writhing against his remaining bonds. Torqual muttered under his breath: 'So this is the purpose of my life? I am mad indeed.'

Shimrod swung his sword in an arc which would have taken Torqual's head from his torso had it struck home; Torqual jerked aside. Emotion came upon him in a frenzy; he flung himself at Shimrod with such wild energy that Shimrod was forced back upon the defensive. So the two fought, in a mutual fury: slash, hack, thrust.

Beside the table the scatter of bones had pulled together to form a random construction with the glittering black eyes looking out, one low, the other high. A spindly arm clawed at the hatchet, raised it high, while from the tangle of bones came a croaking voice chanting the great spell.

Shimrod dodged back from Torqual, threw a chair to impede him, then cut at the arm holding the hatchet. The arm splintered; the hatchet fell to the floor. Shimrod picked up the hatchet and as Torqual charged upon him,

510

flung it into Torqual's face. Torqual's head and face shriveled and disappeared; his sword fell clattering to the floor, followed by his body.

Shimrod turned back to the table. The way into Xabiste was closing; to Shimrod's horror the arms, rather than disengaging, were drawing Murgen, chair and all, back through the slit.

Shimrod hacked at the thin gray arms. The hands fell to the floor, fingers clenching and unclenching. Murgen was free. He stood erect, and stepping forward, looked down at Joald. He uttered four plangent words. Joald's head lolled back; the arm dropped down beside the hulking torso.

In the Atlantic, the island created by the appearance of Joald's black pate sank beneath the surface. The arm fell with an enormous splash, creating a wave four hundred feet high which rolled toward the coast of South Ulfland. It struck full into the estuary of the Evander and sent a monstrous wall of water rushing up the valley, and the fabulous city Ys was lost.

Where Joald had lurched and kicked away the buttresses under Hybras Isle, the ground shuddered and sank, and Evander Vale, with its palaces and gardens became an inlet of the sea.

Up the Ulfish coast, as far north as Oaldes, the shore-side towns were drowned and the populations washed into the sea.

When the waters became calm, Ys of the Ages, Ys the Beautiful, Ys of the Many Palaces, was sunk beneath the sea. In later times, when the light was right and the water clear, fishermen sometimes glimpsed the wonderful structures of marble, where nothing moved but schools of fish.

IV

There was heavy silence in the great hall at Swer Smod. Murgen stood immobile by the table; Shimrod leaned against the wall. On the table the Joald simulacrum lay inert. The splintered bones of the weasel skeleton lay in a heap, showing no vitality save for the glitter of two black eyes. On the table the blade of the hatchet-halberd had altered, swelling and becoming first globular, then gradually taking on the semblance of a human face.

After a moment Murgen turned toward Shimrod. He spoke in a heavy voice. 'So now we have known tragedy. I cannot blame myself – but only because I cannot spare the energy. In truth, I fear that I became complacent, even arrogant, in the fullness of my strength and the certainty that no one would dare challenge me. I was wrong, and tragic events have occurred. Still, I may not allow myself to be injured by remorse.'

Shimrod approached the table. 'These things – are they still alive?'

'They are alive: Tamurello and Desmei, and desperately scheming for survival. This time I shall not dally with them and they shall fail.' Murgen went to one of his cabinets and threw wide the doors. He worked at a whirling apparatus and in due course evoked a glare of pink light and a queer fluting voice: 'Murgen, I speak across the unthinkable gulf!'

'I do the same,' said Murgen. 'How goes your war with Xabiste?'

'Well enough. We ordered the whorl Sirmish and flushed the green from Fangusto. However, at Mang Meeps they came in force, the place is now infested.'

'A pity! But take cheer! I now give you two hybrid demons, Desmei and Tamurello, both reeking with green.'

'This is a pleasant event.'

'Just so. You may send a tendril to take the pair, and to seek out any sops and seepages of green which they might have exuded.'

For an instant the hall flickered with pink light; when it subsided the hatchet and the pile of bones were gone.

Murgen spoke: 'Take the pair to the deepest pits of Myrdal, and seek out the hottest fires. There destroy them utterly, so that not even their last regrets linger in the flux. I will wait to learn of this final disposition.'

'You must be patient!' said the efferent. 'A deed worth doing is worth doing well! I shall be at least ten of your seconds, with another two seconds for my ritual cleansing.'

'I will wait.'

Twelve seconds passed. The efferent from Myrdal spoke once more. 'The deed is done. Of the two demons neither jot, atom, breath, thought nor tittle remain. The pits of Myrdal burn hot.'

'Excellent!' said Murgen. 'I wish you continued success against the green.' He closed the cabinet, and turned back to the table, where he reinforced the bonds which held Joald quiescent.

Shimrod watched with disapproval. 'Joald should also be destroyed.'

Murgen spoke in a soft voice. 'He is protected. Only this much is allowed to us, and then grudgingly.'

'Who protects him?'

'Some of the old gods still live.'

'Atalanta?'

For a long moment Murgen said nothing. Then: 'Certain names should not be named and certain topics are best not discussed.'

12

I

Rumors of the cataclysm along the Ulfish coast reached Haidion three days after the event. King Casmir heard the reports with keen interest and impatiently awaited full details.

A courier at last arrived, telling of the devastation which the ocean had wrought along the South Ulfish coast. Casmir's sole interest was the damage done to King Aillas' military capabilities. 'How far north did the waves strike?'

'Not so far as Oaldes. The offshore islands diverted the waves. They also saved Skaghane and the Ska Foreshore.'

'What do you know of Doun Darric?'

'It is King Aillas' Ulfish capitol, but it sits high on the middle moors and it took no damage.'

'So the army suffered no losses?'

'I cannot say with certainty, Sire. No doubt warriors on leave were lost. I doubt if the army as a whole was much affected.'

Casmir grunted. 'And where is King Aillas now?'

'Apparently he has taken ship from Troicinet and would be at sea.'

'Very well. Go.'

The courier bowed and departed. King Casmir looked around the faces of his aides. 'The time of decision is upon us. Our armies are trained and ready; they are poised for a swift advance and eager for a smashing defeat of the Dauts. When Dahaut is ours, we can deal with Aillas at leisure, no matter what nuisances he inflicts with his navy. What say you?'

One after another Casmir's aides told him what he wanted to hear:

'The armies of Lyonesse are strong, numerous and indomitable! The leadership is good and the warriors are well-trained!'

'The armories are well-stocked; the weaponmakers work both night and day. We suffer no shortages.'

'The knights of Lyonesse are keen and eager; all crave the rich lands of Dahaut for their estates! They await only your command.'

King Casmir gave a fateful nod. He struck his fist on the table. 'Then let it be now.'

II

The armies of Lyonesse assembled in various quarters, marched as unobtrusively as possible to Fort Mael, reformed into battalions and set off to the north.

At the Pomperol border the vanguard was met by a dozen knights commanded by Prince Starling. As the Lyonesse army approached the border, Prince Starling held up his hand, bidding the oncoming host to halt.

A herald galloped forward and delivered a message to Prince Starling. 'The Kingdom of Lyonesse has been prompted to conflict against the Kingdom of Dahaut, by reason of many and troublesome provocations. That we may expeditiously prosecute our campaign, we require the right of free passage across Pomperol, nor will we protest if in your neutrality you extend the same privilege to the troops of Dahaut.'

Prince Starling made a forthright statement: 'To allow you passage would compromise our proper neutrality, and in effect would make us your allies. We must deny the permission you require. Go instead to the west, to Lallisbrook Dingle, then bear north along Bladey Way, and so you will come into Dahaut.'

The herald responded: 'I am empowered to answer in this fashion: "Not possible! Stand aside and let us pass, or taste our steel!"'

The Pomperol knights drew silently aside and watched as the armies of Lyonesse moved north and in due course entered Dahaut.

King Casmir had expected only token resistance from the so-called 'gray and green popinjays', but his invasion infuriated high and low alike. Three great battles were fought, instead of the single perfunctory engagement King Casmir had envisioned, at great cost in men, material and time. At Chastain Field, a makeshift army led by Audry's brother Prince Graine attacked the invaders with reckless ferocity and were defeated after a day of bitter combat. The second battle was fought near the village Mulvanie. For two days the warriors surged back and forth across the downs. Steel clashed on steel; war shouts mingled with screams of pain. In and out of the mêlée rode formations of mounted knights, hacking at the foot soldiers who sought to pull them down with halberds and crowhooks, so that knives could cut aristocratic throats.

The Daut army gave way at last, and retreated toward Avallon. Again King Casmir could claim a victory, though again he had taken heavy casualties and had lost equally valuable time from his schedule of conquest.

The Daut army, now strengthened by reinforcements called down from Wysrod, took up a position beside Castle Meung near Market Chantry, some thirty miles south and west of Avallon. For two days King Casmir rested and reformed his troops, and waited another day for reinforcements from Fort Mael, then again advanced upon the Dauts, intent upon their final destruction.

The armies met on Wild Apple Meadow near Castle Meung, with the Dauts led by King Audry himself. Each side sent out squads of light cavalry, to harass the enemy with arrows. The armored knights, with heavy cavalry and standard bearers at their backs, formed themselves into opposing ranks, their steel gleaming ominously. And the minutes moved one after the other with fateful deliberation.

The Daut heralds, splendid in gray and green, raised their clarions and sounded a sweet shrill call. The Daut knights lowered their lances and charged at a thunderous gallop; the knights of Lyonesse did the same. At the center of Wild Apple Meadow the two ranks collided in a great dull clang of metal striking metal, and in an instant order gave way to a yelling chaos of toppling bodies, rearing horses, flashing steel. The Lyonesse charge was supported by squads of pikemen and archers, using disciplined tactics; in contrast, the Daut infantry arrived in amorphous groups, and were met by shoals of sighing arrows.

The battle at Wild Apple Meadow was shorter and more decisive than the two which had preceded it, since the Dauts now were demoralized and no longer expected to gain the day through sheer élan. They were finally sent reeling from the field.

King Audry and the surviving elements of his army retreated at best speed and took refuge in the Forest of Tantrevalles, where they no longer constituted a threat, and could be dealt with at leisure.

King Casmir marched upon Avallon, and entered without resistance. He rode at once to Falu Ffail, where he would finally take possession of Cairbra an Meadhan the table and Evandig the throne, and send them back to Castle Haidion in Lyonesse Town.

Casmir entered the quiet palace without ceremony. He went at once to the Hall of Heroes, only to find no sign of the furniture which figured so largely in his ambitions. From a portly young under-chamberlain he learned that Cairbra an Meadhan and Evandig had been taken away two days before by a company of Troice marine warriors. They had carried throne and table to a Troice ship and then set sail to a destination unknown.

Casmir's rage was almost too large to be borne. His face became congested with choler; his round china-blue eyes bulged so as to show white encircling rims. With legs planted wide and hands gripping the back of a chair, Casmir stared blindly at the empty areas. His thoughts finally settled into a semblance of order and he chanted vows of revenge which horrified Tibalt, the under-chamberlain.

At last Casmir calmed himself, and thereby became even more baleful than before. The deed had been done with the connivance of the Dauts. Who were the persons responsible? Casmir put the question to Tibalt, who could only stammer that all the high officials of Falu Ffail had fled Avallon, to join their fugitive king. There was no one on hand to punish save underlings.

To Casmir's further displeasure, a courier arrived on a lathered horse with dispatches from Lyonesse, to the effect that Ulfish warriors had stormed down the south ramparts of the Teach tac Teach into Cape Farewell Province, an area where Casmir's strongholds had been depleted of their garrisons for the benefit of the main army. The invaders had reduced castle after castle without difficulty and the town Pargetta was under siege.

Casmir took stock of his situation. He had broken the Daut armies and in effect controlled Dahaut, even though

518

King Audry still survived and still commanded a few dispirited fugitives. Audry must be hunted down and either captured or killed, before he could rally the provincial gentry about him and assemble a new army. For this reason Casmir could not yet weaken his expeditionary forces by detaching a force strong enough to expel the Ulfs from Cape Farewell Province. Instead, he sent Bannoy, Duke of Tremblance, to Fort Mael and there put together as best he could a new army comprising levies currently under training, and contingents of veterans from garrisons at forts along the coast. These in turn must be reinforced by drafts of local yeomen, sufficient to resist the inevitable raids to be expected from the Troice navy.

Bannoy would take his fresh new army into Cape Farewell Province and there send the Ulf bandits scuttling back into the fastnesses of the Troagh. Meanwhile, Casmir's forces in the field would complete the conquest of Dahaut.

A courier from Godelia arrived at Falu Ffail, carrying a dispatch from King Dartweg. The courier paid his formal respects to King Casmir, then unrolled a scroll of glazed sheepskin parchment wound upon rods of birch. The message was written in fine Irish uncial which no one present could read, including the courier himself, and it became necessary to summon an Irish monk from the nearby Abbey of Saint Joilly who opened the scroll and read the message.

King Dartweg first saluted King Casmir, using a dozen florid apostrophes. He reviled their mutual enemies and declared himself, as ever and always, from the start of time to final blink of the sun, Casmir's tenacious ally, ready to join the mutual fray against the twin tyrants Audry and Aillas, until the final grand victory and the sharing of the spoils.

To certify his faith, King Dartweg had ordered his

invincible, if somewhat boisterous, warriors across the Skyre and into North Ulfland, where he hoped to take the old capitol Xounges by crafty infiltration and surprise escapades from the seaside cliffs. So much accomplished, he would sweep south to smite the Troice interlopers. When all were dead, drowned, or fled, the Godelians would stand on guard in the Ulflands, to the perpetual comfort of King Casmir. So declared King Dartweg, Casmir's loving friend and trusted ally.

Casmir listened with a small grim smile, then returned a courteous reply, thanking King Dartweg for his interest and wishing him good health. King Dartweg's cooperation would be appreciated, but no final dispositions could be made at the moment.

The courier, his joviality dampened by King Casmir's manner, bowed and departed. King Casmir returned to his contemplations.

First things first; and first was the final expunction of the broken Daut army. This would seem a routine operation of no great difficulty, which King Casmir put into the charge of Prince Cassander.

King Casmir summoned Cassander and told him of the decision. He appended explicit instructions which, in Cassander's ears, made poor hearing: Cassander must carefully heed the counsel of Sir Ettard of Arquimbal, a crafty and experienced war-leader. Cassander must also listen to and profit from the counsel of six other senior knights, also of proved competence.

Prince Cassander confidently undertook the mission – so confidently, indeed, that King Casmir once more stipulated that Sir Ettard's advice must be heeded. Prince Cassander grimaced and frowned, but made no protest.

On the following morning Prince Cassander, mounted on a mettlesome black stallion, clad in gilded armor with a scarlet jupon and a gilded helmet flaunting a scarlet plume, led his army into the west. King Casmir settled himself to the reorganization of his new lands. As a first priority, he ordered construction of twelve new shipyards along the Cambermouth, where warships equal or superior to those of Troicinet might be constructed.

Cassander's troops marched westward. The manors and castles of the countryside, during the reign of King Audry, had abandoned whatever military function they might once have served, and offered no resistance, which in any case could only have proved suicidal to the occupants.

As Cassander advanced, Audry withdrew: ever westward, gathering reinforcements along the way. Arriving in the Western March, he took his army still further west and out upon the Plain of Shadows. The army of Lyonesse came in close pursuit, never more than a day behind him.

With the Long Dann barring further progress to the west, Audry's options began to dwindle. His counselors, notably Claractus, Duke of the March, urged counter-attack and at last had their way. They selected the ground with care and took concealment in a north-thrusting salient of the great forest.

In the army of Lyonesse, Sir Ettard suspected such an intent and urged Cassander to halt near the village Market Wyrdych, to take local information and to send out scouts, that the Daut army might definitely be located. Sir Ettard had already counseled Cassander to caution on previous occasions and none of his forebodings had come to pass. Cassander, therefore, had come to dislike and distrust Sir Ettard, and blamed him for their failure so far to come to grips with the Dauts. Cassander was certain that Audry intended to take refuge in the Ulfish highlands behind the Long Dann. There he might well join his forces to the Ulfish armies. Far better, insisted Cassander, that the Dauts be intercepted before they escaped by some secret way over the Long Dann. He refused to delay and ordered his armies forward at best speed.

As Cassander rode past the forest, a line of Daut knights charged from cover, lances leveled. Cassander became aware of drumming hooves; he looked around in startlement to find a knight bearing down on him with lance ominously steady. Cassander tried to wheel his horse, but in vain; the lance pierced his right shoulder and carried him from his horse, so that he fell heavily on his back, in a confusion of stamping hooves and clambering warriors. An old Daut, face contorted in battle-rage, hacked at Cassander with an axe. Cassander screamed and jerked; the blow sheered the proud crest from his helmet. The Daut yelled in fury and again struck down with his axe; once again Cassander rolled aside, and one of his aides cut through the Daut's neck with a sweep of the sword, so that the spurting blood drenched Cassander where he lay.

King Audry came lunging forward, swinging his sword back and forth like a man possessed. At his side rode Prince Jaswyn, fighting with equal energy. At their back rode a young herald on a white horse holding high the gray and green standard. The battle swirled in confusion. An arrow pierced Prince Jaswyn's eye; he dropped his sword, clapped his hands to his face, slid slowly from his horse and was dead before he struck the ground. Audry gave a great groan. His head sagged and his sword became listless. Behind him the young herald took an arrow in the chest; the gray and green standard tottered and fell. King Audry called a retreat; the Dauts fell back into the forest.

With Cassander wounded, Sir Ettard assumed command and restrained his forces from pursuit, for fear of the losses which they would surely take from ambush and arrow. Cassander sat on a dead horse, holding his shoulder, his face white and clenched in a dozen emotions: pain, offended dignity, fright to see so much blood, and nausea which caused him to vomit even as Sir Ettard approached.

Sir Ettard stood watching with eyebrows contemptuously arched. Cassander cried out: 'What now? Why have we not given pursuit and destroyed the whelps?'

Sir Ettard explained with patience. 'Unless we advanced with the stealth of ferrets, we would lose two for their one. This is both foolish and unnecessary.'

'Ai ha!' cried Cassander in pain as one of the heralds tended his wound. 'Be easy, I pray you! I still feel the thrust of the lance!' Grimacing, he turned back to Sir Ettard. 'We cannot sit here in a stupor! If Audry escapes us, I will be the laughing-stock of the court! Go after him, into the forest!'

'As you command.'

The Lyonesse army cautiously advanced into the forest, but came upon no Daut resistance. Cassander's dissatisfaction was compounded by the pulsing pain in his shoulder. He began to curse under his breath. 'Where are the skulkers? Why do they not reveal themselves?'

'They do not wish to be killed,' said Sir Ettard.

'So it may be, and so they defy my wishes! Have they nested high in the trees?'

'They have probably gone where I suspected they might go.'

'And where is that?'

A scout came riding up. 'Your Highness, we have discovered signs of the Dauts! They have fared westward, where the forest gives upon the plain.'

'What means that?' cried Cassander in perplexity. 'Is Audry bereft that he would invite a new attack?'

'I think not,' said Sir Ettard. 'While we prowl the forest, peering in nooks and searching the crannies, Audry wins to freedom!'

'How so?' bleated Cassander.

'Across the plain is Poëlitetz! Need I say more?'

Cassander hissed between his teeth. 'The pain in my shoulder has stopped my thinking. I had forgotten Poëlitetz! Quick, then! Out of the forest!'

Breaking once more out upon the Plain of Shadows, Cassander and Sir Ettard discerned the straggling Daut army already halfway to the scarp. Sir Ettard with his knights and cavalry dashed off in hot pursuit; Cassander, unable to ride at speed, remained with the foot soldiers.

The sally port of Poëlitetz showed as a dark blot at the base of the Long Dann; other elements of the fortress, built of native rock, seemed a part of the scarp itself.

Almost in front of Poëlitetz Sir Ettard and his cavalry overtook the Dauts; there was a short sharp skirmish in which King Audry and a dozen of his bravest knights were killed and as many more cut down as they guarded the way into Poëlitetz for the defeated Daut troops.

The portcullis clanged down at last. The Lyonesse cavalry wheeled away to avoid the arrows which were striking down at them from the parapets. On the plain before the scarp sprawled a dismal litter of dead and dying.

The portcullis lifted once again. A herald emerged upon the plain carrying a white flag, followed by a dozen warriors. They circulated among the bodies, giving the *coup de grâce* where needful, to friend and foe alike; and conveying the wounded, again friend and foe alike, into the fortress for such rude treatment as might be practical.

Meanwhile the balance of the Lyonesse army arrived and made camp on the Plain of Shadows, not much more than an arrow's flight from the fortress. Cassander set up a command pavilion on a hummock directly in front of the portal. At the instigation of Sir Ettard, he called his advisers together for a consultation.

During an hour of discussion, interrupted by Cassander's groans and curses, the group considered their present condition. All agreed that they had honorably fulfilled their mission and might now return to the east, if that were to be their decision. King Audry lay dead and twisted out on the Plain of Shadows and his army had been reduced to a rabble. But there still remained scope for greater achievement and further glory. Close at hand and seductively vulnerable was North Ulfland. Admittedly the Long Dann barred the way, with the only feasible access guarded by the fortress Poëlitetz.

However, another fact must be taken into account: so one of the group pointed out. The Godelians were now at war against King Aillas and had in fact invaded North Ulfland. A courier might therefore be sent to King Dartweg, urging him to march south and attack Poëlitetz from its vulnerable rear approaches. If Poëlitetz fell, then both North and South Ulfland lay exposed to the might of the Lyonesse army.

The opportunity seemed too good to ignore, and might well yield victories beyond all King Casmir's expectations. In the end a decision was made to explore the situation.

The army built its fires and cooked its evening rations. Sentries were posted and the army composed itself to rest.

Across the eastern edge of the Plain of Shadows the moon rose full. In the commander's pavilion Sir Ettard and his fellows wearily divested themselves of their armor, spread out horse blankets and made themselves as comfortable as might be. Cassander kept to his own tent where he gulped down wine and ate powdered willow bark to dull the throb of his mangled shoulder.

In the morning, Sir Heaulme and three men-at-arms rode north to find King Dartweg, that they might urge his attack upon Poëlitetz. During their absence, scouts would explore the face of the Long Dann in the hope of discovering another feasible route up to the high moors.

In the fortress Poëlitetz the garrison cared for the haggard Daut warriors to the best of their ability, and kept a vigilant watch upon the activities of the Lyonesse troops.

A day passed and another. At noon on the third day King Aillas arrived, with a strong contingent of Ulfish troops. His coming was fortuitous. News of King Dartweg's incursion had reached him at Doun Darric and he had assembled a force to deal with the situation. New reports had reached him on the previous day. Dartweg had tried to storm the city Xounges but the defenses had been too much for him, and he veered to the west, looting and pillaging along the way. At last he arrived at the Ska Foreshore. Disregarding all sanity and prudence the Celts had stormed into Ska territory. Three Ska battalions struck them like thunderbolts, again and again, killing King Dartweg and driving the hysterical survivors back across the North Ulfish moors and into the Skyre. Then, satisfied with their work, the Ska returned to the Foreshore, so that, when Aillas arrived at Poëlitetz, the Celtic threat had vanished, and he was free to contemplate the Lyonesse army camped before Poëlitetz.

Aillas walked along the parapets, looking out across the plain to the Lyonesse camp. He reckoned the number of armored knights, light and heavy cavalry, pikemen and archers. They considerably over-matched his own forces, both in numbers and in weight of armor, even taking the Dauts into account, and there was no way he could challenge them by a frontal attack.

Aillas thought long and hard. From a grim period long in the past, he remembered a tunnel which had extended from a Poëlitetz sub-cellar to the hillock on the plain where the Lyonesse commanders had raised their pavilion.

Aillas descended by a route barely recalled into a chamber underneath the marshaling yard. Using a torch he discovered that the tunnel was as before, and seemed to be in good repair.

Aillas chose a platoon of hard-bitten Ulfish warriors, who cared nothing for the niceties of knightly combat. At midnight the warriors negotiated the tunnel, silently broke open the far exit and crawled out into the open. Keeping to the black shadows, away from the moonlight, they entered the pavilion where the Lyonesse war leaders lay snoring, and killed them as they slept, including Sir Ettard.

Directly behind the pavilion a paddock constrained the horses of the army. The raiders killed grooms and sentries, broke open the fences and drove the horses out upon the plain. They then returned to the tunnel and under the plain to the fortress.

At the first crack of dawn the sally ports at Poëlitetz opened and the Ulfish army, augmented by the surviving Dauts, issued upon the plain, where they formed a battle line and charged the Lyonesse camp. In the absence of leadership and lacking horses, the Lyonesse army became a chaos of milling men, sleepy and confused, and so was destroyed. Abandoning all order, the fugitives ran eastward, pursued by the vengeful Dauts who showed them no mercy and cut them down as they ran, including Prince Cassander.

The liberated horses were herded together and brought back to the paddock. With captured armor Aillas mounted a new corps of heavy cavalry, and without delay set out to the east.

III

At Falu Ffail King Casmir received daily dispatches from all quarters of the Elder Isles. For a time he learned nothing to cause him dismay or disturb his sleep. A few situations remained untidy, such as the Ulfish occupation of the Cape Farewell province, but this was only a temporary annoyance and surely would be remedied in good time.

From the west of Dahaut the news continued good. King Dartweg of Godelia had invaded North Ulfland, compensating for the Ulfish foray into the Cape Farewell Province. Prince Cassander's great army continued to sweep to the west, smiting the hapless King Audry hip and thigh. According to his last advices, the Dauts had been backed up against the Long Dann and could flee no farther; the end, so it seemed, was in sight.

On the following morning a courier rode up from the south to bring disquieting news: Troice ships had put into the harbor at Bulmer Skeme; Troice troops had landed and had reduced Spanglemar Castle, and now controlled the city. Further, there was a rumor to the effect that the Troice had already taken Slute Skeme, at the southern terminus of Icnield Way, and in effect controlled the entire Duchy of Folize.

Casmir pounded the table with his fist. This was an intolerable situation, which forced awkward decisions upon him. But there was no help for it: the Troice must be dislodged from the Duchy of Folize. Casmir sent a dispatch to Duke Bannoy, ordering him to augment his army with all the power to be had at Fort Mael: raw recruits and veterans alike. All must march south into Folize Duchy and expel the Troice.

On the same day that Casmir sent off the dispatch, a courier arrived from the west, with news of the Celtic defeat and the death of King Dartweg, which meant that King Aillas and his Ulfish armies would not be preoccupied doing battle with the Celts.

A day passed, then late in the following afternoon another courier arrived, bringing news of staggering dimension: in a battle beside the Long Dann Prince Cassander had been killed; his great army had been utterly smashed. Of all the proud host only a few hundred still survived, hiding in ditches, skulking through the forest, hobbling along the back roads disguised as peasant women. Meanwhile, King Aillas with an army of Ulfs and revitalized Dauts marched east at best speed, picking up strength along the way.

Casmir sat slumped for an hour, bewildered by the scope of the disaster. At last he gave a great groan and set himself to doing what needed to be done. All was not yet lost. He sent another courier riding south to Duke Bannoy, ordering him to turn back from Folize Duchy and to march north up Icnield Way, assembling all strength along the way: every knight of Lyonesse capable of wielding a sword; the training cadres at Fort Mael, the raw levies, and every aging veteran or yeoman competent to wing arrow from bow. Bannoy must bring this makeshift army north at best speed, that it might meet and defeat the armies of King Aillas advancing from the west.

Bannoy, who had been well down Icnield Way toward Slute Skeme, was forced to turn his army about and return the way he had come, with an added hardship: the Troice and Dasce they had been sent south to attack now followed them north, harassing the rear guard with light cavalry. Bannoy was therefore slow in arriving at his rendezvous with King Casmir, who already had retreated south from Avallon, by reason of King Aillas' proximity.

King Casmir joined Bannoy's army near Lumarth Town and set up camp on a nearby meadow.

King Aillas brought up his army with deliberation and established a position at Garland's Green, ten miles west of the Cambermouth and a few miles northwest of Lumarth. Aillas seemed in no hurry to come to grips with King Casmir who, in his turn, felt grateful for the reprieve, since it allowed him better to organize his own forces. Still, with growing perturbation, Casmir wondered as to Aillas' delay; for what might he be waiting?

The news reached him presently. The Troice and Dasce who had taken Folize Duchy were now at hand, and joining them were the entire might of Pomperol, Blaloc and also the former kingdom of Caduz, which Casmir had assimilated. These were formidable armies, motivated by hatred, and they would fight like men possessed: this Casmir knew. The combined forces moved northward with ominous deliberation, and Aillas' army of Ulfs and Dauts moved toward Lumarth.

Casmir had no choice but to shift his position to avoid entrapment between the two armies. He ordered a retreat eastward toward the Cambermouth, only to receive news that forty Troice warships and twenty transport cogs had sailed to the head of the Cambermouth and there had discharged a great force of Troice and Dasce heavy infantry, supported by four hundred archers from Scola, so that armies now moved upon Casmir from three directions.

In a tactic of desperation Casmir ordered full and vehement assault upon Aillas' army, which was closest at hand, and included components of the Daut warriors whom he had already chased the width of Dahaut. The two armies met on a stony field known as Breeknock

Barrens. Casmir's warriors knew themselves to be fighting a lost cause, and their assault was listless, almost tentative, and was at once thrown back on itself. The other two armies now appeared and Casmir found himself pressed from three directions, and he realized that the day was lost. Many of his untried troops were slaughtered in the first ten minutes; many surrendered; many fled the field, including King Casmir. With a small troop of high-ranking knights, squires and men-at-arms he broke through the battle-lines and fled to the south. His only hope now was to arrive in Lyonesse Town where he would commandeer a fishing vessel and attempt the passage to Aquitaine.

Casmir and his comrades outdistanced pursuit, and in due course rode unchallenged down the Sfer Arct into Lyonesse Town.

At the King's Parade, Casmir turned aside toward Haidion, where he met a final bitter surprise: Troice troops commanded by Sir Yane. They had overcome the weakened garrison several days before and now occupied the city.

Casmir was unceremoniously clapped into shackles and taken to the Peinhador, where he was confined in the deepest and dankest of the thirty-three dungeons, and there left to brood upon the vicissitudes of life and the unpredictable directions of Destiny.

IV

The Elder Isles were quiet, in the torpor of exhaustion, grief and satiated emotion. Casmir huddled in a dungeon from which Aillas was in no hurry to extricate him. One frosty winter morning Casmir would be brought up and led to the block behind the Peinhador; there his head would be detached from his torso by the axe of Zerling, his own executioner, who, for the nonce, also occupied a dungeon. Other prisoners, depending upon their offenses, had been liberated or returned to the Peinhador, pending more careful judgment. Queen Sollace had been put aboard a ship and exiled to Benwick in Armorica. In her baggage she carried an antique blue chalice, double-handled, with a chipped rim, upon which she lavished a great devotion. It remained in her custody for several years, then was stolen, causing her such distress that she refused to eat or drink and presently died.

When the Troice took Lyonesse Town, Father Umphred went into hiding, using the cellars under the new cathedral for his lair. Upon the departure of Queen Sollace he became desperate and decided to follow. Early one gray and blustery morning he took himself aboard a fishing vessel, and paid the fisherman three gold pieces for passage to Aquitaine.

Yane, at Aillas' instructions, had been seeking Umphred high and low, and had been waiting for just such an occasion. He took note of the priest's furtive embarkation and notified Aillas. The two boarded a fast galley and set off in pursuit. Ten miles to sea they overtook the fishing vessel, and sent aboard a pair of stalwart seamen. Umphred saw them come in sad-eyed dismay, but managed a nervous little wave of the fingers and a smile. He called: 'This is a pleasant surprise!'

The two seamen brought Father Umphred aboard the galley. 'Truly, this is all a nuisance,' said Father Umphred. 'I am delayed in my travels and you must suffer the bite of this brisk sea air.'

Aillas and Yane looked around the deck, while Umphred volubly explained the reason for his presence on the fishing boat. 'My work is done in the Elder Isles! I have achieved wonderful things but now I must move on!'

Yane tied a rope to a stone anchor. Umphred spoke more feelingly than ever. 'I have been guided by divine instruction! There have been signs in the sky, and prodigies known only to me! The voices of angels have spoken into my ears!'

Yane coiled the rope, and cleared it of kinks that it might run freely.

Umphred spoke on. 'My good works have been manifold! Often I recall how I cherished the Princess Suldrun and assisted her in her hour of need!'

Yane tied the end of the rope around Umphred's neck.

Umphred's words tumbled over each other. 'My work has not gone unnoticed! Signals from above have beckoned me onward, that I may achieve new victories in the name of the Faith!'

A pair of seamen lifted the anchor and carried it to the rail. Umphred's voice rose in pitch. 'Henceforth I will be a pilgrim! I will live like a bird of the wild, in poverty and abstention!'

Yane thoughtfully cut away Umphred's pouch, and looking within discovered the glitter of gold and jewels. 'Wherever you are going, you surely will not need so much wealth.'

Aillas looked around the sky. 'Priest, it is a cold day for your swim, but so it must be.' He stood back. Yane pushed the anchor overboard. The rope snapped taut, jerking Umphred across the deck in a stumbling run. He clawed at the rail, but his fingers slipped; the rope pulled him over the side. He struck the water with a splash and was gone.

Aillas and Yane returned to Lyonesse Town and spoke no more of Father Umphred.

V

Aillas summoned the grandees of the Elder Isles to Haidion. At an assembly in the monumental old Hall of Justice he issued a proclamation.

'My heart is too full to speak at length,' said Aillas. 'I will be brief, and you will hear my message in simple words – though the concepts and their consequences are large.

'At the cost of blood, pain and woe beyond reckoning, the Elder Isles are at peace and, in practical terms, united under a single rule: my own. I am resolved that this condition shall continue and remain in force forever, or at least so far as the mind can project into the future.

'I am now King of the Elder Isles. Kestrel of Pomperol and Milo of Blaloc must henceforth use the title "Grand Duke". Once again Godelia becomes the Province of Fer Aquila, and there will be many reapportionments. The Ska will remain independent on Skaghane and the Foreshore; that is the force of our treaty.

'We shall maintain a single army, which need not be large, since our navy will guard us against attack from abroad. There will be one code of law: the same justice will apply to high and low alike, without regard for birth or wealth.'

Aillas looked around the hall. 'Does any person protest or make complaint? Let him air his feelings now; though I warn him that all arguments in favor of the old ways will go for naught.'

No one spoke.

Aillas proceeded. 'I shall rule not from Miraldra, which is too remote, nor from Falu Ffail, which is too splendid, nor yet from Haidion, which is haunted by too many memories. I shall undertake a new capitol at Flerency Court near the village Tatwillow, where Old Street meets Icnield Way. This place shall be known as "Alcyone", and here I shall sit on the throne Evandig and dine with my faithful paladins at Cairbra an Meadhan, and my son Dhrun after me, and his son after him, and so shall there be peace and kindness throughout the Elder Isles, and neither man nor woman will ever claim that he or she lacked recourse for wrongs done to him or to her.'

VI

Castle Miraldra at Domreis could no longer serve Aillas as his seat of government. Haidion, where he had set up a temporary residence, oppressed him by reason of its melancholy associations and he was resolved to move, as quickly as convenient, to Ronart Cinquelon, near the site of his new palace Alcyone at Flerency Court.

To assist in the organization of his government, he transported his council of ministers from Domreis to Lyonesse Town aboard the galleass *Flor Velas*. Madouc, feeling lonely and neglected at dank old Castle Miraldra, took herself uninvited aboard the vessel, and arrived with the others at Lyonesse Town. The counselors were met by carriages for their immediate journey to Ronart Cinquelon. Madouc found herself standing alone on the docks. 'If that is the way of it, so it must be,' said Madouc to herself and set off on foot up the Sfer Arct.

Castle Haidion loomed above her: massive, gray and cheerless. Madouc climbed steps to the terrace and crossed to the front portal. The men-at-arms on guard duty now wore the black and ocher of Troicinet, instead of Lyonesse lavender and green. As she approached they thumped the butts of their halberds smartly down upon the stone by way of salute, and one opened the heavy door for her; otherwise they paid her no heed.

The reception hall was empty. Haidion seemed only the husk of its old self, though the domestic staff, lacking orders to the contrary, unobtrusively went about its usual duties.

From a footman Madouc learned that both Aillas and Dhrun were absent from the premises, but where they had gone and when they would return the footman could not say.

In the absence of a better arrangement, Madouc went to her old chambers, which smelled musty from disuse. She threw wide the shutters to admit light and air, then looked about the room. It seemed a place remembered from a dream.

Madouc had brought no baggage from Castle Miraldra. In the wardrobe she found garments she had left behind, but marveled to discover how small and tight they had become. She gave a laugh of sad amusement which left an ache in her throat. 'I have changed!' she told herself. 'Oh how I have changed!' She stood back and surveyed the room. 'Whatever happened to that long-legged little wretch who lived in this place and looked from yonder window and wore these clothes?'

Madouc went out into the hall and summoned a maid, who recognized her and began lamenting the tragic changes which had overtaken the palace. Madouc quickly lost patience with the recital. 'It is clearly all for the best! You are lucky to be alive, with a roof over your head, since many are dead, or homeless, or both! Now go fetch the seamstresses, since I have no clothes to wear! Then I wish to bathe, so bring me warm water and good soap!'

From the seamstresses Madouc learned why Aillas and

Dhrun were away from Haidion: they had gone to Watershade on Troicinet, where Glyneth was close upon her time.

The days passed pleasantly enough. Madouc was fitted with a dozen pretty new gowns. She renewed her acquaintance with Kerce the librarian, who had remained at Haidion, along with a small number of courtiers and their ladies who, for one reason or another, had been granted residence and now had no other place to go. Among those who lingered at the court were three of the maidens who at one time had attended Madouc: Devonet of the long golden hair, pretty Ydraint, and Felice. At first the three kept themselves warily apart, then, perceiving the possibility of advantage, began to make themselves agreeable, despite the lack of any responsive cordiality from Madouc.

Devonet was especially persistent and sought to remind Madouc of old times. 'Those were truly wonderful days! And now they are gone forever!'

'What "wonderful days" are these?' asked Madouc.

'Don't you remember? We had such glorious fun together!'

'You had glorious fun calling me "bastard". I remember that well enough. I was not all that amused.'

Devonet giggled and looked aside. 'It was just a silly game, and no one took it seriously.'

'Of course not, since no one was called "bastard" but me, and I ignored you, for the most part.'

Devonet heaved a sigh of relief. 'I am happy to hear you say so, since I hope to find a place in the new court.'

'Small chance of that,' said Madouc briskly. 'You may call me "bastard" again if you like.'

Devonet put her hands to her mouth in horror: 'I would never think to be so rude, now that I know better!'

'Why not?' asked Madouc reasonably. 'Truth is truth.'

Devonet blinked, trying to grasp not only the sense but

also the overtones of Madouc's remarks. She asked cautiously: 'So you never learned the name of your father?'

'I learned his name, well enough. He announced himself to my mother as "Sir Pellinore", but unless they undertook marriage vows at almost the same instant they met – and my mother does not remember such a ceremony – I am still a bastard.'

'What a pity, after all your longing for a pedigree and respectable lineage!'

Madouc sighed. 'I have stopped caring about such things, since they are not to be mine. "Sir Pellinore" may still exist, but I suspect that I shall never know him.'

'You need not grieve!' declared Devonet, 'since now I will be your dear friend!'

'Excuse me,' said Madouc. 'I am reminded of an errand I have neglected.'

Madouc went around to the stables to search out Sir Pom-pom, only to learn that he had been killed in the battle at Breeknock Barrens.

Madouc slowly returned to the castle, musing as she went. 'The world now lacks a "Sir Pom-pom", with all his funny ways! I wonder where he is now? Or is he anywhere at all? Can someone be nowhere?' She pondered the matter an hour or more, but could find no decisive answer to the question.

Late in the afternoon Madouc discovered to her delight that Shimrod had arrived at Haidion. He had been with Aillas and Dhrun at Watershade, and brought news that Glyneth had borne a baby girl, the Princess Serle. He reported that Aillas and Dhrun would return by ship in a day or two; Glyneth would remain at Watershade for yet another month.

'I have no patience for traveling either by horse or by ship,' said Shimrod. 'When I discovered that you had come to Haidion I decided on the instant to join you and the next instant I was here.'

'I am happy that you are here,' said Madouc. 'Although, if the truth be known, I have almost enjoyed the time alone.'

'How have you been occupying yourself?'

'The days go by quickly. I visit the library, where I confer with Kerce the librarian and read books. Once I went up the cloisters, through Zoltra Bright-star's Gate and out on the Urquial. I went close to the Peinhador, so that when I looked at the ground I could imagine King Casmir sitting deep below me in the dark. The thought made me feel strange. I went back across the Urquial and pushed through the old gate so that I could look into Suldrun's garden, but I did not go down the path; the garden is far too quiet. Today I went out to the stables, and I found that poor Sir Pom-pom had been killed in Dahaut and now is dead. I can hardly believe it, since he was so full of foolishness. His life barely got started before it was done.'

'Once I spoke along similar lines to Murgen,' said Shimrod. 'His response was not exactly to the point, and it puzzles me to this day – to some extent, at least.'

'What did he say?'

'First he leaned back in his chair and looked into the fire. Then he said: "Life is a peculiar commodity, with dimensions of its own. Still, if you were to live a million years, engaged in continual pleasures of mind, spirit and body, so that every day you discovered a new delight, or solved an antique puzzle, or overcame a challenge; even a single hour wasted in torpor, somnolence or passivity would be as reprehensible as if the fault were committed by an ordinary person, with scanty years to his life".'

'Hm,' said Madouc. 'He gave you no exact information, or so it seems to me.'

'This was my own feeling,' said Shimrod. 'However, I did not assert as much to Murgen.'

Madouc said thoughtfully: 'It might be that he was confused by your question and gave the first answer that entered his mind.'

'Possibly so. You are a clever girl, Madouc! I will now consider the matter an insoluble mystery and dismiss it from my mind.'

Madouc sighed. 'I wish I could do the same.'

'What mysteries trouble you so seriously?'

'First is the mystery of where I will live. I do not care to stay at Haidion. Miraldra is too cold and misty and too far. Watershade is peaceful and beautiful, but nothing ever happens and I would soon become lonely.'

'At Trilda I too am often lonely,' said Shimrod. 'I invite you, therefore, to visit me at Trilda, where you shall stay as long as you like – certainly until Aillas builds his palace Alcyone. Dhrun would come often to join us and you surely would not be lonely.'

Madouc could not restrain a cry of excitement. 'Would you teach me magic?'

'As much as you cared to learn. It is not easy, and in fact surpasses the ability of most folk who try.'

'I would work hard! I might even become useful to you!'

'Who knows? It is possible!'

Madouc threw her arms around Shimrod. 'At least I feel as if I have a home!'

'Then it is settled.'

On the next day Aillas and Dhrun returned to Lyonesse Town. and immediately all departed Haidion. Shimrod and Madouc would turn off Old Street at Tawn Twillett and ride north to Trilda; Aillas and Dhrun would proceed along Old Street to Tatwillow and Castle Ronart Cinquelon.

Along the way the group came to Sarris, where Aillas

540

chose to sojourn for two or three days of banqueting, good-fellowship and irresponsibility.

Dhrun and Madouc wandered out on the lawn which sloped down to the River Glame. In the shade of a great oak with wide-sprawling branches they paused. Dhrun asked: 'Do you remember how you hid behind this very tree to escape the attentions of poor Prince Bittern?'

'I remember very well. You must have thought me a very strange creature to go to such lengths.'

Dhrun shook his head. 'I thought you amusing and altogether remarkable – as I do now.'

'More now than then, or less?'

Dhrun took her hands. 'Now you are begging for compliments.'

Madouc looked up at him. 'But you still haven't told me – and I value your compliments.'

Dhrun laughed. 'More, of course! When you look up at me with your blue eyes I become weak.'

Madouc held up her face. 'All this being the case, you may kiss me.'

Dhrun kissed her. 'I thank you for your permission, although I was about to kiss you anyway.'

'Dhrun! You frighten me with your savage lust!'

'Do I indeed?' Dhrun kissed her again, and again. Madouc stood back, breathing hard.

'Now then,' said Dhrun. 'What of that?'

'I cannot understand why I feel so odd.'

'I think I know,' said Dhrun. 'But there is no time to explain now, since the footman is coming to call us.' He turned to leave, but waited as Madouc knelt beside the oak. Dhrun asked: 'What are you doing?'

'There is someone missing. She should be here.'

'Who might that be?'

'My mother, Twisk! It is my duty as a daughter to invite her to an occasion so merry!'

'Do you think she will come?'

'I will call her.' Madouc selected a blade of grass and made a grass flute. She played a piping note and sang:

> '"Lirra lissa larra lass
> Madouc has made a flute of grass.
> Softly blowing, wild and free
> She calls to Twisk at Thripsey Shee,
> Lirra lissa larra leer
> A daughter calls her mother dear!
> Tread the wind and vault the mere;
> Span the sky and meet me here.
> So sing I, Madouc."'

In a swirl of vapor Twisk appeared. Her delicate features were placid, her blue hair coiffed into a crest along the top of her scalp and engaged in a silver mesh.

Madouc cried out in delight: 'Mother, you are more beautiful than ever! I marvel at you!'

Twisk smiled with cool amusement. 'I am pleased to merit your approval. Dhrun, I must say that you present yourself most agreeably. Your early training has served you well.'

'So it may be,' said Dhrun politely. 'I shall never forget it, certainly.'

Twisk turned back to Madouc. 'Our compliments have been exchanged; what was your purpose in calling me?'

'I wanted you, my dear mother, on hand to share our merriment at a banquet, which even now is about to begin. It is a small but select occasion, and we will take pleasure in your company.'

Twisk shrugged. 'Why not? I have nothing better to do.'

'Hmf,' said Madouc. 'Enthusiasm or none, I am still pleased! Come, we have already been called to the table!'

'I will naturally avoid the gut-clogging impact of your

coarse food; still, I may taste a drop of wine and perhaps the wing of a quail. Who is that handsome gentleman?'

'That is King Aillas. Come, I will introduce you.'

The three strolled across the lawn to where the table had been laid with linen napery and salvers of silver. Aillas, in conversation with one of his escort, turned to watch the three approach.

Madouc said: 'Your Highness, allow me to present my mother, Twisk, often known as "Twisk of the Blue Hair". I have invited her to share our banquet.'

Aillas bowed. 'Lady Twisk, you are more than welcome!' He looked from Twisk to Madouc and back to Twisk. 'I think I see a resemblance, though certainly not in the color of the hair!'

'Madouc's hair was perhaps the only birthright rendered her by her father, a certain Sir Pellinore, of frivolous bent.'

Shimrod approached the group. Madouc called out: 'Mother, I would like to present another of my dear friends!'

Twisk turned, and her blue eyebrows lofted high. 'So, Sir Pellinore! At last you choose to show yourself! Have you no shame?' Twisk turned to Madouc. 'I advise more caution in the choice of your friends! This is the secretive Sir Pellinore, your father!'

Madouc gave a poignant cry: 'I can choose my friends, Mother, but as for my father, the choice was yours!'

'True,' said Twisk equably. 'Indeed, it was from Sir Pellinore that I learned the caution I am now trying to teach you.'

Madouc turned to Shimrod. 'Are you truly "Sir Pellinore"?'

Shimrod attempted an airy gesture. 'Many years ago, I wandered the land as a vagabond. It is true that I occasionally used the name "Sir Pellinore" when the mood

came upon me. And, indeed, I reme..... ... ...
forest with a beautiful fairy, when I thought the name "Sir
Pellinore" rang with romantic reverberations – far more
than simple "Shimrod".'

'So it is true! You, Shimrod, are my father!'

'If the Lady Twisk so asserts, I shall be honored to claim
the relationship. I am as surprised as you, but not at all
displeased!.'

Aillas spoke: 'Let us take our places at the table! Our
goblets are full with wine! Madouc has found her father;
Shimrod has found a daughter and the family is now
united!'

'Not for long,' said Twisk. 'I have no taste for maudlin
domesticity.'

'Still, you must acknowledge the moment. To the table
then, and we will celebrate Lady Twisk's surprising
disclosures!

'First: we shall salute my absent queen Glyneth and the
new Princess Serle!

'Second: to the Lady Twisk, who astounds us with her
beauty!

'Third: to Madouc, one-time Princess of Lyonesse, who
became demoted to "Madouc the vagabond", and now by
royal dispensation becomes once again: Madouc, Princess
of Lyonesse!'